Ion Grant Neville Keith-Falconer

Kalilah and Dimnah

Or the Fables of Bidpai

Ion Grant Neville Keith-Falconer

Kalilah and Dimnah
Or the Fables of Bidpai

ISBN/EAN: 9783337075682

Printed in Europe, USA, Canada, Australia, Japan

Cover: Foto ©Andreas Hilbeck / pixelio.de

More available books at **www.hansebooks.com**

KALĪLAH AND DIMNAH

OR

THE FABLES OF BIDPAI:

BEING AN ACCOUNT OF THEIR LITERARY HISTORY,

WITH AN ENGLISH TRANSLATION OF THE LATER

SYRIAC VERSION OF THE SAME,

AND NOTES,

BY

I. G. N. KEITH-FALCONER, M.A.

TRINITY COLLEGE, ASSISTANT LECTURER AT CLARE COLLEGE, AND
FORMERLY TYRWHITT'S HEBREW SCHOLAR.

EDITED FOR THE SYNDICS OF THE UNIVERSITY PRESS.

CAMBRIDGE:
AT THE UNIVERSITY PRESS.
1885

CAMBRIDGE:

PRINTED BY C. J. CLAY, M.A. & SON,

AT THE UNIVERSITY PRESS.

TO MY FRIEND AND TEACHER

WILLIAM WRIGHT, LL.D.,

PROFESSOR OF ARABIC IN THE UNIVERSITY OF CAMBRIDGE.

PREFACE.

PROFESSOR Wright, when printing his edition of the later
Syriac version of the *Kalilah wa-Dimnah*[1], also known as the
fables of Bidpai or Pilpai, proposed to me that I should prepare
an English translation. This proposal I have carried out in the
hope of being useful to two classes of students. The beginner,
who uses the Syriac text for practice in reading, will, I think,
be glad to have a literal rendering at his elbow, and the student
of folk-lore, unacquainted with Semitic languages, to have access
to a version of this renowned collection of stories, which would
otherwise remain sealed to him. It is true that the Arabic
Kalilah wa-Dimnah, the original on which this Syriac version is
based, has been rendered both into English and German. But
De Sacy's text, from which these translations were made, is
notoriously defective, and Knatchbull's English rendering is far
from literal or correct, while the German versions of Wolff and
Holmboe are now very difficult to get.

In translating the text, which rests on a single, inaccurate
manuscript, often exceedingly corrupt, it has been frequently
necessary to adopt conjectural emendations. A large number
of these were supplied by Professors Wright and Nöldeke, others
by myself[2]. Nearly all of them have been already published in
the foot-notes or list of Additions and Corrections attached to
the Syriac text, while a few appear for the first time in the notes

[1] The book of Kalilah and Dimnah, translated from Arabic into Syriac.
Edited by W. Wright, LL.D., Professor of Arabic in the University of
Cambridge (Oxford: at the Clarendon Press. London: Trübner and Co., 1884).
[2] In a few cases I have ventured to differ from these scholars.

at the end of this volume². Not a few of the conjectures
adopted are confirmed, if not suggested, by the versions.
The square bracket indicates that the enclosed word or
clause represents what has dropped out of the Syriac text².
Where possible, these lost passages have been supplied from
the Arabic version. Additions made for the sake of clearness
are enclosed in parentheses.

Wherever I have been at a loss how to translate or how to
supply a gap, the fact is indicated by dots.

The numbers in parenthesis are those of the pages of the
Syriac text, and indicate where these commence.

I have prefixed to the translation a concise account of the
literary history of this collection of tales. Many readers may be

¹ I regret that M. Duval's notice in the *Revue critique d'hist. et de litt.*
(12 Jan. 1885) did not appear earlier. He proposes a number of excellent
emendations, of which the following are specially noticeable: Syr. text, p. 24,
l. 8, read a(i)kh for ellâ.—49, 4, v'hône for v'hâze, cf. 52, 2.—142, 9, perhaps
deqqath shishân, 'powder of lilies'.—175, 8, delete the dâlath of d'ḥubbeh,
'although separated from his friend by accident, his friendship remains fixed in
his soul'.—188, 11, perhaps no omission need be assumed, the sense being: 'even
if he possessed all the good things of this world, he would not find in them more
than what we have mentioned (nourishment, clothing, and lodging), except to
place them in reserve to enjoy the sight of them, just as those who look at
them enjoy them', comp. Bickell's transl. p. 43, l. 14.—191, 22, read 'al for
'am. 200, 7, the nigr should have been placed after qallt.—202, note 2. the
doubtful word seems to be bâse, comp. 364, 2. 206, 2, by transposing the words, a
satisfactory sense is obtained: v'râḥem ḥarbâthâ v'telânithû, lait yaqir sh'mâ
d'leh narme bâleh, 'and he loves ruins and darkness, no respectable person
pays any attention to him'.—232, 9, add sitar after men.—248, 7, read denô,
'than I', instead of dellâ.—274, 4, read l(e)sdsh ellâ.—277, 17, read: ellâ kadh
h'ôhu, 'the elephant who cannot be tamed except when he is closely surrounded
by others who are tamed', comp. Bickell's transl., p. 81, l. 20.—278, 5, read
madhr'khin for madhr'khd.—282, 22, read d'thamân, 'that he may see where
it is possible for him to apply himself to his work'.—381, 11, read aikan lâ
l(e)ndsh âtya, 'how (shall a great recompense not be payed) to a doctor...'—389,
5, delete the dâlath before m'nihis.

² In a good many unimportant or doubtful cases I have neglected to put the
square bracket, but perhaps the following had better be noted: p. 63, l. 21
[on the ox]; 96, 11 [if]; 132, 3 [without]; 134, 5 [not]; 134, 37 [were missing];
140, 31 [not to]; 149, 19 [in the house]; 153, 29 [although]; 156, 21 [which is];
170, 34 [mouse]; 183, 20 [if]; 183, 22 [subdue]; 189, 18 [not]; 191, 23 [be
considered]; 194, 3 [pleasant to]; 197, 19 [want of]; 205, 2 [not]; 211, 8 [he
who]; 215, 24 [by]; 211, 33 [to everybody]; 253, 1 [a physician].

interested in the wanderings and transformations of a book which has probably had more readers than any other except the Bible, and I trust that the notices of the various printed editions will be of service to the bibliographer and the librarian. Where personal inspection was impossible, I have been careful to refer to the source of statements given at second hand.

The chief printed authorities from which I have derived assistance are De Sacy's dissertations in the *Notices et Extraits des Manuscrits*, Vols. IX., X.; Benfey's brilliant *Einleitung zur Pantschatantra*, and his introduction to Bickell's *Kalilag und Damnag*; and three publications of Prof. Th. Nöldeke, which, though short, are full of condensed information.

The notes contain, besides the conjectural emendations already referred to, explanations of the text where they seemed needful, and corrections of my own translation[1].

My grateful thanks are especially due to Prof. Wright for reading all the proof-sheets which I ventured to send to a scholar who bestows more time on the work of others than on his own, namely those of the introduction and notes, as well as for much excellent advice during the course of my work; to the Rev. R. Sinker, B.D., librarian of Trinity College, who has very kindly read the proof of every sheet from first to last, and given me a number of useful hints on bibliographical points; and lastly to Prof. W. Robertson Smith for several helpful suggestions.

[1] The student is particularly requested, before using the book, to note the corrections made in the notes to p. 2, l. 4; 94, 88; 95, 18; 121, 13; 121, 20, 21; 144, 11—14: 196, 18; 203, 11; 217, 12, 13; 221, 12, 18; 237, 36, 37; 211, 38; 248, 15; 249, 27, 28; 252, 25—28; 253, 89—254, 1.

I. KEITH-FALCONER.

CAMBRIDGE.
19th January, 1885.

CONTENTS.

(The list of chapters in the printed edition stands at the end.)

INTRODUCTION.

I. PRELIMINARY SKETCH.

§ 1. Few books ancient or modern have been so widely circulated or rendered into so many languages as the collection of tales known variously as 'The fables of Pilpay or Bidpai', 'The book of Kalilah and Dimnah', 'Anwári Suhaili', &c. A glance at the translation which follows this introduction will give an idea of what this book is. Each chapter forms a story, which is supposed to have been related at the request of a king of India by his philosopher Bidpai, in order to enforce some particular moral or rule of conduct. The story, simple in itself, generally gives rise to a number of minor parenthetical stories, conversations, and sayings. In many of the tales the parts are played by animals, and that as if they were men and women[1].

[1] In this respect Indian fables differ from 'Æsopic.' In the latter, animals are allowed to act as animals, the former make them act as men in form of animals. This peculiarity of Indian conception Benfey attributes to the belief in metempsychosis, and the exclusively didactic nature of Indian tales. All tales therefore in which animals play the part of human beings are Indian, in form at any rate, if not in origin. As to the remote origin of popular tales and fables in general, Benfey comes to the conclusion that most fables about animals are Western or Æsopic, that the tales on the contrary are Indian. Already at the beginning of the second century A.D. Indian stories had begun to travel East and North. Along with Buddhism they penetrated straight into China, where they found a ready reception. Stan. Julien discovered two Chinese encyclopædias containing a number of Indian tales translated into Chinese. The oldest of these encyclopædias was finished in A.D. 668. From one of these collections he has selected a number of such tales and published them in a French translation under the title, *Les Avadânas, Contes et apologues Indiens*, &c. (Paris 1859). Similarly they reached Tibet, and thence Mongolia. Anton Schiefner has published in the *Bulletin de l'Acad. Impér. des Sciences de St. Pétersbourg* German renderings of a number of Buddhist tales found by

§ 2. Originating in India and forming a part of Buddhist literature, this collection of stories passed not later than 570 A.D. into Persia. The story of how Khosrū Nūshīrvān, king of Persia (A.D. 531—579), heard of its existence, and despatched the physician Barzūye to India in order to procure and translate a copy of it into Pehlevī, the literary dialect of Persia, is one which has been embellished with much pleasing fiction. This Pehlevī version (to which a Persian element became added) has, along with its Indian original, unfortunately vanished. From Pehlevī the book was rendered about A.D. 570 into Syriac by an ecclesiastic named Būd (or Bōd), and about A.D. 750 into Arabic by 'Abdullah Ibn al-Moḳaffa'. The latter version contains besides the original Pehlevī book a considerable element of undoubted Arab origin.

If Buddhism originated these stories, it was Islām which transmitted them to Europe. For while the old Syriac version just mentioned had no offspring as far as is known, the Arabic passed into not less than five distinct languages : Syriac, Greek, Persian, Hebrew, and Spanish.

The Syriac version must be assigned to the tenth or eleventh century and ascribed to a Christian priest. Of this later Syriac version an English translation is given in this volume.

The Greek version, made about A.D. 1080 by Symeon son of Seth, gave rise to an old Italian one first published in 1583.

Several Persian translations were made, both in prose and verse, ranging from about A.D. 940 to 1600. I will here only mention three; that of Naṣrullah, the *Anwārī Suhailī* of Ḥusain Wā'iz, and the *'Iyārī Dānish* of Abu'l-Faḍl. The version of Naṣrullah was made about A.D. 1120, and was based

him in Tibetan writings. The Mongols possess their own version of the *Pañ-chatantra* (their *Sadâi-Kûr*), and of the *Sinhâsana-dvâtrinçati* (their history of *Ardshi Bordshi Khan*). The 200 years of Mongol rule in Europe opened a wide door for the entry thither of Indian conceptions, and the Arab invasions contributed to the same end. The chief literary vehicles which conveyed these tales into Europe were the *Tūtīnâmah* of Nakhshabī, Arab writings, and probably Jewish ones. The European authors who have preeminently helped to naturalise them in Europe are Boccaccio for the stories and Straparola for the fables. From the literature they passed to the people, whence changed they returned to the literature, and so on. Though very numerous, they reduce themselves to a limited number of elementary forms. (Benfey's *Einleitung zur Panchatantra*, Preface, pp. xii., xxi. xxvi., and pp. 94—96.)

on the Arabic: but the author treated his original with some
freedom, accommodating it to his age and country, and produced
a book suitable rather for the learned and literary than for the
people. It has never been edited. On it is based the well-
known *Anwâri Suhailî*, made more than three centuries later,
and intended by its author for a popular and simplified edition
of the work of Naṣrullah. The *'Iyâri Dânish* ('Touchstone of
knowledge') is quite late, having been completed in A.D. 1591,
and is merely a modernised edition of the *Anwâri Suhailî*. The
Turkish *Humayûn Nâmah* of 'Alī Chelebī is a close translation
of the work of Husain Wā'iz.

A Hebrew translation of the Arabic, of uncertain date and
authorship, was the parent of a Latin one, made between
A.D. 1263 and 1278 by John of Capua, a converted Jew, and
styled by him *Directorium humanæ vitæ*. This Latin version
had a numerous progeny, including translations in German,
Spanish, Italian, French, English, Danish and Dutch.

I should mention here a Latin poetical imitation of the
Kalîlah wa Dimnah, namely Baldo's *Alter Æsopus*, of uncertain
origin and probably belonging to the thirteenth century.

The Spanish version made directly from the Arabic was
written by an unknown author in A.D. 1251, and on it was
mainly based the later Latin version of Raimund de Béziers
(Raimundus de Bitorris), made for Queen Joanna of Navarre,
wife of Philip le Bel, and finished in A.D. 1313, though Raimund
certainly used the *Directorium* as well.

All these numerous versions mark the circulation of the
book in the West. To Anton Schiefner belongs the credit of
discovering a Tibetan version of one of the most interesting
chapters in the book, made directly from the Sanscrit. That
other portions of the book found their way to the East and
North of India is very probable.

For the sake of clearness I exhibit the names of these
versions in a genealogical table (p. lxxxvi).

§ 3. Thus the great majority of the versions of this collection of fables and stories are based directly or mediately on the
Arabic of Ibn al-Moḳaffa', the Pehlevī original of which, now
lost, is reflected in the old Syriac version perhaps more perfectly
than in the Arabic. The striking likeness between the two latter

in the parts where they correspond goes far to shew that they are both faithful reflexes of their common prototype.

Beyond this point the history of the book is wrapt in deep obscurity. All that we know for certain is that it originated in India and belonged to the Buddhist literature. Whether Barzōye, the Persian, found the stories in a collected form or made his own selection from various sources is doubtful. And further, supposing that he found such a book, it is still doubtful whether it was a compilation or proceeded from some one author.

§ 4. The history of the Indian element of the *Kalīlah wa Dimnah* on Indian soil has been exhaustively treated in the late Professor Benfey's *Einleitung zur Pantschatantra* (Leipzig, 1859). Suffice it here to say, Firstly, that the extant Sanscrit writings which most nearly represent that Indian element are (1) the *Panchatantra*, or 'the five books', which corresponds to chapter 5, 7, 8, 9 and 10 of De Sacy's Arabic text[1]; (2) three tales in the *Mahābhārata*[2], identical with chapters 11, 12 and 13 in De Sacy; (3) one story in the first chapter of the *Panchatantra*, identical with De Sacy's 17th chapter: Secondly, that the *Panchatantra* and, to a lesser degree, the part of the *Mahābhārata* in question are artificially elaborated expansions of that original writing or writings of which the *Kalīlah wa Dimnah* contains a substantially faithful reproduction.

II. THE ARABIC AND OLD SYRIAC VERSIONS.

§ 5. To the Dutch scholar H. A. Schultens belongs the credit of having first published any portion of the Arabic *Kalīlah wa Dimnah*[3]. The part he chose was the chapter of the lion and the ox. Guidi, judging from this specimen, is inclined to think that the MS. used by him was a most incorrect one[4].

The Arabic version as a whole lies before us in Silvestre de Sacy's *Calila et Dimna ou Fables de Bidpai en Arabe; précédées d'un mémoire sur l'origine de ce livre, et sur les diverses traduc-*

---

[1] See H 5, 6.   [2] The great national epic of India.
[3] *Pars versionis arabicæ libri Colailah wa Dimnah sive fabularum Bidpai philosophi Indi* (Lugd. Bat., 1786, 4°.).
[4] See p. 5 of Guidi's *Studii.*

tions qui en ont été faites dans l'orient (Paris, 1816, 4°.)[1]. De Sacy's edition leaves much to be desired. His text (unpointed) is faulty in two respects. First, it is not the copy of any one manuscript, but is compounded out of several[2]. Second, it is based chiefly on a manuscript which turns out to be an inferior one. Nöldeke says rightly: ' one can almost say that the mere printing of any bad manuscript which might be chosen would be of more use to criticism'[3]. That the MS. on which the great French savant chiefly relied was exceedingly defective has been proved by the labours of Guidi, Nöldeke and Zotenberg.

Guidi, in his *Studii sul testo arabo del libro di Calila e Dimna* (Roma, Spithöver, 1873), has supplied from three Arabic manuscripts a large number of supplementary extracts, wanting in de Sacy's text. All, or nearly all of these, are to be found in their proper places in the versions. See for instance the table on p. 317 of this book.

Nöldeke in his *Die Erzählung vom Mäusekönig und seinen Ministern* (Göttingen, Dieterich, 1879)[4] gives German renderings of this story as found both in the unique manuscript of the old Syriac and in an Arabic text represented by four manuscripts of the Paris National library[5]. A complete transcript of the text of the passage in *Ancien Fonds* 1489, with a collation of the three other manuscripts, was supplied to him by Zotenberg and accompanies the translation. Nöldeke found that *Anc. Fonds* 1489, the MS. which De Sacy made least use of, agrees best (at any rate in this chapter) with the old Syriac, and therefore contains the most ancient text, while the MS. which he used most is very much abridged.

Of modern editions there are several. They all reproduce De Sacy's text with slight alterations. There is an Egyptian one published at Būlāķ in A.H. 1249 (A.D. 1833)[6]; Guidi[7] says that he has used an Egyptian edition of A.H. 1251 (A.D. 1835), and

---

[1] The volume also contains the Muʻallaķa of Lebīd, in Arabic and French.
[2] De Sacy, *op. cit.* pp. 57—61.
[3] *Göttingische gelehrte Anzeigen*, September 1884, p. 676.
[4] Printed in the *Abhandlungen d. k. Gesell. d. Wissenschaften zu Göttingen*. Bd. xxv. hist. phil. Classe 5.
[5] Anc. f. 1489; Anc. f. 1502; Suppl. ar. 1794; and Suppl. ar. 1793.
[6] In Camb. Univ. Library.
[7] *Studii sul testo &c.*, p. 5.

K. F.   *b*

its reprint of A.H. 1285 (A.D. 1865); and Zenker mentions another lithographed at Delhi in 1830. I possess a Mosul edition, by the Dominican fathers of that place, published in 1876 and freely pointed, and a Beirūt edition, published in 1882, partially pointed. In the Mosul edition the coarser passages have been altered.

Of modern translations there are three: an English one by Knatchbull[1], a German by Holmboe[2], and a German by Wolff[3]. Knatchbull's is a free translation of the original, as he says in his preface. Like the good Dominicans of Mosul he has altered the indelicate stories.

§ 6.   De Sacy's edition contains 18 chapters : viz.

1.   The preface of 'Ali son of ash-Shāb the Persian.

2.   The mission of Barzōye to India to procure a copy of the book.

3.   Exposition of the subject of the book by 'Abdullah son of al-Mokaffa'.

(A list of contents follows here)

4.   Biography of Barzōye, and his search after a true religion.

5.   The lion and the ox; or two friends between whom a crafty interloper sows dissension.

6.   Investigation of Dimnah's conduct, and his defence of himself.

7.   The ring-dove; or the love of sincere friends.

8.   The owls and the crows; or an enemy of whom one should beware.

9.   The ape and the tortoise; or the man who, having grasped something, lets it slip.

10.   The ascetic and the weasel; or the hasty man.

---

[1] *Kalila and Dimna, or the Fables of Bidpai. Translated from the Arabic. By the Rev. Wyndham Knatchbull, A.M.* (Oxford, 1819). Knatchbull was a pupil of De Sacy.

[2] *Calila und Dimna, eine Reihe moralischer u. politischer Fabeln des Philosophen Bidpai, aus dem arabischen von L. H. Holmboe* (Christiania, 1832).

[3] *Das Buch des Weisen in lust- und lehrreichen Erzählungen des indischen Philosophen Bidpai. The book is one of a series entitled Morgenländische Erzählungen verdeutscht v. Ph. Wolff.* The Camb. Univ. Lib. contains a Stuttgard edition of 1839, preface dated 1837, 2 parts in one vol., marked 2ᵉ Auflage large 12°.   Zenker mentions a Stuttgard edition of 1837, 2 vols., large 12°.

11. The mouse and the cat; or the man who has many enemies.

12. The king and the bird; or the vindictive man whom one should not trust.

13. The lion and the jackal; or the man who seeks to be reconciled with one whom he has illtreated.

14. Story of Ilādh, Bilādh, and Irākht.

15. The lioness and the horseman; or the man who refrains from hurting another, because of the harm he would thereby bring upon himself.

16. The ascetic and his guest; or the man who abandons his craft for another, and forgets the first without learning the second.

17. The traveller and the goldsmith; or the man who does good to those who are unworthy.

18. The king's son and his companions; a chapter shewing that God's decrees are inevitable.

Three additional chapters appear in some manuscripts, viz.:

19. The king of the mice; or the advantage of having a wise counsellor.

20. The heron and the duck.

21. The dove, the fox and the heron; or the man who can give good advice to others but not to himself[1].

§ 7. In the preface of 'Alī an account is given of the origin of the book. Alexander, having defeated Porus (فور) king of India, appoints one of his own officers to succeed that monarch. But scarcely are the troops withdrawn, than the people depose their alien ruler and replace him by a descendant of their own ancient kings, named Dabshalīm. The new king soon abandons

[1] The first known mention of the Arabic *Kalilah wa Dimnah* occurs in the ante-Islamic history of Ibn Wādih (Al-Ya'kūbi), ed. M. Th. Houtsma, pp. ٦٧—٦٦, where only ten chapters are enumerated, as follows: 1. Lion and ox, 2. Trial of Dimnah, 3. Owls and crows, 4. Bilād, 5. Goldsmith and traveller, 6. Ape and tortoise, 7. Cat and mouse, 8. Lion and jackal, 9. Ring-dove, 10. Lioness and horseman.

This list would seem to have no value, because it omits three chapters found in the old Syriac version (§§ 24, 28) viz. Ascetic and weasel, King and bird, King of the mice. These must always have belonged to the Arabic. The title too of the 5th chapter is inaccurately given.

Ibn Wādih lived into the first years of the tenth century of our era.

himself to caprice and cruelty. A Brahman philosopher Baidabā
(Bidpai, Pilpai) determines, if possible, to restore him to the
paths of moderation and justice. His disciples attempt in vain
to dissuade him from his enterprise. He goes to the king and
makes representations to him. The king flies into a passion,
and condemns the philosopher to death, but immediately after
commutes the sentence to one of strict imprisonment. One
night the king, unable to sleep, is thinking about the move-
ments of the heavenly bodies and the system of the universe,
and is thereby reminded of Baidabā. Reproaching himself for
his injustice to him, he sends for him out of prison and makes
him his minister. In this capacity, Baidabā employs his spare
time in composing treatises on government, and the king, by
following the rules of conduct thus laid down for him, becomes
an object of adoration to his people, and receives the submission
of neighbouring princes. While studying the history of his
predecessors, Dabshalīm notices that each of their reigns had
been marked by the publication of some particular book, and
thus conceives the wish of leaving to posterity some work which
will perpetuate his name. Accordingly he commissions Baidabā to compose a book containing useful lessons for the conduct
of kings who would secure the loyalty and obedience of their
people, and enlivened by light and amusing stories. One year
is allowed him in which to complete his task. Baidabā thereupon retires with a disciple to a private chamber and dictates to
him the work in fourteen chapters, each of which contains a question with its answer. These he collects into one book and calls it
the book of Kalīlah and Dimnah. At the expiry of the year it
is read to the king, who offers handsome presents in return for
it. Baidabā declines them all, merely expressing the wish that
the work may be carefully preserved, lest it be stolen and fall
into the hands of the Persians. The preface concludes by
mentioning briefly that Nūshīrvān king of Persia afterwards
heard of the book, and by means of the physician Barzōye
obtained a copy which he deposited among the royal treasures.

The reputed author of this preface Nöldeke would identify
with 'Alī ibn Muhammad ibn Shāh al-Ṭāhirī, a frivolous writer
and a descendant of Shāh ibn Mikāl who died A.H. 302[1]. But

---

[1] *Mänzckönig*, p. 6 : referring to the *Fihrist*, p. 153.

whoever the author was, it did not gain admission into Arabic manuscripts until late. For not only is it wanting in some of these, but it is absent from all the off-shoots of the Arabic version. It no doubt owes its existence to the wish to give some account of so celebrated a book, and should be classed with the introduction to the Panchatantra[1] and to that prefixed to the *Anwári Suhailí*. It is based on a fabulous connection between king Dabshalīm, known to them solely through the *Kalīlah wa Dimnah*, and Porus, familiar to them as a contemporary of Alexander the Great, not so much from history as from the mass of popular traditions about the latter. Such is Benfey's account of this chapter[2].

§ 8. The contents of the second chapter are briefly as follows. Nūshīrvān king of Persia, having heard that there exists in India a book containing every kind of instruction, directs his vizir Buzurjmihr to find a man of literary ability and zeal, acquainted with Indian and Persian. The vizīr selects Barzōye[3]. The latter then receives the order to procure the book, which is supposed to be in the library of the king of India. Arriving in India, he meets with great difficulties, but at last makes friends with a certain Indian through whose assistance he obtains not only the book he is seeking for but also other works of great value. Barzōye works day and night translating the book into Persian, fearing lest the king of India may ask for it. This done, he returns home. A large assembly is convened, and the book is read aloud. It is universally admired. The king offers him the costliest presents, but he declines them all except a robe, asking however that the king may command his vizīr to write a short account of his (Barzōye's) life, to be placed before the chapter of the Lion and the Ox, that is at the commencement of the book proper. His

[1] Benfey's *Pantschatantra*, pp. 1—8.

[2] Benfey's *Einleitung zur Pantsch.* pp. 54, 55.

[3] Persian authors write the termination ويه *ōye*, or وى. The pronunciation proscribed by Arab grammarians, namely ـوَيْه *awaihi* should probably be rejected as pedantic. So Nöldeke in the *Z. D. M. G.* xxx., p. 753. See further Olshausen in the *Monatsbericht der k. Akad. der Wissenschaften zu Berlin*, 16 June, 1881; and De Lagarde in the *Göttingische gelehrte Anzeigen* for 1883, pp. 707—709.

request is granted. The vizir retires and writes the history of
Barzōye 'from the period when he first frequented the schools;
describes how he journeyed to India for the purpose of extending
his knowledge in chemistry and medicine, and learnt the language of the country, bringing the story of his life down to the
time when Nūshirvān sent him thither in search of the book;
and takes care to omit nothing that can illustrate all the good
qualities which Barzōye possessed.' The history, when finished,
is read aloud to an assembly of nobles and courtiers.

Such is the substance of this chapter as found in De Sacy's
edition, in the Persian of Naṣrullah, and in the Greek of Symeon
Seth. It is not represented in the later Syriac version, and
of course not in the old Syriac. In the remaining offshoots of
the Arabic, it appears in a different place and in a different form.
The Hebrew version, reflected in John of Capua's Latin[1], the
old Spanish, and Raimund's Latin (a compound of the first
two[2]), all place it after De Sacy's 3rd chapter, which in these
versions heads the book. In the *Directorium* De Sacy's 3rd
and 2nd chapters together form the Prologue, after which come
the words 'Explicit Prologus. Incipit liber.' De Sacy's 4th
chapter (Biography of Barzōye) comes next as first chapter, after
which his order is preserved throughout (except that his 13th
chapter is placed after the 16th). Since in the Hebrew version
the 3rd chapter corresponds to De Sacy's 6th, the first chapter
must have been De Sacy's 4th, and De Sacy's 3rd and 2nd no
doubt together formed the prologue, just as in the *Directorium*.

In the old Spanish and in Raimund's Latin, the chapters
follow precisely the same order as in the *Directorium*. Only
in the old Spanish the Prologue corresponds to De Sacy's third
chapter *alone*, the first chapter being his fourth, the second his
fifth, and so on; while in Raimund's Latin there is no prologue
at all, his first chapter being De Sacy's third, his second
De Sacy's second, and so on.

The substance of the chapter too is very different in these
versions, and agrees with Firdausī's account in the section of the
Shāh-nāmah which he has devoted to describing the acquisi-

---

[1] Unfortunately the unique MS. of the Hebrew version is mutilated and only
begins in the middle of its third chapter (= De Sacy's 6th).

[2] See § 54.

tion of the *Kalilah wa Dimnah*. According to this form of the
story it is not the Persian king who hears of an Indian book and
procures it with difficulty, but the physician Barzōye who reads in
some book that in India are high mountains on which certain
trees and plants grow, out of which a preparation can be made
capable of raising the dead. This information he makes known
to the king of Persia, who promptly sends him to India in order
to search for them. For a year he tries a number of plants in
vain. At length he has recourse to the wise men of India, one
of whom tells him that the passage he has read is allegorical, that
by the mountains are meant wise and understanding men, by
the trees and plants the wisdom and understanding of the same,
by the medicine their books of instruction and wisdom, and
by the dead those who are destitute of wisdom. He now procures
these writings and translates them. One of them is the book of
Kalilah and Dimnah.

Since this form of the story exists in two independent
versions of the Arabic, viz. the Hebrew and the Old Spanish,
Benfey infers[1] that Firdausi read it in his copy of the *Kalilah wa
Dimnah*, and not that Firdausi was the source whence it found
its way into the Arabic version. He holds that it is older
than the form in De Sacy's text, and should be assigned to the
publisher of the Pehlevi translation, by whom it was intended
to stand as a kind of preface at the head of the whole book and
before the table of contents, the book commencing with the
biography of Barzōye. This theory, Benfey points out, agrees
with the fact that in all the versions the table of contents
stands before the biography and after the mission of Barzōye.
De Sacy's third chapter, the preface of Ibn al-Mokaffa', was no
doubt originally intended to stand before the mission of Barzōye.
Otherwise it is difficult to avoid the conclusion that Ibn al-
Mokaffa' wrote two prefaces, which is unlikely both in itself
and because Ibn Khallikān records that *the* treatise at the
commencement of the *Kalilah and Dimnah* is by Ibn al-
Mokaffa', in other words that in his copy De Sacy's third chapter
stood at the head of the book.

Benfey further thinks that the reason why the primitive

---

[1] *Einleitung zur Pantsch.,* pp. 61 sqq.

form of the story was replaced in some copies by the other and
longer one, was that the discovery of the book, as related
originally, was thought by some reader to be unworthy of so
celebrated a book. Too large a part was played by chance. So
he wrote the story differently and so as to assign the book a
prominent place from the commencement of the narrative to
the end[1].

How much truth there may be in the older form of the
story it is impossible to say.

§ 9. There is nothing in De Sacy's third chapter (which as
noticed in § 8 originally occupied the first place) to forbid us
accepting the statement of the superscription, namely that
Ibn al-Moḳaffa' was the author of it: nor is there any external
evidence to the contrary. It is simply a preface explaining the
nature and object of the book. Several tales are introduced.
They are all fully investigated by Benfey[2].

§ 10. The biography of Barzōye is of great interest. The
heading of the chapter ascribes it to Buzurjmihr, vizir of
Nūshīrvān, in harmony with the account given in the second
chapter[3], which account further agrees with the fact that in all
the versions (except the *later* Syriac) this biography stands at the
head of the book proper, that is immediately before the chapter
of the Lion and the Ox and after the table of contents. In the
later Syriac it stands last of all. That Buzurjmihr had little
or no share in writing the chapter is probable enough: for not only
is it written in the first person throughout, but it contains too
much about the inner life of Barzōye to have been written by
any but himself. Further, the long and detailed anatomical
description (pp. 262, 263) betrays the physician unmistakeably.
What Buzurjmihr had to do with the writing of the chapter is
uncertain. At most he could not have done more than arrange
materials supplied him by Barzōye. More probably, he merely
lent his name as a compliment.

The substance of the chapter is as follows: Barzōye, a young
man of good birth and education, conceives an ardent desire
to study medicine. Having acquired extensive knowledge of
the art, he pauses and considers whether he will live for worldly

1 Benfey's *Einleitung zur Pantsch.*, p. 64.
2 *Ibid.*, § 14.   3 See § 8.

gains or heavenly joys. He decides to make the latter his
object, and accordingly treats the sick for nothing, looking for
recompense to God alone. To the poor he gives money as well
as medical aid. He becomes the object of royal favour even
before his journey to India. Finding however that it is
impossible to cure a person so completely as to make a recur-
rence of disease impossible, he ceases from his zeal for the
medical profession and resolves to lead a purely religious life.
But here a difficulty meets him. There are many religions:
which is the right one? Men, ho finds, embrace a religion
either by compulsion, or because their fathers professed it, or
from sordid motives. He consults teachers belonging to all the
various creeds. Each one extols his own religion and reviles
that of his fellow. The arguments of none are convincing.

He is inclined to devote himself for a season to meditation
and research, but the thought occurs to him that the time for
dying may bo near. Thereupon he casts himself on the mercy
of God, and also on the good deeds ' which have gone before
him.' In the meantime he endeavours to live as harmless and
virtuous a life as he possibly can, eschewing all crime and unlawful pleasures. At length ho wishes to devote himself entirely
to asceticism and piety. For a time he hesitates, fearing lest,
having set out on this course, ho may not have strength and
perseverance to continue in it, on account of the hardships and
privations it involves. He becomes more and more convinced
that earthly pleasures are empty and transitory, that human
life is full of sorrows, and that the majority of men sacrifice
their final bliss to present and fleeting gratifications. Finally
he resolves to remain as he is and to strive to become as perfect
as be can, hoping that at some future time be may meet with
' a guide for his path, a power to rule his soul, and one who will
order his affairs.'

Barzōye ends his story by saying that ho returned from
India after copying out many of the Indian books, and in
particular the book of Kalilah and Dimnah [1].

A large number of tales and illustrations are introduced.
These are fully treated of by Benfey (*Einleitung zur Pantsch.*,

---

[1] According to John of Capua, Barzōye resolves in the end, not to remain a
physician, but to become an ascetic.

pp. 77—83). The prominent part which asceticism plays
in this biography Benfey connects with Buddhism, then in full
vigour in India. Barzōye's study of Indian books and sojourn
in India cannot fail to have familiarised him with this phase of
Buddhism [1].

The short notice of Barzōye by Ibn Abī Uṣaibi'a [2] adds
little to the information given in the chapters relating the
mission and biography of Barzōye. According to that notice,
ho was born at Merv esh-shāhjān and was private physician to
Nūshīrvān.

§ 11.   With the chapter of the Lion and the Ox we enter on
the original Indian book. This and the 7th, 8th, 9th and 10th
chapters of the *Kalilah wa Dimnah* correspond respectively to
the five chapters of the *Panchatantra* [3]. The 6th chapter is not
Indian at all, but Arabic, and first appears in Ibn al-Mukaffa''s
version [4].

The story of the lion and the ox illustrates how two loving
friends may be set at variance by a crafty interloper. It runs
briefly as follows. A merchant has extravagant sons who
squander his money and earn nothing. He admonishes them.
The eldest son in consequence turns over a new leaf and sets
out on a trading expedition. He has with him a waggon drawn
by two oxen. One of these, named Shanzabah, becomes exhausted by over-exertion, and is left behind in charge of
an attendant. The latter, growing tired of waiting, leaves
Shanzabah, overtakes his master, and declares that the ox
is dead. Shanzabah recovers strength, finds pasturage and
water, and becomes sleek and fat. A lion, who lives in the
neighbourhood and is king of the beasts in that part, hears
Shanzabah bellowing, and is very much frightened, never having
heard or seen an ox before. Two jackals, named Kalilah and
Dimnah, are courtiers at the king's gate. Kalilah is content

[1] Benfey's *Einleit. zur Pantsch.* p. 76.

[2] Wüstenfeld's *Geschichte der arabischen Aerzte und Naturforscher* (Göttingen, 1840) p. 6. But in Müller's edition of Ibn Abī Uṣaibi'a (Part i., p. 808)
even these particulars are absent.

[3] The order of the chapters in De Sacy's edition from the 5th to the 12th
inclusive is the same in all manuscripts and versions, except in the old Italian,
where the 14th occupies the place of the 11th. On the Panchatantra and its
relation to the *Kalilah wa Dimnah* see § 83.

[4] See § 12.

with his position and pay, but Dimnah is ambitious and
grasping. Dimnah, perceiving that the lion's mind is not at
ease, determines to approach him, offer his services, and if
possible relieve his distress, and by that means improve his
position and his salary. Kalilah warns him of the danger of
approaching princes. Dimnah, nothing daunted, enters the
lion's presence and makes an offer of his services in a general
way. Finding that he has made a favourable impression,
Dimnah at length makes bold to ask why the king is not at his
ease, and refrains from hunting and amusing himself as usual.
The lion only replies that it is not on account of fear that he
does so. But at this moment the ox is heard to bellow. The
lion out of sheer fright confesses the truth. Dimnah, after
soothing the king's fear and telling him the story of the fox
and the drum (p. 14), offers to go to the ox, take stock of him,
and bring back a report. The offer is accepted, and the
account Dimnah gives is reassuring. Dimnah is sent a second
time, and comes back bringing the ox with him, having in the
meantime inspired him with that respect which is due to
kings, and at the same time given him the most solemn
promises of safety.

The lion and the ox speedily make friends with one another,
and the ox is exalted beyond all his fellows before the king.
Dimnah now envies the ox exceedingly, and is specially vexed
to think that *he* should have been the cause of Shanzabah's
prosperity. He complains bitterly to Kalilah, who then tells
him the story of the ascetic and the rogue, or 'Don't complain
of what is your own fault' (pp. 18—21). A long conversation
between the two jackals ensues, in which Dimnah announces
his intention of compassing the death of Shanzabah by guile,
and tells two very clever stories (pp. 23—28) to shew that mere
strength is no match for cunning. He then goes to the lion,
tells him that the ox has treasonable designs against him, and
advises him without delay to make an end of him; relating the
story of the three fishes (p. 31) or the danger of carelessness and
inattention, and then that of the louse and the flea (p. 34)
or the danger of making friends with strangers. The lion is
unwilling to believe in the perfidy of Shanzabah, and Dimnah
only succeeds in arousing his suspicions. Before leaving, Dimnah

tells him that the ox, when he comes again, will present
the appearance of one on the point of making an attack. From
the lion, Dimnah goes to the ox, and succeeds in making him
equally suspicious of the lion; though he will not believe that
the lion himself is guilty, but that his advisers have out of envy
stirred him up against his friend. This reflection suggests the
clever story of how the wolf, the crow and the jackal brought
about the death of the honest camel (pp. 43—47). The ox,
determined to face the lion boldly and not to plot against him
behind his back, enters the royal presence, naturally wearing a
downcast face. The lion, as Dimnah has anticipated, thinks he
means to do battle, and rushes at him. Kalilah and Dimnah
look on at the battle. It must have lasted a very long time,
for before the lion has killed the ox outright, Kalilah has time
to administer a protracted lecture, including the story of the
man, the bird and the apes (p. 53), that of the rogue and the
simpleton (p. 56), and that of the merchant and his iron (p. 59).
The lion, having killed his friend, repents of his hasty conduct,
reflecting that the ox may have fallen a victim to the calumny of
envious persons. The brief statement at the end that Dimnah's
treachery was afterwards discovered and punished is wanting in
the Panchatantm and in the old Syriac version, and is therefore an Arabic addition, which either suggested or was suggested
by the next chapter, namely the account of the trial, defence
and punishment of Dimnah.

§ 12.   That the 6th chapter in De Sacy's edition formed no
part of the original Indian book is certain.   It is wholly
wanting in the Panchatantra, the last chapter of which ends by
saying that the lion troubled himself no more about Shanzabah,
promoted Dimnah to be minister, and reigned happily[1].   Nor
can any trace of such a chapter be found in any of the Indian
offshoots of the Panchatantra[2].   Moreover, however much this
may offend against our moral feeling, it is yet in thorough
harmony with Indian politics, of which the pervading spirit is a
selfish egotism.   This chapter is also wholly wanting in the
old Syriac version[3], in which, as in the Panchatantra, the
chapter of the lion and the ox ends without the slightest hint

---

[1] Benfey's *Pantsch.* p. 121.   [2] Benfey's *Einleitung zur Pantsch.* p. 298.
[3] *Kal. u. Dam.* Transl. p 32.

that Dimnah was ever brought to trial and punished. Hence it is reasonable to assume that the Pehlevi version did not contain it, and therefore that it first appeared in the Arabic.

Though it is perhaps the least interesting chapter in the book, the author of the later Syriac version has spun it out to a preposterous length.

§ 13. The story of the ring-dove is perhaps the most pleasing in the book. It corresponds to the second book of the Panchatantra, and runs briefly thus. A certain crow, perched on a tree, espies a fowler coming towards it. He spreads a net on the ground and scatters some seeds over it. Presently, a ring-dove and a number of her companions, tempted by the bait, are all caught. But before the fowler comes up, the doves by a united effort pluck up the net, and fly with it into the air. The crow, wishing to see the end of the affair, flies after them. The ring-dove conducts her companions to the hole of a certain mouse, her friend, who in a short time gnaws through the net and liberates them all; whereupon they fly home again. But the crow remains, having conceived an ardent desire to make a friend of the mouse. The mouse, distrustful at first, is at length persuaded to accept the proffered friendship. One day the crow remarks to the mouse, that his dwelling is dangerously near the public road, and proposes that they both retire to a more secluded place, where a certain tortoise, a friend of the crow, lives. The mouse consents, and the crow, taking hold of the mouse's tail, flies away with him to the pond where the tortoise lives. They are well received, and the mouse at once proceeds to entertain his two friends by giving them an account of the circumstances which led to his becoming acquainted with the crow. He had formerly lived in prosperity and affluence, the envy and pride of many other mice, for whom he procured food. But fortune forsook him and his means of sustenance were cut off, whereupon the other mice turned their backs upon him, and mocked at him. And this was why he had left that place and come to live in the fields, where he was visited by the crow. After they have conversed together yet awhile, there comes running towards them a gazelle, seeking refuge from a huntsman who, he thinks, is pursuing him. The tortoise, seeing him eye the water as if thirsty, begs him

to drink without fear, and then invites him to live with them,
assuring him that no huntsman ever comes that way. This
select society makes a habit of meeting together from time
to time to enjoy each other's company. But one day the gazelle
is missing. The crow soars into the air, and lo the gazelle
lying captive in a net! He flies back with the sad news. The
mouse forthwith sets out in order to liberate his friend by
gnawing through the meshes of the net. Hardly has he
reached the gazelle, than the tortoise also comes up, declaring
that he could not bear to be left all alone without his friends.
While they are yet conversing together, the huntsman draws
near. But the meshes are severed, the gazelle runs swiftly
away, the crow ascends rapidly into the air, and the mouse
hides himself craftily; the tortoise alone remains. The huntsman, on finding the tortoise, binds him with a cord and carries
him over his shoulder. His friends, the gazelle and the crow,
then beg the mouse to devise a means of rescuing him. Acting
on the advice of the mouse, the gazelle lies down where the
hunter can see him, as if wounded, and the crow settles on him
as if pecking the wound. The huntsman lets go the tortoise,
and runs after the gazelle. The gazelle retires slowly, so as to
induce the huntsman to continue his pursuit for a while. The
mouse thus gets time to gnaw through the cord which binds
the tortoise, and they are all saved. They end their lives in
peace and happiness.

§ 14. The next three chapters[1]—De Sacy's 8th, 9th and
10th—correspond to the remaining three books of the Panchatantra. The story of the owls and the crows (pp. 129—157) is
long and not very interesting. That of the ape and the
tortoise (pp. 158—168), on the other hand, is a most entertaining tale. It is too short to require an outline here. The
chapter of the ascetic and the weasel (p. 169) is made up of two
stories, both of which have become naturalised in the literature
of every civilised people.

§ 15. The next three chapters[2]—De Sacy's 11th (mouse
and cat), 12th (king and bird), and 13th (lion and jackal)—
though not to be found in the Panchatantra, appear in the

[1] Knatchbull, pp. 214—273: my translation, pp. 129—171.
[2] Knatchbull, pp. 273—318: my translation, pp. 172—203.

Mahābhārata[1], whence they are translated at length by Benfey in his *Einleitung*[2]. The story of the king and the bird is also to be found in the *Harivança* (v. 1117 ff.).

§ 16. The next chapter in De Sacy's edition, the 14th[3], is of considerable interest.

A certain good king one night has eight dreams, which alarm him so much that he sends for the Brahmans to interpret them. The Brahmans, deeply embittered against his majesty for having recently put to death 12,000 of them, resolve to utilise this opportunity for the purpose of gaining political ascendancy, and, if necessary, of taking the king's life. Accordingly they tell him that he has good reason to be alarmed by his dreams, but that, having searched in their books, they have discovered means of averting the threatened danger. Namely, the king must deliver up to them his favourite wife, his favourite son, his confidential adviser, his secretary, his swiftest horse, his matchless sword, his two best war elephants, his powerful Bactrian camel, and last and chiefly, the wise Kibariūn. These they must put to death, and mix their blood in a caldron. The king must then sit in this caldron. When he gets out, they must stand round him, mutter incantations, spit upon him, and wash him with water and sweet oil. After this he may return to his palace. By this means the danger will be averted. But if the king refuses to adopt this course, his kingdom will be taken from him, and he himself lose his life. The king retires, falls on his face and weeps, and 'turns himself about on the ground as a fish does when it is taken out of the water,' not knowing which is the worst of the two evils. The favourite queen, acting on the advice of the king's confidential adviser, goes to him and asks what his trouble is. In a little while he tells her. She answers very calmly that she will be delighted to give up her life to serve the king, but advises him at the same time to place no confidence in the Brahmans and to have no communication with them until he has consulted the wise Kibariūn. To the house of Kibariūn the king then

[1] Namely, *MahābhĀ.* XII. vv. 4930 sqq., XIL. vv. 5183 sqq., and XIL. vv. 4064 sqq., correspond to these three chapters respectively.
[2] Benfey's *Einleitung zur Pantsch.* §§ 219, 221, 223.
[3] Knatchbull, pp. 311—338; my translation, pp. 219—247.

repairs. The wise man bids him cheer up, and interprets the
dreams to signify the very reverse of bad fortune. Each dream,
except one, means that a king is going to send messengers
bearing valuable presents. That one dream the sage declines
to interpret fully, merely saying that it portends a little dis-
pleasure against one whom the king loves. In a few days, the
messengers arrive with the presents, as Kibariûn had predicted.
The king, overjoyed, distributes the presents, sending some
gold-embroidered garments and a diadem to the women's
apartments. He directs his favourite wife to choose either tho
diadem or one of the garments. Sho takes the diadem.
Another of his wives, who is jealous of her, decks herself in tho
garment which she had refused, and excites the king's admira-
tion to such an extent that he blames his favourito wife for
having chosen the diadem. She, in a moment of irritation,
throws a dish of rice over the king's head. The king instantly
summons his confidential adviser, and bids him lead her away
and have her put to death. As he takes her away, he determines to spare her life until the king's wrath subsides, thinking
that perhaps then he may repent of his order. In the meantime he will keep her in close custody. The king repents, as
the minister has foreseen. The latter, guessing the change in
the king's feelings by his altered demeanour and countenance,
bids him moderate his grief and endure patiently what cannot
be remedied. He then relates to him the story of tho two
doves', showing that a sensible man should not punish hastily ;
and then that of the ape and the lentils, teaching that one
should not grieve for a single thing that is lost, but rather be
thankful for all that he still possesses. Then follows a very long
conversation, in which the monarch proves no match for his
minister at repartee. As the interview goes on, the situation
becomes more and more strained ; at length, having taxed the
king's temper and patience to the very utmost, he announces
that the queen is still alive. The king, delighted, confers
supreme power and rich presents on his minister, and promises
never to neglect taking the advice of his friends in any measure
of importance. The Brahmans are put to death.

¹ Knatchbull. p. 331 ; my translation, p. 306.

The long passage of arms between king and minister is given very briefly in De Sacy's text, but Guidi has supplied the missing portions[1]. These supplementary extracts of Guidi are nearly all to be found in the later Syriac version[2].

The whole chapter really consists of two stories pieced together, the second being a slender frame-work for the long conversation. The first story ends with the fulfilment of Kibariūn's interpretation of the dreams.

Of all the chapters in the book, this one is the most unmistakeably Buddhist. Throughout, the Brahmans are pictured in the most hideous light. But if further proof be wanted, it may be had in the fact that a Tibetan version of the chapter has been found in the Kanjur by Anton Schiefner[3]. Just as so many of the Buddhist tales passed along with Buddhism to the east and north of India[4], so this particular story (or rather these two stories) reached Tibet.

§ 17. De Sacy's 15th chapter, that of the lioness and the horseman[5], is too short to require an outline here. There can be no doubt that it is of Indian and Buddhist origin. The idea that the lioness ceases to eat flesh and lives only on fruit, and that, on hearing from the dove that the animals complain of the consequent scarcity of fruit, she eats only grass, could only have been conceived originally by Buddhists. See further Benfey's *Einleitung zur Pantschatantra*, p. 599.

§ 18. De Sacy's 16th chapter, that of the ascetic and his guest[6], contains nothing distinctively Indian, while on the

---

[1] Guidi, *Studii*, pp. 78—95.

[2] Pp. 235—244 of my translation. See table, p. 319.

[3] *Mahākātjdjana und König Tshaṇḍa-Pradjota. Ein Cyklus buddhistischer Erzählungen.* Mitgetheilt von A. Schiefner. Contained in the *Mémoires de l'Académie Impériale des Sciences de St Pétersbourg.* Series VII. Vol. XXII. Nr. 7 (St Petersburg, 1875, 4°, viii pp. of introduction, 67 pp. of German text). The tales are twenty in number, and the last two correspond respectively with the two parts of De Sacy's chapter 14. In the same year with the above, Schiefner had published the Tibetan text of the last of these tales, together with a Latin translation. (*Viro illustrissimo Victori Bosniakowsky...gratulatur Imperialis Academia Scientiarum Petropolitana classis historico-philologica. Dharatæ responsa Tibetice cum versione latina ab Antonio Schiefner edita.* St Petersburg, 1875, 4°, 46 pages.)

[4] See p. xiii, note [1].

[5] Knatchbull, pp. 339—343: my translation, pp. 214—216.

[6] Knatchbull. pp. 343—346: my translation. pp. 217, 218.

other hand it does present indications of foreign origin. Such
are the mention of eating dates[1], and of learning Hebrew.
This view is confirmed by the fact that the chapter is not to be
found in the old Syriac version. It was no doubt a subsequent
addition.

§19. The two concluding chapters of De Sacy's edition,
namely that of the traveller and the goldsmith[1], and that of
the king's son and his companions[2], are entertaining, but too
short to require an outline here. That of the traveller and the
goldsmith appears in the first book of the Panchatantra (our
chapter of the lion and the ox), according to the Berlin manuscript,
and is undoubtedly Buddhist, being also found in a Buddhist
collection of legends known as the *Rasavâhinî*, as well as in the
Buddhist *Karmaçataka*[3]. As to the story of the king's son and
his companions, there is one bearing some resemblance to it in
the first book of the Panchatantra, according to the Berlin
manuscript and H. H. Wilson's manuscripts; but the resemblance
is so slight that it is doubtful whether the two have
a common source[4]. Benfey pronounces it to be of Indian and
Buddhist origin[5].

§20. Thus far have been enumerated the 18 chapters of
De Sacy's edition, but the manuscripts present three more;
namely
19. The king of the mice and his ministers.
20. The heron and the duck.
21. The dove, the fox, and the heron.
The chapter of the king of the mice is certainly of considerable
antiquity, for it appears in the old Syriac version,
where it stands last. It is also found in Symeon Seth's Greek
version of the Arabic (where it occupies the last place but one),
as well as in the old Italian translation of the Greek version.
So far as I know, it appears nowhere else. It has been made
the subject of a monograph by Professor Theodor Nöldeke of
Strassburg[6]; De Sacy has given an outline of it in the *Notice*

[1] Knatchbull, p. 344 ; see note on p. 217. ll. 12, 18 of my translation.
[2] Knatchbull, pp. 346—354 : my translation, pp. 204—207.
[3] Knatchbull, pp. 354—366 : my translation, pp. 208—213.
[4] Benfey's *Einleit. zur Pantsch.*, p. 603.   [5] *Ibid.* § 104.
[6] *Ibid.* pp. 288, 289   [7] See § 5.

des Manuscrits prefixed to his *Calila et Dimna;* and Benfey
says a few words about it in his *Einleitung zur Pantschatantra,*
pp. 605, 606. The story runs as follows. The king of the mice
consults with his ministers as to the possibility of freeing themselves from the cats. He himself thinks that there must be
some means of doing so. Two of his ministers agree with him
and are subservient to his wishes, but the third and wiser one
gives it as his opinion that an evil of long standing cannot be
so easily abolished, and that any attempt to cure it may easily
cause a great calamity. This view he confirms by a story.
But since the king adheres to his resolution, he yields, and his
colleagues bring forward proposals. The proposal of the first
one, to hang a bell on every cat as a danger signal, is pronounced
by the second not to be feasible. The proposal of the second, to
go into the wilderness for a year that people may do away with
the cats thus rendered superfluous, is declared by the third to
involve great hardships and to be an uncertain method. He
then makes a proposal himself, which is to act and weave plans
in such a manner as to induce men to ascribe to the cats the
harm done by the mice, and to exterminate them, not as being
merely superfluous but as evil doers. This plan succeeds, the
cats are exterminated, and men of a later generation relate
extraordinary stories of the harmfulness of the cats.

The parenthetical story of the third minister is as follows.
A king has a castle at the foot of a mountain. Out of a hole
in this mountain comes a great deal of wind. He consults his
minister as to how the evil may be remedied. Though the
minister warns him not to attempt to do away with an evil
of long standing and tells him a story to confirm what he says,
yet the king persists in his plan, and the minister yields. So
the king causes the hole to be stopped up. Since no more
wind comes out, there is no more moisture. All the plants and
trees wither, and men and animals are in great need. The
king's subjects then rebel, kill the king and his family as well
as the minister, break open the hole, and set fire to the wood
which had been used to stop it up. The pent up wind rushes
forth with terrific force, scatters the burning wood all over the
land, and everything is destroyed by the wind and the fire.
The story introduced parenthetically in this story is that of the

ass, who wishing to escape from the misery inherited by his race, attempts to get the horns of a stag as weapons, but is robbed of his ears by the stag's keeper.

Professor Nöldeke argues[1] that this chapter is of Persian, not Indian origin. His principal reasons are briefly as follows. 1. None of the proper names which occur in this section, (except of course those of the king *Dabsharm* (Dēvaçarman) and his philosopher *Baidabā* or *Baidanā*,) can be pronounced Indian. On the other hand several are clearly Persian. 2. The phrase "the land of the Brahmans" occurs. Such an expression would be entirely out of place in a book written in India. 3. It would be difficult to find in India proper such an immense wilderness as the one mentioned. But in Irān there are notably many such. 4. The idea that to withhold the wind would cause the trees to wither has been found in a genuine Persian myth (Bērūnī, 217). 5. A passage occurs in which suicide is condemned, which sentiment is in perfect harmony with the Zoroastrian religion, but is certainly not Indian.

Since this chapter is only to be found in some Arabic manuscripts, in the old Syriac version, and in Symeon Seth's Greek (whence it found its way into the old Italian), it must have been lost at an early period. Its original position was probably at the end of the book, as in the old Syriac. Though it follows the story of the cat and the mouse in most of the Arabic manuscripts in which it occurs, this is merely because in both sections the relations of cats and mice are treated of.

§ 21. The chapter of the heron and the duck was found by De Sacy in one Arabic manuscript, but the copyist says in a note that it forms no part of the original book, having been added afterwards[2].

Both this chapter and that of the dove, the fox, and the heron, are found at the end of the old Spanish version, of the Hebrew version, (whence they were taken by John of Capua,) and of Raimund's version. Neither of these chapters is contained in the later Syriac, in Symeon Seth's Greek, or in Nasrullah's Persian version.

The story of the heron and the duck is entitled in the

---

[1] *Mäuselänig*, p. 5.
[2] *Notice des Manuscrits*, prefixed to De Sacy's edition, pp. 59, 60.

Directorium "De avibus et est de sociis et proximis qui se invicem decipiunt," in the Hebrew version merely 'Chapter of the birds' (שִׁיר הָעֵיפוֹת), in the old Spanish "De las garzas é del zarapico[1]," and in Raimund's Latin "De duabus avibus habentibus tibias longas et colla longa; et vocatur hæc avis *gurca* vulgariter et arabico *holgos*[2] et de quadam ave quæ ambice *marzam*[3] (furtber on *masiam*) dicitur bahens longum rostrum et dicitur vulgariter *moratico*..." In the Hebrew text the names are given as עֶלֶבֶּם (for עֶלְנוּם)[4] and מְרֹם[5], in the *Directorium* as *holgos*[4] and *mosan*[5].

An outline of this stupid story is given by Benfey in his *Einleitung zur Pantschatantra* (pp. 607—609).

The remaining chapter of the Arabic version, that of the dove, tbe fox, and the beron, being contained in two independent translations (tho Hebrew and the old Spanish), must have found its way into some recension of tho Arabic version. Besides, it is actually contained in the Mosul edition[6] of the *Kalilah wa Dimnah*, where it is entitled 'Chapter of tho dove, the fox, and tho bird called māliku 'lḥazīn[6], or the man who gives good advice to others but not to himself.' Tbe heading in tho old Spanish version is tho same, except that tho name *alcaravan*[4] appears instead of *māliku 'lḥazīn*. In the Hebrew version the bird is called simply צִפּוּר, rendered in tlie *Directorium* by *passer*. Raimund's Latin bas *alcharam* in one codex, *acharam* in another[7].

The story is a good ono. A fox terrifies a dove, who is perched on a tree, to such an extent that to save her life she throws him down her young ones. After the fox has departed, a bird comes to the dove and says, 'You should have dared him

---

[1] I.e. the herons and tho whimbrel (or curlcw). *Zarapito* is the word as given in Spanish dictionaries.

[2] I.e. عَلْكُوم, a species of beron.

[3] I.e. مِرزَم, of which Damiri in his Natural History (p. ٢٠٢) says: 'a sea-bird with long legs and neck, a curved beak and wings tipped with black. It feeds mostly on fishes, and may be used for food.'

[4] P. ٢٢٠.

[5] A species of heron. See Damiri's Natural History, p. ٢٠٢.

[6] I.e. a sort of bustard. See Dozy and Engelmann's Glossary.

[7] *Notices et Extraits des manuscrits &c.*, Vol. x., Pt. 2.

to do his best, and threatened, in the event of his climbing up the
tree, to devour your young ones and fly away.' When the fox
returns, she gives him this answer. He promises to spare her
young ones, if she will tell him who prompted her to say this.
She tells him. The fox then goes to the bird and says, 'When the
wind catches you on the right side, where do you lay your head?'
The bird replies 'Under the left side.' 'When it catches you
in front, where then?' 'Towards my hinder part.' 'But when
it blows from every side, where then?' 'Under my wings.'
The fox says that he cannot believe it, but that if the bird
really can do this thing, he has never seen the like of it before.
The silly bird does it, to convince him. The fox promptly
catches him, saying, 'You could give good advice to the dove
but not to yourself,' and devours him. See further Benfey's
Einleitung zur Pantschatantra §§ 237, 118.

§ 22. The *Kalilah wa Dimnah*, then, is made up of three
elements; Indian, Persian, and Arabic. Twelve chapters are
of Indian and Buddhist origin (viz. chapters 5, 7, 8, 9, 10, 11, 12,
13, 14, 15, 17 and 18); three are pronounced by good critics to
be Persian (viz. chapters 2, 4, and 19); six appear first in the
Arabic version (viz. chapters 1, 3, 6, 16, 20, 21).

Of the twelve Indian chapters, five (5, 7, 8, 9, 10) correspond
to the five chapters composing the *Panchatantra*, two (17, 18)
appear in the first book of the *Panchatantra*, three (11, 12, 13)
are found in the *Mahābhārata*, and two (14, 15) seem to have
fallen out of the Indian literature altogether.

§ 23. No account of the Arabic *Kalilah wa Dimnah* would
be complete without some notice of the man to whom we are
indebted for this translation.

'Abdullah son of al-Mukaffa' was born about A.D. 725[1] in
the province of Persia, and brought up in the Zoroastrian
religion. His father al-Mukaffa', whose real name was Dâdûyeh,
had been appointed receiver of the revenue of Fârs. Convicted
of embezzling the public money, he had been put to the
torture, which had had the effect of shrivelling up his hand,
whence his name al-Mukaffa' ('the shrivelled'). The son
'Abdullah was a man of great ability, learning, and wit. While

---

[1] He certainly died about 760; and al-Madâinî, as reported by Ibn Khallikan (De Slane, 1. p. 434), states 'Ibn al-M. lived (it is said) thirty-six years.'

still a young man he made profession of Islamism to 'Īsā son of 'Alī, paternal uncle of the first two 'Abbāsī caliphs, as-Ṣaffāḥ and al-Manṣūr, and governour of the province of Ahwāz in 'Irāḳ. He then became intimate with him and acted as his secretary. Another person of note whom 'Abdullah knew intimately was Sufyān son of Mu'āwiya al-Muhallabī, governour of al-Baṣra. This Sufyān he offended deeply by habitually calling him *Ibn al-moghtalimah*[1], by alluding to his large nose, and generally treating him with contempt.

It is well known that 'Īsā's brother 'Abdullah aspired to the califate and rebelled against his nephew al-Manṣūr, but being defeated by an army sent against him, fled for refuge to his brothers 'Īsā and Sulaymān. These interceded for their brother with the caliph, who consented to forgive them and sign a letter of pardon. The two brothers instructed 'Abdullah son of al-Muḳaffa' to draw up the letter and word it in the strongest terms, so as to leave al-Manṣūr no pretext for evading his word. He even inserted the following clause amongst others : *And if at any time the Commander of the faithful act perfidiously towards his uncle 'Abdullah ibn 'Alī, his wives shall be divorced from him, his horses shall be confiscated for the service of God (i.e. for war), his slaves shall become free, and the Muslims loosed from their allegiance towards him.*

The caliph, on reading the paper, was highly displeased, and when he found out who had drawn it up, directed Sufyān, the governour of al-Baṣra, to put him to death. Sufyān, willing enough, waited for an opportunity. One day, 'Īsā sent his secretary to see him on some business. He was seen to enter Sufyān's house, but he never came out again. How the murder was accomplished is uncertain. According to al-Madāinī, Sufyān ordered an oven to be heated, and the limbs of Ibn al-Muḳaffa' to be cut off and thrown in one by one. He then threw his body in, and closed the oven, saying : 'It is not a crime in me to punish you thus, for you are a Zindiḳ ('heretic'), who corrupted the people.' According to another account, Sufyān sent him into the bath, and kept the door locked till he was suffocated. The brothers 'Īsā and Sulaymān, having ascer-

[1] *Filius luxice.*

tained that their secretary had been seen to enter the palace of
Sufyān but not to come out, cited him before the caliph. But
the latter intimidated the witnesses, and the two brothers,
perceiving that the caliph had prompted the crime, held
their peace[1].

The author of the *Fihrist*[2] describes him as a forcible and
eloquent writer and an elegant poet, and states that he translated a number of books from Pehlevi into Arabic, being
thorough master of both languages[3]. Certainly his version of the
Kalilah wa Dimnah is written in the most elegant and classical
Arabic. Al-Aṣmaʿī, perhaps the greatest authority on the *lughu*
or classical language, speaking of another work by Ibn al-
Muḳaffaʿ, could only point out one mistake in point of language[4].
The well-known wezir Ibn Muḳla (died A.D. 939) reckoned him
among 'the ten most eloquent men'[5]. One specimen at least of his
poetry, an elegy, was admitted into the Ḥamāsa[6], the well-known
collection of Arabic poetry by Abū Tammām (born A.D. 808).

Both the author of the *Fihrist* and al-Masʿūdī mention a
number of the books translated by Ibn al-Moḳaffaʿ from Pehlevi
into Arabic. The *Fihrist*[7] names the following: "the *Kho-
dhāi-nāmah*[7], consisting of history; the *Aīn-namah*; the book
of Kalilah and Dimnah; the book of Mazdak[8]; the *Tāj*

---

[1] This notice is a brief resumé of that of Ibn Khallikan (De Slane's translation, I. p. 431, ff.), who lived A.D. 1211—1282.

[2] الفهرست, or 'The Index,' is a reference book treating of general history
and literature, by a writer known best by the name of An-Nadīm, who died
towards the end of the 10th century, A.D.

[3] *Fihrist* (ed. Flügel), p. 118. For a rendering of the whole passage, see
De Sacy in *Notices et Extraits des Manuscrits*, Vol. I. Pt. 1, p. 266.

[4] *Muzhir*, II. 86. [5] *Fihrist*, p. 126.

[6] *Ḥamāsa* (ed. Freytag), I. p. 394; II. Pt. 2, p. 62. The lines are also quoted
with a translation by De Sacy in *Notices et Extraits*, I. Pt. 1, p. 266.

[7] I.e. 'Book of Kings.' This book, not extant even in the Arabic, Nöldeke
would identify with one mentioned in the introduction to Firdausī's *Shāh-nāmah*
as forming one of his sources, and containing the history of the Persians from
the creation down to the end of the reign of Khosrū II Parwēs, A.D. 628.
(*Geschichte der Perser u. Araber*, p. xv.)

[8] A person who advocated communist doctrines in Persia, during the reign
of Kawādh. For a full account of Mazdak and the Mazdakites, see Nöldeke's
Geschichte der Perser und Araber, pp. 455 sqq. Though Ibn al-Muḳaffaʿ's translation is not extant as a whole, it is preserved more or less perfectly in Eutychius,
Ibn Ḳotaiba and Tabarī.

('diadem'), containing the history of the reign of Nûshirvân; the
large treatise concerning belles-lettres (or good manners); the
small treatise concerning the same; and a book called 'the
incomparable pearl'."

According to al-Mas'ûdî[1], he also rendered from Pehlevî into
Arabic a book, in which are related the exploits of Isfendiâr, and
another book containing accounts of the defeat of Afrâsiâb by
Zû, of the wars between the Persians and the Turks, of the
death of Siyâwaksh, of the history of Rustem, how he killed
Isfendiâr, and how he in turn was killed by the son of Isfendiâr,
and of other extraordinary events in the old history of Persia.
This latter book, al-Mas'ûdî tells us, was highly valued by the
Persians, containing as it does, accounts of their ancestors and
histories of their kings. Finally, al-Mas'ûdî says in another
passage[2]: 'He (al-Mahdi) exterminated without pity the
heretics, and all those who renounced Islamism; for it was
during his chalifate that these religious heresies appeared and
gained strength, after the publication of the books of Manes,
Ibn Daiṣân and Markion, which were translated from Persian
and Pehlevî into Arabic by 'Abdullah son of al-Muḳaffa' and
others.'

'Nikbi ben Masoud'[3] represents Ibn al-Moḳaffa' as an infidel
who professed Islamism but remained at heart attached to the
Zoroastrian religion. According to the same writer, Ibn al-M.
together with several of his co-religionists, attempted to imitate
the style of the Ḳur'ân, but in vain.

It is certain then that Ibn al-Muḳaffa' was a man of distinguished literary abilities and a translator of a high order. It
is therefore reasonable to assume that if his version, known as
the Kalîlah wa Dimnah, is not a substantially faithful rendering
of the Pehlevî original, the fact is not due to any want of
ability on his part. We may at least assume that he perfectly

[1] II. pp. 44, 118. Al-Mas'ûdî was born at Bagdad about A.D. 900, and died at
Fosṭâṭ (Old Cairo) A.D. 956. He travelled in Persia, India, Ceylon, Madagascar,
Palestine, Syria, and Egypt; and wrote a large number of books, of which only
one has been published in Europe, namely the Murûju 'l-dhahab ('meadows of
gold'), a book of history, travel, and geography.
[2] VIII. p. 293.
[3] Cited by De Sacy in the Notices et Extraits des Manuscrits, Vol. X. Pt. 1.
pp. 160, 161.

understood the text which he had before him. If he altered or
left out anything, he did so deliberately. Now it has been
conjectured[1] that he did alter and omit certain passages, lest
they should offend Muslim readers and serve to increase the
suspicion in which he was held. One such omission is said to
have been found[2]. But it is difficult to understand why the
man who helped to translate the books of Manes, Ibn Daiṣān,
and Markion, should think it worth his while to make alterations
in a story-book for fear of being convicted of heresy. Further
it should be remembered that he is represented by Arab writers
as the reverse of prudent.

The old Syriac Version.

§ 24. Besides the Arabic version there is another one which
flowed directly from the Pehlevī, namely the old Syriac—old
as distinguished from the later Syriac version made from the
Arabic[3]. As this old Syriac translation was made nearly 200 years
before that of Ibn al-Muḳaffaʿ, it might well have been taken
first, were it not for two things. First, it is incomplete as
compared both with the Sanscrit original, with the Pehlevī, and
with the Arabic version. That is, it does not contain three of
the original Indian chapters, namely those numbered 15, 17,
18 in De Sacy; nor the Persian chapters numbered 2 and
4 in De Sacy; nor, of course, those chapters which are of Arabic
origin, namely those numbered 1, 3, 6, 16, 20 and 21.
Secondly, every known version of the book (except the old
Syriac) is descended directly or mediately from the Arabic,
while the old Syriac version remained childless. So for con-
venience sake I have noticed the Arabic first, and that too at
some length, that I may describe its numerous offshoots to some
extent by comparing them with it.

§ 25. ʿEbed-Jesu, bishop of Nisibis, mentions in his catalogue
of Syriac writings a certain 'Būd (or Bōd) periodeuta'[4] as
having composed various works, principally against the Mani-

[1] Kalilag u. Damnag, pp. xcii, sqq.
[2] Ibid. pp. xlvii, xlviii. The passage omitted relates to the doctrine of the transmigration of souls.
[3] See § 35.
[4] I.e. a chorepiscopus.

chæans and the Markionites. This person, he says, was entrusted with the oversight of the Christians in India and Persia, and lived about 570 A.D. He further adds: '*and it was he who translated from the Indian the book of Kalilag and Damnag.*' This catalogue of 'Ebed-Jesu was published by Assemani in his *Bibliotheca Orientalis Clementino-Vaticana*, III, Part 1 (Rome, 1725). On page 325 Assemani shows that it must have been written between 1200 and 1318, that is at a time when both the Pehlevi version and the Indian original (if indeed the Indian fables ever existed in a collected form) had long ago perished. Hence 'Ebed-Jesu in mentioning the 'book of Kalilag and Damnag' must have taken the name from the Syriac work itself and not from the Pehlevi version or an Indian original. Again, according to page 219 note 2 in the same volume, Bûd lived about A.D. 570, or just at the time when Barzôye was sent by Khosru Nushîrvân to procure the Indian original and translate it into Persian, i.e. Pehlevi. As many other works are assigned to Bûd in this catalogue of 'Ebed-Jesu, he must have been a well-known littérateur, and so the date given is likely to be correct. Now it is highly improbable that just about the same time two persons should both have conceived the idea of translating the same Indian book, the one into Persian and the other into Syriac. Besides, as Nöldeke has said[1], the literary conditions of the Syrians make a direct translation from the Sanscrit so improbable that we must assume at the outset a Persian writing as a connecting link, unless convincing proofs to the contrary are forthcoming. Finally, the names *Kalîlag* and *Damnag* point to this Persian medium, for from what is known of Pehlevi, these names, if Pehlevi, are easily and naturally derivable from the Sanscrit *Karataka* and *Damanaka*[2]. From all these considerations it follows that there are ample *a priori* grounds for discrediting the statement of 'Ebed-Jesu, and for thinking that this Syriac version must have flowed from the Indian through a Persian version. Assuming, for the moment, that such was the case, we may further conjecture that the translator Bûd was a Persian Christian acquainted with Syriac, not that he was a Syrian familiar with Persian. It is notorious, says Prof. Nöldeke, that at that time the colloquial and literary

[1] Z. D. M. G. xxx. p. 751.   [2] Ibid. p. 758.

language of the king's province properly so called (*Beth Armayē*), the ecclesiastical language of nearly all the Christians in the kingdom, was held in high estimation. 'The Persian Paul' dedicates his compendium of logic, written in Syriac, to no less a personage than the king Khosrū. On the other hand, it must have been exceedingly difficult for a Syrian (i.e. Aramæan) to penetrate into the secret writing of the Pehlevī literature, even though he himself might speak Persian with fluency[1].

§ 26. All doubt as to the existence and origin of the old Syriac version has been set at rest through its discovery and publication. It lies before us in the joint work of Professors Gustav Bickell and Theodor Benfey entitled '*Kalilag und Damnag. Alte Syrische Uebersetzung des indischen Fürstenspiegels. Text und deutsche Uebersetzung von Gustav Bickell. Mit einer Einleitung von Theodor Benfey*' (Leipzig, F. A. Brockhaus. 1876)[2].

The circumstances of the discovery of this precious document are narrated at length in Benfey's introduction[3]. In the summer of 1870, Pius IX. summoned a council of all catholic bishops, which met at Rome. Professor Bickell, remembering the statement of 'Ebed-Jesu, determined not to let slip this opportunity for making enquiries, and wrote on the subject to Professor Benfey, who then put himself in communication with his friends Professors Schöll and Ignazio Guidi, then at Rome. Guidi, while conversing with a Chaldæan bishop, was told by him that on his journey to Rome he had come across a Syriac manuscript of *Kalilah and Dimnah* in the episcopal library at Mārdīn. As luck would have it, Professor Socin (now of Tübingen) was then travelling in this part of Asia. He was accordingly written to and asked to look for it. He found it at the library named. Unfortunately he was not allowed to purchase the manuscript, for the Patriarch's permission was necessary, and this dignitary was absent. All that Socin could do was to arrange for a transcript. This reached him in Bâle in April 1871, and was

[1] *Z. D. M. G.* xxx. p. 754.
[2] Reviewed by Nöldeke in the *Z. D. M. G.*, xxx. pp. 752—772; by Prym in the *Jenaer Literaturzeitung*, 1878, p. 98; and by Weber in the *Literarisches Centralblatt*, 1876, no. 31, 1021 f.
[3] Pp. xlä—xxxii.

subsequently bought by the Royal Scientific Society of Göttingen and presented by them to the University Library in that town.

§ 27. The original manuscript is written in Nestorian, the Göttingen copy in Maronite-jacobite characters, and contains (1) the Ḳalilag wa Damnag, (2) the Revelation of St Paul, (8) a poem purporting to be by Ephraem concerning the final Judgement and the punishment of sinners, (4) a number of disconnected notices, treating of the development of the embryo, the names of unnamed biblical personages, the parents of the Virgin, the star of the Magi, the crucifixion and burial of Christ, the nourishment of John the Baptist, the names of the two disciples whom he sent to Christ, the situation in the body of the various affections and feelings, and lastly, the human microcosm as compared with the macrocosm. The whole book ends with two notices. The second one is written by the copyist employed by Socin and need not be noticed further. But the first one presents difficulties. It runs thus in the transcript: 'This original manuscript which we have copied was finished by the hand of a deacon named Hormuzd, son of Simeon, in the village of the convent of the holy Mār 'Ebed-Jesu which is near to Amedia, which is called the town of Rēthūnū, in the year of the Greeks 1837[1]. Glory to God! Amen.' It is not certain who was the author of this notice. It must be referred either to the person who wrote the Mārdin manuscript from which Socin had his copy made—an unlikely supposition because the copyist would in that case be omitting the customary mention of his own name— or more likely to the copyist employed by Socin, so that Hormuzd is the name of the person who wrote the Mārdin manuscript from which the copy now at Göttingen was made. This copy swarms with errors, some (perhaps many) of which are certainly to be referred to the Mārdin original[2]. Bickell in the foot-notes to his edition of the text, and Nöldeke in his *Mäusekönig*, have shown how much may be done towards restoring the right text by means of conjectural emendation. Further, the original Mārdin manuscript is not complete. Two marginal notes in Arabic draw attention to the fact that the first and last leaf of the *Ḳalilag wa Damnug* are wanting. The fact is that a sheet

---

[1] I.e. A. D. 1526.　　　　　[2] *Kal. u. Dam.* p. xxix.

has become detached. As the last leaf of the *K. wa D.* contained
also the commencement of the Revelation of St Paul, the text of
this is not complete either. There is also a long gap in the
chapter of Bilār (De Sacy's 14th), due perhaps to the fact that
Socin's or an earlier copyist turned over two leaves by mistake[1].

§ 28. According to the Mārdīn manuscript, the contents of
the old Syriac version are arranged as follows:

1. The lion and the ox (De Sacy's 5th chapter).
2. The ring-dove (De Sacy's 7th ch.).
3. The ape and the tortoise (De Sacy's 9th ch.).
4. The ascetic and the weasel (De Sacy's 10th ch.).
5. The mouse and the cat (De Sacy's 11th ch.).
6. The owls and the crows (De Sacy's 8th ch.).
7. The king and the bird (De Sacy's 12th ch.).
8. The lion and the jackal (De Sacy's 13th ch.).
9. The story of Bilār (De Sacy's 14th ch.).
10. The king of the mice (contained in Arabic MSS. but
not in De Sacy's text)[2].

The sixth chapter (De Sacy's 8th) has no doubt been displaced, and ought to stand after the second (De Sacy's 7th).
Possibly the disturbance points to a copy in which the chapters
of the book were contained in separate fasciculi which might
easily become disarranged[3]. This ingenious suggestion of Benfey
may perhaps also explain why so many chapters undoubtedly
Indian or Persian, and contained in the Arabic version, are
wholly wanting in the Mārdīn manuscript.

§ 29. What light is thrown by this old Syriac version on
its relation to the others? Benfey in his introduction to
Bickell's edition of the text seems to have established satisfactorily from internal evidence the following propositions.

1. The variations of the old Syriac version from the Arabic
version and its offshoots furnish proof that the Syriac cannot
have flowed from the Arabic, but do not decide that the Pehlevi
and Syriac are independent of one another[4].

2. There is proof to show that the Pehlevi and old Syriac
versions are not independent, but that only one of them was

---

[1] *Kal. u. Dam.* pp. xxiv—xxvii.   [3] *Kal. u. Dam.* pp. xxxvii, xxxviii.
[2] See §§ 6, 20.   [4] *Ibid.* pp. xxxi—xlviii.

made directly from the Sanscrit original and then gave rise to the other[1].

3. There is proof to show that it was the Pehlevī version which was made directly from the Sanscrit, whereas the old Syriac flowed from the Pehlevī[2].

In support of the first proposition Benfey draws attention to the following points.

(a) The old Syriac version contains none of the introductory chapters which appear first in the Arabic and its offshoots (viz. De Sacy's chapters 1, 2, 3), nor the biography of Barzōye the physician (De Sacy's 4th chapter)[3]. But let me remark, with all due deference, that the absence of De Sacy's chapters 1, 2, 3, proves nothing, for they are all absent in the later Syriac version, which undoubtedly flowed from the Arabic. Indeed De Sacy's chapter 1 is wanting in all the offshoots of the Arabic. And as to the chapter about Barzōye, Benfey himself admits that it may have been lost by accident, and that its nature is such that a Christian priest might naturally have shrunk from reproducing it. To my mind the most significant omission in the Syriac is the omission of *all* the chapters of Arabic origin, namely those which are numbered 1, 3, 6, 16, in De Sacy, and the two chapters which I designate as 20th and 21st[4]. Surely, if the old Syriac version had flowed from an Arabic copy, it would have contained some of these.

(b) The names *Kalilag* and *Damnag* cannot be derived from the Arabic *Kalilah* and *Dimnah*[5]. And there are other instances of this terminal *g* which has been preserved in the Syriac but not in the Arabic.

(c) A few Sanscrit names are reproduced more or less faithfully in the old Syriac, which do not appear in the Arabic or any of its offshoots. At the beginning of the chapter corresponding to De Sacy's 11th the names of the questioner and answerer are given as *Zedashtar* and *Bisham*[6]. These forms reflect as nearly as could be expected (considering the lapse of time and the ambiguities of the Pehlevi writing[7]) the original

[1] *Ibid.* pp. xlviii—lxvii.
[2] *Ibid.* pp. lxvii—lxxxiv.
[3] *Ibid.* p. xxxi.
[4] See §§ 6, 20, 21.

[5] See § 25.
[6] Bickell's text, p. 57.
[7] Nöldeke in the Z. D. M. G. xxx., pp. 752 sqq.

Sanscrit names *Yudhishṭhira* and *Bhishma*[1]. As these names are replaced by the more usual *Dabshalīm* and *Baidubā* in the Arabic version and all its offshoots, it seems that Ibn al-Muḳaffa' suppressed them, perhaps intentionally.

The same remarks apply to a passage in the chapter of the owls and the crows[2], where the Sanscrit names of two heroes *Arjuna* and *Bhīma* survive in *Arzeg* and *Bīmadh*. It may be added that several Pehlevī names occur in the Syriac which do not appear in Ibn al-Muḳaffa''s version[3].

(*d*) At the commencement of the chapter of the lion and the jackal[4], tho old Syriac version introduces the jackal thus: "In the land of the Turks, in the place Rapūḳan, was once a king who had committed many sins and evil deeds. And because of his many sins, when ho died his soul entered the body of a jackal, who in due time gave birth to him. And because ho had done so few good deeds, he remembered while in the jackal's body that he had formerly been a king, but on account of his crimes had come into tho jackal's body. And ho repented of the sins which he had committed, and as he roamed about with jackals, wolves and foxes, his companions, be neither hurt nor killed animals nor ate flesh." This passage also appears in the corresponding place in the *Mahābhārata* (XII, 4084), but not a trace of it is to be found in the Arabic version or in any ono of its descendants. Hence very probably Ibn al-Muḳaffa' omitted it for some reason or another[5]. If so, then we have here another proof that the old Syriac version did not flow from tho Arabic.

Assuming then that the old Syriac version did not flow from the Arabic, then either it was made from the Pehlevī of Barzūye or from the Sanscrit original. By comparing a number of the proper

[1] Benfey's *Einl. zur Pantech.* p. 545.

[2] Bickell's text. p. 76 lin. ult., 77, l. 2; Benfey's *Pantech.*, Bk. III., strophes 234, 235.

[3] See the ond of this section.

[4] Bickell's text, p. 87, ll. 6 sqq.

[5] Benfey thinks that he purposely suppressed it. A Muslim proselyte, he says, whose orthodoxy was seriously doubted, and a man who had many powerful enemies, would not have dared to reproduce a doctrine which to his coreligionists must have appeared ridiculous and abominable. Perhaps so, but see the end of § 23.

names which occur in the old Syriac with the corresponding ones in the Sanscrit and the Pehlevi (as reflected in its Arabic translation) Benfey has established his second proposition.

The Syriac and Pehlevi forms of a name, while differing from the Sanscrit, *often present the same differences.* This similarity of difference is frequently so striking that it is impossible to avoid the conclusion that the Syriac and the Pehlevi are mutually connected, i.e. that either the Syriac flowed from the Pehlevi or *vice versâ.* Thus, take the name the Sanscrit form of which is *Karaṭaka.* The Pehlevi form is reflected in the Arabic *Kalîluh,* and the Syriac has *Kalîlag.* Thus both the Pehlevi and the Syriac have changed Sanscrit *r* to *l* and Sanscrit *ṭ* to *l,* and both have substituted *i* for *a*[1]. Would both versions have hit on the same differences, had not one of them flowed from the other?

Again, the name of the king in the chapter of Bilār (De Sacy's 14th chapter) appears in Schiefner's Tibetan text[2] as *Chanda-Pradyota.* The Arabic MSS. give variously *sîdkrm, sâdrm, sâdât*[3]. Of these we should *a priori* select the first, as containing most consonants. The old Syriac gives *shtprm*[4]. By writing ــ (*f*) for ک (*k*) in *sîdkrm,* we get two almost identical forms: Arabic *sâdfrm* and Syriac *shtprm* (for *s, d, f* are radically the same as *sh, t, p*). Now these two forms, while differing widely from the original *Chanda-Pradyota,* are yet exceedingly like one another. In both the *n* is absent, in both *dyota* is replaced by *m.* It seems reasonable to infer that either the Syriac form is a transcription of the Pehlevi one, or *vice versâ.*

Lastly, the cat in the chapter of the mouse and the cat is called in the *Mahābhārata* by the name *Lomaça*[5]. The old Syriac has *Rômâ,* De Sacy's text *Rûmî.* In each of these Sanscrit *l* has become *r,* in each the Sanscrit termination *ça* has been dropped. This is a remarkable coincidence if the Syriac

---

[1] For an explanation of this latter substitution, see Nöldeke in the *Z. D. M. G.* xxx., p. 766.

[2] See end of § 16. The Sanscrit text of this chapter is not forthcoming.

[3] Guidi's *Studii sul testo Arabo del libro di Kalila e Dimna,* p. 72.

[4] Bickell's Syriac text, p. 95, lin. penult.

[5] Benfey's *Einleit. zur Pantsch.,* p. 540.

K. F.   *d*

and Pehlevī versions are independent translations of the Sanscrit[1].

Benfey establishes his third proposition, namely, that it was
the Pehlevī version which was translated from the Sanscrit,
whereas the old Syriac flowed from the Pehlevī, in two ways:
first, by appealing to the authority of Firdausī[2] and to that of Ibn
al-Mukaffa'[3]; secondly, by showing that the old Syriac contains a
number of Pehlevī words.

Firdausī's account of the matter I have already detailed
(§ 8); Ibn al-Mukaffa''s is contained in the second chapter of
De Sacy's text (§ 8). 'Ebed-Jesu's statement that the book
was rendered from Indian into Syriac must certainly give way
to the authorities just quoted. For in the first place, 'Ebed-Jesu
wrote about A.D. 1290, or two centuries later than Firdausī and
five later than Ibn al-Mukaffa'. Next, Firdausī was preeminently
well versed in the ancient history and literature of Persia.
Lastly, since in our MS. of the Syriac, the introductory chapters
are missing, it is quite possible that they were also missing in
'Ebed-Jesu's copy; and the Pehlevī had very likely disappeared
by then. Hence his mistake was a very natural one; how
could he have known that between the Sanscrit and the old
Syriac version, written according to J. S. Assemānī about A.D.
570, intervened another, namely a Pehlevī version?

The following are a few of the cases in which Benfey descries
Pehlevī words.

In the chapter of the owls and the crows (De Sacy's 8th,
old Syriac 0th) we read of a certain lake called in the Sanscrit
chandrasaras[4], i.e. 'basin of the moon,' in the old Syriac
mahōkhanī[4], a name which Benfey pronounces to be compounded of Pehlevī *māh* ('moon') and *khān* ('well').

In the same story occurs the name of a hare. This name is
given in the *Panchatantra* as *Vijayadatta*, 'victorious.' The
old Syriac has *Pirūs*[5], a word surely identical with Persian
Pīrūz and Pehlevī *Pirudshi*, also meaning 'victorious.'

---

[1] For more examples of this kind the reader is referred to chapter VIII. of
Benfey's Introduction to Bickell's *Kalīlag und Damnag*.
[2] Persian writer and author of the national epic known as the *Shāh-Nāmah*
('book of kings'). He lived A.D. 960—1030.
[3] Benfey's *Pantsch*. Pt. II., p. 226.   [4] Bickell's text, p. 65, l. 7.
[5] Benfey's *Pantsch*. Pt. II., p. 229.   [6] Bickell's text, p. 48, l. 0.

In the chapter of the lion and the ox (De Sacy's 5th), a story occurs in which the fabulous king of birds plays a part. His Sanscrit name is *garuda*, but the Syriac has *Sīmūr*. In this word Benfey recognizes the Persian *Sīmurg*, who figures in the heroic lore as the nourisher and bringer up of Rustam's father Sāl, and also as king of the birds[1].

The first and last of the instances just cited also tend to prove that this Syriac version is not descended from the Arabic. For while in both cases the Syrian translator has *copied* the names, the Arab has *translated* them. In the Syriac we find *Mahōkhanī* and *Sīmūr*, both Pehlevī words; but in Ibn al-Mukaffa''s version the Arabic expressions عين القمر and المُنْقا[2]. If then the Syrian translator had the Arabic text before him, why did he represent Arabic expressions by rendering them into Pehlevī? Of any other Arabic text besides that of Ibn al-Mukaffa' there is not the smallest trace[3].

§ 30. Having settled the question of the origin of the Syriac version, Benfey gives reasons for thinking that, so far as it goes, it is substantially a more faithful reflex of the Sanscrit original than the version of Ibn al-Mukaffa'[4]. He thinks that on the one hand the circumstances of the Arab translator were such as to induce him to deliberately omit passages, while on the other the Syrian Būd had every inducement to render faithfully what he found before him. Islām was then comparatively young, and hence more sensitive and intolerant of rival creeds, than a religion more firmly established and which had lasted for centuries. This would be specially true of Muham-

---

[1] For more examples of Pehlevī words, see Chap. ix. of Benfey's Introduction to *Kalilag und Damnag*.

[2] De Sacy, p. 126, 8. For المُنْقا see Lane.

[3] As was only to be expected, several of the instances cited by Benfey in his learned investigation of the *Kalilag wa Damnag* have been challenged by reviewers. Prym has pointed out that ܩܒܠ (Bickell's text, p. 3, line 7 from the bottom) is not a proper name but an adjective ('imperitus, rudis'), and hence that the whole of Benfey's elaborate argument based thereon (pp. lxxvii.—lxxx.) falls to the ground. Again, Nöldeke has no hesitation in saying that ܚܨܘܣܘ (Bickell's text, p. 1, l. 8), on which Benfey has a good deal to say (pp. lxxxi., lxxxii.), is merely a corruption and should be read ܚܪܦܘ.

[4] Pp. xcii.—xcv.

d 2

medanism, founded as it was on a very simple creed, originating
as it did among a people of no very deep psychical feeling, and
propagated by the force of arms. Add to this that Ibn al-
Mukaffa' was a proselyte whose sincerity was always suspected.
It follows (so thinks Benfey) that he must have been strongly
tempted to avoid reproducing in his version anything which
might excite the ridicule, horror or suspicion of his brethren.
One instance of such an omission is adduced, namely, a passage
containing the doctrine of the transmigration of souls, omitted
in the Arabic but found in the Syriac. On the other hand
Benfey urges that Büd was a Christian, belonging to a people
who notoriously held Indian philosophy and literature in the
highest respect, (a fact illustrated by the Syriac version of
the biography of Buddha in *Barlaam and Josaphat*[1]), and also
points to the slavish fidelity which was notably a characteristic
of their translations of foreign literature. I have already shown
that there is a fact which runs in the teeth of Benfey's theory
with respect to these intentional omissions of Ibn al-Mukaffa'[2].
As to the Syrian translator, it is very likely that his rendering
was a slavishly faithful one. But, as Benfey admits, both the
Mārdīn manuscript and its copy swarm with errors and
omissions, a fact to be carefully remembered in considering
the textual problems presented in the book.

After all, such *a priori* arguments as Benfey advances on
this head are of little value. The special peculiarities of
particular individuals often override and set at nought the
conclusions arrived at by reasoning from anterior probabilities.
There is nothing to argue from with safety except positive
evidence.

§ 31. Benfey devotes the last and longest chapter[3] of his
learned introduction to Bickell's text to the examination of a
number of differences between the old Syriac and the Arabic

---

[1] A religious romance attributed to St John of Damascus, once in office at
the court of the Chalif al-Mansur. It is the history of an Indian prince who
was converted by Barlaam and became a hermit. The book exists in many
languages. It has been shown that Josaphat (who has been canonised by the
church of Rome) is none other than Bodisat or Buddha. (See T. W. Rhys
Davids in his *Buddhist Birth Stories*, pp. xxxvi. sqq. On p. xcv. a conspectus
of the Barlaam and Josaphat literature is given.)

[2] See end of § 23.   [3] Pp. cv.—cxliv.

version in the chapter of the lion and the ox (the first book of the *Panchatantra*, the first chapter of the old Syriac, and the fifth of De Sacy's text). I must confess that the impression produced on my own mind by the reading of this chapter is, not that the two versions differ in some points, but that on the whole they are strikingly in harmony. This agreement of the Arabic and old Syriac is a proof that they are both substantially faithful witnesses to their common Pehlevi original. Some of the differences indeed are not real differences, but are due to the carelessness of copyists or possessors of manuscripts, as Benfey admits.

§ 32. In attempting to settle the textual problems introduced by a comparison of the Syriac version with the Arabic version and its offshoots, it seems that the main guiding rules are as follows:

1. Whatever is found in the Sanscrit as well as in the old Syriac or the Arabic *Kalila wa Dimnah* should be accepted as having belonged to the original text.

2. Whatever is found in the old Syriac and in the Arabic, or in one of its offshoots, should be recognized as authentic. It is very doubtful whether any of the descendants of the Arabic version have been influenced by the old Syriac.

3. What is found in the Sanscrit, but not in the old Syriac or in the Arabic version or any of its offshoots, should be rejected as a later Indian addition, unless there is strong reason to the contrary.

§ 33. It may appear strange that the Sanscrit texts should be considered as second-rate witnesses to the text of an Indian book, but Benfey's investigations, set forth in his brilliant *Einleitung zur Pantschatantra*, published in 1859 (or 17 years before the discovery of the Syriac manuscript), led him to the conclusion that the Arabic *Kalilah wa Dimnah* (i.e. the Indian part of it) represents with substantial accuracy an Indian book (or rather, as some think, a collection of tales selected from various Indian sources), of which the *Panchatantra*, the *Mahābhārata* and the *Hitopadesa* contain each a part, but that part in a modernised and artificially elaborated form. While there is no reason to doubt that Barzöye's rendering of the Sanscrit original was a faithful one, it is easy to understand

how that original became altered and enlarged, curtailed in parts and elaborated in others, as time went on. *A priori*, it was likely that this should be so, in view of the tendency to 'übertriebene Raffinement' (to use Benfey's phrase) which characterises later Indian writings. It is in the extant *Panchatantra* that this tendency most clearly shows itself. Compare it with the *Kalîla w. D.* The latter is terse and brief, simple and vigorous, evidently the relic of a hoary antiquity. The other is elaborate and lengthy, subtle and philosophical. Its form, too, is artificial, for the parts of the book which are not narrative appear in the form of poetry. It bears on the face of it the stamp of later times. The sketch of the first three books of the *Panchatantra* contained in Somadeva's *Kathâ-Sarit-Sâgara*, a work composed at the commencement of the twelfth century, shows that these chapters still retained at that time the form they had when they passed into Persia[1]. Since the *Kathâ-Sarit-Sâgara* and the Pehlevî (as reflected in the Arabic and old Syriac) are independent witnesses, this agreement is a strong proof that they are both substantially true, and that the *Panchatantra* as we have it gives a false idea of its original form as known to Barzôye.

It is of course possible, though unlikely, that he did not take all that he found in the copy before him; which might account to some extent for the absence of certain passages in the *Kal. w. D.* which appear in the Sanscrit *Panchatantra*.

§ 34. It is doubtful whether the source of the Pehlevî book was a single book, a connected whole, or whether Barzôye did not make a selection from various sources, a kind of anthology, or (which amounts to the same thing) found it made for him. Benfey held that there was originally such a 'Gesammtwerk' or 'Grundwerk,' that is a book whose contents formed a complete, connected, organic whole; that the first five chapters of this book became detached from the rest and formed the *Panchatantra*; that the next three chapters were preserved in the *Mahâbhârata* ('retteten sich ins Mahâbhârata'); that two

[1] Benfey's *Einleitung zur Pantsch.*, Pref. p. xviii., and p. 18; and Tawney's *Kathâ Sarit Sâgara* in English, chapters lx. lxi. and lxii. (Fasc. vii. of the *Bibliotheca Indica*, Calcutta, 1881).

chapters were taken up into the first book of the *Panchatantra ;*
and that the rest dropped out of the Indian literature altogether[1].
What evidence does he adduce for this ? Absolutely none. On
the contrary, Prym[2] has pointed out that there are facts which
make it highly improbable that there ever was a single united
Indian book such as this. First, strongly marked differences of
form appear in the chapters. The five chapters corresponding
to the *Panchatantra*[3] are characterised by their endless number
of inserted stories; the three chapters found in the *Mahābhārata*[4]
by their simple, didactic, or homiletic nature; while the curious
chapter of Bilār[5] is strikingly different from all the others. In
this chapter none of the parts are played by animals; its ruling
purpose is evident from beginning to end, namely, to hold up
the Brahmans to execration ; and the very long series of simili-
tudes is something quite *per se.* Next, the fifth chapter of the
old Syriac[6], which is one of the three sections found in the
Mahābhārata, is introduced by the words 'Zedashtar said to
Bisham : Show me how, &c.', whereas all the other chapters, like
those of the Arabic *Kalīlah wa Dimnah,* are said to have been
narrated by *Bēdawīg* or *Bīdūg* (De Sacy's *Baidabā*) to *Debashram*
(De Sacy's *Dabshalīm*). Now *Zedashtar* and *Bisham* are merely
corruptions of *Yudhishthira* and *Bhīshma,* names which in the
Mahābhārata appear at the head of each of these three chapters[7].
It is therefore certain that in the Pehlevi version, each of these
chapters commenced in this manner, and that the Syrian
translator or a subsequent scribe substituted in the case of
two of them the commoner *Bēdawīg* and *Debashram,* but
inadvertently allowed the old names to stand at the head of
the third. In the Arabic translation they have disappeared
altogether, giving place in all three instances to *Baidabā* and
Dabshalīm. If therefore these three chapters belonged to the
same book or 'Gesammtwerk' as the five which are represented
in the *Panchatantra,* why are they differently introduced ?
Lastly, I may add, Schiefner's publication in the *Mémoires de*

---

[1] *Einleitung zur Pantsch.,* Pref. p. xviii. : *Kalilag u. Dam.,* p. viii.

[2] *Jenaer Literaturzeitung,* 1878, p. 98.

[3] De Sacy's chaps. 5, 7, 8, 9, 10.   [5] De S. 11, 12, 13.

[4] De S. 14.   [6] De Sacy's 11th.

[7] Benfey's *Einleitung zur Pantsch.,* pp. 545, 561, 575; also *Kalilag u.
Damnag,* p. xxxviii.

l'*Académie Impériale des Sciences de St Pétersbourg*' shows
that the Sanscrit original of De Sacy's 14th chapter formed the
two concluding tales of a cycle of twenty sections, all relating to
king Chanda-Pradyota'.

III. THE OFFSHOOTS OF THE ARABIC VERSION.

A. THE LATER SYRIAC VERSION.

§ 35. The later Syriac version, made directly from the Arabic,
was discovered and edited by Prof. W. Wright of Cambridge'.
The edition is an exact reproduction of the greater portion of a
single and unique manuscript belonging to the library of Trinity
College, Dublin, marked B. 5. 32 and lettered *Scientia Mundana
Syriac*, consisting of 209 leaves, of which the first 184 com-
prise the *Kalilah wa Dimnah*. A small portion of the manuscript (ff. 161—184 and 200—207) the editor assigns to the
latter part of the thirteenth century; the rest he considers to
be a century or two later and to have been written by two
scribes, except a few leaves which were added in 1613 to replace
others which had somehow dropped out at different times.
The MS. contains, besides the *K. w. D.*, a collection of fables
entitled *Fables of Josephus* (*sic*, i.e. Æsopus), various questions
or riddles with the solutions, a section on the different ways of
putting a question, sayings of Pythagoras, and sayings of other
Greek philosophers.

The text of the *K. w. D.* in this MS. teems with errors, as
may be seen from the quantities of conjectural emendations
proposed in the foot-notes and in the long list of additions and

---

¹ End of § 16.
² See also A. Weber's remarks in the *Literurisches Centralblatt*, 1878,
col. 1020.
³ *The book of Kalilah and Dimnah, translated from Arabic into Syriac.*
Edited by W. Wright, LL.D., Professor of Arabic in the University of Cambridge.
(Oxford, at the Clarendon Press, and London, Trübner, 1884.)
The above has been reviewed by Prof. Nöldeke in the *Göttingische gelehrte
Anzeigen* (nr. 17, 1 Sept. 1884), and by M. R. Duval in the *Revue Critique d'hist.
et de litt.* (12 Jan. 1885).
Professor Wright had some years before published an account of the MS.,
together with the text and translation of the first few pages, in the *Journal of
the Royal Asiatic Society*, New Series, Vol. VII. Part I., 1871, Appendix.

corrections. To aggravate matters, the oldest portion of the MS. has been largely retraced by a later hand. This retracing, being most faulty, obliterates the old writing without shedding light upon it. What was obscure before is now pitch dark.

§ 36. The contents of the later Syriac version according to this MS. are :—

1. The lion and the ox. (5th in De Sacy.)
2. The defence of Dimnah. (6th in D.S.)
3. The ringdove. (7th in D.S.)
4. The owls and the crows. (8th in D.S.)
5. The tortoise and the ape. (9th in D.S.)
6. The ascetic and the weasel. (10th in D.S.)
7. The mouse and the cat. (11th in D.S.)
8. The king and the bird Pinzīh. (12th iu D.S.)
9. The lion and the jackal. (13th in D.S.)
10. The traveller and the goldsmith. (17th in D.S.)
11. The king's son and his companions. (18th in D.S.)
12. The lioness and the jackal. (15th in D.S.)
13. The ascetic and the traveller. (16th in D.S.)
14. The story of the wise Bilār and queen Ilār. (14th in D.S.)
15. The biography of Barzōye. (4th in D.S.)

§ 37. As this version contains several of the distinctively Arabic chapters, it must be descended directly or mediately from the Arabic.

That it was made directly from the Arabic follows from several considerations. Not only does the translator tell us so[1], but there is also decisive internal evidence of the fact. Prof. Nöldeke has pointed out[2] a number of Arabisms. Namely o ﺍﻻ =ﻭ, ﻳﻻ (illa with wāw alḥāl), e.g. ܣܝܡܝܢ ܡܕܡ ﺍﻻ (p. 189, 23) = ﻳﻻ ﺩﺍﺭﺝ ﻗﺮﺕ ﺍﻳﻪ; the partitive use of ܡܢ in ܡܢ ܡܠܟܐ ܩܕܡ ﺍﻟﻤﻘﺪﻡ ﻣﻦ ﺑﺎﺭﺍ ܘܡܩܒܠ (p. 394, ult.); the Arabic ﺻﺎﺣﺐ with following genitive reproduced by ܡܪܐ with suffix, e.g. ܡܪܗ (p. 238, 5) = 'he who has it' (the illness), compare p. 269, 4; verbs of purely Arabic origin, as ܡܝܙܬ ܐܢܐ (used six times, see

---

[1] Syr. Text, p. 402, 4: Engl. Transl. p. 264, 23.
[2] In his review above quoted.

the glossary) = ' I hope,' derived it would seem from Arabic رجا,
and ܡܬܚܙܐ (p. 70, 8) ' looking, glancing,' which Prof. Wright
explains in his glossary by Arab. طَرْف (' a look '). Further,
numbers of Arabic words appear in a transliterated form. Thus
ܐܠܡܢܨܐ (p. 77, 22) or rather ܐܠܚܕܨܐ, which was no doubt
meant, is merely the الْمَنْصَة of the Arabic text (De Sacy, p. 126,

8); ܡܥ؟ (p. 150, 10) is the Ar. ديوان; ܐܚܡܐܡܨܡ (المطرنة),
p. 160, 4 and 167, 16; ܪܨ؟ (مُفْرِد), p. 209, 21; ܡܨܠܐ (سَبَل),
a disease of the eye), p. 297, 4'; ܢܨ؟ a corruption of صص (بَيَر),
p. 313, 20; ܪܝܡ؟ (جَرَاد), p. 335, 2; ܨܡܚܐܒ (بَنْخَنِي), p. 335, 5;
and ܐܡ؟ (ايران), p. 346, 13. In all these cases the translator,
not understanding the Arabic word before him, has simply
transferred it bodily to his translation; as may be seen by
referring to the corresponding passages in the Arabic version.
Further, words occur which are evidently translations of Arabic
words wrongly read. Thus ܕܛܐ؟ (p. 169, 5), which yields no
intelligible sense, is the translation of حَجَر (' stones '), a misreading of حَجَر (' holes '), the word in the Arabic text (De
Sacy, p. 162, 3)[2]. Again ܐܛܡܐ؟ (p. 278, 17) is the rendering of
الْحَمَر (' wine ') misread for الْحَمَر (' ashes,' De Sacy, p. 231,
l. ult.)[2]. Again, at p. 172, 15, the ' enmity between precious
stones' rests on a misunderstanding of the عداوة الجوهر (De
Sacy, p. 163, l. ult.)[3], the translator having understood جوهر
(' nature ') in its other sense of ' jewels '. Natural enmity is meant.
Lastly, ܕܐܠܕ؟ ܥܨܕܪܡ؟ (p. 237, 21) is no doubt a rendering of
الدين (' religion '), instead of الدَّيْن (' debt,' De Sacy, p. 205, 8)[4].

[1] See Additions and Corrections prefixed to the Syriac text.
[2] As Prof. Wright has observed.
[3] As Prof. Nöldeke has pointed out in his review above mentioned.
[4] As Prof. Wright has pointed out.

The four things to be feared are debt, fire, a powerful enemy, and disease[1]. See too my notes on pp. 159, 28 and 163, 8 of the English translation (due, I ought to have said, to Prof. Nöldeke), and my note on p. 258, 35.

§ 38. By whom and when was this version made? On pages 264, 205, of my English translation[2] will be found two passages which have been clearly inserted by the Syrian translator. These show clearly that the author was a Christian priest, living at a time when the Syrian church lay in an utterly degraded state, and when the power of the Caliphate was on the wane. Indeed apart from these passages, the numbers of Scriptural quotations and allusions which embellish almost every page of the book, are amply sufficient to betray the Christian translator. These of course have no place in the Arabic version. Further, our Syriac version must have been made at some time after the middle of the eighth century, when the Arabic version was published, and some time before the latter part of the thirteenth century, the date of the oldest part of our Syriac MS., which, apart from the faulty retracing, is in such a bad state that the text must have previously passed through the hands of several scribes[3]. Further, the translator, whoever he was, has used a number of rare and antiquated words[4], and on the other hand occasionally retained an Arabic word, often merely as a gloss to explain a Syriac word where we should hardly have thought an explanation necessary[5]. This shows that he was a person whose conversational language was Arabic, whereas he had only acquired Syriac in the schools, to study the Bible and the translations of the Greek fathers. These considerations have led Prof. Wright to assign the version to the tenth or eleventh century.

[1] Compare Bickell's text (p. 79, 8), which has ‌ܠܐܘ ; my English transl. p. 154, 56; Knatchbull, p. 253, 5.

[2] Syriac text, pp. 402, 403.

[3] If the reader will take the trouble to go through the list of conjectural emendations made on the text of this portion, he will see that large numbers of them affect words not retraced but written by the first hand. These are to be found partly in the foot-notes to the Syriac text (pp. 367—406), partly in the Additions and Corrections (pp. LXXIX.—LXXXI.).

[4] Explained in the glossary prefixed to the text.

[5] But see my note on p. 215, 38 of the English translation, from which it appears that not all these explanatory glosses proceed from the translator.

§ 39. The chief value of this Syriac version is that it sheds light on the original text of the Arabic *K. w. D.* The Arabic text which the Syriac translator had before him must have been a better one than De Sacy's, because numbers of Guidi's extracts, which are not found at all in De Sacy's text, appear in their proper places in the later Syriac; as may be seen by referring to my table (p. 317).

Unfortunately the translator was a bad one. He did not always understand the text before him, as we have seen; and he often gave a different turn to a passage in order to bring out a Christian sentiment[1]. His ignorance of natural history has led him into other mistakes[2]. A regard for decency has led him to alter many of the coarse passages[3].

B. THE GREEK VERSION.

§ 40. The Jesuit father, Peter Possinus (Poussin), when about to edit a Greek manuscript containing the history of the emperor Michael Palæologus by George Pachymeres, found cited therein (Bk. VI. Cap. XVIII.) τὰ τοῦ Ἰχνηλάτε Παραβολικά, as if it were an excellent and well-known book. Being wholly ignorant both of its author and subject-matter, he made further inquiries and obtained from the library of Leo Allatius a Greek codex, hitherto unedited, containing these very Παραβολικά. Possinus was so pleased with them that he turned them into Latin, and appended this Latin version (without the Greek text) to his edition of Pachymeres[4].

In 1697 S. G. Stark published the Greek text from a

---

[1] See for instance my note on p. 264, 2 f. of the English translation.

[2] E. g. he imagines that sea-water is suitable for drinking (Syr. text, p. 290, 12). The text has 'I drink water from the sea.' Prof. Nöldeke, in his review, has drawn attention to other instances of similar ignorance, which make it unlikely that the text here is corrupt, as I thought when I rendered 'water from the pool' (Engl. tr., p. 189, 22; see Add. and Corr., 290, 12).

[3] E. g. see my notes on p. 34, 1 and p. 117, 38 of the English translation.

[4] *Georgii Pachymeris Michael Palæologus* (Rome, 1666, fol.). The appendix is entitled *Appendix ad observationes Pachymerianas. Specimen sapientiæ Indorum veterum. Liber olim ex lingua Indica in Persicam a Perzoe medico: ex Persica in Arabicam ab Anonymo; ex Arabica in Graecam a Symeone Seth, a Petro Possino Societ. Jesu novissime e Graeca in Latinam translatus.* [Copy in British Museum.]

Hamburg MS., adding a new Latin translation[1], as he thought
that Poussin had treated his original too freely.

In § 23 of his preface Stark says: 'Restat ut etiam de
Græca versione dicamus. Eam quemadmodum statim in fronte
libri patet, adornavit *Simeon Seth*[2] Medicus, ex Arabico. Atque
idem etiam ob alios libros, quos ex eadem lingua vertit, famam
inter eruditos meritus est. Qui quidem si Codici Florentino
fides habenda est, quem ex amicorum literis allegat *Possinus* in
Glossario ad Pachymeris Andronicum, hunc librum vertit,
jussu ALEXII COMNENI *Imperatoris*. Exstat adhuc ea
versio Manuscripta in Bibliotheca et *Vindobonensi* et *Florentina*
et *Augustana* teste *Allatio*. Extat etiam, quod ex Catalogis
patet, in *Oxoniensi* in *Anglia*[3], in *Belgio* in *Lugdunensi*, atque
etiam Cl. Lucæ *Holstenii* beneficio in *Johannea Humburgensi*.
Atque ipse eam quoque *Allatius* possedit. In manus meas
illa pervenit ante annos aliquot opera *B. Hinckelmanni*, ut
erat cura *Holstenii* descripta. Non potuit me tum abstinere,
quin statim in *Latinum* verterem: sed posteaquam rescivi,
eandem librum jam Latine ex Græco redditum a *P. Possino*, ac
Georgii Pachymeris Historiæ Michaëlis Palæologi subjunctum
esse: pene me subiit laboris hujus poenitentia. Sed facile
patuit, ubi librum ipsum videre datum est, ita illam versionem
exactam esse, ut cum Græco textu non passu pari ambulet.
Nam neque ipsi Possino id in animo fuit, ita presso insistere
vestigiis *Simeonis*. Qui et in præfatione fatetur aliqua se
omisisse, neque negare potest, alicubi esse sua opera hunc
librum auctiorem. Proinde quum mereri videretur Græca
versio, ut typis exscripta tibi, *Lector Benevole*, communicaretur;

---

[1] *Specimen sapientiæ Indorum veterum. Id est, liber ethico-politicus pervetustus, dictus arabice,* ك ل ي ل ه و د م ن ه *grece Στεφανίτης και Ιχνηλατης, Nunc primum grece ex MSS. Cod. Holsteiniano prodit, cum versione nova Latina, opera Sebast. Gottofr. Starkii* (Berlin, 1697, 8°). [Copy in British Museum.]
The Greek text has been reprinted at Athens (1851. 8°).

[2] For information as to Symeon and his writings see Leo Allatius in his *De Symeonum scriptis diatriba* (Paris, 1664), pp. 181—184; and De Sacy in the *Mémoire historique* prefixed to his *Calila et Dimna*, p. 31.

[3] There are at least three manuscripts of the old Greek version in the Bodleian Library. One belongs to the Barocci collection (no. 131, extending from fol. 507b to 523b), another to the Laudian collection (no. 8), while the third is classed among the miscellaneous Greek manuscripts (no. 272). [Coxe's catalogue of the Greek MSS. in the Bod. Lib.]

quæ etiam in aula Imperatorum Grajorum ita celebrata fuit, ut
Michaël Palæologus in frequenti suorum concilio ad eandem, ut
omnibus satis notam, provocaret, ut narrnt Pachymeres: eidem
non dubitavimus adjungere hanc novam nostram *Latinam*, ut
quantum fieri posset, in utraque lingua sibi esset liber quam
simillimus.' In § 25 he says: 'De cætero…monendum est in
Possino tria Prolegomena adesse quæ a Græco Codice nostro
abfuerunt.'

Stark's text contains 15 chapters. The first thirteen
correspond respectively to De Sacy's chapters 5, 6, 7, 8, 9, 10,
14, 11, 12, 13, 17, 18, and 15; the fourteenth is the chapter of
the king of the mice; and the last chapter is De Sacy's 16th.

The missing 'Prolegomena' were edited in 1780 by
Aurivillius from an Upsala codex[1]. They consist of three
sections (Auriv., pp. 1—22; 22—33; 33—44) corresponding respectively to De Sacy's chapters 2, 3, and 4. Aurivillius has
appended to his edition a number of specimen readings from
the rest of the codex. The 'Prolegomena' have been re-
edited recently by V. Puntoni in his *Directorium humanæ vitæ*
…*accedunt Prolegomena tria ad Librum Στεφανίτης και Ἰχνηλατης* (Pisa, 1884), with the Latin text of Possinus subjoined.

The Greek version, then, as a whole, contains all the chapters
found in Arabic MSS., except the profaco of 'Alī, the chapter
of the heron and the duck, and that of the dove, the fox and
the heron (see § 6).

The text both of the Hamburg MS. and of the Upsala MS.
is very incomplete and faulty. Thus, in the former, of Stark's
14th chapter (king of the mice) only the beginning remains, and
the cats as enemies of the mice have disappeared altogether, τὸ
πλῆθος τῶν κρειττόνων having taken the place of τὸ πλῆθος τῶν
κάτων[2].

In the case of proper names, Simeon has often substituted
others of his own inventing. Στεφανίτης was suggested by
the resemblance of *Kalīlah* to the Arabic *Iklīl* ('crown'),

---

[1] *Prolegomena ad librum . Στεφανιτης και Ἰχνηλατης e cod. suer. biblioth.
Acad. Upsal. edita et latine versa, dissertatione academica, quam…Præside Mag.
Johanne Flodero…publico examini modeste submittit Petrus Fabrian. Aurivillius
&c.* (Upsala, 1780, 4°.) [Copy in the British Museum.] The first 'prolego-
menon' according to Aurivillius commences with a very curious 'Ἀνακεφαλαίωσις.

[2] Nöldeke's *Mausekönig*, p. 1.

Ἰχνηλάτης ('vestigia persequens') by a fancied connection of *Dimnah* with the word *dimn* explained in the Ḳāmūs to mean 'traces of tents and of men.' *Dabshalim* becomes Ἀβεσαλώμ. In the chapter of the king of the mice and his ministers the king-mouse is named Τρωγλοδύτης, and the three ministers are styled Τυροφάγος, Κρεοθόρος and Ὀθονοφάγος. Often he omits proper names altogether. The names *Baiḍubā, Shanzabah, Rōzbah, Kibariūn, Finzah* have all disappeared.

A critical edition of the whole Greek text is promised by Puntoni. The materials would seem to be numerous. Besides those already noticed, De Sacy mentions two MSS. in the National Library of Paris, both very incomplete : the first numbered 2231 ; the second entitled Βιβλίον λεγόμενον τοῦ Ἰχνιλάτου. (*Calila et D.*, Mémoire historique, p. 33.) There are also two Florentine MSS. (Cod. Laur. XL 14 ; Cod. Laur. LVII. 30), which have been examined by Prof. Emilio Teza and described by him in *Orient und Occident*, II. pp. 709 sqq. Teza (*ibid.*, note 1) quotes Leo Allatius (*De Symeonum scriptis*, p. 184) as saying of the Greek version 'asservatur praeterea in bibliotheca augustana inter libros manuscriptos, plut. 7 cod. 3, et Viennae Austriae iu bibliotheca imperatoris.' And Puntoni says that in preparing his promised edition he has consulted, along with other authorities already mentioned, three MSS. which he designates as Vat. 704, Vat. 867, Barber. L 172, and Lugd. 93 Vulc.

The old Italian version.

§ 41. An Italian rendering of Simeon's version was published at Ferrara in 1583[1] and reprinted at Bologna in 1872[2].

[1] Del governo | de' regni. | Sotto morali essempi | di animali ragionanti | tra loro. | Tratti prima di lingua | indiana in agarena. | Da Lelo Demno Saraceno. | Et poi dall' Agarena, nella Greca. | Da Simeone Setto | Philosopho Antiocheno. | Et bora tradotti di Greco in Italiano. | In Ferrara per Dominico | Mammarelli. MDLXXXIII. (8°.) [Copy in British Museum.]

The title is followed by a dedicatory preface addressed by Mammarelli to the 'Illustre Sign. Lvigia Malpigli de Bvonvisi,' dated June 12, 1583, and a sonnet to her by Givlio Nuti.

The book seems to have been republished at Ferrara in 1610 (see Stark's preface to the Greek text).

[2] In the 'Scelta di Curiosità Letterarie inedite o rare dal secolo XIII al XVII in Appendice alla Collezione di Opere inedite o rare. Dispensa CXXV.'; and entitled 'Del Governo de' Regni sotto morali Esempi di Animali ragionauti tra

The Ferrara edition comprises:

1. An 'Introduzione,' containing an abridgement of De Sacy's chapters 3 and 4, the 'Introduzione' being simply Aurivillius' prolegomena 2 and 3 pieced together.

2. The story of 'Stefaneto & Ichnilato,' which heads a fresh paragraph (p. 9) but is not otherwise separated from the 'Introduzione.'

3. Secondo Essempio, Terzo Essempio, &c., corresponding respectively to De Sacy's chapters 7, 8, 9, 10, 14, 12, 13. The next, i.e. the ninth, 'essempio' is the story of the king of the mice. The tenth consists of De Sacy's chapters 17, 18, and 15. The eleventh and last is De Sacy's chapter 16 [1].

Dr W. Pertsch in *Orient und Occident* (II. pp. 261 sqq.) gives a careful description of the Ferrara edition and a list of (a) the chief points in which the Italian version differs from the texts of the Greek translation (Possinus, Stark or the Athens reprint, Aurivillius) but does not agree with some other offshoot of the *Panchatantra*; where, that is, the Italian translator has drawn on his imagination : (b) points in which divergencies of one or other of the above mentioned texts of Symeon Seth from the rest are supported or rejected by the Italian : (c) cases in which the Italian differs from all known texts of the Greek translation but *agrees with de Sacy's Arabic text*. On pp. 707 sqq. of the same volume Prof. Emilio Teza shows that there are reasons for thinking that Nuti was not the author of the Italian translation, as Pertsch assumes, gives some useful information about the two Florentine codices of the Greek, and draws attention to a Spanish translation of the Turkish *Humāyūn-nāmah* by Vincenzo Bratuti of Ragusa (died A.D. 1680).

loro' (Bologna, Gaetano Romagnoli, 1872), edited by E. Teza. 200 copies only were printed. [Copy in British Museum.]

[1] As compared with Stark's edition

Ferrara	II.	=	Stark	3
	III.	=	,,	1
	IV.	=	,,	5
	V.	=	,,	6
	VI.	=	,,	7
	VII.	=	,,	9 (Stark 8 is missing in the Italian.)
	VIII.	=	,,	10
	IX.	=	,,	14
	X.	=	,,	11, 12, 13
	XI.	=	,,	16

§ 42. The Greek version passed also iuto old Slavonic[1]; and according to H. F. von Diez[2] and Schulteus[3], Stark's text was rendered into German under the title *Abnschalem und sein Hof-philosoph oder die Weisheit Indiens in einer Reihe von Fabeln*, vom Rector Lehmus (Leipzig, 1778, 8°).

C. PERSIAN VERSIONS.

§ 43. The oldest extant Persian version of the Arabic *Kalīlah wa Dimnah* is that composed by Abu 'l-Ma'ālī Nasrullah ibu Muḥammad ibn 'Abd al-Ḥamīd, partly at the direction of Bahrām Shāh, 13th Ghaxnevī Sultan and a great patron of literary men (died A.D. 1151). We are indebted to De Sacy for a notice of this translation, which he knew from six Persian manuscripts iu the Paris library[4]. The author has prefixed to his work a long preface in which he explains how he was led to set about the translation and encouraged by the Sultan to finish it, and describes the plan on which he made it. The preface is followed by an introduction, attributed to Ibn al-Muḳaffa', relating the mission of Barzōye to India and identical with De Sacy's 2nd chapter. Then comes the index of chapters. These are sixteen iu number and correspond respectively to De Sacy's chapters 3, 4, 5, 6, 7, 8, 9, 10, 11, 12, 13, 15, 16, 14, 17, 18. De Sacy remarks[5] that although the author announces in his preface his intention to take very considerable liberties with his original, yet he has only done so at the commencement of the chapter of the lion and the ox. De Sacy shows[6] that Nasrullah must have made his version about A.H. 515 (A.D. 1121).

---

[1] [Stephanitw i Ichnilate] edited by Th. J. Bulgakoff. (St Petersburg, 1877.) [Copy in Bodleian.]

[2] *Ueber Inhalt u. Vortrag...des königllchen Buchs* (Berlin, 1811, 8°).

[3] *Pars versionis arabicæ libri Colailah wa Dimnah*, p. xvi.

[4] *Notices et Extraits des Manuscrits*, Vol. x. Pt I. pp. 91—196. Besides several shorter extracts De Sacy gives the complete text of the chapter of the king and the bird (pp. 176—196). On earlier Persian versions no longer extant, both in prose and verse, see De Sacy in the *Mémoire historique*, prefixed to his *Calila et Dimna*, pp. 37—39; and in *Notices et Extraits*, Vol. x. I. pp. 101, 102, 110, 111, 171—175.

[5] *Ibid.* p. 112.   [6] *Ibid.* pp. 133 137.

K. F.   e

The 'Anwār-i-Suhailī.'

§ 44. On Naṣrullah's version is based the well-known *Anwār-i-Suhailī* ('Lights of Canopus')[1]. The best edition is that of Lieut.-Col. J. W. J. Ouseley[2], and the best English translation that of E. B. Eastwick[3]. The author—Ḥusain Ibn 'Alī al-Wā'iẓ, known by the name al-Kāshifī—gives in his preface a brief history of the book. After mentioning Naṣrullah's version, he says, according to Eastwick's rendering: 'Although those who sit on the throne of the court of style are unanimous

---

[1] First printed at Calcutta (1804, fol.) and again there in 1824; there is also a lithographed Bombay edition (1828, fol.). *Suhailī* is the relative adjective formed from the noun *Suhail* (the star Canopus), and the name of the person in whose honour the author entitled his book.

[2] *Anwār i Suhelī: or lights of Canopus: being the Persian version of the fables of Bidpāi,* by Husain Vāi̇. Kāshifī (Hertford, 1851, 4°).

[3] *The Anwār-i Suhailī; or, the lights of Canopus; being the Persian version of the fables of Pilpay; or, the book "Kalīlah and Damnah," rendered into Persian by Ḥusain I'ā'iẓ u'l-Kāshifī: literally translated into prose and verse,* by Edward B. Eastwick, F.R.S., &c. (Hertford, 1854, 8°).
There is another, by A. N. Wollaston (London, 1877, 8°). There is also a French rendering of the first four chapters of the *A-i-S* untitled; *Livre des lumières ou la conduite des Rays composé par le sage Pilpay, Indien; traduit en français par Darid Sahid d'Ispahan, ville capitale de Perse. A Paris chez Siméon Piget* (1644, 8°). De Sacy (*Notices et Extraits,* ix. pp. 450 sqq.) shows that Ganlmin had a hand in the book and wrote the introduction. The book was reprinted under the title, *Les Fables de Pilpay philosophe indien: ou la conduite des rois* (Paris, Delaulne, 1698, 12°). [Copy in Bodleian.] The name of the translator and the dedicatory epistle were suppressed, and the rest slightly retouched. For later editions see De Sacy in *Notices et Extraits,* x. p. 431; Diez's *Ueber Iuhait u. Vortrag ..des königlichen Buchs* (Berlin, 1811), pp. 143 sqq.; and Grässe's *Trésor de livres rares,* s.v. *Bidpay.*
This French book was rendered into English and passed through several editions. I have seen copies of two editions in the Bodleian, viz. *The instructive and entertaining Fables of Pilpay, an ancient Indian Philosopher. Containing a number of excellent Rules for the Conduct of Persons of all Ages and in all Stations: under several Heads. Corrected, improved and enlarged; and adorned with near seventy Cuts neatly engraved* (London, 1747, 12mo), and *The fables of Pilpay. With numerous illustrations, by Thomas D. Scott* (London, E. Lumley, 1852, 12mo). The edition of 1747 contains Ganlmin's preface, but in that of 1852 a new one is substituted and the spelling of the whole modernised.
There is also a Dakhni translation of the *Anwār-i-Suhailī* entitled *Dukhnee Unwari Soheilee. A translation into the Duknee tongue, of the Persian Unwari Soheilee for the use of the military officers on the Madras establishment.* By Mohummud Ibraheem Moon-shee (Madras, 1824, fol.]

in praise of the magnificence of the words, and in applauding the eloquence of its compounds,...nevertheless, through
the introduction of strange words and by overstraining the
language with the beauties of Arabic expressions and hyperbole
in metaphors and similes of various kinds, and exaggeration
and prolixity in words and obscurity of expression, the mind of
the hearer is kept back from enjoyment of the meaning of the
book, and from apprehending the pith of the subject...Hence,
too, it all but came to pass that a book of such preciousness [as
this is] was almost neglected and abandoned, and that the people
of the world were deprived of its advantages and excluded from
them.' Then, after mentioning the Amír Shékh Aḥmad Suhailí
(generalissimo of Sultan Ḥusain Mírzá, king of Khurásán and
descendant of Tamerlane), he continues: 'With a view to the
universal diffusion of what is advantageous to mankind, and
the multiplying what is beneficial to high and low, he condescended to favour me with an intimation of his high will
that this humble individual, devoid of ability, and this insignificant person of small capital, Ḥusain-bin-'Alí-u'l-Wá'iẓ...should
be bold enough to clothe the said book in a new dress, and
bestow fresh adornment on the beauty of its tales of esoteric
meaning, which were veiled and concealed by the curtain of
obscure words and the wimple of difficult expressions, by presenting them on the stages of lucid style and the upper chambers
of becoming metaphors, after a fashion that the eye of every
examiner, without a glance of penetration or penetration of
vision, may enjoy a share of the loveliness of those beauties of
the ornamented bridal-chamber of narrative, and the heart of
every wise person, without the trouble of imagining or the
imagining trouble, may obtain the fruition of union with those
delicately reared ones of the closet of the mind '.'

The version of Ḥusain Wá'iẓ includes a large number of
stories not found in the *Kalílah wa Dimnah*, and is written in
a style of which the extract just quoted affords a fair specimen.

The exact date is not certain. The king of Khurásán alluded
to in the preface reigned A.D. 1470—1505[2].

The contents are:

¹ Eastwick, pp. 8—11.
² Diez, *Ueber Inhalt u. Vortrag. des königlichen Buchs*, p. 99.

(1) Author's preface, ending with a list of chapters.

(2) Chapter I., consisting of (α) a new introduction relating the remote origin of the book, and (β) a section corresponding to De Sacy's chapter 5.

(3) Chapters II.—XIV. inclusive, corresponding respectively to De Sacy's chapters 6, 7, 8, 9, 10, 11, 12, 13, 15, 16, 14, 17, 18.

De Sacy's chapters 1, 2, 3, 4 are not represented at all.

The introduction is briefly as follows:

One of the emperors of China, Humāyūn Fāl, goes out hunting with his vezir, Khujistāh Rāī. Returning in the heat, they take rest on a hill-top. The emperor sees a swarm of bees in a hollow tree. Their manner of living gives rise to a conversation, in the course of which the vezir mentions Dabshalīm and Bīdpāi, and at the emperor's request tells him about them. Dabshalīm, said he, had once in a dream heard an old man bid him go to the east, that he might there find a treasure worthy of a king. He journeyed into the desert, and found in a cave a mass of treasures, including a richly ornamented box containing a piece of white silk on which was written in Syriac characters the testament of king Hūshang, especially deposited for Dabshalīm, whom the writer had foreseen by inspiration would find it. It contained fourteen rules of life, to be expounded by means of tales, but with regard to these the king was directed to repair to the holy mountain in Ceylon. After some hesitation, he went thither, and discovered a cave in which lived the wise Brahman called by some Bīdpāi, by others Pīlpāi[1]. The king told him his dream, and Pīlpāi then communicated to him the lessons of wisdom. Herewith commences the book proper.

This introduction, Benfey suggests[2], is due to the wish to represent the book as a united whole, and the particular form of it may have been suggested by the *Jāwidān Khired* ('Eternal wisdom'), a Persian writing attributed to king Hūshang, known also as the *Testament of Hūshang*[3].

---

[1] I.e. 'Elephant-foot.'

[2] *Einleit. zur Pantsch.* § 19.

[3] De Sacy in *Notices et Extraits*, x. p. 93.

The "Iyār-i-Dānish" of Abu 'l-Faḍl.

§ 45. The *Anwār-i-Suhailī*, like its predecessor, became anti-quated and gave place to a later and simplified edition, the '*Iyār-i-Dānish* ('Touchstone of knowledge'). It has never been edited, but De Sacy has given an account of it as found in two Persian manuscripts of the Paris library, together with extracts[1]. The author, Abu 'l-Faḍl, says in his preface, according to De Sacy's version: 'Djélaleddin Acbar[2], empereur conquérant, étant tombé sur ce livre, ce chef-d'œuvre d'éloquence, et ce recueil où sont offertes, sous le masque de la fable, les maximes de l'ancienne sagesse, eut le bonheur de plaire à Sa Majesté. Aussitôt le serviteur de cette cour, Abou 'Ifazl, fils de Mobaree, dont l'humble soumission est sans bornes, reçut l'ordre de faire une nouvelle rédaction de l'Anvari Suhaïli dans un style clair, en conservant l'ordre primitif, mais en retranchant certaines expressions, et raccourcissant les périodes de trop longue haleine, afin que ce livre devînt d'une utilité plus générale, et que le but qu'on s'était proposé fût parfaitement atteint : car bien que l'Anvari Suhaïli, si ou le compare à la traduction connue sous le nom de Calila et Dimna, se rapproche davantage du styl de notre siècle, il n'est point cependant exempt de termes arabes et de métaphores extra-ordinaires[3].'

The version of Abu 'l-Faḍl contains (*a*) his preface, concluding with a list of 16 chapters, (*b*) chapter I., corresponding to De Sacy's chapter 3, (*c*) chapter II., consisting of two parts which correspond respectively to De Sacy's chapter 4 and to the intro-duction of Ḥusain Wā'iẓ in which are related the adventures of Humāyūn Fāl, (*d*) 14 chapters corresponding respectively to De Sacy's chapters 5, 6, 7, 8, 9, 10, 11, 12, 13, 15, 16, 17, 18, (*e*) a long epilogue giving the date of the completion of the work (Monday 15th Sha'bān, A.H. 996 = A.D. 158⅔)[4].

[1] *Notices et Extraits*, x. pp. 197—223.
[2] The great Mogul who reigned at Delhi A.D. 1552—1605.
[3] *Notices et Extraits*, x. p. 208.
[4] *Ibid.* p. 215; and Rieu's *Catalogue of the Persian MSS. in the British Museum*, p. 757.

The 'Iyār-i-Dānish' has been translated into Urdu and edited by Capt. Thos. Roebuck (*Khirad U'rāz*, Calcutta, 1815, large 8vo).

The Turkish 'Humāyūn-nāmah.'

§ 46. In the first half of the 16th century A.D., under the reign of the Ottoman emperor Suleymān I., the work of Ḥusain Wā'iẓ was rendered into Turkish by 'Alī Chelebī, professor of Muhammedan law at Adrianople, at the college founded by Murād II. He entitled his work *Humāyūn-nāmah* ('Imperial book').

This version is known to us principally by the French translation commenced by Galland and completed by Cardonne[1]. The part by Galland comprises the first four chapters, of which the first (extending over 177 pages) includes, as in the *Anwār-i-Suhailī*, the story of Humāyūn Fāl and Dabshalim and that of Kalīlah and Dimnah (De Sacy's 5th chapter). The mention of Lokmān on the title page is quite out of place.

There exists also a Spanish translation of the *Humayūn-nāmah*, of which some account has been given by Teza in *Orient und Occident*, II. pp. 714 sqq. The first part was published in 1654, and a second in 1658. The first part is entitled *Espejo politico, y moral, para principes, ministros, y todo genero de personas, Traducido de la lengua turca en la castellana, por Vicente Bratuti raguseo interprete de la lengua turca, de Felipe quarto el grande rey de las Españas... Parte primera En Madrid anno 1654. Por Domingo Garcia y Morras.*

The *Humāyūn-nāmah* is treated of in H. F. von Diez's *Über Inhalt und Vortrag, Entstehung und Schicksale des königlichen Buchs, eines Werks von der Regierungskunst, als Ankün-*

---

[1] *Les contes et fables indiennes, de Bidpai et de Lokman. Traduites d'Ali Tchelebi-Ben-Saleh, Auteur Turc. Oeuvre posthume. Par M. Galland. (Paris, chez G. Cavelier, 1724, 2 vols. sm. 8vo). [Copy in Bodleian.]

Contes et Fables indiennes, de Bidpai et de Lokman; Traduites d'Ali Tchelebi-ben-Saleh, Auteur turc. Ouvrage commencé par feu M. Galland, continué et fini par M. Cardonne... (Paris, 1778, 3 vols. 12mo). [First two vols. in Bodleian.]

Galland and Cardonne's work has been reprinted in the *Cabinet des Fées*, Tom. XVII, XVIII (Geneva, 1760). Galland's work passed also into modern Greek (Vienna, 1783), Hungarian (1783), and Dutch (*sine loco et anno*). See De Sacy in *Notices et Extraits*, X. p. 480: and Graesse's *Trésor de livres rares et précieux*, s.v. *Bidpay*.

digung einer Uebersetzung nebst Probe aus dem Türkisch-Persisch-Arabischen des Waassi Aly Dschelebi (Berlin, 1811).
The author has related the literary history of the *Kalilah wa Dimnah* with special reference to the Turkish version, and given in German a specimen taken from the commencement of the story of Humāyūn Fāl together with a list of the chapters. These are 14 in number and correspond with the 14 of the *Anwār-i-Suhailī.*

Diez devotes several pages (146—151) to a slashing criticism of Galland and Cardonue's work. Its only merit, he says, is that it is printed in clear, readable type. Otherwise it is faulty and fragmentary, and skips or alters the difficult passages. Diez also gives some information about Bratuti's version (p. 151).

Ed. von Adelburg in his *Auswahl türkischer Erzählungen aus dem Humajun-name* (Erstes Heft, Wien, 1855) gives the Turkish text (with a German translation) of a fragment of the introductory chapter.

D. THE HEBREW VERSION AND ITS OFFSHOOTS.

§ 47. There are two Hebrew versions of the Arabic. One of these formed the basis of the celebrated *Directorium* of John of Capua (which in turn gave rise to German, Danish, Dutch, Spanish, Italian, French and English versions), and is therefore critically of great importance. It is contained in a unique and unfortunately mutilated manuscript of the Paris National Library [No. 1282, 2]. De Sacy has described this MS. at length in the *Notices et Extraits des manuscrits*, Vol. IX. Pt. I., pp. 413 sqq., and given the Hebrew text of the chapter of the king and the bird (pp. 451—466); Ad. Neubauer published the text of the chapter corresponding to the fourteenth in the Arabic, accompanied by a German translation, in *Orient und Occident*, I. pp. 483—496, 657—680; and Joseph Derenbourg has published the entire text, together with a French translation, a collation of the *Directorium*, and a number of excellent conjectural emendations (*Deux versions hébraïques du livre de Kalilah et Dimnah...*Paris, Vieweg, 1881; being fasciculus 49 of the *Bibliothèque des hautes études*).

Both the date and the author of this version are unknown[1]. It cannot have been made later than about 1250, the approximate date, as will be seen, of its Latin translation by John of Capua. The volume in which this unique MS. is contained belonged formerly to Gilbert Gaulmin, and comprises four distinct writings, the third of which is a large portion of the *Kalilah wa Dimnah*. The text of the *K. w. D.* commences abruptly at a point towards the end of the chapter numbered 6th in De Sacy's Arabic. The next chapter in the Hebrew MS. is headed 'Fourth chapter,' and the rest are numbered in order as far as the seventeenth and last. By comparing the contents of the *Directorium*, it seems that there was originally a prologue or introduction corresponding to the 3rd and 2nd chapters in the Arabic, followed by an index or list of chapters, at which point the book proper commenced, the first chapter corresponding to De Sacy's 4th, and the 2nd to his 5th; so that the complete text contained a prologue or introduction and seventeen chapters. The extant chapters correspond respectively to the Arabic chapters 6 (in part), 7, 8, 9, 10, 11, 12, 14, 15, 16, 13, 17, 18, 19, 21. It is quite certain that this Hebrew version gave rise to the Latin and not vice versâ, for (1) John of Capua expressly states the fact in the first sentence of his prologue, (2) renderings occur in the *Directorium* which can only be explained on the assumption of a Hebrew original; e.g., when the author renders *ignis* where the sense requires *humo*, it is evident that the mistake is due to a misreading of שֵׁא for שֵׁא.

This Hebrew version is wholly distinct from the *Mishlē Sandabār* (substantially the same book as the Greek 'Syntipas the philosopher' or the story of the seven vezīrs in the Arabian nights), with which it has been confounded owing to the unfortunate fact that the name of the philosopher (Baidabā) appears in this version as סֶנְדְּבָּאר (Sandabār), in which of course the ר (*r*) may be a corruption of an original ד (*d*). The mistake is no doubt due partly to a misunderstanding of the

---

[1] It has been ascribed to a certain Rabbi Joel, of whom nothing is otherwise known but the name. See Benfey's *Einleit. zur Pantsch.* pp. 10 sqq. ; Comparetti's *Researches respecting the book of Sindibad* (Publication IX. of the Folklore Society). pp. 64 sqq. ; and De Sacy in *Notices et Extraits*, IX. pp. 401, 402.

Arabic (perhaps unpointed) سندباد and partly to a reminiscence of the familiar *Sandabâr*. The mistake is of course repeated in all the offshoots of the Hebrew, except where a totally different name is purposely substituted.

The other Hebrew version is partially contained in a manuscript of the Bodleian library (No. 2384), and was made by Jacob ben Eleazar, a writer of the thirteenth century and author of a Hebrew dictionary entitled *Sĕfer hash-shâlēm*. The text is complete as far as a point near the end of the chapter of the owls and the crows, where it terminates. The extant chapters correspond respectively to De Sacy's Arabic chapters 3, 2, 4, 5, 6, 7, and (in part) 8.

This version is the second of the *Deux versions hébraïques*, etc., edited by M. Deronbourg, who gives the text together with critical notes, but no translation.

While the version attributed to Rabbi Joel is a link in the chain of the transmission of the fables, that of Rabbi Eleazar is merely a literary product of modern Judaism, being little more than a cento of Bible verses, possessing hardly any critical value[1].

The 'Directorium' of John of Capua.

§ 48. The Hebrew version attributed to Joel was rendered into Latin by John of Capua, a converted Jew who flourished towards the end of the thirteenth century. Until Puntoni's reprint of 1884, only a single (and now very rare) edition of this work is known to have been published. The copy in the library of Trinity College, Cambridge, is entitled *Directorium huma'ne vite alias parabo!le antiquorū sapientā* (sine loco et anno, gothic type, folio, 82 leaves, 50 lines to a page, woodcuts). The book seems to have been slightly corrected from time to time while in the press[2]. It cannot have been published later than 1483, if, as Benfey says[3], the editor of the 1483 Ulm edition of the German version had the printed Latin text ' before his eyes.'

[1] It was unknown until Steinschneider drew attention to it in the *Z. D. M. G.*, Vol. XXVII. 1873, p. 553.
[2] See Benfey's *Einleitung zur Pantschatantra*, p. 17, notes 1 and 2.
[3] *Einleit. zur Pantsch.* p. 16.

The *Directorium* commences with a prologue, which opens
with a short prefatory statement of the author, followed without
a break by a section corresponding to De Sacy's 3rd chapter,
and ending with the words 'Explicit prologus, Incipit liber.'
The next section answers to De Sacy's second chapter (Mission
of Barzōyē), and is followed by an index or list of chapters,
whereupon the book proper begins, containing 17 chapters,
which correspond respectively with the chapters numbered 4, 5,
6, 7, 8, 9, 10, 11, 12, 14, 15, 16, 13, 17, 18, 19, 20, and 21, in the
Arabic version.

The clue to the date at which this Latin version was made
is furnished by the short prefatory notice which forms the
commencing part of the prologue.

'Verbum Johannis de capua, post tenebrarum olim pulpa-
tionem ritus judaici: divina sola inspiratione ad firmum et
verum statum orthodoxe fidei revocati. Cum plura diversarum
scientiarum genera esse prospexerim in lingua fundata hebraica:
non parve utilitatis in eruditionem christianorum consortii, ut
in sacris scripturis, et divinis moralibus atque medicinalibus:
ipsa ex predicta lingua in latinam reducere meus animus
aspiravit. Inter quo nunc hunc libellum dictum kelila, ex
illa lingua in hauc: nunc esse vidi non etiam immerito trans-
ferendum. Est enim opus virorum intelligentie animarum
multe informationis, et nihil earundem non modico delectationis.
Ad honorem autem divine trinitatis, sanctissimique ejus nominis
exaltationem, salutem et meritum anime, fortitudinem cor-
poris et roborationem, atque dierum productionem. Reverendi
patris et domini domini matbei dei et apostolice sedis gratia.
Tituli sancte marie in porticu diaconi cardinalis, motus sum
praesens opusculum in lingua latina interpretari. Ad te igitur
prefato pater domine dirigitur hic libellus et ut tuarum aliarum
gratie (? gratiarum) protectione, pusillus interpres, ad alia majora
utiliora et nobiliora, manum imponat, ex altera prefatarum
linguarum in alteram cum audacia reducenda.

Pro sapientibus et insulsis hic liber factus est. Hic est liber
parabolarum antiquorum sapientum nationum mundi. Et vocatur liber kelile et dimne, et prius quidem in lingua fuerat
indorum translatus. Inde in linguam translatus persarum.
Postea vero reduxerunt illum arabes iu linguam suam, ultimo

ex inde ad linguam fuit redactus hebraicam. Nuuc autem nostri propositi est: ipsum in linguam fundare latinam.'

From this point onwards the 'Prologus' substantially agrees with De Sacy's 3rd chapter.

From the above extract (taken from the copy of the *Directorium* in Trinity College Library) it appears that this version was made from the Hebrew by John of Capua, a converted Jew living in the time of a certain Matthew, cardinal deacon of the 'title' of *Holy Mary in porticu.*

This Matthew, identical with *Matthæus de Rubeis* or *de'Rossi,* nephew of Pope Nicholas III., was created cardinal deacon by Urban IV. in 1262 or 1263. Hence John of Capua wrote his translation not earlier than 1263. Further, since Matthew was created archpriest of St Peter by Nicholas III. in or about 1278, and protector of the order of the *Fratres minores* in 1279, while yet these titles are not accorded to him by John of Capua, De Sacy infers that the translation was made not later than 1279[1].

The Latin version is a slavish reproduction of the original Hebrew, and for this very reason of special critical value[2].

Eberhard's German Version.

§ 49. The *Directorium* was rendered into German at the instance of Graf Eberhard of Württemberg about 1480.

The latest and best edition of this excellent translation is that of Holland, entitled *Das Buch der Beispiele der alten Weisen......herausgegeben von Dr Wilhelm Ludwig Holland* (Stuttgart, 1860, 8vo, pp. iv and 261), being Vol. LVI. of the *Bibliothek des Litterarischen Vereins in Stuttgart*[3]. The edition is based on three Heidelberg manuscripts and the printed texts. Dr Holland has given in his introduction a very full bibliography of the first twenty editions[4]. The earliest dated edition

---

[1] De Sacy in *Notices et Extraits,* III. p. 401.

[2] The *Directorium* has been reprinted by V. Puntoni in his *Directorium humanae vitæ...accedunt Prolegomena tria ad librum Στεφανιτης και Ιχνηλατης* (Pisa, 1884, 8°).

[3] Briefly reviewed by Theodor Benfey in *Orient und Occident.* I. p. 383.

[4] See too K. Gödeke's article in *Orient und Occident.* I. pp. 641 648 (where a concise bibliographical list is given), and Benfey's dissertation in the same volume (pp. 138—187), where he shows that the German translation was

is one by Lienhart Holle (Ulm, 1483, May 28, 195 leaves, folio)[1]. Three editions are *sine loco et anno*. The editions previous to the Strassburg one of 1536 are all entitled, either at the beginning or end, *Das Buch der Weissheit der alten Weisen*, but that of 1539 bears a new title, viz. *Der Alten Weisenn exempel spriüch, mit vil schönen Beyspileu und Figuren erleüchtet. Darinnen fast aller menschen wesen, Händel, Untrew, List, Geschwindigkeyt, Neyd, und Hass, Figuriert vnd angezeygt werden*, &c., the old title being retained at the end.

The German version passed into Danish and Dutch.

There are two editions of the Danish, one *sine loco et anno*, the other of Copenhagen (1618).

In C. V. Bruun's *Bibliotheca Danica* (col. 960) I find the following entries:

'De gamle Vijses Exempler oc Hoffsprock, met mange skiöne Ligneleer forklarede: hnorvdi mangfoldige Menniskens Væsen, Handel, List, Behendighed, Had oc Avjnd affmalis oc tilkiende giffnis. Kbh. 1618 Paa Christen Nielszöus Borgers oc Bogfürers Bekanntning [oversat af hain].

—U. St. o. A. [Kbh. paa Chr. Geertscns Bogh. Bekostn.]

The Bodleian library has a copy of a Dutch version entitled ' Voorbeelsels | der | onde wyse, | Handelende | Van trouw on-trouw list haet ghelswindicheyt ende alle andere Menlsche-lijcke gheneghenthcden...Door Zacharias Heyns, t'Amsterdam, Ghedruckt by Broer Janaz....1623.' (8vo, goth., 136 leaves, 40 lines to a page, 99 woudcuts.)

Schultens, in the preface to his *Pars versionis arabicæ libri Colailah wa Dimnah*, after mentioning Heyns' version, says "Quam versionem deinde refinxit, pluriumque rerum alien-arum admixtione a veteri fonte longius abduxit, Johannes Duikerius in ' Voorbeehlzels der oude Wyzen ; uit meest alle de Oostersche, Griekache en Romeinsche Taalen vergaderd (Am-sterdam, 1714).'"

---

printed before the Latin (*ibid.* p. 166), and that the Spanish *Exemplario* was considerably influenced by the German. Compare Benfey's *Einleit. zur Pantach.*, pp. 16 sqq.

[1] The Bodleian library contains copies of two editions, viz. of Ulm by Cnorad Dinckmut (1485, fol.), and of Strassburg (1545, fol.).

The Spanish 'Exemplario' and its offshoots.

§ 50. Another translation of the *Directorium* is the Spanish *Exemplario contra los engaños y peligros del mundo*, first printed at Saragossa in 1493 by a German. De Gayangos describes eight editions of this work in his introduction to 'Calyla é Dymna' in the *Biblioteca de autores españoles*, Vol. LI. (Madrid, 1860), p. 5, note 3: Benfey notices two other editions in *Orient und Occident*, I. pp. 166 sqq., 501: and K. Gödeke gives a complete and concise bibliographical list in the same volume, p. 688. The oldest edition Gödeke describes as 'Çaragoça de Aragon, Paulo Hurus, Alcman de Constancia, 30 March 1493. 87 leaves, fol., 117 woodcuts.'

Firenzuola's 'Discorsi degli animali.'

§ 51. The *Exemplario* seems to be the source whence Agnolo Firenzuola derived the substance of his *Discorsi degli animali ragionanti tra loro*, first published at Venice in 1548, and frequently since.

It consists of a dialogue between 'Lutorerena' (Dabshalim) and the philosopher 'Tiabono' (Bidpāi). After a short introduction the king asks him to relate a story illustrating the case of two dear friends between whom a third person wishes to sow discord. Tiabono then relates the story of the lion, the ox, and the sheep. The ox, Bioudino, is of course Shanzabeh, and the sheep, Carpigna, is Dimnah. Carpigna's companion, Bellino, is Kalilah. The rest agrees substantially with the chapter of the lion and the ox (De Sacy's 5th). Firenzuola has transported the scenes to various places in Italy, and has often changed the names of the animals.

Firenzuola's work was rendered in French by Cottier under the title *Plaisant et facécieux discours sur les animaux*, trad. par *Gabr. Cottier* (Lyon, 1556, 16mo) [Grüsse's *Trésor de livres rares*, s. v. Bidpai].

A. F. Doni's 'Moral filosophia.'

§ 52. De Sacy (*Notices et Extraits*, IX. p. 441) says: 'C'est une chose reconnue que Doni, dans sa *Filosofia morale*, n'a fait

presque autre chose que mettre en italien la traduction latine
du livre de Calila, faite par Jean de Capoue.'
    Doni's work was first printed at Venice in 1552'. It consists
of two main parts, the *Moral Filosophia* and the *Trattati diversi
di Sendebar Indiano filosopho morale.* The first is entitled
'La Moral | Filosophia del Doni, | Tratta da gli antichi scrit-
tori; | Allo Illustriss. S. Don Ferrante Caracciolo dedicata.
[Engraving with the motto Η ΓΑΡ ΣΟΦΙΑ ΤΟΥ ΚΟΣΜΟΥ
ΤΟΥΤΟΥ ΜΩΡΙΑ ΠΑΡΑ ΤΩ ΘΕΩ ΕΣΤΙ] Con privilegio.
In Uinegia per Francesco | Marcoliui MDLII' (4to), aud is
divided into three books, of which the second and third have
special title-pages, though the paging is continuous. The
Moral Filosophia contains the complete history of Dimnah (De
Sacy's chapters 5 and 6). Kalilah appears as *l' asino* and
Dimnah as *il mulo.* The other part (with fresh paging) is
entitled 'Trattati | diversi | di Sendebar Indiano | filosopho
morale. | Allo illustriss. et excellentiss. S. | Cosimo de Medici
dedicati. [Engraving bearing the motto 'Fiorenza'] In
Uinegia | nell' Acadenia Peregrina. MDLII'; and at the end
(p. 103) stands 'In Uinegia per Francesco Marcolini. MDLII.'
The *trattati* are six in number, with continuous paging.
    The whole volume has very fine woodcuts.
    In the *Trattati diversi* the king and the philosopher appear as
Fr. Sforza, duke of Milan, and *maestro Dino filosofo Fiorentino*,
respectively. *Dino* may be an anagram of *Doni.* In fact the
scenes and personages are all Italian. The fables contained in
the book are mostly found in the *Directorium[2].*
    The *Moral Filosophia* (without the *Trattati*) was rendered
into English by Sir Thomas North, and published in 1570 and
1601. The edition of 1570 is entitled 'The Morall Philosophie
of Doni: | *drawne out of the auncient writers.* | A worke first
compiled in the Indian tongue, | and afterwards reduced into
diuers other languages: | *and now lastly englished out of Italian
by Thomas North.* Brother to the right Honorable Sir Roger
North Knight, Lord North of | Kyrtheling. | [Here follows
an engraving, a bad copy of the original, with the motto 'The
wisdome of this worlde is folly before God.'] ¶ Imprinted at

---

[1] There is a copy in the Bodleian.
[2] See further *Notices et Extraits*, IX. p. 442.

London | by Henry Denham.' (Small 4to, in four parts, of
which the third and fourth have separate title-pages', each
having a different engraving and motto and bearing the date
1570, which also appears at the end of the book; paging continuous, 116 leaves, woodcuts) [Copy in Bodleian]. The book
was republished in 1601. (London, 4to.) [Copy in British
Museum.]

On Firenzuola's *Discorsi degli animali* and Doni's *Moral
Filosophia* is based the work of De la Rivey entitled *Deux
livres de filosofie fabuleuse. Le premier prins des discours de
M. Ange Firenzuola Florentin. Par lequel sous le sens allegoric
de plusieurs belles fables, est monstrée l'envie, malice, & trahison
d'aucuns courtisans. Le second, extruict des Traictez de Sande-
bar Indien Philosophe moral, traictant soubs pareilles allegories
de l'amitié & choses semblables. Par Pierre de la Rivey
Champenois.* A Lyon, par Benoist Rigaud, M.D.LXXIX. (Small
8vo, pp. 377, continuous text, pages headed *Livre I* and
Livre II.) In both the books the king is called *Lutorcrène*
and the philosopher *Tiabou.* The second book, excepting the
introduction, the joinings of the several stories, and the substitution of the names of the king *Lutorcrène* and the philosopher
Tiabon for those of the duke *Sforza* and the philosopher *Dino*,
belongs wholly to Doni.

E. THE OLD SPANISH VERSION.

§ 53. As might have been expected from the contact of the
Arabs with Spain, the Arabic *Kalilah wa Dimnah* also passed
directly into Spanish. This Spanish version (to be carefully
distinguished from the later one based on the *Directorium*) has
been edited by De Gayangos in the *Biblioteca de Autores
Españoles, desde la formacion del lenguaje hasta nuestras dias.
Escritores en prosa anteriores al siglo xv recogidos é ilustrados*

---

¹ The reason why only two out of the last three parts have separate title-
pages is that North's title-pages are imitations of Doni's, of which there are
only three. North's four sections correspond to Doni's three.

² There is a copy in the Bodleian. Graesse in his *Trésor de livres rares*, s.v.
Bidpay, mentions an earlier edition (Paris, Abel l'Angelier, 1577, 12mo).

por don Pascual de Gayangos (Madrid, 1860). Vol. 32 (but not so named)[1].

The edition is based on two independent manuscripts of the Escurial, the oldest of which (marked iii. h. 9) dates from the end of the fourteenth century. Each contains a note at the end saying that the translation was made by the order of the infante D. Alfonso. This note in the older manuscript runs thus: 'Aquí se acaba el libro de Calina é dygna, et fué sacado de arábygo en latyn, é romançado por mandado del infante don alfonso, fijo del muy noble rey don fernando, en la era de mill é dozientos é noventa é nueve años' (= 1261 of our era). In another manuscript, described by Sarmiento[2], the same notice occurs, but the year given is 1389 (Spanish era). None other than Alfonso the Wise can he meant. As he was already reigning in 1261 of our era, he was then no longer Infante. On the other hand, Raimund's Latin version, based largely on this one, was finished in 1313 (1351 Spanish era). Hence both the dates 1299 and 1389 must be wrong. If we accept the 2 in 1299 and the 8 in 1389, the date 1289 (= 1251 of our era) is obtained, which was the year preceding Alfonso's accession to the throne, and therefore the latest possible date.

The version contains a prologue (corresponding to De Sacy's 3rd chapter), followed by 18 chapters, corresponding respectively to the Arabic chapters 2, 4, 5, 6, 7, 8, 9, 10, 11, 12, 14, 15, 16, 13, 17, 18, 20 and 21.

Notwithstanding the statement in the above-quoted note, there is no doubt whatever that this Spanish translation is based directly on the Arabic. There is no evidence that any Latin version existed when it was made, and it is a far truer representative of the Arabic than is the *Directorium* or the Hebrew. Thus many of the proper names are accurately reflected in the Spanish, but not in the Hebrew and Latin[3].

---

[1] A small though important part of it (the chapter corresponding to De Sacy's 2nd) had been published by Rodriguez de Castro (*Biblioteca Española*, 1, p. 636). See too De Sacy in *Notices et Extraits*, ix. 1, 431. A review of the old Spanish translation by Th. Benfey appears in *Orient und Occident*, Vol. 1, p. 409.

[2] *Memorias para la historia de la poesia*, Madrid, 1775.

[3] For examples see my notes to the English translation on pp. 1, 1, 116, 88 (O. Span. *Sirac*); 135, 38; 308, 20—28 (in the Heb. and O. Span. *Gôhar* is simply called 'primogenitus')—and the works cited there.

Perhaps the most striking example of the independence of the *Directorium* and the old Spanish is to be found at the beginning of the chapter about Barzöye. In the *Directorium* it runs thus: 'Inquit Berosius caput sapientum Persic,...Fuit pater meus de tali progenie, et mater mea de nobilibus talium.' In the old Spanish, according to one MS., thus: ' La hestoria de Berschuey, el filósofo. Mi padre fué de Mortedilla, et mi madre fué do los del Algabe, et do los legistas '; according to the other ' Yo padre fuè de Merceeilia, et mi madre fué do las fijasdalgo do asemosana et de los legistas[1].' The Arabic has: ' Barzöye......said : 'My father belonged to the army (المقاتلة al-mukātila) and my mother was descended from the chiefs of the houses of the magi (الزمازمة al-zamāzima) [2].'

Mortedilla and *Mercecilia* are corruptions of *mukātila*, and *asemosana* of *al-zamāzima*. These Arabic words are avoided in the *Directorium.*

Again, in the chapter of the ring-dove, the dove is called in the old Spanish *la paloma collarada ó torcas*[3], a literal translation of the Arabic *al-ḥamāmatu 'lmuṭawwaḳatu*[4]. But both in the Hebrew and the *Directorium* the epithet is wanting. Several Arabic words too appear transliterated in the old Spanish, but translated in the Hebrew and the *Directorium*: e.g. in the story of the wolf, the crow, the jackal and the camel (p. 43), the jackal is called *abnue*[5], *abnue* being simply an imitation of the Arabic ابن اوى (ibn āwā). The *Directorium* has *vulpis*. In the story of the sand-piper (p. 48), the sand-piper is named in the old Spanish *tittuy* and *tittuya*[6], which is only a transliteration of the طيطوى in the Arabic[7]. The *Directorium* has merely *avis aquatica*, and so the Hebrew translator was probably puzzled too. This was because the word is really not Arabic, but the Sanscrit *ṭiṭṭibha*[8]. In the chapter of the lion and the jackal (p. 186), the jackal is called *anzahar*[9], *anzahar* being merely the Arabic الشعر, but the Hebrew gives שעל (' fox ').

[1] *Cal. é Dym.* p. 14.
[2] *Cal. é Dym.* p. 41.
[3] *Cal. é Dym.* p. 29 note [2]; p. 30 note [2].
[7] De Sacy, p. 124, L. 10.
[5] *Cal. é Dym.* p. 67.

[2] De Sacy, p. 61.
[4] De Sacy, p. 160.
[6] *Ibid.* p. 30.
[8] *Kal. u. Dam.* pp. xlii, xliii.

Raimund's Latin Version.

§ 54. De Sacy in *Notices et Extraits*, Tom. x. Pt. II. pp.
3—65, has given a detailed account of two manuscripts in the
Royal (now National) Library of Paris, each containing a Latin
version of the *Kalilah wa Dimnah.* Of these two MSS., one is
merely a copy (but with certain deliberate alterations) of the
other. The copy was made in 1496. From the introductory
and dedicatory notices at the beginning of the original MS. it
appears that Raymundus de Biterris (Raimond de Béziers), a
physician, was commissioned by Queen Joanna of Navarre, wife
of Philip le Bel, to translate from Spanish into Latin the book
of Kalilah and Dimnah, which had been offered to that princess;
that this translation had been interrupted by her death in
1305; that subsequently Raimund wishing to gain an audience
of Philip, thought to do so by completing his translation; and
that he had the honour of presenting it to the king in 1313,
after the festivities which took place at Paris on Whitsunday
and the following days.

The dedicatory and introductory notices are followed by a
'proemium,' of which one passage at least was borrowed by him
from the *Directorium*[1]. The 'proemium' is followed by a
lengthy index (covering 30 pages of the manuscript) of the 19
chapters contained in Raimund's version, which correspond
respectively to the Arabic chapters 3, 2, 4, 5, 6, 7, 8, 9, 10, 11,
12, 14, 15, 16, 13, 17, 18, 20, 21.

De Sacy, who knew nothing of the old Spanish version
except what had been said by Rodriguez de Castro, saw clearly
that Raimund must have used (*a*) a Spanish text which had
flowed directly from the Arabic, and (*b*) the *Directorium*. An
examination of the proper names found in Raimund as compared
with the corresponding ones in the *Directorium* convinced him
that a Spanish-Arabic text had been employed; while the
verbal identity of whole passages with the corresponding ones in
John of Capua was proof positive that the *Directorium* must
have been at his elbow. The publication of the old Spanish

[1] *Notices et Extraits*, x., pt. 2, p. 12.

version has most decisively confirmed all De Sacy's arguments.
Thus for instance De Sacy notices that in the chapter corresponding to his 7th the queen of the doves is called *columba
dicta coronata*, and remarks that this epithet is wanting in the
Directorium and in the Hebrew, and reflects the *muṭawwaḳa* of
the Arabic. Turning to the Spanish version (p. 41), we find
mention of the ' paloma collarada ó torcaz.'

Raimund was by no means a faithful translator. He does
not scruple to introduce numbers of quotations from the Bible
and from classical authors. The chapter containing the biography of Barzöye has suffered most. He is represented as a
model christian monk. Long discourses on the christian virtues
are introduced. Barzöye sees in a vision paradise, the Virgin
Mary, the angels and all the saints of God. This vision is
described in hexameters and is illustrated by miniatures.

Not less curious is the way in which Raimund has embellished the end of the chapter containing the trial of Dimnah;
for by introducing the leopard as father confessor, a fine
opportunity is afforded for a discourse on the seven mortal
sins.

The later MS. of Raimund's version is a copy of the first, but
the index has been abridged, and nearly all the verses and
quotations with which Raimund overloaded his version have
been judiciously suppressed. Raimund's translation contains all
the chapters found in the old Spanish and the *Directorium*, and
in the same order.

Raimund's version has never been edited. Besides De Sacy's
descriptive notice of the work, we have some citations from it
in Édélstand du Méril's notes to his edition of Baldo's *Alter
Æsopus*, found in his *Poésies inédites du moyen âge* (Paris, 1854),
pp. 217 sqq.

§ 55. This *Alter Æsopus* is a poetical imitation of *Kalîlah
and Dimnah*, containing only the chief stories set to inferior
hexameters, and succeeding one another without any connecting
thread. It is assigned by the editor to the thirteenth century.

An Ethiopic version would seem to have been made from the Arabic. In Prof. Wright's 'Catalogue of the Ethiopic manuscripts in the British Museum' (p. 82, col. 2) a manuscript is described which contains an adaptation of the book of Psalms. The author, enumerating the books he has used, mentions the *Kalîlah wa Dimnah.*

To the offshoots of the old Greek version should be added a Croatian translation, mentioned by Puntoni under the title 'Indijske price prozvane Stefanit i Ihnilat (Starine II, U Zagrebu, 1870),' i.e. 'The Indian princes called Stefanit and Ihnilat (Miscellany of ancient documents, Vol. 2, Agram, 1870).'

In the 'Actes du sixième Congrès international des Orientalistes, tenu en 1883 à Leide' (p. 79) appears the following: 'M. Etbé fait une communication relative à quelques traductions turques, inconnues jusqu'ici, des fables arabes de *Kalila et Dimna.* Cette communication paraîtra dans les Travaux du Congrès.'

The University of Leiden possesses a Malay version in manuscript, made probably from the Arabic.

There is no evidence that an Armenian version exists. Grässe (*Trésor de livres rares*, s.v. *Bidpay*) says: 'Il existe aussi une rédaction arménienne du livre de Calila et Dimna, que nous connaissons d'une traduction française, *L'abrégé géographique de Moïse de Khoren, avec un recueil de fables, connu chez les anciens sous le titre du Livre de renard* (Marseille, 1676).' The book referred to is the composition of an Armenian writer of the thirteenth century, named Vartan. He has appropriated not a few of the fables found in the *Kalîlah wa Dimnah*, but his book cannot be called a version of that work.

Attention has been drawn to Vartan's book by Prof. Emilio Teza in *La Cultura*, 1882, Nr. x. (Rome)[1].

On p. lii I have quoted Benfey as alluding to a Syriac version of Barlaam and Josaphat. Mr W. Rhys Davids (in his *Buddhist Birth-stories*, p. xcv) also mentions a Syriac version of this romance, existing in manuscript only. But neither of these writers gives any authority for his statements, and it is very doubtful whether any such version exists.

With this account of the versions of the *Kalilah wa Dimnah* and their various editions may be compared:—

Loiseleur Deslongchamps' *Essai sur les fables indiennes et sur leur introduction en Europe, suivi du Roman des sept sages de Rome*......(Paris, 1838), pp. 6—70;

Prof. F. Max Müller's lecture *On the migration of fables*, in his *Chips from a German workshop*, Vol. IV. pp. 145—209 (London, 1875);

Mr T. W. Rhys Davids' introduction to his *Buddhist Birth-stories*, especially p. xeiii; and Grässe's *Trésor de livres rares et précieux*, s.v. *Bidpay*.

[1] For these facts I am indebted to the kindness of the Rev. Dr L. M. Alishan (of the Mechitharist monastery, San Lazzaro, Venice) and of the Rev. Dr John Thumajan (of the Mechitharist monastery, Vienna).

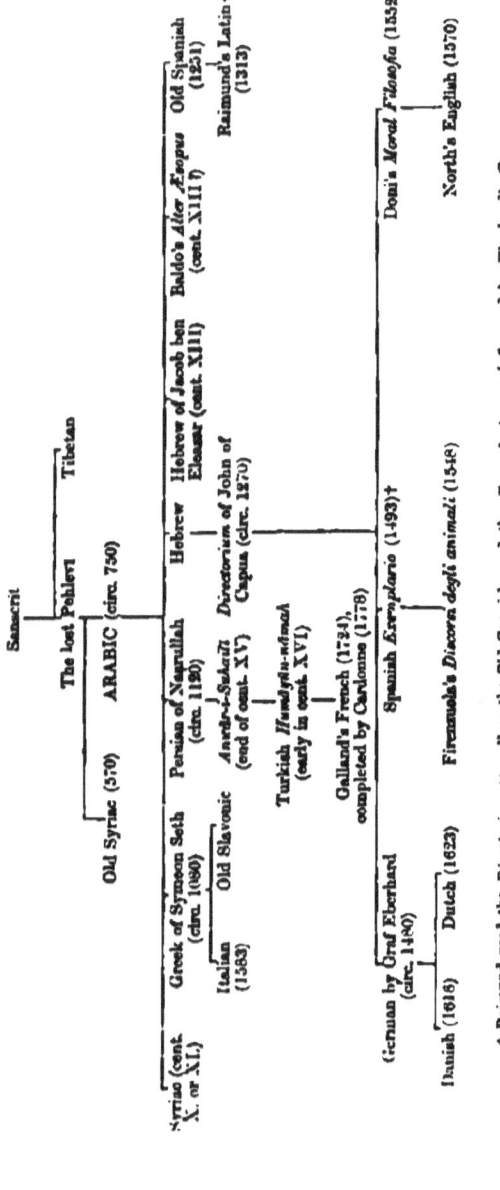

† Raimund used the *Directorium* as well as the Old Spanish, and the *Exemplario* was influenced by Eberhard's German.

THE BOOK

OF

KALĪLAH AND DIMNAH.

In reliance upon God we write the tales and instructive stories
of Kalílah and Dimnah, as translated by the wise.

THE STORY OF THE LION AND THE OX.

ERRATUM.

At p. 272, line 18, *for* "(Geurgia)" *read* "(Jurgán)."

Nadrab the philosopher answered: When a false man comes 10
between two loving brothers, ho disturbs their brotherly feeling
and destroys their harmony. It is said in the parable that in
a certain region called ———— there was a (+) merchantman,
who was possessed of no little wealth. And he had sons, who
when they came to be young men, began, all with one accord, 15
to squander their father's property, not being careful to gather
in, but only to spend. Then their father reproved them, saying:
'My sons, every one in the world considers how he may procure
three things, which however cannot be obtained except by four
means. The first of these three things is ample and abundant 20
sustenance; the second is the respect of men and a good name;
and the third, provision for the world to come. And the following are the means (to get these things): first, tho amassing of
wealth by lawful means; second, the good use of the same;
third, provision for the wants of nature; and fourth, generosity 25
to one's neighbours, charity to the poor, (and) supplying the
wants of the needy. He who attends to these four things

K. F.   I

In reliance upon God we write the tales and instructive stories
of Kalilah and Dimnah, as translated by the wise.

THE STORY OF THE LION AND THE OX.

It is related that Dabdahram, king of India, said to Nadrab the philosopher, the wise man, and chief of the wise men: 5 Show me the similitude of two men, companions or friends, between whom a false or astute cunning individual has produced dissension, so that they have been turned from mutual love and harmony to hatred and enmity.

Nadrab the philosopher answered: When a false man comes 10 between two loving brothers, he disturbs their brotherly feeling and destroys their harmony. It is said in the parable that in a certain region called ———— there was a (4) merchantman, who was possessed of no little wealth. And he had sons, who when they came to be young men, began, all with one accord, 15 to squander their father's property, not being careful to gather in, but only to spend. Then their father reproved them, saying: 'My sons, every one in the world considers how he may procure three things, which however cannot be obtained except by four means. The first of these three things is ample and abundant 20 sustenance; the second is the respect of men and a good name; and the third, provision for the world to come. And the following are the means (to get these things): first, the amassing of wealth by lawful means; second, the good use of the same; third, provision for the wants of nature; and fourth, generosity 25 to one's neighbours, charity to the poor, (and) supplying the wants of the needy. He who attends to these four things

K. F.   1

pleases his Creator; but he who does not gather these four into
his garners, or neglects one of them, derives no benefit from his
wealth, and attains not to the summit of his hope. Now if he
amasses nothing, and despises his wealth, and cares not at all
5 for his own interest, he can neither relieve others nor himself,
and without doubt will find himself destitute of property and
be left without sustenance. And if he manages his property
fittingly and quietly, with discernment and steady attention,
and yet adds nothing to it, it is like the eye-paint or kohl,
10 (5) of which the portion taken is like a little fine dust or smoke
which flies before a breath of air, but which, in spite of the
very minute quantity that is taken of it (each time), is surely
used up (at last). And if it be not fittingly managed,
rightly laid out, nor justly spent, besides losing his wealth,
15 he will be recompensed with justly deserved affliction and
with ill treatment by enemies. And if it is amassed, and not
dispensed compassionately nor distributed charitably, but is
hoarded up and concealed in the bosom of the earth in a
miserly way, while its possessor becomes like a needy and
20 destitute man who owns nothing, most assuredly it will be lost,
pass to others, or remain in the heart of the earth. It will
be like a tank of water which has many entrances but not a
single exit : for when there is much water in such a tank,
in some cases breaches are made in it, and the water runs out
25 of it, and it becomes useless ; while in others the tank is saved
from accident or bursting, and the water remains in it, but the
parching wind dries it up. So it happens to the wealth that is
not dispensed compassionately to the needy, when death withers
the limbs of its owners.'
30   Then the sons of that merchant took the advice of their
father, inclined to him the shoulder of obedience, and displayed the fruits of energy. And his eldest son set out on
a trading expedition, and journeyed towards a region called
Mathwâ. And he and his party crossed a certain place where
35 there was much clay or stinking mire. (6) Now he had with
him a waggon drawn by two oxen, one of whom was called
Shanzabeh and the other Banzabeh. Then Shanzabeh became
weary, stumbled in the mire, and fell. And the merchantman and his party made haste, and drew, and pulled the ox out

of the mire. And the merchant left the ox in that place, letting one of his young men remain with him, till he should recover
from his fall, and the young man should bring him along after
him. But on the morrow the hireling got tired of the place,
went after the merchant, and said : 'The ox has died in yonder 5
place.' Then the ox recovered strength and proceeded little by
little till he entered on a fen abounding in water and dense
with rich pasture. When he had remained a long time in that
place, he became very sleck and stout, and his reins thick with
fat. Then he thrust his horn into the ground, hollowed valiantly, 10
and roared vehemently. Now in that region was a certain lion,
who was king of all the animals therein, and was named Pingalaka ; and there were with him many animals of every kind.
Now this lion was exceedingly haughty in spirit, and whatever
he wished to do, he did independently, without employing 15
the advice of anyone. Notwithstanding, his knowledge was
not very perfect ; and when he heard the voice of the ox, he was
sore afraid, for he had never yet heard such a sound or seen an
ox. But he did not like to make known the fear of his heart,
and (so) remained in the place where he was for a time, and 20
did not move from it. Now in his camp, that is at his royal
gate, there were two (7) jackals, who were brothers, and named,
the one Kalîlah, and the other Dimnah. These were very crafty,
and trained too in learning or wisdom. And Dimnah was very
grasping, and not content with his pay ; but he was not ac- 25
quainted with his own feebleness, and did not know himself.
Dimnah said to Kalîlah: 'I see that the king has been staying
in one place without moving from it to another ; I should like
to know for what reason he does so, and why he does not amuse
himself as usual.' 30

Kalîlah. And you, why do *you* ask about such a thing as
this, which is none of your business or your affairs ? As for us,
we fare well, and dwell in comfort at the king's gate, receiving
sustenance from God, the Nourisher of all. But we are not of
those who are worthy to look into the king's actions, and to 35
track out the knowledge of his secret matters ; neither are we
of those who are entitled to speak with him. Nay, be quiet,
brother, and know that if a man longs and craves for something
which does not befit him or lies outside the range of his

mental vision, there will happen to him what happened to the
ape.

Dimnah. How runs the story about him ?

Kalilah. They say that a certain ape came upon a carpenter,
5 whom he saw mounted on a log, and splitting another log into
two pieces : the carpenter being like a man riding in a carriage (8). And he saw the carpenter take a small wedge of
wood from the fissure of the log which he was splitting, and
place another like it in its place in the cleft. Then the car-
10 penter went away on some business of his, while the foolish
ape took a leap and mounted on the log like the carpenter,
with his back towards the cleft of the log, and his face toward
the little wooden wedge, while his tail hung down and lay in
the middle of the cleft of the log. [Then he pulled out the
15 wedge.] But the fool forgot to put another in its place, and
his tail was crushed between the two parts of the log which
was being split. Whereupon the poor wretch fell back, smitten
by deadly pangs : and his senses left him from the violence of
the pain which came upon him. He also got punishment from
20 the carpenter, by whom he was chastised with blows more
severe than the violence of the pain caused by the log of wood.

Dimnah. I have heard your discourse, and understood what
you have said ; but know, O brother, that not everyone who
approaches kings, or gains intimacy with them, (does so) merely
25 to receive a salary whereby to fill his belly ; because the belly
may be filled anywhere. But he who is anxious to approach
a king (should wish to do so) that his position may become
distinguished and his horn exalted, and that he may be more
highly thought of ; that his nobility of character may be
30 examined and his knowledge tried ; (9) so that his friend may
rejoice in him and exult, and his enemy be vexed and cut to
the heart. Now those who are without good qualities, destitute
of fine spirit, void of wisdom and bereft of knowledge, exult
and rejoice over a single small and miserable scrap, and when
35 they find it, cling to it like a hungry and exhausted dog, who,
on finding a bare bone, void of all savour or marrow, holds
fast to it. But he whose discernment is clear-eyed, in whose
brain resides sound intelligence, and whose knowledge is clear,
does not hold fast to small things, or put up with trifles, but

studies to attain to great honour, and to be exalted to a high
rank, and sit on a seat of honour; just as a lion who finds a
hare and seizes it that it may serve him for food, as soon as he
sees a sheep or a goat, lets go the hare that is in his mouth,
and takes the goat (or sheep). Or have you never seen, O 5
brother, a dog fawning on a man and seeking to please him,
and coaxingly wagging its tail until he throws him a scrap of
dry bread? But the elephant who is trained in knowledge and
acquainted with the extent of his strength, and conscious of his
own magnificence, inasmuch as he serves as a chariot to the 10
king; when his food is brought to him, will not partake or (10)
eat of it until he is groomed by his keepers and his body is
washed clean of dust, and he is caressed with kind words.
Therefore he who lives in this world so as to please his Creator;
whose place is exalted, his horn lifted up, and his honour dis- 15
tinguished; whose necessity is relieved, while he in turn relieves
his fellows:—such a man, although he may only live a short
life, is reckoned to have lived many years. But he who spends
his days in abasement, and whose years run out in distress of
mind, who departs from this life through want of food and need 20
of good things, who has not enjoyed wealth himself nor caused
others to enjoy it:—such a man, though many and prolonged
be his years, is called sad of days, and named much-sighing.
And they say of him who is without good things and whose
pay is small, and who cares for nought but filling his belly 25
and sexual gratification, that though his days be many and the
years of his life prolonged, he is reckoned with the irrational,
and with him who is destitute of all true virtue.

Kalilah. I understand what you say: but examine your
thoughts, my brother, by means of subtle reason, and know 30
that every man has his distinct rank; and when a man sees
that his position is one in which he fares well among his companions, and his years do not pass away badly with his associates, he ought assuredly to continue in that his position, and
not to leave it for others that are too high for him, and not to 35
lust after abundance, but to be content with his pay. Now I
see that this our position is one in which our affairs do not
proceed badly.

(11) *Dimnah.* High rank and honourable situations are

(only) gained by sharpening the wits and by great energy, and in proportion to a man's nobility of disposition, freedom from base qualities, and loftiness of mind. Thus he (alone) makes progress who sets his mind to it. But he who is not stirred 5 by all his nobility of character, nor longs with all his heart, nor strives with all his might, to become great;—let him know that of his own accord he debases and degrades himself. And the quest of high rank or exalted position is very arduous, and they are only gained by great labour, and grasped by intense 10 struggling: while a low position or a mean situation may be gained in a twinkling. Now these opposites are like a stone of heavy weight, for when a man attempts to take it up from the ground and place it on his shoulder, it is only with great labour and much exhaustion that he can raise it from the earth: 15 but when he tries to take it off his shoulder, he can do so in an instant. Therefore, O brother, let us in truth plan, scheme, and strive that our position may be raised, our rank exalted, and our seat distinguished, and, if possible, let us cease to remain in this mean estate in which we are at present.

20   *Kalilah.* What idea has suggested itself to you, and what have you resolved to do, and on what basis do you found your plan?

Dimnah. I wish to approach the lion: because he is weak in his intellect and lacking in mind, and all the more so (12) at 25 this time, for his thoughts are distracted, as is also the case with all his associates; so that perhaps while he is cast in this state of anxiety, and his spirit tortured with distress and misery, I may open before him the door which is now shut in his face, and that by means of my good and sound counsels our position 30 with him may become distinguished, and that we may become great in his eyes and intimate with him, and be honoured by him.

Kalilah. How do you know that the lion's thoughts are distracted, and his mind troubled, and his knowledge withheld 35 from him?

Dimnah. I know these things by acuteness of mind, and attained to them by deep thought; because he who investigates much, finds out secret things, inasmuch as they are perceived by the change of outward appearance.

Kalilah. But how can you expect these high things, as you have never been attached to kings nor served princes, and are not acquainted with what is due to them?

Dimnah. A powerful man, or one mighty in strength, is not vanquished or defeated by a burden, though it be very heavy, 5 because - - - - - - - -; and a wise and knowing man, with discernment and ingenuity, is not daunted by novelty of situation.

Kalilah. It is not every man who is assisted by a prince, but only he who is very near him is accounted worthy of his 10 honour, and receives his gifts. And he (the prince) is like a garden; for the extremities of its branches only entwine and overspread those trees or walls that are near to it. But you, O brother, are one who is stepping beyond his sphere, and is ignorant of (13) the smallness of his stature, and unacquainted with 15 his own insignificance. How is it that you have set your mind upon the promotion which you are to gain yourself and to procure for another from the lion, seeing that you are one of the mean persons at his gate, and not esteemed?

Dimnah. I understand, brother, what you say; but know 20 that those who are near the king (now) were not so once, but have attained to a high position, though they used to occupy a mean one; only little by little they pushed forward, and their position became distinguished, and they were promoted to high rank. As for me, I shall try with all my might to approach 25 the lion, and (then) I expect to captivate his mind by my excellent counsels. Because it has been said by the wise that unless a man patiently stands at the gate of the palace, bears annoyances, pockets indignities, endures hardships, does not disdain to eat and drink with the crowd, fawns on those who go in, and 30 pays court to the servants, he fails to realize his hope, or to receive what he asks for.

Kalilah. And suppose that you do gain access to the lion, what gentleness, clearness of mind, subtlety of knowledge, or depth of thought have you got, that the lion may be helped 35 by you, and that you may have boldness towards him and look on him with confidence?

Dimnah. If I can gain access to him, search into his thoughts and weigh his intelligence, (14) fix my regard on

his actions and look at his disposition with my mind's eye, I
shall constantly run in the track of his will, and (never) in the
least degree verge on opposing his wishes. When he seeks to
do anything, and I have investigated its fitness in my mind, and
5 weighed its harmlessness in the balances of my intellect, I shall
recommend it to him, and urge him to accomplish it, and show
him how excellent it is, so that he will take increased pleasure
in it. And when he seeks to do something from which I fear
trouble, and apprehend disgrace, and sadly anticipate loss, I shall
10 show (him) in a hinting way the calamities flowing from it, and
how many losses are involved in it, and what advantage and
renown he will gain in abandoning it. And I shall speak gently
and advise prudently; and when he hears these my words, whose
like he did not hear from his counsellors who preceded me, I do
15 not doubt that I shall find confidence before him, and that he
will count me worthy of presents and of great honours. For
a man who walks with his companion in prudence, subtle
knowledge and sound intelligence, if he wishes to obliterate the
truth and stultify the right, and establish and accredit the false,
20 so that his companion may believe a lie, may sometimes be able
to do so; and resembles a skilful painter who paints portraits of
every kind on the walls, for these pictures that are imprinted on
the walls [look some as if they were coming out of the wall,
though they are not, and others as if they were entering into it,
25 though they are not]. (15) And if the lion sees my skill in
matters, and considers my profitable counsels, he will be prompt
to confer honours upon me, and upon my associates along
with me.

Kalílah. Since then you are thus resolved to carry out your
30 intention, I warn you of princes; because attachment and
proximity to them make a man to stand in great dread, and
constant suffering and hard trials are incurred by him who is
anxious to gain intimacy with princes. A wise man has said
that there are three things with which only a madman of weak
35 discernment will meddle, and whoever meddles with them shall
in no wise escape from them. One of them is approach to a
prince, [the second,] confidence in women concerning matters
which are secret and terrible, and [the third, the conduct of] the
man who took deadly poison to try or test it. And a wise man

has compared a prince to a high mountain whose ascent is very arduous, and on which are fruits and trees and useful things and produce of all kinds, but also harmful beasts (of prey). And not only is the ascent of it arduous, but to dwell in it is most exceedingly horrible and dreadful.   5

Dimnah. You have spoken the truth; but know, my brother, that everyone who shrinks from hardship and despises not trials and scorns not sufferings, fails to gain access to the nobility, and cannot acquire wealth. He who trembles at sufferings and is afraid of (16) trials, through his cowardice fails to approach 10 exalted things, and sits not on a lofty throne. It has been said that there are three things which a man cannot get, except when fear has been taken away from him, and cowardice removed from him, and weariness of anxiety is hidden from his eyes. The first of them is proximity to a prince, the second 15 trafficking on the ocean, and the third fighting with enemies. Again it has been said by a wise man that a high-minded and high-spirited man will not choose a seat except either at the head of the table, in honourable places, or in kings' palaces, where he commands and is obeyed; or with hermits and ascetics, 20 where he is quiet and modest. Like the elephant, all whose glory is seen in two places (namely) first in a wilderness full of wild beasts, and secondly where he is the king's chariot.

Kalilah. May the Lord God establish your actions and level the hill before you, may He direct your steps in the paths 25 that lead to joys, and effect for you and for us a safe and peaceful issue.

Then the crafty Dimnah made straight for the lion, entered his palace, and inquired concerning his welfare. And the lion asked his courtiers: 'Who is this person?' They told him: 30 'So and so, the son of So and so.' Whereupon the lion said to them: 'I was acquainted with his father.' Then they brought him to the lion, who said to him: 'Where have you been, and in what region have you been living?'

(17) *Dimnah.* I have not been far from the king's gate, and 35 I have been hoping that some occasion would arise to the king, or some other matter (would happen), in which I might help his victorious and most triumphant Majesty with my person and counsels. For many things go on in the king's gates, in which

there is need of someone who is not esteemed or well known.
Because there is no man who is utterly useless. Just as a small
bit of wood lying on the ground, which a man takes up to clear
his ear of the wax which descends into it from the brain, or of
5 some little insect which has got into it while he was asleep,
(may be useful). And if so, certainly rational beings who have
life and intelligence, may sometimes fill up mighty breaches.

The lion, on hearing these words from him, inclined to him,
and thought to find in him uprightness and good counsels, crafty
10 in a good sense, and clear from wicked devices.

Then the lion turned to his courtiers, saying: 'If a man has
nobility of disposition, a soul too high for greed, a mind free
from guile, thoughts cleansed from envy, lips remote from false-
witness, and a religion or faith void of slander, and is withal
15 rich in knowledge and profound in understanding, all these traits
will in the end raise his horn and exalt his position ; like burning
tow, which, when the person who tends it or (18) lighted it
seeks to extinguish it, or to allay its fierceness, persists in raising
its flames aloft.'

20   Dimnah, perceiving that the lion was pleased with him,
that is, agreed with what he had said, spoke as follows: 'O king,
mighty in power, there is no man who appears before you, or is
honoured with a seat beside you, but he ought to acquaint
you with all the learning he has, make known all the pleasant
25 fruits of peace his mind is laden with, and not conceal aught
whereby he may satisfy the king's wish and rejoice his heart ;
because the king is not profited by what is hidden with
them. And when they disclose what is concealed in their heart,
and the balance which is in the chambers of their minds is tried
30 like gold in the fire, and like honey in the clarifier, then he
whose purity stands the test, and who gratifies the palate by his
sweetness, is chosen by the king and admitted to his honours,
and his horn is raised, and his position distinguished. The
secrets of the heart are like the seed hidden in the heart of the
earth ; for no one knows about it until it sprouts, and then men
know what it is. And in the balance of intelligence ought the
king to weigh justly each one of his confidants ; and he who
weighs down the scale by his knowledge, and in whom real
nobility is manifested, and purity of affection and humility of

demeanour is displayed, and abundance of intellect and sincerity
of speech shines forth, (19) into his hands should he commit his
affairs, and ho should be made the confidant of the king's secret
matters, and he should make use of his advice.　For it has also
been said by the wise that it is not right for a king—though 5
he ho supreme over all rational beings—to raise a man above
his due, nor to degrade another who has done no harm beyond
measure.　As one ought not to put the feet in the place of the
head; and as a collection of pearls and jacinths does not match
with lead or tin, because although tin does not injure pearls or 10
detract from their value, still he who matches them together
is not considered wise.　For this reason again a wise man has
said that a man should not follow another whose right hand he
does not know from his left.　And what peace is hidden in a
man's mind is only known by the investigation of the prince 15
who is over him.　Again the sincerity of (a man's) profession of
faith in God the Exalted can only bo shown by teachers who
expound the truth and elucidate doctrine.　And it has been
said that there are three classes where tho individuals resemble
one another in name only, while they differ in their actions; 20
namely, men and men, elephants and elephants, teachers and
teachers.　And sometimes it happens that a number of individuals try to assist in some affair, but through their want of
education and the unsoundness of their knowledge, (only) bring
great loss upon the person whose affair it is, notwithstanding 25
their great number.　For an affair which succeeds is not established by a multitude of helpers, (20) but by helpers who are
prudent of understanding and skilled in the knowledge of tho
decrees of tho most High.　In like manner, a man who carries
on his shoulder a stone of great weight has no profit from it 30
except by its miserable, paltry value; while another man,
subtle of understanding, clear of brain and free from stain,
carries a jacinth.　It is called a stone just as much as the stone
of heavy weight and small value, but it is not heavy on him as
be carries it; but its value is heavy, for it yields a shekel, satis- 35
fies hunger, supplies what is due, pays the debt, and satisfies
justice.　Similarly too a matter which is established by nobility
and gentleness, and not settled by impetuous zeal.　And a prince,
though he be head of a nation, and ruler of peoples, ought not

to despise a wise man, for though his horn is low and his place
not distinguished—because he is despised now—yet in time
he may be exalted. He is like a sinew or tendon which is taken
from a dead animal, and, when the bow has been furnished with
5 it, is honoured and required by the king for his amusement and
prowess in battle.'

Now Dimnah on being honoured by the king, wished that
those present should know that the lion honoured him, not
merely because he had known his parents, but on account
10 of his intelligence, perseverance, subtle knowledge and ele-
gance of speech. So he said: 'A king or a prince does not
choose a man (21) for his service and admit him to intimacy
with him on account of his parents, or, on the other hand,
repulse him because his parents were without rank; but he
15 summons and selects for his service everyone the gold of
whose nobility he pours into the furnace of affliction, and the
clearness of whose mind and the purity of whose thoughts he
weighs in the balance of justice; and he whose good qualities
turn the scale, whose soul is not corrupted by guile and his
20 mind not defiled by the viper (of) jealousy,—him he selects
and makes his confidant. For there is nothing so near to a man
as his own body; but sometimes a part of his body is diseased,
and he is only healed of his disease by a drug that has come
from a distant place. And sometimes there is a mouse in the
25 house who is a loved neighbour: but when it destroys anything
that is in the house, it becomes an enemy, and is chased away
altogether. And the hawk or the eaglet is wild and fierce, but
on account of the use and assistance expected from it, it is
caught and tamed.'

30 When Dimnah had finished speaking, the king was doubly
pleased with him, and began to praise him, and to show his
companions the excellence of his discernment, saying to them:
'It is not lawful for a prince, or right for a king, to refuse what
is right, or to repulse noble men, or to neglect the humble,
35 especially those who have been brought up in independence of
spirit and nourished in the fear of God, and take pleasure in
purity (22) of heart. And though he neglect them for a little
time, from not knowing about them, chance circumstances
(which make them known to him) should cause him speedily to

invite them and promote them, and give them power over his affairs. But those unlettered men who used to be with him, and have been found useless in his camp, he should expel and burn with the chaff. For men are of two sorts. The one is he whose understanding is founded on a weak basis, that is, built 5 on sand; and badly and bitterly - - - - - -. And ho is like a serpent; for though a man tread on it, and it does not hurt him, let him not be sure that if he tread on it again, he will not be hurt by it. And the other (sort of man) resembles a foundation that has been laid entirely on the adamant of sincere love; 10 and his fruit is gentleness, his leaves humility, and the object of his behaviour the fear of the Creator. And ho is like white sandal-wood which is cool and sweet to smell; for if a man treads upon it, and rubs his body with it, it cools him in the heat of noon, and refreshes him in the raging of fever; but 15 if it is scraped on a sharp stone, it departs from its natural state, and becomes hot and injurious.'

Then Dimnab had confidence, knowing that he had pleased the lion's heart, and became bold towards him. And when they were sitting together alone, Dimnab said : ' For what reason do 20 I see that the king, glorious in victory, has ceased from his pleasure, and refrained from hunting, and not departed or moved from his place ? What thing has caused (23) this delay, so unusual for the king's most illustrious Majesty?'

The lion, not wishing to betray to Dimnah his cowardice, 25 said: 'It is not on account of fear, that is, apprehension of anything.' While they were yet speaking together, the ox gave a terrible bellow. And when the lion heard that bellow, he was induced by fear to reveal to Dimnah the secrets of his heart. 30

The Lion. The sound that I hear,— I know not from whom it proceeds, nor what his strength may be; but if his strength is like his voice, we cannot live in this region any longer.

Dimnah. Perhaps something else, besides this, has troubled the king? 35

The Lion. Nothing else.

Dimnah. It is not fitting that on account of an unknown voice, the king should leave his royal place, and give way before it; for a wise man has said that water forces open a small dam,

that a lofty spirit troubles a weak intellect, that crafty men, or
talebearers, destroy affection, and that a loud voice terrifies a
craven heart. And in one of the parables someone says that
'not everyone who is heard, alarms; and not everyone who
5 makes a noise, inspires fear.'

The Lion. How does that parable run?

Dimnah. It is said that a certain fox, being very hungry,
went and stood by a pool or fountain of water, and found a
drum or tabret lying by one of the trees there. As the north
10 wind was blowing, (24) it stirred the branches of the tree,
which kept smiting the drum, so that it gave out a great noise.
When he perceived that the sound of the drum was very loud and
terrible, the greedy creature thought that it contained a quantity
of meat and satisfying flesh, went up to it, and began to beat it
15 about, until he rent it. Finding it quite empty and destitute of
all fatness, the fox said within himself: ' It appears that there
is no coward but he who has a fat appearance and a loud voice.'
Now this parable I have related before you, O glorious king,
to let you know that if your Majesty wishes and your Highness
20 commands, I will proceed to the author of this sound, inquire
into his business, examine his strength, learn the height of his
stature and the measure of his thickness, and bring a plain and
certain report of him, being confident and assured that in appearance and strength he will not be found such as to justify
25 the terror he has caused.

This proposal pleased the king, who consented that Dimnah
should set out and go in the direction of the sound.

So Dimnah departed from the lion and bent his steps
towards the locality from which the sound had proceeded. And
30 when he had departed, the king considered within himself and
repented having sent Dimnah, saying to himself: ' I have not
acted safely, nor done that which is fitting, in sending him and
relying on his faith, though I have never tried him, and on the
sincerity of his religion, though I have never tested it. Because
35 he is a man who has stood for some time at the royal gate; (25)
but no honour has been awarded to him, nor have his kinsfolk
been raised, nor his income been increased. And perhaps he is
in want of nourishment, and his distress has not been relieved.
Or perhaps he is sorrowful in spirit, and his sorrow has not been

comforted. Or perhaps he has been oppressed by some one, and has not been avenged on his oppressor. Or perhaps he has been entrusted with some of the king's business, and it has been taken from him, and committed to other hands. Or perhaps he has had an associate in some affair of a prince, and his associate 5 has been honoured while he has been dishonoured. Or they were both (equally) offenders, and his associate was let off the stripes that his offence deserved, and ho alone was scourged. Or perhaps he and those with him have repaired some great breach, and the gifts bestowed on his companions were dis- 10 tinguished, while ho (himself) was defrauded of (all) recompense. Or perhaps he had enemies, who bribed an unjust judge, so that vengeance for him was not required of them. Or perhaps his religion has been corrupted, and his faith not tried by faithful teachers. Or perhaps he was doing something for a prince 15 by which the prince was profited, and he has been expecting to receive gifts and presents in return for it. And in view of all these possibilities, it is not right that a prince should hastily condescend to any man, and reveal to him the secrets of his heart. Now Dimnah is one who is crafty and practised in speak- 20 ing and trained in wisdom; yet he used to lie at our royal gate despised and not esteemed, and perhaps he has suffered (26) hardships in finding means to do something. So now I think he has done something deceitful, and has deceived me, and is about to act craftily against me. And all the more, if he 25 finds that the author of the sound is stronger than I and his power extensive and warlike, will ho make friends with him and hatch a plot against me, and reveal to him all my secrets.' When this opinion had strengthened in the lion, it caused him to leave his place; and ho rose and went little by little in a downcast 30 and terrified manner. Then ho sat down and gazed into the distance; and he saw and lo! Dimnah coming alone, deliberately and gently, joyfully and not sadly. Whereupon the king's downcast mood was turned to joy, and his mind cheered up, and the trembling of his heart ceased. And he turned back hastily 35 and sat down in his place; for he was anxious that Dimnah should not perceive that these thoughts had proceeded from him. Dimnah on entering the lion's presence, saluted him cheerfully and not as if terrified. And tho lion asked him

concerning the report, on account of which he had set out.

Dimnah. I saw a single ox grazing, and he is the author of the sound which the victorious king heard.

5   *The Lion.* What is his size and how great is his strength?

Dimnah. His figure is burly, his appearance handsome, and his fatness excessive. However I did not try his strength. And I stood before him, and despised him inwardly. And I spoke with him. He was not afraid of me, and I again was
10 not alarmed at him.

The Lion. You must not rely on this, or think that from weakness or feebleness he dealt gently with you, and spoke quietly and not (27) violently, mildly and not boldly. Because the north wind is mighty, but it does not hurt the weak, or
15 terrify the feeble; still it uproots thick and beautiful trees, blows down lofty towers, and destroys great cities. So too warriors or men of might do not fight with the weak, or take captive small caravans; but they lie in wait for captains of thousands, and take captive great armies.

20   *Dimnah.* Let not such a thought as this come up in the king's heart. Nor let his mind hesitate in any of his actions. For if the king wishes and commands (it), I will soon make him stand before the king like a servant.

When the king heard this, he rejoiced with great joy, and
25 said: 'Do as you have said, and delay not: and make haste and tarry not.'

Then Dimnah went off to the ox, and without being afraid or terrified, said to him: 'The lion has sent me to you, in order that you may speedily appear before him. And he has
30 commanded me saying: "If the ox comes quickly and obediently and without tarrying or delay, he shall not be blamed for his delay hitherto, and he shall be absolved from all his penalties." And I will give you an oath on his behalf, besides my own oath (that this shall be). But if you do not do these things
35 and are not obedient, I will quickly return to him and bring him tidings of your disobedience.'

The Ox. Who is the lion of whom you speak, and where is he?

Dimnah. (28) He is the king of the beasts, and their ruler.

Then was the ox alarmed at hearing of the beasts. And he
said to Dimnah: 'If you will give me the right hand of truth,
and will make a faithful covenant with me, and take the Immortal to witness concerning you, I will come with you.' Then
Dimnah gave him the right hand of sincerity, and made a 5
sacred covenant with him.   And they each called on Him
who seeth secret things to witness concerning the other.   And
the ox's soul consented and his mind was pleased.   And they
proceeded both together, and went in before the king.   When
the lion saw him, he received him cheerfully and spoke with 10
him joyfully.   And he asked him quietly, saying: 'When did
you come to this region? And what is the cause of your coming
hither? And how do you fare here?'
   Then Shanzabeh related to him his whole story.
   And the king said to him : 'Then remain with us, and do 15
not remove from beside us.   For you shall be honoured in our
camp, and I will make you great and renowned before me.
And I will attend to your needs, and will not neglect (to
provide) the things that befit you.'
   Then the ox opened his mouth, saying: "I return thanks 20
and am grateful to my lord the king for (all) this solicitude
and attention.   May the Lord God who gives strength to the
weak, and puts wisdom into the minds of the ignorant, and
the word of knowledge into the simple, be the stablisher of
your kingdom.   May your arm extend like a bow, your right 25
hand reach all that hate you, (29) and your sword destroy
all your enemies.   May you trample with the heel on all the
might of the adversary, and may the fame of your exploits fly
to all the limits of your kingdom.   May you rejoice in all the
good things of Jerusalem all the days of your life, flourish on 30
the mountains like the cedars of Lebanon, and yield pleasant
fruits seasoned with the salt of truth.   May you be envied and
renowned, victorious and not put to shame.'
   When the lion heard these words, he rejoiced in Shanzabeh
with great joy.   And he admitted him to intimacy and honoured 35
him.   And he made a covenant with him and gave him an
oath, and made him his confidant and counsellor.   And after
that the king had placed him in the furnace of trial, and
poured out his noble character like gold in the fire of pro-

K. F.   2

bation, he committed to his hand the management of all his
affairs, and he received gifts and honours from the lion, and
every day (new) excellencies appeared in his conduct. In short,
he was exalted beyond all his fellows before the king.

5   Now when Dimnah saw that the ox was exalted thus, he
envied him exceedingly. And his mind became infected and
his soul disturbed, and the eye of his discernment blinded.
And he complained to his brother Kalilah, saying: 'Do you
not wonder, my brother, and marvel at my imbecility, and at
10 the way in which I have injured myself? For why did I study
the lion's advantage at the expense of my own? For when I
began to be great and to advance and to rise to a high rank,
lo! suddenly I fell backwards, and caused another to sit on
the lofty seat.'

15   Kalilah.   What happened to the ascetic and befell the
hermit has happened to you.

Dimnah. (30) How did it fare with him?

Kalilah. It is said that an ascetic had some beautiful garments given him by a king. A certain rogue seeing it, desired
20 to take them from him. So ho came to the hermit craftily,
and said to him: 'I wish to stay with you and conform to
your discipline, and learn of your ways, and walk with you.'
And lo! the ascetic, in the innocence of his heart and the
simplicity of his mind, did not repulse him from beside him,
25 nor drive him away, nor doubt his honesty, but admitted him
to intimacy and made him his companion. And the crafty
fellow clave to him eagerly, and walked cunningly with the
innocent minded ascetic, falsely feigning himself one also. And
he began to work craftily on the ascetic, and to wheedle him in-
30 sidiously, until he was able to steal the garments boldly. Having
taken them, he went fraudulently away. When the good man
sought for the thief, and for the garments which had been
unjustly taken, and found them not, he knew that that rogue
had taken them. So he pursued after him along a certain
35 road in the hope of overtaking him. And he saw on that road
two rams butting one another. And they fought a long time
on that road with one another, until each of them cut open the
other's head. And a fox came up, and began to lick up the
blood which was flowing from them. And while that greedy

fox was intently fixed on the blood, the two rams turned, and
butted him until they killed him. And the ascetic departed
and went his way.

* * * * * *

[18 lines left untranslated. See note.]

(31. 18) And the ascetic rose in the morning to search for 5
another lodging. A certain shoemaker found him and took
him into his house. And the shoemaker directed his wife,
saying: 'Attend to this ascetic, and prepare for him all things
that he needs, because I am about to go to a feast at the house
of a friend of mine.' Now whenever the shoemaker left (32) 10
his house, his wife had a certain lover (at hand). And the
negotiator between them was a certain woman who had sold her
good character, the wife of a barber. And the shoemaker's wife
sent to the barber's wife, with the message : 'My husband is
going to a feast to-night; go to my lover and tell him that my 15
husband has gone to a feast to-night, and that the house is
empty. Let him come and eat and drink.' So when it was
evening, he came and stood at the outer door, so that she might
call him. At that moment her husband the shoemaker arrived
at the door of the house drunk. When he saw that lewd man, 20
he was angry, and went into his house, and smote his wife
with hard blows and bound her firmly to one of the columns
which were in his house. When it got dark and the shoemaker
was asleep, the barber's audacious wife came secretly, and gave
the shoemaker's wife a hint that her lover was sitting at the 25
outer door, and waiting for her. Then the shoemaker's wife
begged earnestly of the barber's wife (saying): 'Undo these
my bonds quickly, and bind yourself in my stead for a little
while, that I may get to my dear one; and I will return to you.'
So the barber's wife bound herself, having loosed the shoe- 30
maker's wife, who went to that lewd man. The shoemaker,
awaking before his wife came (back), called her by name; but
she answered him nothing, for fear lest he should know her
voice. (33) When he had waited (sometime) without her
answering a word, he became very angry indeed, and got up 35
[and went] to the barber's wife, and cut off her nose, saying:

'Take this, base woman, and give it to that wicked lover of
yours.' When the shoemaker's wife returned, she perceived
that the barber's wife had had her nose cut off. And she loosed
her bonds, and bound herself in her stead. And the barber's
5 wife took her nose in her hand, and went to her house in great
shame. Then the shoemaker's audacious wife raised her voice,
saying: 'O Lord God, if my husband has wronged me, do thou
by thy swift commands make my nose as it was before, that the
fame of my innocence may be proclaimed in all our city.' Her
10 husband hearing these (words), said to her: 'What are these
babblings, O sorceress?' She said: 'O unjust man, rise up and
behold. Because God the Pitiful knew the wrong done to me,
he has sent his angel, and made my nose again as it was before;
because that I am innocent.' Then that stupid man rose and
15 lit the lamp, and saw that his wife's nose - - - - - - as before.
When he saw (it), he repented, so that she became reconciled to him. And the barber's wife, as she went away, thought
much on how she should escape from her husband, and from
public disgrace. When day dawned, her husband awoke from
20 his sleep, and said to his wife: 'Pray give me my shaving
gear, because I want to go early and serve one of the nobility.'
But she delayed. Again he said to her: 'Give it me, and delay
not.' And becoming angry and wrathful, because she went
slowly, (34) he took up a razor in the dark, and threw it at her.
25 Whereupon that audacious woman cried aloud, saying: 'Woe,
woe is me! My nose is cut off.' Her neighbours heard her,
and all came together, and saw her nose that had been cut
off, and the razor lying. Whereupon they seized her poor husband and took him to the judge, who ordered him to be
30 scourged. As the poor man remained without any defence,
the ascetic got up and approached the judge, saying: 'The truth
shall not be concealed from you by means of artifice, O judge.
For it was not the rogue who took my garments, nor yet the
rams that killed the fox, nor the - - - - - - - - - - - - - - - - -
35 to God and said: 'If I am innocent and this man has wronged
me, do thou heal me, that it may be proclaimed in all our city
that I have been wronged.' And the shoemaker heard (her)
and said: 'What are these babblings?' She answered him: 'O
unjust man, rise and see. For God has looked on the wrong

done me, and sent an angel, and restored my nose.' Then the
poor man rose and saw that it was healed. And he offered
repentance and made apology. - - - - - - - Then the ascetic
said: 'It was not the rogue who took my garments, nor yet the
rams that killed the fox, nor the poison that killed the dealer 5
in pleasure, (35) nor the barber who cut off his wife's nose; but
we have all done wrong.' And Kalilah said to Dimnah: 'And
you too have sinned against yourself.'

Dimnah. I have listened to this parable, and it is very like
what I have done myself. But now what plan can we carry out 10
to get back what we have lost?

Kalilah. What do you think of doing?

Dimnah. I meditate on doing something, not that I may
be raised to my former rank, but that I may get back the occupation which I used to have. For three things are required of 15
everyone who is rational and intelligent; let him not neglect
one of them. One is that a man examine what profitable things,
and what harmful things, he is doing; so that he may beware of
the harmful things, and pursue after the profitable things which
he has neglected. Another is that he be watchful, so that he 20
may not suffer hurt, and that he beware lest his good things be
snatched from him. (And) the other is that he discern with
the clear eye of his mind, what good things he expects to receive; that he may be active and eager to get them, and afraid
of the harmful things lest they touch him. And when I look 25
at my future, and consider my past, there is nothing which will
help me, or by which my honour may return to its place, and I
may recover what has been taken from me, except the death of
the ox. For (so) both my own condition will be remedied, and
the lion will be profited and freed from blame. For the lion's 30
heart has been captivated by the talk (36) of the ox, and lo! he
is reviled by all who are near him.

Kalilah. I find no reason for blaming the lion for admitting
the ox to intimacy; nor do I see in him any shortcoming.

Dimnah. Do not entertain, my brother, such an idea, nor 35
hold such an opinion. Because the lion, through admitting the
ox to intimacy, has inflicted a great injury on himself. For he
is insulted by all his fellows and reviled by the whole army,
and they have all withheld their services from him. For the

bad or damaging circumstances of a ruler are produced by six different things. One of these is bad luck. Another is local disturbance, that is, sedition which breaks out in one place and another. Another is demoralisation, when the understanding is
5 ensnared by whatever it may be. Another is remissness when it prevails, or warlike policy when extolled by inconsiderate generals. Another is bad weather, fewness of springs, sterility of land, and dearth of necessaries. And the other is the breaking out of fire.
10 On the other hand the advantageous circumstances of a king, and the good things which a prince has in abundance, spring from other six different causes. One of these is sincere confidants, well-known for all excellent qualities, intimate with the good, skilled in knowledge, large-minded, [removed] from
15 all greed, free from all envy, remote from pride, (37) with conscience clear of fraud. One is warriors and nobles and powerful men. One is plenty of silver and abundance of gold. One is the stability of towns, and peace in all places. One is strong walls and high and mighty strongholds. And one is good laws
20 and prudent subjects.

Now seditions and tumults are stirred up against a king, and arise against a prince by the hand of a helper, when he is deprived of his rights and his pay is taken from him. (For) then he studies to disturb the sound mind of the nobles, and to
25 corrupt the mind of the generals, until they set the king's army in commotion, and distract the captains of his forces. And if the intellect is ensnared and the mind is enfeebled, it is due to the beauty of women. Drunkenness by wine, and field sports, spring from having nothing to do. Stiffneckedness and haugh-
30 tiness of soul and want of modesty, these are the things which procure for the man who is guilty of them, a swift course to bloodshedding, rouse the tongue to calumnies, and teach the lips falsehood. Oppression and the demanding of what is not due, and the seizing of what ought not to be seized, are
35 engendered by bad times, scarcity of springs, and dearth of necessaries. And burning by fire, and war, and disease, and spoiling of fruit, are caused by rarity of the atmosphere. Frost, (38) and intensity of heat, spring (respectively) from abundance of rain and want of water. Vermin in quantities, and cattle

plague, and loss of horses, are caused by parching wind, when it blows and destroys everything.

Now like all these things, is a contentious man who is not grounded on the fear of God, nor trained in knowledge, nor labours to get understanding, and puts bitter for sweet, 5 darkness for light, the fool for the wise man, the infidel for the believer, and the enemy for the friend. And when he seeks to set a cunning ambush for an enemy, he proclaims it on the housetops with a loud voice. And when he seeks to join battle with a band of robbers with horsemen and with 10 arms, he becomes exhausted through his weakness, so that he turns his back and flies in shame, and becomes a laughing-stock for his defeat.

Kalilah. How can you cope with the strength of the ox by fraud, and under what standard are you going to fight with 15 him ? For he is stronger than you, and more splendid and glorious in knowledge and height of stature than you, and stands nearer to the lion than you, and has more brothers and kinsmen than you.

Dimnah. You must not look at the small stature and 20 weakness of my person, or on the having plenty of brothers and kinsmen. Because such affairs as these (which I have in hand) do not proceed according to strength or weakness, and are not engaged in by the brave or weak (as such), nor are carried out by means of a great number. Because many have been small 25 in stature and deficient in number, who by their artifices (39) and subtlety of knowledge have attained to lofty things which the mighty in strength and lofty in dimension, and distinguished in race and rich in numbers, have not reached. Or have you not heard, O brother, of the raven of hateful appearance and 30 stinking odour, who planned against a black serpent of great power and terrible fame, so that she killed him quietly and warily, by a subtle plan and a clever artifice ?

Kalilah. What did she do ?

Dimnah. They say that a certain raven lived in one of the 35 trees on a mountain. And near her was a large hole, in which there lived a powerful black serpent, who, when the raven was rearing her young ones, used to go and eat them. When this thing became grievous to the raven, and she had no heir left to

her, she complained to a friend of hers, a jackal, saying : 'O
brother, I wish to take advice from you in a certain deed that
I am about to do, and which I cannot achieve without your
counsel.'

5   *The Jackal.* What is it ?

The Raven. I wish to attack a serpent while he is asleep,
and pick out his eyes ; for he does not spare me any young
ones that I may rejoice in them at all.

The Jackal. You have devised neither justly nor fittingly;
10 but plan some subtle scheme, that you may take your revenge
on the serpent quietly. and destroy (40) his life craftily.   And
let not your deed be publicly (done), lest you rashly destroy
yourself with your young ones, and become like the heron,
when he sought to destroy a crab, and from lack of knowledge
15 destroyed himself.

The Raven. How runs the story about him ?

The Jackal. It is said that in a certain marshy lake was a
heron.   And there were many fishes in the lake.   [But in time
the heron got too old to catch any,] and became very hungry,
20 and his soul languished.   A certain crab seeing him from afar,
approached him, saying : ' Why is your soul distressed, and why
are you sad ? '

The Heron. And how should I not be sad who until to-
day have lived on these fishes, but this day have seen two
25 fishermen, one of whom said to the other: 'Let us not catch
(all) these fishes at one time,' his companion replying : ' I have
seen another lake in which there are plenty of fishes.   Let us
go and catch them (first), and then we will come and catch all
these in a twinkling.'   I know that when they return from
30 their journey, they will not leave anything in this lake, and I
shall utterly perish from life !

Then the crab spoke to the fishes.   And all the fishes
gathered to the heron, and said to him : ' Although you are
an enemy to us, because we are your food and you feed on
35 us, still he who has the fear of God, in time of trouble does
not refuse what is right, or profane the emblem of the faith.
Lo ! we are all knocking at your door, that you may hearken
to us and ease (41) the distress of our soul, and counsel us what
to do in this distressful time.'

The Heron. To do battle with the fishermen I am not able, and expel them from this region I cannot. But I know of a certain pool in which there is water abundant, fresh and clear. And there are green reeds in it. If you could remove thither from here, you would gain advantage to yourselves.   5

The Fishes. But how is it possible for us to do so without your help?

The Heron. I will do what you wish and consent to you. But I am sore afraid of those fishermen, lest they come hastily. But I will begin to carry some of you every day, as many as I 10 can, until I have exhausted (you and taken) you all away from here.

And he began to carry off one or two every day, and to convey them to a certain region, and to eat them there; the others being ignorant of it. It came to pass one day (that) 15 the crab said to the heron: 'I too find this place unpleasant. Pray carry me off too and convey me with my companions.' So the heron carried off the crab. When he reached the place where he had eaten the fishes, the crab beheld and saw the bones of his companions. And he perceived that the heron 20 had done this wickedness, and was about to devour him too. And the crab said within himself: 'He that goes forth to battle and encounters his enemy wherever it may be, if he knows that his enemy will not hesitate to destroy him if he can, whether he make war with him (the enemy) or remain at 25 peace with him, he ought to fight for himself (42) strenuously, and not destroy himself for want of exertion. For if he is vanquished and perishes, still his honour goes with him, and his glory (remains) on his head.' Then the crab grasped the heron's throat with his pincers, and kept gripping him with his 30 claws, until he throttled him and took away his life. So the crab escaped from slaughter. And he went little by little until he got (back) to the fishes, whom he acquainted with the story about the heron.

The jackal said to the raven : 'This parable I have related 35 to you, [that you may know] that when a man engages in fraudulent plans and transactions and schemes, his wickedness returns on his own head, and he himself perishes by his own artifices. But I will give you a piece of advice, so that if you

can put my counsel into practice you may destroy the slayer
of your young ones, without danger to yourself.'

The Raven. What is the piece of advice, so that I may
embrace it?

5   *The Jackal.* Fly upwards and hover in the air, and look
about and see whether you can spy out of the trinkets belonging to the women on the housetops, one that is very precious
and of great value. When you have taken it, do not soar very
high, but fly a little and rise, and then descend again. And
10 fly before all who see you gently and slowly, so that they may
follow after you, until you reach the hole of the serpent your
enemy. And whatever you have taken, introduce and place in
the hole, that its owners may come and take it, and put an
end to the serpent.

15   So the raven flew away and soared, and, spying out an
article of gold laid (in a place), took it according to the jackal's
advice. And people saw her, and pursued after her till they
arrived in sight of the serpent's hole. Then the raven went
in, and put (43) the necklace in the hole. And the people
20 coming up, took the necklace and killed the serpent.

Dimnah said to Kalilah : 'I have told you [this] parable, O
brother, that you may know that plans and artifices overcome
all forces, and vanquish inaccessible strongholds.'

Kalilah. Know, O brother, that the ox, besides having
25 strength and a lofty stature, is prudent and sagacious; and
courageous and able to fight. So how can you cope with his
strength? And under what standard are you going to fight
with him?

Dimnah. Although the ox is courageous and sagacious,
30 valiant and able to fight, he will incline to my words, and
consent to my wishes, agree to my advice, and not disbelieve
what I say. And all the more since he remembers the oath
of sincerity which I gave him, and recollects the sacred covenant that I made with him, and trusts and adheres to the
35 witness whom I called to witness between me and him, do I
expect to humble his might, and to cast him into the abyss (of
destruction), just as the hare did the lion.

Kalilah. How runs the story about him ?

Dimnah. They say that there was a lion (who lived) in a

certain region abounding in water and thickly grown with grass.
And in it were a number of animals of different kinds. But
in none of those things did they take any pleasure, on account
of their fear of the lion who lived in that region. Then those
animals came in a body to the lion, and said to him: 'O king, 5
it is only by hard toil and severe labour that you can get
one (44) or two of us in a whole day. Now it has seemed
good to us to make a treaty with you, and that you give us
a sacred oath that you will not molest us any further. We
(on our part) will send you every day one animal at your feed- 10
ing time; so that you may not have labour and fatigue, and fill
your belly with bean food, and that we (too) may not be frightened away from grazing, but may take our food without fear.'
Then the lion inclined his ear to their words, and made a compact with them, conditional on this thing. After a little time, 15
the lot fell on a certain hare, that she should be food for the
lion. Then the hare said to the animals: 'If you will grant me
a little favour, as the thing will not inconvenience you, perhaps
I shall be able to free you and myself from the evil of this lion.'
The animals answered: 'Lo we are all before you, and willing 20
to hear you.' The hare said: 'Instruct your messenger to convey me to the lion slowly and not hurriedly, deliberately and
not hastily; so that I may linger on the road a little until his
dinner-time is past, and the lion, being hungry, gets angry.'
And the animals did as the hare had said. Then the hare 25
began to go along by slow degrees. And she drew near to the
lion when he was hungry and vexed, enraged and incensed.
And he came out walking in an angry mood. On seeing the
hare, he said to her: 'Who are you? And whence do you
come?' The hare said: 'I am the messenger of the animals to 30
you, who sent me with a (fine) fat hare (45) for your food. But
when it reached this region, a certain lion came out and seized
it, saying to me: 'This land, with these animals that are in it,
belongs to me.' And I said to him: 'This land is the property
of such and such a lion.' But my words profited nothing with 35
him, for you he reviled, and me he drove empty-handed from
before him.' Whereupon the lion got angry and said to her:
'Come and show me this lion who dared to seize my food.' And
the hare went on till she reached a certain deep pit in which

there was clear water. And she said: 'Here is the lion and the
fat hare with him. But I fear to go near him. (So) pray place
me against your breast that I may not be afraid of him, and I
will show you where he is.' When he had placed her against
5 his breast, she showed him his own reflection and hers in this
clear water. Whereupon the lion leaped in to snatch the hare
from the breast of the other lion. And he fell into the pit,
while the hare escaped to the other side.

Kalilah. If then you can destroy the ox without afflicting
10 the lion, do (so); because you say that the proximity of the ox
to the lion has much distressed you and others with you. But
if you know that when your desire has been accomplished in the
destruction of the ox, the lion will be afflicted and distressed,
then this thing does not commend itself to me.

15   Then Dimnah for many days abstained from this thing, and
did not go in to the lion. But (at length) he went in to him
with a gloomy countenance, while the lion was sitting alone.
The lion said: 'Wherefore have I not seen you for (some) days,
and (why) is your countenance altered?

20   *Dimnah.* (46) Nothing is hid from you, O king.

The Lion. Perchance some accident has happened?

Dimnah. It is fitting that language which ought not to be
spoken except in the absence of others, should fall on a mind
clear of thought and not preoccupied, and in private too.

25   *The Lion.* Lo the mind is unoccupied, and the sitting place
removed from the crowd.

Dimnah. No utterance from which the hearer shrinks in
abhorrence, is the mind of the speaker encouraged to make
known. And although the speaker be a good and upright man,
30 yet is it certainly heard from him with abhorrence. However,
when the hearer of the utterance is rich in brain and sound in
intellect, prudent in knowledge and versed in understanding,
practised in observation and perfected in (making) trials, intelligently he listens to the words (spoken), and patiently
35 he bears their grievousness. And when the utterance is profitable, the profit of it (falls) to him who hears it. - - - - - - - -
the speaker of it and nothing more, except he be reckoned
upright in purpose and sincere in (his) love for his friend, and
be honest in his friendship. And you, O king, are valiant in

strength, extolled for knowledge, and glorious in honour, watchful in all your actions, and illustrious for all your personal
qualities. And I am cast in great doubt by something that I
wish to let your pure ears listen to. But because I rely on the
excellence of your mind, the subtlety of your knowledge, and 5
the depth of your reflection, and am (47) free from all blemish
before the king—and specially from slander—and remote too
from the viper jealousy, (and) pure from wicked speech, not
concealing the right nor hiding what is fitting, not smitten with
greed, but one who rejoices in the tranquillity of the kingdom, 10
and delights in the welfare of the king, zealous for your advantage, striving for the success of your affairs, loving the plenitude
of your army, afraid of all things which would impede you, [I will
not fear]. And lo! a little thought occurs to me and a slight
suspicion has been born in my mind, that perhaps I shall not 15
appear trustworthy and honest before the king in what I (shall)
utter before him. In such doubts as these am I cast. Then
I turn to my soul, and bring it to account, saying: 'O my soul,
weak in thought, knowest thou not that, owing to (our) animal
nature, our soul is bound up with the soul of the king, our 20
vitality subsists in him, our eyes look to him, and our nourishment is prepared at his court?' So that on all accounts there
rests on me an obligation which can never be (adequately) performed, (and which compels me) to disclose to the great king
something which has come to my ears, the truth of which is 25
firmly established in my heart: although you, O valiant king,
have made no inquiry or investigation concerning the truth,
and (so) perhaps by reason of a miserable suspicion which
attaches to many, these words of mine, (48) which in due time
shall have been spoken before you, will not be believed. Because 30
it has been said and well said, that he who conceals from the
king what he ought to hear, his disease from the physician, or
the account of his suffering from a brother, is called one who
deceives his own soul.

The Lion. What is the report which is so dreadful to hear? 35

Dimnah. A certain upright and faithful man, true and not
given to falsehood, whose word is accepted by me, and whose
evidence is in my soul as trustworthy as adamant, has told me
that Shanzabeh, the eater of grass, has dealt craftily and gone

te the king's chief men, and said to them: 'I have examined
the king's power, explored his secret matters, and weighed his
plans in the balance of my mind: and I have not found in
him one of the requisites of a king. And lo! I am prepared to
5 do a mighty deed with him. And I will disclose all his secret
affairs, and reveal to every man and show the badness of his
disposition, and his want of education.' When I heard these
things, I perceived that Shanzabeh is one who denies the goodness of God, and does not observe good faith, or hold to integrity,
10 or discharge obligations, and has no gratitude, and is not free
from guile, and that his soul is steeped in envy. You know,
my lord the king, that when you increased his honour and
exalted his rank and raised his seat, and put him in your own
place, that he craved to obtain your royal rank, and raised his
15 neck, yea hardened it, and studied to seize your crown by fraud;
while captivating by devices and artifices the hearts of your
nobles, and your Majesty's generals, at the same time promising
them (49) many things. But may the Lord not bring his edifice
to perfection, may his plan not succeed, and may his fall be
20 speedily, like the house that was built on the sand. Aforetime
it was said by a wise man that when a king sees a man to
be like him in appearance, and sees him to be possessed of
oratorical power, and not far distant from him in wealth, the
king should make haste and abase him, lest he rise and over-
25 throw the king. And you, O illustrious king, are one who makes
vexations to cease, and whose mind is versed in affairs. So in
whatever way it seems good to you to stamp out this ulcer
which on a sudden has broken out upon us, and to heal this
sickness which, like a gangrene, must, if neglected, destroy the
30 whole body, make haste and without delay do (it): and do not
leave him alone until he fixes his roots in the ground, and his
branches grow strong and put forth leaves, and bear bitter and
abominable fruits, when the uprooting of them has become
difficult. Again it has been said by teachers and wise men that
35 there are three (types of) men. Two are vigilant and prudent,
and one is slumbering in the sleep of inattention. Now one of
those who are vigilant in knowledge and rich in prudence, when
he looks out into the distance and sees evil creeping gradually
up and seeking to get near him, hastens by means of subtle

devices to lay hidden snares for it with careful reflection; and it is removed from him so that it does not approach him. But the other is wiser than he, (namely) he who does not suffer a single bad affair (even) to be born, but as soon as it is conceived in thought, roots out the thought, the mother of it, and buries 5 the seed of tares that springs up by it in the dust of the ground. And the (50) third is lazy, that is, sunk in the sleep of inattention, cast among doubts, and wrapped in thoughts; and by reason of procrastination he destroys himself. And they are like the three fishes that were in a certain pool of 10 water.

The Lion. What is the story about them?

Dimnah. It is said that in a certain pool were three big fishes; an intelligent one, a second who was more intelligent and prudent than he, and a third one lazy and forgetful. And 15 no one (ever) approached that pond on account of its depth. But one day there passed by the pond two fishermen, skilful in their craft, who agreed with one another to cast their nets, and to bring about the capture of these fishes. But the intelligent and prudent fish, when he no more than scented 20 the smell of a single word from the fishermen, made haste and got out of the pool by the conduit which brought the water into it, and saved himself from fear and distress of mind. But the one who was inferior to him in knowledge, remained in the pond until the fishermen came. And when he saw them 25 he fell to deliberating and thinking, and began to form plans. And he said to himself: ' Now you need patient care, and if you strive cleverly, you will not fall into the net; but if you remain inactive and perplexed, you are doomed to destruction.' Then that reflection made itself a subtle plan (51), (namely) 30 that he should throw himself on his back, like one that having been killed is dead in the water. And the fishermen began to dam up the conduit which brought the water. And they found this crafty one floating on the water after the manner of fishes who when dead float on the surface. Seeing him thus, they 35 took him and put him on the bank of the other pool. And when he saw the fishermen wholly intent on the dam, he took a leap, fell into the water and escaped from them. But the lazy, idle one began to consider and hesitate until the fisher-

men caught him and took him. Nay, it seems to me, O king, that you must make haste and put the ox to death, before the thing becomes difficult, and gathers strength, and resists force.

5   *The Lion.* I understand what you say, but I cannot imagine that the ox will deal fraudulently by me after I have put upon him such honour, and placed him on a glorious throne; because he cannot remember having lacked anything.

Dimnah. His mind was not corrupted, nor did he become 10 exalted in his own eyes, or arrogant, except by reason of honour, and exaltation of seat. For he who is of base origin and poor in wealth, whose sustenance is scanty and his place low, and who is degraded in his rank, when he is admitted to friendship, or honoured, exalted and made great, satiated with good 15 things and fattened on rich food, and becomes wealthy after being indigent, and becomes rich out of poverty, shows obedience (52), activity, justice and energy, until he is exalted and sits on a throne that does not befit his base origin, or accord with his low estate. Then arrogance of spirit instigates him and 20 he begins to form plans and weave deceits. For a low born man does not submit himself to a prince except for two reasons: one of them is fear of justice, and the other is that he hopes to snatch something from him. But when he attains his object and has reaped from the prince the accomplishment of his 25 desire, he returns to his former wretched state of mind. And he resembles the curly tail of a dog which is bound. As long as it is bound, it presents a straight appearance, but on being released from the cord, becomes curly again as before.

Know O King, (that) if a prince does not hearken to one who 30 loves the stability of his kingdom, cares for the peace of his flock, and is eager for the prosperity of his affairs, although grievous - - - - - - - - , his knowledge is not to be praised, his judgment is not sound, and his mind is not healthy. He is like a sick man or one smitten with hard ulcers, who neglects the 35 directions of the physicians and desires things that are hurtful to his wounds. For the debt can never be (fully) paid by any of those who enjoy the king's nourishment, and live under the hand and wing of his care, (53) who pasture in the folds of his power, and bear the yoke of his service. There is a definite

rule for them (namely) to show their care and manifest their zeal,
and supply what is lacking and fill up breaches by means of their
sound and excellent counsels.   And among pupils or servants, or
among friends and kinsfolk, ho alone is praiseworthy who does
[not] conceal the truth; by which his kindness is made manifest 5
in the end.   And good is that friendship which strife touches
not. Good too is the praise that comes from upright men.   Good
is that gentleness which conducts to the fear of God, and gives
sound counsels. Good is a ruler when he does not oppress.   Good
is a rich man when greed does not overpower his noble character. 10
Again it has been said: 'If a reckless man put serpents for his
pillow, and spread fire under him, he ought not to enjoy life
(any more) even though his enemies he put down under him'.
And tho meanest of kings is he who casts behind him matters
pregnant with evil and ready to cause destruction and confusion, 15
and pays no attention to them.   He is like an untrained elephant, for when his knowledge and nobility of disposition is
tested, he is accounted as nought.   And if anything happens to
the mean man, vengeance is taken on his neighbours, and he
becomes a laughing-stock and a mockery.   20

  The Lion.   You have spoken very hard words.   But the
words of a friend or confidant are to be received, (54) oven
though they be grievous to hear.   But Shanzabeh cannot do us
any harm.   For how can he do any harm, since he feeds on
grass while I feed on flesh?   And he too is food for me.   For 25
this reason I am not afraid of him.   Besides, I cannot be false
to my promises to him, and (to) the right hand of truth that I
gave him, and (to) the faithful Witness whom I took to witness
between me and him.   In addition, I remember his frequent
services and renowned exploits, and how he served me without 30
deceit, his obedience to my orders, and his zeal towards all the
army, and what honours I put upon him, and to what high rank
I exalted him and the glorious throne on which I set him, and
with what great praises I extolled him to all my companions.
If I reverse these things and am false to my promises, and insult 35
my own nobility, I shall be ashamed before my companions,
who are educated and skilled, subtle in thought and versed in
scrutiny.

  Dimnah.   Let not this idea entice you nor let this opinion
  K. F.   3

get the better of the king's mind, (namely) that the ox is food
for you.   For although he is not a match for your strength,
and cannot accomplish his desire concerning you by himself
alone, yet he will devise a plan for you, employ deceitful
5 artifices against you, and resort to others (for help), until he
secures his object and his intention is realized.   But God forbid
that this should be.   Now it has been said by a wise man that
when a traveller meets you, and you are not acquainted with his
character, and he asks you for a night's lodging, you should
10 not reveal your mind to him nor trust (55) yourself to him, lest
he defile you with his own mire, and some of his misfortune
befall you, as it happened to the louse after meeting with a flea.

   The Lion.   What befell him?

   Dimnah.   Why they say that a louse took up her quarters
15 in the bed of one of the chief men of the town, and fed on his
blood a long time, and when he was asleep, used to suck small
quantities from him, he not perceiving her, and used to creep
on his body softly and gently.   Now one night there met her a
flea and made friends with her, she being unaware of his folly.
20 And he asked of her a lodging for one night.   And when this
rich notable had fallen asleep, the flea bit him severely, so that
the man awoke from his sleep, and ordered his place to be
searched.   And when they began to search, the flea took a
jump and escaped, while the louse was caught and slain.   Now
25 I have related to you, O mighty king, this parable [that
you may know] that he whose conscience is not clear of evil,
and his mind not too high for envy, his soul not free of deceit,
and his eye not void of greediness, if he cannot do by his own
strength something whose end leads to destruction, and prepares
30 affliction in no small measure and brings many trials, (yet)
accomplishes his desires by means of many plans and hidden
tricks.   And though you are not afraid of the ox, have fear of
the strength of your nobles and captains of your troops, whom
he has stirred up (56) and tutored into enmity against you, and
35 whose peaceable minds he has corrupted: although he is going
to complete this matter by himself, that is in his own person, as
my heart testifies to me.   For he did not think of practising
such deceit as this, until he got fat from your good things, and
his reins were steeped in the wealth which he gathered from

your kingdom. As it has been said by the ancients: 'A certain one got fat and trampled on his liberator.'

Then was the lion troubled at the speech of Dimnah. And the lion began to take counsel with Dimnah, saying, 'What do you think then that we ought to do?' 5

Dimnah. A man's tooth which is fixed in his mouth is firmly rooted there, but when it is injured or loosened by some small thing which strikes it, or by decay that is in it, or by some malady that troubles it, there is no rest for that man, and he has no enjoyment from this life, until he removes it from 10 his mouth. And when with an iron forceps he extracts it, with great pain it comes out thence, but after this bitter pain he finds great rest and reaps great joy without measure. And when food is foul in the stomach, the body is in pain because of it, and finds no rest until it expels it by vomiting, and then 15 it enjoys rest. And there is no rest from an enemy who is terrible in evil, (57) until the sight of him is taken away and he is placed in the earth.

The Lion. So according to what you say, you do not permit me to live in the neighbourhood of the ox. Lo! I will send 20 and tell him to depart from me and choose him such a region as he likes.

But when Dimnah heard this, it did not please him, because if the ox heard these things, he would make a plausible defence of himself, and by prudence and perseverance would bring to 25 nought his lying counsels, and with the subtlety of his knowledge would take captive the king's heart, until he returned to his former honour, and sat on a glorious throne, and he himself would be sent into banishment when his deceitfulness became manifest and known. 30

Dimnah. A message to the ox, and a change of the old love that you show him, will not lead up to a good result or bring any advantage; because the ox, without having the least idea that you know his wickedness, is turning over his plans and continues secretly in his crafty ways. But if he gets to 35 know that his wickedness has been manifested before you, I fear that he will go forth against you with a rush. For if (which God forbid) he is able to vanquish the king valiant in strength, the king will become a laughing-stock and a derision before all

3—2

his companions. And if he is able to escape from you, his
harmfulness will be increased, and his plans and tricks will
multiply. Prudent and wise kings do not reveal to offenders
with what stripes they are about to chastise them, just as they
5 do not reveal their private affairs, but first in their own minds
proportion every chastisement to the offence, and then order
(it). For offences are of different kinds. One offence happens
openly, (58) and openly must its author be chastised; and
another happens in secret, and in secret he is chastised.

10   *The Lion.* Every king who chastises a man when his offence is not evident, is considered unjust, and makes himself a
laughing-stock and a mockery.

Dimnah. Therefore only let the ox appear before you when
your face is gloomy and your countenance is changed, and let
15 him not find freedom of speech before you; because I know
that when he enters into your presence, he will show you his
appearance according to the evil of his heart, for you will
see that his colour is changed and that his limbs totter, and
that his face looks to the right and left, and you will see his
20 horns extended like arrows that he may thrust and do battle
with them.

The Lion. Now I shall be on the alert, when he enters
into my presence, and I note the marks in him. If those that
you have mentioned appear in him, I shall have no doubt about
25 the corruption of his way and the fraud in his heart.

When Dimnah was certain that he had corrupted the
lion's mind and made turbid all his friendship, with the evil
dregs of counsels which corrupt good principles, he wished also
to go to the ox, cast bitter tares into his heart, and cut
30 down from off his peaceful field all perfect love and friendship
and pleasantness. But he desired that his going should be
at the command and wish of the lion, so that no evil suspicion
should rest upon him. So Dimnah said to the king: 'If it
seems good to the king glorious in exploits, that I should go
35 to the ox and search out his sentiments, (59) perhaps I shall
be able to wrest from him the secrets of his heart, and he will
reveal to me, through my winning way towards him, what he is
going to do, and on what foundation he is about to base his
plan.'

And the lion permitted Dimnah to go to him. So Dimnah
the crafty set out and reached the ox, and, entering his presence,
stood as if sorrowful (and) sad—a liar far from the truth. When
the ox saw him thus, he urged him until he made him sit
down. And he sat with his face gloomy and his appearance 5
altered. The ox, seeing that his countenance was thus changed
and that he was downcast, said to him : ' Wherefore have I not
seen you so long ? What is the cause of your delay ? And why
has all your cheerfulness forsaken you ? Is there peace in the
midst ? Or has a change in anything come upon us on the 10
king's part ?'

Dimnah. How can a man be at peace who is not certain
of his life, and whose soul is placed in the hands of another,
and who serves before unbelievers and is subject to infidels
and promise-breakers ? For the fear of God is not before their 15
eyes, and they keep not the faith, walk not in uprightness,
render not what is due, and forsake virtue. When a man
goes about with such, how can he be at peace ? And what
peace falls to his lot ? Nay but he is continually in fear and
spends his days in trembling, because he subjects his soul 20
voluntarily to a man of greed, and sells his liberty knowingly
to a knave, and to sum up, ruins himself for both worlds by
his ambition, and does not attain to his desire.

The Ox. What has happened that (60) your soul is thus
troubled thereat and your mind sad on account of it ?   25

Dimnah. Something has happened which is fixed and determined in evil..., and who can escape ? Who (ever) walked with
a man of high degree and attained to an exalted rank, and
was recompensed with gratitude ? Who (ever) went after his
desire and fulfilled his lust, and did not perish ? Who that 30
kept company with women, was not ensnared by them ? Who
was (ever) attached to a ruler, without being envied and
slandered ? Who (ever) asked anything of a greedy man, and
had his request granted him ? Who (ever) begged and asked
from one niggardly-minded and unused to giving, and was not 35
contemned and abused ? And who (ever) became intimate
with wicked men, and was not injured by their wickedness ?
And he spake the truth who said that a prince, in his
lack of good faith and his false affection towards those who are

attached to him, is like a harlot, for one goes and another
comes.

Shanzabeh. Lo! I hear from you words which make me
fear that you have seen a change on the lion's part.

5 *Dimnah.* I have seen a change on his part, (but) not against
myself. And you know, O my brother, what solicitude I have
for you and what claims you have on me. Firstly, your obedience to me and your readiness to come with me. Secondly,
the oath of God the Exalted, that I gave you, and the faithful
10 covenant of truth that I made with you, and the Witness the
Searcher of secret things, whom I took to witness between me
and you. Great and laudable then is the affection that we
have got for one another while (61) serving the same unjust
master. How can I treat lightly any one of these things and
15 be false to them?

The Ox. What have you seen in him and heard?

Dimnah. One who is faithful, upright, truthful and not
deceitful, told me that the lion said to his companions: 'I much
desire the fat of the ox, and wish to eat him and to give you
20 to eat of him with me, because I do not need him in any one
of my affairs.' When these things came to my ears, I hastened
and came to you to acquaint you with his treachery, and that
not believing his promises or trusting in him any longer, you
might seek some plan for yourself.

25 Shanzabeh, on hearing what Dimnah said, thought that he
had come to him in friendship and honesty. And he said to
Dimnah : 'It was not right for the king to change the love he
had towards me and to entertain such an idea about me, because I have not committed any offence, whether small or great,
30 against him or against any one of his companions. But I am
fully persuaded that bad men, cunning, that is, and slanderous,
crafty and deceitful, envious and hating good things, who love
not peace but seek oppression, these have corrupted the lion's
mind ; since many of them attached themselves to him, (being)
35 greedy and mischief-makers. Thus it happens to him who
makes friends of bad men, and allows the perverse to approach
him, for they not only envy him extremely, but deprive him
of good things, and, what is worse than all this, place sins
upon his head and make him inherit dismay. (62) To many

such as these there happens the like of what happened to
the goose, who, seeing the shining of a star in some clear
water, thought she saw a fish in it, but when she came
near it, she found nothing. And the next morning she
saw in a stream a great fat fish, but, thinking him to be a 5
similar appearance to the former one, did not go near him.
Now if some one has told the lion something against me in the
wish to disturb his friendship and change his faithfulness, and
corrupt his mind and disturb his opinion, and has been credited
by him because of the experience he has had of the many who 10
served him before me, this does [not] call for wonder and astonishment. But if no deceitful man has accused me before him,
and if no mouth that is far from the fear of God has defamed
me, and no sharp sword of a tongue has slandered me, but he
of his own accord has come to hate (me) thus, it calls for weep- 15
ing and lamentation. And aforetime it was said by a wise
man : ' It is wonderful that a man should seek reconciliation
with one who is implacable ; but ten thousand wonders (that
he should seek it) with a man in whom, when one asks for
reconciliation with him, that is for the soothing of his feelings, 20
the soreness only increases and the mind is corrupted.' When
a man's heart is grieved on account of some annoyance, its
cure is easy and its conciliation not difficult. But when it
happens that the heart is vexed without cause and by no
offence, all hope of conciliating him is cut off. For when the 25
vexation is on account of an offence, apology can be offered
for it, that is regret at the offence. And falsehood will not
stand for ever. And though (63) I exchange many thoughts
between myself and my soul, I cannot find in myself a single
small offence. (And yet) I must surely have committed one at 30
some time, because he who is with his companion a long time
cannot escape altogether, or be free (from them). Especially
(is it so) when a man is a confidant, a counsellor, and ruler of
a kingdom.'

Dimnah. Of what kind was the change which you have 35
mentioned ?

The Ox. Sometimes the lion would think of doing something (or other); and when, on weighing it in the balance of my
intelligence, I discovered that the losses involved by it would

outweigh the benefits of it, I used to restrain him from it
gently and warily and by hints, while showing him from whence
the evils of it sprang, and by what door on the other hand the
advantages of it went out. And when he looked at (facts) such
5 as these, and extended his vision to the termination of the thing
in question, that is to the end of the matter, he used to find
great peace, and evil without end did he put out of his house.
But I did not do this thing foolishly and clumsily, before any of
the generals, but intelligently and warily, alone and secretly,
10 as a servant speaks before his master. Briskly too, as a child
prattles cheerily before his father. Thus continually did I
manage him. And everyone who is noble in his character and
pure in his birth, prudent in his knowledge and sound in his
religion, exercised (64) in his doctrine and skilled in his wisdom
15 and just in his conduct, when a man commits some offence
against him or is guilty of a slight error or inflicts an injury
productive of loss, weighs his offence and examines accurately
the harm he has done; and if his offence has proceeded from
want of knowledge, according to his want of knowledge is his
20 censure; but if his fault was committed knowingly and his
offence proceeded from hatred, his stripes are multiplied. And
if his transgression proceeded from enmity and deceit in the
heart, his stripes are made severe, and he is sent away to
judgment and handed over to the executioners. I know too
25 that everyone who walks with his companion in uprightness
and performs his service with perfect love, and with all his
soul desires for his peace, and with all his strength studies
his advantage, yet does not wholly escape from sin, nor is freed
either from all blame and censure. For matters which are not
30 accomplished in uprightness hold together only so long as
falsehood is wrought among them. In the same way too if a
physician employs flattery and behaves hypocritically towards a
patient, he is eager for his ruin and not for his recovery. In
the same way too, if teachers, that is resolvers of knotty ques-
35 tions, employ falsehood to one who asks concerning the truth of
his religion, they add darkness to his mind and spread a veil of
thick darkness (65) over his thoughts. But if the matter is not
thus, this has been effected by the insolence of a prince. (For)
one prince is steeped in ignorance; another is eaten up with

conceit and confused by pride, which brings its victim to ruin;
and another is deceived by the emfty, inclines his ear to listen
to the deceitful, and allows those who wish, to approach him,
when they ought to be kept at a distance, and insults those
who should be allowed to approach.   On account of this it has 5
been said by the wise, that he who sails on the ocean brings
himself near to hard trial, but still more so does he who has
attached himself to a prince.   For he who has approached a
prince, and walks with him in uprightness of heart and serves
him with love remote from deceit, and with a friendship remote 10
from all dissension continues in all the things that gave him
satisfaction, and then, alas, by accident or ignorance offends in
some little thing, as happens to one who is mortal and com-
passed by passions, this little thing becomes the cause of his fall
and of his ruin.   If this is not it, the profits that I served to 15
reap, and the breaches that I filled up, and the good things that
I did, and the deficiencies that I supplied, these have been
the cause of my ruin.   For when a tree is famed for its fruit
and desired for its appearance, and its fruit is sweet, these very
excellencies that are combined in it cause its destruction.   For 20
when men see that its leaves are beautiful, and its fruit abundant
and clustering together and sweet, they cut down a branch
together with the fruit upon it.   The peacock too, owing to
the greatness of its beauty, do men rob of its feathers, and
they are the cause of its destruction.   And a man (66) who 25
walks in uprightness, and is envied on account of his wealth and
the copiousness of his sustenance, the excellence of his character
and the abundance of his successes, his enviers being many and
his enemies clamerous, does not easily escape from ruin.   But
if it is not (this), it is something that is decreed and determined 30
by God, (and) who can avoid it?   For that which is decreed
and ordained by God, causes the lion to be humiliated and
caught by the hands of weak men and imprisoned in cages.   It
is this too which gives the charmer power over the serpent, so
that he can make it come out of a cleft in the earth, and take 35
hold of it with his hand like a cord, and in the sight of many
make sport of it.   It is this too which relieves the poor man
and causes his good things to abound, and sometimes distresses
the rich and parts them from their wealth.   It is this too which

humiliates the strong man in battle, and gives victory to the
humble and weak. Says Dimnah, full of deceit: 'If the lion is
seeking to do this evil thing by you, it is not for any of these
reasons which you have enumerated that he is doing (it) to you.
5 For no one, as you suspect, has incited him to do this, and
opened this door to him; but he of his greediness and of the
badness of his nature and bitterness of his heart and corruptiou
of his principles and his bad faith, has sought for this hatred
and meditated this deceitfulness, not having kept his covenant,
10 or trembled at the retribution of justice, or feared the Witness
who searches deep places and sees the secrets of hearts. In the
beginning of his friendship he is like a mouthful of honey that
is sweet to the palate (67) for a little while, but in the end of
the matter more bitter than aloes of Sokotra and wormwood.
15 And in truth I say that he is deadly poison.'

Shanzabeh. That honey which I tasted was (only) a mouthful: but now I see that I have come to taste bitter morsels
spiced with the venom of a basilisk. But whom shall I
blame except myself? And whom shall I accuse except my own
20 choice? And whom shall I censure except my own free will,
which by reason of greed has ruined me? Wherefore did I
remain with the lion who is an eater of flesh while I am a
feeder on grass? Therefore fie upon greed! and out on vain
flesh! For these made me fall into the pit, and brought me to
25 Gehenna, made me inherit dismay, got sighs for me, and led me
into straits, and made me like bees, that settling on a lotus-leaf
and smelling the smell, enjoy it a little while and destroy themselves, because the wings with which they fly no longer remain
to them, and they die where they are. And as to him who is
30 not contented with his pay, and will not put up with what (only)
satisfies the hunger of his belly, covers the nakedness of his
secret parts, and affords a shelter to protect him from scorching
heat, and looks not into the distance nor examines his course of
action and fears not the evils of the result, the wretched man
35 knows not that his eye will be filled with (only) a little thing,
that is, with one handful of earth, and that his body will be
put in three cubits of all the breadth of the land. There befalls
him what befell the fly who was not satisfied (68) with being
nourished by his tree and enjoying all the trees of the field, so

that he longed to drink of the liquid flowing from the ear of an
untamed, that is untrained, elephant, and the elephant shook his
ear and killed the fly. And he who contends with all his might
and endeavours with his whole soul and exhausts all his knowledge, to bring about peace and get tranquillity for him who is 5
devoid of gratitude, is like him who sows his seed on thorns,
and he who counsels the proud and arrogant, like him who
whispers to the deaf.

Says Dimnah, the liar and far from the truth: 'Leave off this
talk, and devise for yourself plans of rescue from this severe 10
contest that is set before you, and an escape from this snare that
is hidden for you, that is for your destruction, and an avoidance
of this cup that is mixed for your drinking.' Says Shanzabeh,
the poor and injured: 'What plans am I to employ if the lion
wishes to kill me? For I am well acquainted with him and 15
his disposition, and I know that though he may desire my
welfare and be anxious to repay the obligations of my service to
him, yet he is not left alone by his associates, who hate me
without a cause, and by counsellors of evil things and enviers of
excellent things, and by those who will utterly destroy them- 20
selves by deceit. He will be urged until he accomplishes their
evil desire by compulsion, and fulfils their wicked longing
against his will. Because cunning and deceit are joined together, and darkness and lying are wedded together, and envy
conceives and deceit is born. Then is light hidden, justice con- 25
cealed, and uprightness buried, and falsehood raises her head
(69) and truth perishes; high too and exalted and successful is
wickedness, although despicable and base. Just as the wolf,
the crow, and the jackal destroyed the honest and strong camel,
all three of them having agreed on his destruction.' 30

Dimnah. What did they do?

The Ox. They say that a certain lion dwelt in a place near
a public road, and had three companions: a wolf, a crow and a
jackal. Some merchants passing along that road, left behind
them a camel. And the camel entered the marsh where the 35
lion dwelt. The lion said to him: 'What do you want?' The
camel answered: 'I want to be a servant of the king.' The lion
said to him: 'Will you deal kindly with me in prosperity and in
distress, in panics and in happiness?' The camel answered:

'Until death will I remain with you.' The lion said: 'Then
remain with us, and I will not neglect your comfort, or diminish
aught of the things you need.' Then the camel consented, and
remained with the lion. Now it happened one day that the lion
5 went out to hunt for some prey, and there met him a certain
powerful elephant. And he did hard battle with him, so that he
tore the lion's body with his tusks, and the lion (only) escaped
with his body bathed in blood. By reason of weakness he
remained some days unable to catch anything for their sus-
10 tenance; and these three animals who were nourished on the
lion's leavings remained [for some days without getting food,]
and became very famished and afflicted. And their condition,
that is the news of their hunger, became known (70) to the lion,
who (himself) was troubled by reason of want. And he showed
15 them his sadness and manifested to them the trouble of his
heart in view of their need. (And) they said to him: 'We are not
anxious about ourselves, nor do we grieve at the diminution of
our own nourishment, nor are we sad because of our own hunger.
But all our fear is on account of you, our lord the king, and all
20 the anguish of our heart is because of your weakness, O glory of
the race of animals. We glance to the right and we look to the
left, to find something fitting for the nourishment of the crown
of our pride and glorious diadem of our forlorn estate, but we
find nothing.' The lion replied: 'I thank you for your solicitude,
25 and do not doubt about your love, nor will I neglect to repay
you. But want has much enfeebled me, and hunger in no small
degree has afflicted me, and need of food has brought me near
to contempt. But go a second time in reliance on the merciful
Provider; perhaps He will make ready for you something that
30 we may partake of, and that may support the hearts of all four
of us.' Then those three went forth and sat and framed a
secret plan between them, saying to one another: 'What have we
to do with this camel, who is not of our race or profession, and
no messmate of ours, but who is food and we the eaters? No-
35 thing will keep us except that we counsel the king to devour
him, and to let us share his meal.' The jackal said: 'No one
could make this proposition to the lion, because he has made
promises to the camel, and cannot (71) turn back from them.'
Says to them the crow of cursed life and foul odour: 'Be quiet all

of you, and remain in this place, and I will go alone to the lion,
and do my deeds and mix my bitter cup.' So the crow set
out by himself, and stood before the lion in his deceit. The
lion, on seeing him come (thus) hastily, said to him: 'Have
you found or observed anything?' The crow replied: 'No one 5
can run and hunt, or observe either, except he be well-fed, and
can see from afar. As for us, all our strength is gone, and our
eyeballs are covered over, and the eyes of our knowledge are
darkened, through hunger and affliction, and all our devices have
failed through the distress of our soul; and our heart is agitated 10
by the king's anxiety as to what he must do. But lo! we have
conceived an excellent idea, if our victorious king will help us.'
The king said: 'And what is it?' The crow replied: 'This idle
camel who feeds on grass that comes not from his seed, and
drinks water that he did not dig for with his own hand, and 15
enjoys the air, but repairs not the breach and saves not from
the enemy, what profits us his dwelling with us?' When the
lion heard (it), he was indignant, and said to the crow: 'Faugh,
insolent fellow! How evil is your counsel, and weak your intellect and feeble your mind! Remote are you from the truth, 20
and devoid of compassion, and stripped of virtue. You were not
faithful in being so insolent as to make this speech before me.
Why, have you not heard that I made a promise to the camel,
and gave him an oath, (72) and made a faithful covenant between myself and him? And have you not heard that a man 25
may distribute many talents to the poor, and not be so profited
as a man who saves one soul from slaughter? How are you so insolent as to say to me: "Falsify your promises and be unfaithful
to your covenant, and anger your Creator, and provoke your
Judge for a little food that perishes, and inherit eternal tor- 30
ment?"' The crow replied: 'I know that what the valiant king
says is true and not false: but one soul may redeem the souls of
a family, [and a family may redeem a tribe, and a tribe may
redeem a large city, and a large city may ransom a king. Now
necessity has come upon the king, and I will propose him a 35
means of evasion from his duty of protection, so that the king
may undertake this without having anything to do with it
himself, and without his ordering anyone to do it. For we will
practise a trick, by which success and victory shall be ours.' The

lion made no answer to this speech of the crow. The crow,
on knowing that the lion had assented, went to his companions
and said: 'I have talked to the lion and argued with him for a
long time, and ceased not until he gave me his consent to our
5 proposition. So come, let us scheme how we may deal craftily
with the camel.' His companions replied: 'We trust to your
ability for the achievement of the matter.' The crow said: 'I
think we should go (to the lion) in a body, we and the camel,
and remind (him) of his condition and the inability to move
10 which has come (upon him), and then say: "You have (always)
treated us well, and been kind and helpful to us, so now we
must discharge our debt of gratitude to you and recompense
you." Whereupon each of us must say: "Eat me up and suck
my bones, and do not die of hunger; for I give you myself." As
15 each of us says this, the rest must bring forward a pretext to
show that he is not fit for it. And perhaps the camel will
imitate us, and say the same. But we will make no excuse for
him, and the lion will not let him go.' Having agreed with one
another, and hatched this plot, they came and presented them-
20 selves before the lion. And the crow said: 'You have need, O
king, of something to strengthen you, and it is right that we
give you ourselves. For by you do we live, and if you perish,
we can have no further existence after you, nor any more
pleasure in life. So let the king eat me up, for I am quite
25 willing.' But the wolf and the jackal objected to him, saying:
'Be quiet, for it is not good for the king to eat you, for your
flesh can give no satisfaction.' (Then) the jackal said: 'But I
shall satisfy the king's hunger, so let him eat me; for I am
agreeable to this and willing.' But the wolf and the crow
30 objected to him, saying: 'You are stinking and foul.' Then
said] the wolf: 'But I am not thus: so let the king eat me.'
(Then) the crow, the camel and the jackal said: 'Let him who
would destroy himself eat of you; because it has been said by
learned physicians that the wolf's flesh brings on strangling
35 pains.' Then thought the simple-minded camel that thus they
would make excuse for him too. So he said at once: 'But my
lord the king, I am not thus. For my flesh is sweet-tasting and
my fat is pleasant; physicians too make use of my fat because
it brings healing to those who lie (ill) with consumption of the

belly. Pray let the valiant king begin and eat *me*.' (Whereupon) the crow, the jackal and the wolf, wicked companions all, said: 'You have spoken the truth and been true to your noble character, and performed what was due and discharged your obligation.' Then they fell upon him and tore him to pieces. 5

Now I have related this fable to you, (73) because I am persuaded that if the king's companions are agreed on my slaughter, envied that I am, they will accomplish their desire; even though there be kindness in the lion's mind, and ho were able to place me between slain and slain, and not consign *my* 10 body to slaughter. But even if the lion's mind is pure, and his love sincere and his inclination to true goodness perfect, (yet) since envious men abound, and deceitful men incite, and crafty men clamour, they will succeed in corrupting his mind; for tho foolish stories of men who deny the goodness of God take away 15 a wholesome mind. And I know, O brother, that water is more tender than tho speech of men, and (yet) when it flows with force against a rock, it tears away part of tho stone.

Dimnah. And what are you going to do?

The Ox. I do not think fit to appear a coward, but as I see 20 him about to act, so shall I act (too). If he is anxious for peace, lo I am his servant and subject. But if he does otherwise, I shall not fail to put forth all my strength. For it has been said by tho wise that neither the man of prayer who is constantly praying, nor he who distributes his goods to the 25 poor, nor he who frees himself from evils, reaps such advantages as be who does battle in his own defence, when he is wronged and envied. If he conquers, it is a matter for boasting to him; and if he is defeated, ho is called praiseworthy, because (74) ho died for the truth by the hand of wicked men. 30

Dimnah. It is not right for a man to hazard his life, even though he have confidence in his strength; because if he conquers, his victory is the result of chance, and if he is defeated, bo destroys himself. But a man who is wary and shrewd does not despise a single one of his enemies, even though ho be 35 weak: lest that weak one resort to others, and lay plans, and accomplish his desire against his powerful foe by means of many (helpers), by fraud in some hiding place, and there befall him what befell the sea through a bird called tho sandpiper.

The Ox.   What did he do?

Dimnah.   It is related about a bird called the sandpiper, that she and her mate formed the plan of building their nest on the sea-shore.   When the time came for young ones, that is
5 for eggs, the hen-bird said to the cock : 'We must needs look out for some other place, lest, when we get young ones and before we have pleasure in them, the water of the sea destroy them.'   The cock replied: 'This place is admirable for us, for it contains clear water and herbs of every kind.   So let us
10 produce our young ones here, and not fear.   For the sea is great in his knowledge, and looks at far-off matters, and will be afraid of evil consequences, and (so) will not hurt us.'   His mate said to him : 'O how weak is your mind and puffed up your spirit, and how simple is your knowledge, and how grand
15 you are in your own eyes ; since you neither recognise your species, nor consider your own diminutiveness.   (75) For he who is wise and prudent compares himself only with that which is like him.   So do not attempt a thing which is easy to you in empty speech, but far from you in deed.   For nothing is more
20 abominable before God, and more evil and hateful in the eyes of men, and weaker, than he who does not recognise his own nature and attempts things which are too high for him.   Nay, listen to me, and do not resist and destroy our young ones as they are growing up and the time approaches for us to take
25 pleasure in them and rejoice.'   When the hen-bird saw that the cock resisted her words, and sought to go after his own desire, she said to him: 'When a man wishes to satisfy his longing, and does not take the advice of his friends and those who love him, that is, his welfare, and are anxious for his peace
30 and wish for his advantage, there happens to him what happened to the tortoise, when she did not listen to profitable counsels.'   The cock said: 'And what happened to her?'   The hen-bird replied : 'It is related that in a certain marsh abounding in water were two geese.   There was also in that marsh
35 a tortoise.   And all three of them made friends with one another.   When all the water in that lake had dried up, the geese said to one another : "Let us depart hence and seek a place where there is clear water, free of evil mud, and herbage, and where we may find rest and build our nest."   [And they said

to the tortoise:] "Lo we are going away now. Farewell." The
tortoise said (76): "As for you, my companions, it is easier
for you to depart, and easier for you to remain on dry land,
than for me. For I am an aquatic animal, and apart from water
I should lose my life. Pray now deal kindly with me and save 5
my life from destruction, and devise a plan for me that I too
may depart with you." The geese replied: "We will carry you,
trusting that you will observe silence." The tortoise said: "How
can this be?" The geese replied: "We can put down a stick,
and do you take hold of the middle of the stick with your 10
mouth; and we will take hold of its ends and (then) fly." And
the tortoise consented that they should do thus to her. So
they put down the stick, and the tortoise took hold of the
middle, and the geese took hold of its ends and flew. While
they were flying, people saw (them) and wondered, and began 15
to make sport and laugh, saying: "See a great wonder, some
geese carrying a tortoise and flying!" When the tortoise perceived the large crowd shouting, she opened her mouth and
said: ["God pluck your eyes out, O people!"] Whereupon, the
tortoise fell from the stick and destroyed herself by her wilful- 20
ness and disobedience.' The cock-bird said: 'I hear what you
say, and I tell you not to fear; because the sea is very wise,
and will not dare to hurt us, since he is afraid of the consequences and considers the remote result of an action.' Then
the hen-bird laid (77) eggs; and when she had produced young 25
ones, they rejoiced in them. But the sea had inclined his ear
and heard everything that they said to one another, and wanted
to know what the cock-bird could do to him. Then he lifted up
his waves and took away the young ones, together with their
nest. But he preserved them and did not destroy them, since 30
he wished to know how matters would end. (And) the hen-bird
said: 'This was pictured before my eyes when I told you that
if you recognised your nature and remained in (an attitude
befitting) your weakness, our young ones would not be lost to
us, and you would not bring upon us this sorrow and sigh- 35
ing.' The cock-bird replied: 'And I too said to you that which
I said. But now watch and see what I am about to do.' Then
the cock-bird went to all the birds, and complained to them
and informed them what the sea had done to him, and how he

had wronged him by taking his children and heirs from him.
And he said to them: 'You all know that tho trials of the
world are many. And he who is tried resists and seeks assistance from his companions. But now I seek help from you all,
5 that possibly I may be able by your intervention to exact
vengeance from my oppressor.' The birds replied: 'Lo, we are
all before you: tell us what you want.' The cock-bird said to
them: 'The king of all the birds and the head of them is
the Sîmurg. If we all go in a body to him and (78) all lift up
10 our voice in weeping and sighing, he will hear our voice and
come out to us. And we will say to him: "You are our King,
and our glory and strength are you. And lo the sea has dared
to wash away our young ones and our nest, and has bereaved
us of our heirs. Pray now avenge us on him, because you are
15 stronger than he."'

So all the birds came to the Sîmurg, and told him their
whole story; and the Sîmurg perceived that the sea was their
oppressor. And the Sîmurg and the whole crowd of birds
drew near to the sea and rebuked him, so that the sea took
20 fright at them, made obeisance, and restored their young ones.

I have related this fable to you in order that you may not
go forth to the lion with a great rush; because he that is
versed in knowledge does not hasten into battle, but allows time
for stratagem.

25 *The Ox.* I say I will not hurry into battle with the lion or
show him an angry countenance, but will speak to him with a
cheerful face in an affectionate, friendly and submissive way,
until I see a change on his part. But when I see something
which leads me to apprehend my destruction, then I shall
30 employ other means, and call God to my help, because his
deliverance is near to them that fear him.

Dimnah, not being pleased to hear from the ox that he was
going to appear before the lion peaceably and affectionately and
submissively, and fearing lest if those false signs which he had
35 mentioned to the lion did not show themselves in him, (79) all
his cunning should be lost and he himself turn out a liar, then
changed the peaceable disposition of the pure-minded ox, saying: 'At the moment when you see the lion you will know the
anger of his heart.'

The Ox. How shall I become aware of (it)?

Dimnah. If you see that the lion's face is gloomy, the gaze of his eyes inteut, his ears extended like arrows, and his mouth growling, and that he is stamping on the ground with his paws, then know that he is ready to slay you.   5

The Ox. If I see in him these tokens that you have mentioned, I shall not doubt that he seeks the destruction of my life.

Having cast all these arrows of suspicion into the lion and the ox, and incited them against one another and corrupted 10 their peaceable dispositions, he then left and went away to Kalilah his brother. Kalilah, on seeing him, said: 'How far has your affair progressed, O man who diggest a pit, and where are those tares of yours which you sowed in peaceful fields?'

Dimnah. The seed has sprung up and the harvest has 15 come; and lo the trap springs and causes the bird to fall into the pit. Do not doubt about this, or think that a cunning workman who employs artifices cannot sever the concord between two brothers and set at variance two associates, even as water cuts through a stone.   20

Then came Kalilah and Dimnah together to see what course their affair was taking. And they saw the ox going in to the lion with his face downcast and the beauty of his appearance altered. And when the lion saw the ox coming in to him he became downcast in face, extended his ears like two arrows and 25 began to stamp with his paws. (80) Then the poor ox, fool of heart, thought that the lion wished to leap upon him. And the ox said to himself: 'No one who fears God and no one iu whom is sound intelligence, (ever) attached himself to a prince, because lo I see that he does not keep his promise or observe his oath, 30 and his love does not abide. And he resembles ouo who places a serpent in bis bosom, and knows not when it may turn upon him and bite him. He also resembles one who swims in a lake in which is a crocodile, for the swimmer knows not whether it may not suddenly snatch him away. And the ox thought on 35 these things with his appearance altered and his body trembling. When the lion saw him thus, he remembered what Dimnah the deceitful had said, and thought that the poor ox was about to do battle with him. Whereupon the lion leaped on the ox, and

4—2

they began to fight (so desperately) that the lion's body and
that of the ox were torn and dabbled with blood.

Kalïlah, on seeing the lion with his body torn and dabbled
with his own blood and that of the ox, said to Dimnah: See,
5 O insolent wretch, far from all nobleness and remote from all
knowledge, what you have brought about by your devices and
tricks, and what an evil end you have brought on both sides.

Dimnah. And what is the evil of the end I have brought
about?

10 *Kalïlah.* The ignominy of the lion, and the misery and ruin
of the ox, and the sin that you have inherited, and what is worse
than all these, the laughing-stock that the King has become
before the chiefs of his army (81) and the generals of his troops;
for a king who does battle in his own person is despised, ridi-
15 culed, and insulted by all. And when I looked, I saw that your
devices were fruitless, and that you framed your tricks without
knowledge. For he who is the counsellor and confidant of
a king, and makes it necessary for the chief, who is the diadem
of the kingdom, to do battle in person and defile his hands with
20 slaughter, is he not mad and senseless and considered foolish
and possessed? Or have you not heard that sometimes matters
are established for a man without war and ignominy and labour
and strife, when a holy and God-fearing man is counsellor?
For then he will shrink from ignominy. Again, an intelligent
25 man with plenty of brains, who, being a confidant and a counsellor, advises a king to do battle with his subjects in person,
is more harmful to the king than his enemies who strive with
him. And as harm befalls a man and a plague-spot fixes itself
on him when his heart trembles and his face is ashamed, so
30 does abasement befall a strong man when he is deficient in
sense and good counsel. Because sound intelligence and understanding, void of stupidity, accomplish many things. And not
by force or battle can this thing be grasped and acquired, but
by subtle intelligence, deep investigation and discriminating
35 thought. And he who seeks to devise plans, or to invent sly
tricks, or (82) to set hidden snares, or to abuse the exalted and
humiliate the mighty, and does not know a door or an entrance,
his beginning is like your beginning and his end is as your end.
And I was well assured of the arrogance of your spirit, and the

insolence of your mind was evident to me, and the badness of it
was depicted in my mind, from the time that you began to talk
in my presence. When I had no more than an inkling of that
foundation that you laid for your edifice rising up to wickedness,
and perceived your greediness, I pictured (to myself) this igno- 5
miny and took note of this snare that you made for yourself
and me. This your wickedness is on the door before our eyes.
Because he who is about to build an edifice or to do something
whatever it may be, or is about to start along a road, first makes
sure of the foundation of the building. And he who is about to 10
do something, ought to project his gaze into the distance, and
look at the result of the matter, with sound intelligence and
discerning eye, lest he gain for himself distress instead of joy,
and trouble instead of satisfaction. And he who is about to
start along a road, ought to enquire whether it is quiet, and ask 15
whether it is undisturbed, and examine honest men who walk
in it. And if it is free from fear and void of snares and clear of
bravoes and robbers, he may walk in it. Otherwise he will
lose his life, and become a laughing-stock to all his companions.

Nor, when you paid your visit to me, did I abstain from 20
censuring you, or keep silence and not reprove you, or neglect
to open your blind eyes, or refuse (83) to inform you that the
matter would end badly, and of the loss that would result to
you in the completion of this your journey. But I was sure
concerning you, that you would not listen to my words or em- 25
brace my counsels, and leave your wickedness. The fear of the
Exalted one you put away from your heart, and did not shrink
from ignominy and shame and disgrace. And to call God to
witness between me and thee for this horrible thing I was not
able; because it was right that I should bury in the heart of 30
the earth this transaction of yours so full of harm. But
now that you have satiated your dog-like appetite and given
effect to your evil desire and achieved your tricks, and shewn
your badness by a quarrel that has cast loss on many and
brought misery on kings and commoners, renounced justice, 35
been false to your promises and broken your oath, been over-
powered by your greediness and have counselled perverse things,
and reaped punishment and inherited dismay and prepared hell
for yourself, I will show you all your defects. One is that you

know how to talk, while you are bad in your actions. And it has been said by the wise that there is nothing worse for a prince than a confidant who knows how to talk but not how to act. On account of this the lion was ruined when he believed
5 your lying words and relied on your perverse speeches, as he perceived in you beauty of language and heard from you smooth and gentle utterances, but did not recognise the barbs hidden in them. And not praiseworthy is the speech (84) which is far from the deed, as cooked food is not pleasant without salt, and
10 as drink is not enjoyable without thirst, and as a rule of life is not wholesome which is destitute of the fear of God. Nor again is a face beautiful unless it have bright eyes; wealth profits not except with goodness of disposition and liberality in giving, largeness of heart and open-handedness: intelligence,
15 wealth and wisdom avail not, unless combined with love of the Creator: alms profit not except with purity of intention: life is not desirable except with perfect health: and rest cannot be found except in freedom from all things that distress. Lo you have journeyed, O brother wretched of heart and wanting in
20 prudence, along this road of yours whose miles are snares and its leagues groans, its end destruction, and its termination the punishment of justice. You have taken distress into your treasuries, and filled your garners with bitter weeping; because you walked not in uprightness, nor proceeded with caution, nor
25 set your building on the truth, nor inclined to quietness by means of your words, nor loved peace in your interference. And the sum of my speech is that that you did not keep your promise to the injured ox, and desired not the satisfaction of the lion. And this your affair is like (the case of) a man who
30 is attacked by a combination of the four passions which are rooted in the constitution of his nature. For no one can allay them except a skilful physician who in the first place fears God, and longs for the Kingdom of the Most High, and is versed in symptoms, skilful in examination, and acquainted with roots
35 and drugs. So too one who is lost (85) to faith in God no one can turn back to the truth, except a faithful teacher who fears the decrees of the Most High, and is versed in books and in the natural sciences. And him who is sickly of appearance and wretched of heart and wanting in prudence the light of the sun

profits not at all; but darkness is added to his outward eyes, and haughtiness of spirit clothes his mind. Now the lion is like a lofty mountain, which the wind, though it be very strong, cannot overthrow; even as greed cannot move his terrible tower nor wickedness overpower it.   5

Your story has reminded me of something that I heard you say, namely that when a prince is good, simple in mind and pure in disposition, while his counsellors are bad and greedy, underhand and shuffling, and not simple and pure, no one derives enjoyment from the king's wealth, or pleasure from his good things. 10 Just as a man who seeks to swim in the ocean and refresh himself from heat, has no enjoyment, since crocodiles are in it. And the virtue of kings and their society and their excellence and the uprightness of their companions, are like the ocean of which only the surface is known. And you in your avarice and 15 greediness wished to enjoy all the king's wealth by yourself and to drive away all other men from his good things. On this account God has not suffered your plan to succeed. And when a man seeks for his own satisfaction at the expense of others, and is consumed with the illicit love of women, arrogance rules over 20 his members and a veil of ignorance is spread over his mental faculties (86), and of his own accord he does all his affairs, without employing advice or betaking himself to a prudent person. Because learning is (only) gained by labour, and wisdom is (only) grasped by toil and trouble. But what do these words 25 now profit me? I know that your case resembles (that of) the man who said to a certain bird: 'Seek not to teach him who will not hearken, nor to correct him who cannot be corrected, and labour not for the wisdom of him who cannot act wisely.'

Dimnah. How runs the story about him?   30

Kalilah. It is related that on a certain mountain was a herd of apes. One cold night they saw a glow-worm, and, thinking it was fire, collected a number of logs of wood, placed (them) on the glow-worm, and began to blow upon it. Now there was a tree in that place with a bird on it. And this bird 35 began to say to the apes: 'That which you have seen is not a spark of fire, so do not fatigue yourselves with blowing at (imaginary) fire.' But the apes obeyed not nor hearkened. Then the bird came down from her place and began to upbraid

them. And a certain man, passing by and seeing her, said to
her : 'Do not try to correct him who cannot be corrected, nor
to instruct him who cannot understand; and do not counsel
him who cannot hearken to counsel. Because he who speaks
5 in the ears of one who cannot hear, repents (of it). For men
do not try swords on a stone, which cannot be cut through, or
make bows of wood that will not bend' (87). Then the bird
hearkened not to that man, nor listened to what he said, but
drew near to the apes to let them know; and one of them took her
10 and flung her on the ground and killed her. But this is a parable
of you, since you have not been established by faithful teachers,
nor again have you attached yourself to the pure, nor hearkened
to wise and God-fearing men, nor been a disciple of ascetics or
hermits. On this account haughtiness of spirit has taken you
15 captive, arrogance has got sway over you, greediness has vanquished you, avarice has slain you, and feebleness of knowledge
has abased you. Now deceitful companions are worse than
madness, and remind one of the simpleton who allied himself
to a rogue.

20   *Dimnah.* How runs the story about them ?

Kalîlah. It is related that a certain crafty rogue, and a
certain innocent simpleton found on the road a purse containing
a thousand darics. And the two being partners together in
every transaction, when they reached their town sat down to
25 divide them. (And) the simpleton said to his partner: 'Take
the half of these darics, and give me half.' The crafty one,
resolving in himself to take them (all) by fraud, replied: '(Nay)
but let us take of them, you and I, as much as we need, and
bury here what remains. And when we are in need again, we
30 will take (more) of them ; because the blessing of God rests
on partners so long as they are not separated from one another.'
The simpleton replied : 'Be it as you say.' So they took a
small quantity of the darics, and buried the remainder in the
earth under a tree. Then that crafty rogue returned by an-
35 other road (88) and took away the darics, and returned to his
house, after rearranging the place deceitfully and wrongfully.
Some time having passed, the simpleton said to the rogue :
'We are in need (of money) for expenses. Come, that we may
take of those darics which God has supplied to us.' So the

two went together, until they reached the tree.   And they dug
in that place and found nothing.   Whereupon the rogue began
to cry out, and pluck his hair, and strike his head, and beat
upon his breast, and tear out the hair of his head and beard,
and to lift up his voice and say: 'No one ought to be trusted 5
in these times, and no one should believe in the good faith of
his companion, nor a brother in his brother, nor a partner in
his portner.'   And he seized the simpleton harshly and wrongfully and said to him: 'You took a different road, and came
and took the darics.'   Then the poor simpleton began to swear 10
and to curse himself, saying: 'I did not take anything, nor did
I return to this place.'   Then the rogue in his dishonesty seized
him, led him to the judge, and related before him their whole
story.   Then the judge asked the rogue: 'Have you witnesses?'
The rogue replied: 'The tree under which we placed them, will 15
witness for me.'   Then the judge wondered at his saying:
'The tree will witness for me.'   And he directed that a surety
be taken from the simpleton for himself.   And the judge directed
the surety to bring him on the morrow to that tree.   And the
rogue went to his house, and related his whole (89) story to his 20
father and said: 'O father, I told the judge that the tree would
witness for me.   So if it seems good to you, O father, we will go
to the tree under cover of night, and do you get into a certain
great cleft that is in the tree, that when the judge comes, you
may witness for me in his presence, that this simpleton took 25
these daries, so that by fraud we may not only take these
daries, but return and take those (besides) which the simpleton
has taken.'   Then the silly man consented to his dishonest
son, and went and hid himself in the cleft of the tree.   And
the judge rose up early in the morning, and the poor simpleton 30
and the greedy rogue.   The judge, having approached the tree,
said to it: 'Which of these two partners took those daries,
which were placed under your roots?   Fear God and lie not;
because, according to the word of your mouth I shall issue
judgement against the guilty one and cause the oppressed to 35
prevail over his oppressor.   Woe from God on the oppressor!'
Then the shameful old man in confusion opened his mouth
within the cleft and said: 'The simpleton took the dinars.'
And directly he had spoken, he came out of the cleft and hid

himself above on one of the branches of the tree. Then the judge was astonished, and collected all his wits, and began to look here and there, until he saw that cleft in the tree. But he did not see any one in it, because the old man who witnessed had got 5 high up in the tree, whither a man's sight could not reach. And they brought a number of logs of wood, placed them in the cleft of the tree, and set fire to them. And tho smoke ascended to the old man, who cried out with a loud voice, and fell (90) from the tree, knocking at the door of death. So 10 he witnessed to the truth without intending (it). And the rogue was severely beaten, and the dinars were taken from him and given to the simpleton. This parable that I have related to you is to show you that no one who is crafty and digs a pit for others and hides a snare, should forget that he 15 will certainly fall into them himself. As for you, O Dimnah, in you are combined many tricks and perverse, crooked, and turbulent ways, avarice and haughtiness of spirit, and what is worse than all these, feebleness of knowledge and absence of fear of the judgement of hell. These are the bitter fruits which 20 you have gathered for yourself and for many others. Doubt not that you will fall into one of all these snares which you have hid.

How tranquil are tho members of a household so long as there is no disturber among them, and no talo-bearer in their 25 family! How quiet and peaceful are brothers and kinsmen so long as a double tongue does not speak among them! Because he who speaks with a double tongue resembles the serpent from whose mouth proceed two substances: one deathly, and one curative. And I was sore afraid of your tongue, when 30 you began with these your crooked and evil ways. And I sought to upbraid you and pacify your mind and strip your wickedness off you. But I feared that I should not avail anything with my words. Because he who counsels and upbraids a serpent, does not save himself from its harmfulness nor escape 35 from its bites. It has been said by a wise man: 'Cleave to the wise (91) and make friends with the godfearing and those who are exercised in and distinguished for goodness of disposition and accustomed to liberality in giving. Pour out your heart before them like water; and do not remove yourself from

them at all. Nor shrink from attachment to prudent, knowing
men, although not perfect in their exterior, for you may be
helped by their intelligence and reap from their wisdom, while
you are free from the deformity of their exterior. But from
those who are perfect in their exterior, while their minds are 5
perverse, and they lie with their tongues, and keep not their
promises, nor tremble at their Creator, from these keep far and
do not even eat bread with them; because the beauty of their
exterior will not profit you, while the badness of their morals
will pollute your good character. And if you find a man whose 10
gifts are abundant, and his soul free from envy, and clear of
deceit, while his knowlege is a little inferior, attach yourself
to him, that he may be helped by your intelligence, while you
may reap of his liberality and enjoy his wealth. But from men
who are distressed in mind and deficient in sustenance, not 15
accustomed to good things nor distinguished for gifts, from such
as these fly many leagues, lest they corrupt the goodness of
your disposition, darken the light of your eye-balls, and pollute
the soundness of your religion; or perhaps your case will resemble (that of) the merchant who was obliged to affirm that 20
a mouse had eaten up a hundred pounds of iron.

   Dimnah. How runs the story about him?

   Kalilah. It is related that in a certain region was a merchant rich (92) in property and goods. And he wished to set
out on some journey or other, in order to add to his wealth. 25
Having by him a hundred pounds of iron, he placed them with
one of his friends in whose integrity he had confidence; and,
having given him the deposit, he set out on his journey. On
returning from his journey, he claimed his deposit from his
friend. (But) he who had had the deposit by him, said: 'I put 30
the iron in one of the corners of the house, and the mice ate it
up.' The merchant replied: 'I have heard that nothing can cut
through iron except something which is like it. So this thing
is quite clear to me: specially so since I have (always) found you
honest and good, upright and not false.' He who had the 35
deposit was exceedingly pleased at the merchant's speech. And
the merchant said: 'Come, brother, let us enjoy ourselves to-day
at my house with wine-drinking.' And the merchant managed
to take away his friend's son and hid him. Then he went to the

boy's father, and seeing him with his mind troubled and the
appearance of his face altered, said to him: 'What has happened
to you?' The boy's father replied: 'I had a little son, and I
know not where he is.' The merchant said: 'As I was getting
5 near your house, I saw an eagle carrying a boy and flying: perhaps he is your son.' The boy's father replied: 'But who (ever)
saw an eagle carry off a boy?' The merchant said: 'In the land
where the mice can eat up a hundred pounds of iron, it is no
wonder that the eagles carry off boys.' The boy's father replied:
10 'In truth it is I who took your iron; because (93) it is impossible that mice should eat iron. But tell me whether you have
taken my son. (If so), restore (him) and take your iron.'

I have related to you this parable to let you know that if a
man is lying in his counsel and practises deceit towards the one
15 who provides his salary, and exalts his low estate, and raises his
mean condition, without doubt his fall will come suddenly. And
you now whose frauds have impoverished many and whose deceits have destroyed honest men, how can you be of use to any
man, seeing that deceit is planted in your soul and honesty is a
20 fugitive from your disposition? And there is no one so hideous
and bad as he who invites and admits you to his friendship;
because love is a stranger to you and kindness is not found
with you, and a man's secret you do not bide in the ground, but
on the housetops is your badness proclaimed. And you are
25 like the aloe tree, which, though it be smeared with honey, does
not diminish from its bitterness. And I was very afraid of
associating with you or mixing with you or companionship with
you as a brother. Because it has been said, and excellently
said, that associating with good men bequeaths good, and asso-
30 ciating with bad men like yourself bequeaths sighing, and what
is worse than this, conducts to hell. Just as the wind which,
when it blows, bears and conducts with it all (kinds of) smells
both sweet and foul. Now I perceive that my talk is very
burdensome to you. For it was said aforetime that there is
35 nothing so burdensome to the hearing of a fool as (94) the talk
of wise men. And nothing is so desired by a wise man and
extolled by a knowing man as good and godfearing men, and as
the quiet and pure-minded. Hateful also to a calumniator is
the quiet, thoughtful conversation of humble men.

When Kalīlah had got thus far, the lion had killed the envied, injured ox outright.

Then, when the ox had perished by the counsel of Dimnah the deceitful, the lion repented; and he groaned and his mind also was troubled, and he rebuked himself saying: 'Very prudent 5 was Shanzabeh, aud simple and pure was his mind, and good his counsels and upright. Perhaps he was clear from crime and free from wickedness, and envious men charged him with guilt and incited me to destroy him.'

Then Dimnah the illstarred left Kalīlah and ceased to con- 10 verse with him, and, approaching the lion, said to him: 'My lord the King, live for ever. Wherefore is your mind troubled and the appearance of your countenance altered, now that God has taken vengeance on your enemy and you have placed your hand on the neck of those that hate you, and their design has 15 not succeeded?'

The Lion. I am grieved at the death of the ox, for very excellent were his counsels and acceptable his utterances. Grief too is laid upon me that I did not keep my promise to him or observe the compact which I gave him. I think that I have 20 angered the Witness whom we called to witness, and am sore afraid of the punishment that will come upon me on his behalf.

Dimnah. Pity him not, O King. Because he who is wise is not afraid of one who is afraid of him. And it is customary 25 for kings, when they hate any one, (95) to drive him from beside them, and not entrust the affairs of the kingdom to his hand. And when they like a man, they place him in the furnace of trial and test his noble character; and if he comes out pure like purified gold from within the fire, they bring him near to them, 30 and also entrust the affairs of the kingdom into his hands. Sometimes too they abhor some useful man; just as medicine is abhorred by a sick man, but when he expects healing from it, he drinks it in spite of his dislike. And sometimes a man likes his companion and his liking for him becomes great, but in spite 35 of his liking for him, he removes him from his presence, because he fears lest perchance he may deal deceitfully towards him. And sometimes a serpent bites a man's finger or toe, and he cuts it off his hand or his foot, lest it infect his whole body.

And the lion believed what he said, and he quitted the King's presence.

After a little while the craftiness of Dimnah was manifested and proved to the lion, who learned for certain that with
5 envy and deceit he had brought about the killing of Shanzabeh. Then the king ordered that Dimnah should be put to an evil and bitter death.

Here ends the first story; (namely) of two brothers whose brotherhood was severed and their concord destroyed by an
10 interloper and an envious counsellor, a lying confidant and a false friend.

DIMNAH'S DEFENCE.

King Dahdahram said to Nadrab the Philosopher: I have heard your speech about the falsehood and deceit which corrupted (96) harmonious minds so as to root out love from them, and sow enmity within them.

Now tell us if you please how Dimnah defended himself to 5 the lion about the killing of the ox, and how he came to know. of Dimnah's tricks and ordered him to be put to an evil and bitter death; and whence also Dimnah's deceit was proved against him, and by what token the judges found out that Dimnah was worthy of punishment, and how he did not prosper 10 when he stood before the judges and councillors of the king.

Nadrab the Philosopher replied to Dabdabram the King: We have found by parable and narration, that when the lion had put the ox to death, Kalilah the upright began to reproach the lying Dimnah and denounce his frame of mind, censure his 15 bad counsels, condemn his ignorance, manifest his folly before his eyes, and call him a stranger to all truth, far from all fear of God and stripped of all nobility of disposition. And when he began to speak to him, he thus upbraided him : That which moved you to corrupt the lion's mind and to bring 20 trouble on the ox with the lion, and sow hatred for them and sever their concord and corrupt their mind, was the bitterness of your fruits and your double-dealing propensity, the perverseness of your thoughts and the cunning of your heart, the greatness of your avarice and your greediness, and the reckless- 25 ness of your intelligence and the unsoundness of your mind, for when it espied some small gain and hoped for some trifling advantage, you became envious, and incited to evil and clamoured for slaughter, (97) and became a mischief-maker and corrupter. You sowed tricks and reaped shame of face. You put on dis- 30 grace and covered yourself also with confusion. You sold love and bought destruction. You brought sighing on your friends and clothed them with shame. You caused your haters to ride

in carriages, and plunged your lovers into foul ignominy. To
sum up, you have prepared for yourself eternal torment. Now
unless I remove from beside you and renounce your brotherhood, become a stranger to your society and withhold myself
5 from your company, I shall have no confidence for my life, nor
escape from your tricks, nor save myself from your harmfulness.
It has been said by a wise man and well said: 'Get far from
those who practise evil things; lest you become like them, and
do not smell their scent, lest some of their foul odour adhere
10 to your garments.' Lo henceforward I shall separate myself
from your companionship, restrain my tongue from conversing with you, and cry aloud to God to save me from your
wickedness; because I am convinced that you brought about
enmity between the king and his good confidant and upright
15 counsellor, and in your wickedness urged the king and incited
him to falsify his promises, belie his oath and not keep his compact, stained his hand with innocent blood, and cast an honest
leader out of his army.

Dimnah. What has been done, has been done. That the
20 slain one should return is impossible, and that he should live
again cannot be. So pray leave off these useless chidings, and
refrain from distressing yourself (98) as well as me. And con-
trive something which may appease the lion's mind. For
I too am vexed as well as sorry for what has happened. But
25 envy incited me and avarice overcame me and greediness got
possession of me. These are the things that urged me on to
those things which have taken place.

Now there was one of the king's companions called the
leopard, who was highly trusted by the lion, and his place was
30 distinguished, and his seat exalted, and he was upright in all
his ways. Now the leopard had remained till late with the
lion on the night when the conversation between Kalilah and
Dimnah took place; and when the leopard came out from the
lion, it was very dark, because clouds had obscured the light of
35 the moon and stars. And the house in which were Kalilah
and Dimnah lay by the roadside; and so, bearing the sound
of conversation, he went near and listened, and heard all
the words which Kalilah exchanged with Dimnah, and how
Kalilah rebuked Dimnah about the wrong he had done, and

how Dimnah confessed and revealed it, and could not deny (it).
When the leopard had listened to them attentively, he set off
hastily and went in to the lion's mother, and related to her the
whole matter as he had heard it. And she made a compact
with him, and he took the living and true God to witness 5
between himself and her, that, as far as possible, she would not
let any one know that he had related this story to her. When
the lion's mother heard from the leopard that Dimnah of cursed
life had thus confessed without being able to deny (it), (99) she
made up her mind that it was he who had destroyed the faultless, 10
guileless ox. When day dawned, the lion's mother went in to
her son. And she perceived that his face was very downcast,
and his mind troubled, and his thoughts perturbed, on account
of the killing of Shanzabeh. Then she opened her mouth and
related to him the whole story, as she had received it from the 15
leopard's mouth; after which she spoke to him as follows:
'This sorrow that possesses you, and this grief that wrings you,
will not avail anything now. And you will not find rest by
these, and they cannot yield a tranquil end or a - - - of
peace. On the contrary, they trouble the understanding and 20
perturb the mind, vex the heart and weaken the body; and,
what is worse than all this, envious men rejoice at you and
enemies despise you, while friends and lovers are distressed on
account of you. Now you, my son, by the strength of God
are acquainted with things fitting, and instructed in things 25
necessary, and versed in signs, and an investigator of things,
and one who invites good men but repulses bad ones. And if
you got any peace of mind or advantage by this grief that
possesses you, let us have a little partnership with you, that
we may bear some of the burden that is on you. But if you 30
got no rest by it, and find no advantage in it, then case yourself
of your distress and cheer up from your sadness, and track out
the truth of this thing which has been done to poor Shanzabeh.
For I have investigated it a great deal, and its comprehension
is not difficult.' 35

The Lion. How is it possible that I should comprehend
(100) the matter, and be certain about the truth of the report
of it?

The Lion's Mother. The wise say: 'Every one who seeks

to try his friends and to know his enemies and haters, his
intimates as well as those who are far from him, let him observe
what sort of feeling is in his own heart towards each one,
whether friendship or hatred.' Thus too does each man judge
5 his companion in his heart, (even) according to what is in his own
heart concerning his companion. And you, O my son valiant in
strength, seek as a witness concerning the ox the feeling which
was in your own heart towards him. If friendship, sincerity,
and concord, than thus (too) was the heart of the poor creature
10 with you. But if your heart was angry with him, and hatred of
him was fixed in your soul, it was the same too with him. And
see, O mighty King; if this punishment which you have
brought upon him proceeded from your own wish and was
planted in your mind and fixed in your heart, then is your grief
15 and vexation superfluous, and instead of being as you are now,
you should appear joyful and keep exulting, because you have
accomplished your desire, obtained what you were wishing for,
and carried out your intention. But if you are sad on account
of his death, and through his slaughter have clothed your limbs
20 with sadness, then these things only took place through the
speech of the envious and the advice of the crafty, and you
have only fulfilled the desire of a deceiver. And as my mind
witnesses to me, so does your holy soul witness to you that the
envied and injured ox was a good friend to you, a sincere
25 adviser, and an honest associate, and was an excellent confidant
(101) with you and walked before you in purity of heart, filled
up all the breaches in your kingdom, and supplied all defects to
the members of your army by his good and prudent counsels.
On account of all these things, demand the truth from your own
30 self and ask *yourself* about the truth (of the matter), for a more
truthful witness than that you cannot seek ; because it has
been said by a wise man that from him in whose brain is fixed
a wise understanding and in whose mind perfect knowledge is
implanted, the truth about matters is not concealed. Because
35 thought receives ideas from the understanding, even as an
infant receives nourishment from its mother's breasts. And
then are excellent things distinguished and discerned from
hateful things, just as a mirror of steel distinguishes youth from
old age, and a bald man from another who has locks of hair.

The Lion. I have examined the matter of the ox a great deal in my heart, and investigated (it) in my mind, and weighed it in the balance of my understanding, but I have not found in the ox a single defect towards me. On the contrary, my whole understanding witnesses to me of his perfect love and sincere 5 brotherhood, his unmurmuring obedience, sincere love of peace, and unselfish ways. I have reaped dismay from the death of the ox, and gotten for myself vexation with distress. All the worse then and more harmful is my want of acquaintance with matters, and the unsoundness of my faith, and the insincerity to 10 my compact. And as far as I remember the matter of the poor ox, I know that he has been wrongfully killed: because I was ensnared by the envious, overcome by men who fear not God, (102) and made to fall by the speech of liars, so that I was induced to destroy the ox. And there is no one who draws away 15 the veil of darkness from my heart in the matter of the ox except you. Now I have awaked from the sleep of ignorance, and perceived that by deep searching and accurate investigation secret things may be reached, hidden things known, and mysteries revealed. Pray now, O blessed mother, declare to me 20 who has related this story to you.

The Lion's Mother. The Searcher of hearts has heard what I said to you, and witnesses to the truth of my words that I have not added or diminished (aught). I do not think that if you knew him, he would be believed by you more than I am. To 25 inform you of the narrator's name would not profit or procure advantage. For I heard it from one of your associates, one who is trusted by you, and is honest, pure and without stain, free from deceit and destitute of envy. But I cannot divulge his name, because I made a compact with him and gave him 30 an oath, and took to witness between me and him the Witness who holds truth, that I would not divulge his name. If I am compelled by your Majesty, and am false to my compact, then I shall be abused by all my acquaintances, and deprived of knowing any one's secret again. It has been said 35 by a wise man, and well said, that no one is more unfortunate, sustains heavier loss, has a greater fall, and perishes sooner, than he who does not keep his promise, observe his compact, or abide in good faith. Nor would he give you any additional

satisfaction (103) nor would you derive any advantage from him.

The Lion. Not every man commands, nor is every commander obeyed : but only he whose good faith is true, his place distin- 5 guished, his rank honourable and exalted, and his knowledge lofty and renowned. And when a matter is hidden, such as if made manifest would bring profit, if made evident would effect release, and by its report confer happiness and drive away sadness, the mischief increases and waxes strong, be- 10 cause the good is not made evident. For it has been said that he who looks and sees the wickedness of an offender and perceives the wrong doing of a criminal, and conceals it from his prince, is not accounted faithful, but is worthy of punishment. And as for this matter, I see in it great advantage for you, 15 as well as for the narrator of it, and strong confidence and great excuse before me, if you name him and do not conceal from me (the name). For he who related (it) to you removed all the blame from his own shoulders, and did not withhold what was due, transgress the law, or conceal the truth. And all his 20 delinquency, offence, and blame have you taken on your own person ; and you are now subject to censure in regard to me, since you have procured two injuries, of which one is sin, great- est of all, and the other, prolongation of our trouble and pertur- bation of our thoughts, sadness of our soul and distress of our 25 mind. And your informant has been unrewarded ; because he is worthy of thanks, and is going to receive large presents in return for the obligations which he has discharged (104) and the duty which he has performed and the rules which he has observed, and is safe from punishment both now and hereafter, 30 is freed from censures, has escaped from blame, and is worthy of high honours.

The Lion's Mother. I am fully persuaded of these things that you have enumerated, and it is very difficult indeed for me to resist your words and disobey your commands. Because 35 I know that God upholds the punisher of transgressors, the scourger of wicked men, the buffeter of the insolent, the liberator of the oppressed, and the rewarder of the good and unstained, who are remote from wickedness and free from deceit. But doubt not concerning what your ears have heard from me and

seek not a hundred additional witnesses, though all proclaiming
in one assembly and narrating the same story and proceeding
along the same road and holding one truth.

The Lion. I do not doubt concerning the uprightness of
your words or fear for the sincerity of your religion or deny the 5
purity of your conduct. You are only considered in my heart
and soul as upright and faithful, just and far from wickedness,
righteous and separated from falsehood, noble and free from
slandering. Notwithstanding, you are blameworthy and under
censure, since you have not informed me of the narrator's name, 10
who was not the injurer of that illustrious one, but who loved
the truth and laboured for our welfare.

The Lion's Mother. To do that would procure me three
injuries: First, that I should have departed from honesty in
not keeping my promise and not observing my compact with 15
(105) the narrator; secondly, the enmity that would exist between me and the possessor of this secret; and thirdly, that all
those who used to reveal to me their secrets would become
strangers to me, and not one of them would come near me
again, or reveal to me the hidden things of his heart as before. 20
Wherefore do you desire to disgrace the good character of her
who reared you? It would not effect anything, nor bring peace,
nor increase the truth.

The Lion. You have told the truth, and made trial with
your understanding, and fulfilled the fear of God, and I will not 25
compel you against this your sound will, nor urge you again to
transgress the divine commands. Because ever since I knew
myself, and discerned, too, good from evil, I have found no fault
in you, nor found any change in your words, nor heard falsehood proceed from your tongue. This alone suffices me as 30
a witness concerning you. I will not demand from you the
narrator's name; only relate to me what your ears heard from
that narrator, and let your account be the same as his account,
without diminution or addition.

Then she told him as she had heard, saying: 'I do not 35
forget the saying of the wise, that those who are clement to
offenders are praiseworthy; and praiseworthy are humanity and
clemency, when the matter of their offence is short of actual
murder; because a limit is set to transgression. And an ordi-

nance is decreed by God against murderers, that they shall be
punished with death; not only against those who murder (106)
with the hand, but also against those who murder with the
tongue.   And we see that those murdered with the tongue are
5 more in number than those murdered with the sword.

Now this offence has brought many disadvantages on the
King.   First, it has made him a prey to that liar, that he should
not keep his promises; secondly, with regard to himself, gloomy
and distressed, foolish and not prudent, impetuous and unre-
10 strained, hasty and not deliberate; thirdly, in the eyes of all
his subjects, a madman and not sensible, a liar and not honest,
a destroyer of his friends, the murderer of one who gave good
counsels, the oppressor of one who brought tranquillity to his
subjects, and one who bides not by his good faith or keeps his
15 promises; and what is worse than all these is that the King
with his own hand has polluted himself with shedding the innocent blood of a sincere confidant, remote from all deceit and
separated from all evil.   Besides all this, their mind is corrupted
and their harmony spoilt.   They are severing the King's bonds,
20 and breaking off the yoke of government from their shoulders.
Nor will any man who is prudent and intelligent, sound in
knowledge and lofty in mind, care to perform his obligations
to the King after this, or render to the King a sincere opinion
as to the appearance presented by his enemies; but every one
25 of them will remain in a sullen mood.   On this account princes
and nobles ought not to spare him who does not keep faith, but
should destroy with severity whoever makes mischief between
a king and his companions, especially those who speak with a
double tongue; as it has been said: "The Lord will destroy dis-
30 sembling lips."   (107) For those who are anxious for the destruction of just men are overcome by avarice and greed, men
who are stung by envy as it were by a viper.   And there is
nothing so much required of a king and his kinsmen and all
princes as the destruction of turbulent men and corrupters of
35 healthy minds.   It has been said by the wise one: "When one of
your members causes you to stumble, cut (it) off and cast (it)
from you, lest it corrupt your whole body."   There is nothing
which would bring you so near to God, O my son, and so wash
the filth from the hearts of your companions and attract them

to your society, and make them so obedient to your commands,
as the destruction of the deceitful Dimnah. And aforetime it
has been said by the wise that nothing is worse for a king
than one who reveals his secret, divulges his private affairs,
and severs his concord. For it has been proved to me that 5
he who has sown this evil seed, from which thorns and dismay
have been reaped, is Dimnah. And now that all his deceit has
been made us manifest to you as the sun, and that all his tricks
and evil ways have appeared to you as in a polished mirror,
take away his life, that your mind may be set at rest and your 10
kingdom stablished and your whole army freed from deceit, lest,
when he sees the gloominess of your countenance and the
change in your face, he oppose you little by little, and corrupt
your kingdom by means of his evil counsels and crafty devices,
and trouble the captains of your troops and incite them to a 15
rupture of your kingdom. And if in the balance of your understanding you weigh all (108) the transgressions of men, the evil
that this Dimnah of cursed life has done outweighs them all.'

The lion, on hearing his mother say these things, became
agitated, and moved from his place, being afraid to leave Dim- 20
nah destroying his welfare by means of his deceits. And he
commanded that a herald should make proclamation in his
camp, and all his magnates were gathered to him. Then he
commanded, and they brought in Dimnah before them. And
Dimnah, when he saw what the king had done, began to speak 25
quietly and deliberately, as if unaware of anything that had
happened to any of those present, (saying:) 'I see the King,
who is illustrious and mighty in strength and extolled for his
exploits, with a very gloomy face and an altered appearance of
countenance. Perhaps he has become aware of some malady, 30
or perhaps an enemy has come out against him, or perhaps he
has seen some deterioration on the part of his subjects?'

The Lion's Mother. What has distressed the king and disturbed his subjects and brought together all his generals, is
your own evil counsel, deceitful perversity, lying talk, and un- 35
equalled craftiness; from all which things you have inherited
destruction for your life, and have fallen into the pit which you
digged.

Dimnah. And what is the wrong that I have done, and

which is the offence that I havo commited, for which I am guilty
of death?

The King's Mother. The wrong you have done is without
equal, and your offence is unexampled; for you have corrupted
5 the king's mind by your deceit, and destroyed his upright confidant by your wickedness.

Dimnah. I see that the parables (109) of the wise aro true;
for the ancients said that he who fatigues himself and labours
for the good of his companions has many enemies, and that his
10 companions depart from him. Again it has been said: 'Thou
who hast brought thyself nigh to the truth, hast delivered thyself over to all manner of trials.' But God forbid that this
parable should bo true of our victorious King or his honest
soldiers. And I endorse this parable which was spoken,
15 (namely) that if a man attaches himself to a bad man and
subjects himself to a reprobate and associates with an avaricious
man and serves a fool, in order to know their wickedness, and
has taken to their employ and submitted himself to their service
and laid on his shoulder the yoke of obedience to them, those
20 things that have been mentioned before happen to him. The
wise, becauso they perceived with tho eye of intelligence and
discernment that the wickedness of the cruel was great and the
merit of the puro disallowed, and that ho who walked uprightly,
served honourably, and counselled honestly, was without reward,
25 relinquished the world, despised its satisfactions, contemned its
wealth, and trampled under foot all its delights, and removed
themselves from human society and chose them abstinence and
solitary abode; since they perceived that the good were punished
for the wrongs done by the bad, and well-principled men chas-
30 tised with the stripes of the wicked. Having investigated these
things with sound understanding, they submitted their necks to
the divine service, laid upon their shoulders the yoke of obedience to their Creator, and loved their Lord and walked in all his
ways; despising the service (110) of men, for their love to one
35 another does not abide, and their servants do not escape from
their wickedness, and their princes who are honest are not delivered from tho envy of their courtiers. On this account does
the friendship of many now ccase. Now there is no one who
so adorns justice and is so consistent with integrity and so cou-

forms to goodness, as our victorious King of many excellencies,
renowned for exploits and glorious in victory; whose noble disposition the talk of envious men cannot change, and the strong
tower of whose honesty the clamour of fools and the babbling of
stupid men cannot move. For his most earnest wish and long- 5
ing is to discharge obligations, and to give distinguished and
abundant honour to those who give good counsels. He looks
afar in the wisdom of his mind, and investigates the truth with
the subtlety of his knowledge, and looks into the polished mirror
of justice which reflects the vanities of the deceitful and the 10
envious and the calumniators and those who run after bloodshed.
And nothing is so evident and manifest to the victorious King
as my affair, poor, injured, lonely, and afflicted that I am, distressed and broken-hearted, a stranger and helpless. Because
that with all my strength I laboured for him, and with all my 15
soul I loved his welfare, and gave no sleep to my eyes or slum-
ber to my eyelids, until I clearly showed him the deceit of his
enemy, and his right-hand took hold of the neck of his hater,
that false friend and perfidious associate, crafty counsellor and
lying confidant; (111) who, when he beheld and saw the lofti- 20
ness of his seat, and perceived the exaltation of his rank, and
became fat from the greatness of the honour bestowed upon him
by our victorious King, lifted his neck on high, exalted his mind
heavenwards, trampled on the ground, trod upon things with
his foot, set his heel on a lofty rock, and sought to crush both 25
the king and his subjects, and to take his life from him as well
as his kingdom. All these things our valiant King saw with his
own pure eyes at the time when he appeared before him; and a
second witness to these things besides our victorious King I do
not want. Therefore he who openly warned the King of all these 30
things and saved the soul of the lion, valiant in strength, from
evil, is worthy of gifts and honour and gratitude and abundant
reward, and not that he should be punished with hostility, as I
am, injured wretch. Our valiant King well knows, and you, O
mother of illustrious character, know well, and all the blessed and 35
renowned assembly, companions of the King clothed in victory,
know that nothing ever passed between me and this ox who
deceived the King, such as made me friendly with his enemies, .
and removed me from the fear of God, that I should seek for

vengeance on him, or plan his destruction; but on account of
the duties I have to our King and the obligations to him that
can never be (fully) discharged, his unequalled virtues, our life
that is bound up in him (112) and our eyes that look to him,
5 did I make evident to him that which he saw with his own
pure eyes, and heard with his own holy ears, and touched with
his own just hands; because many of the perverse and crooked,
even the crafty and deceitful, the avaricious as well as dishonest,
made plans for me that I should become intimate with them
10 and assist them to their wickedness, that they might deal
deceitfully against the King and raise the heel against the lion.
But I repulsed them from me and threatened them, and they
became enemies to me, and all my haters meditated evil against
me, and they all spoke the language of wickedness against me
15 and made plans for the destruction of my soul.   But God did
not help them, and I am confident that He will deliver mo,
poor and lonely that I am, from their wickedness, by His justice
and uprightness and the kindness of our peace-loving King.
     When the king heard these words from him, he ceased from
20 the intensity of his indignation, and commanded him to be
taken from out of his presence, and delivered him to the judges
and the examiners, at the same time calling God to witness concerning them, and commended them to the righteous Judge, and
charged them to listen to the prisoner with just and upright
25 judgment, and in the fear of God to investigate and track out
the truth of this matter, and not with ill-will or hatred fixed
in the heart and enmity hidden in the mind, or to forward
the cause of others, calumniators and haters of the truth.
     Dimnah, on hearing these things from the king's mouth,
30 sat down on the ground before him, and opened his mouth
boldly, saying : ' My Lord the King, (113) live for ever !   Hear
a couple of words from your servant, injured that he is, and
troubled and oppressed in spirit.   It does not befit the wisdom
of the King, fearing God (as he does) and being his sword on
35 the earth, that he should take away my life for the words of
bobblers who fear not God, but that he put forth to (examine)
this matter of poor me, men skilful in knowledge and acquainted with wisdom, and distinguished for the fear of God,
who are no respecters of persons and conceal not the truth for

a bribe, nor comply with the wishes of others, even though
they be near friends of the King. And let him command that
they report to him how my affair progresses and whatever of
my statements is shown to be true from day to day. For I
rely upon the mercy of God to bring me out like purified gold 5
from the furnace of trial; since it has been said by the wise
that he who could bring fire out of the stone in which it was
hidden, can bring out hidden things by just trial and investigation coupled with the fear of God. From this it is evident
to our good King that I am innocent and pure, wronged and 10
oppressed, (namely) because I ask of him to investigate and
try these accusations which have been made against me by
men who hate the truth and are smitten with envy. But he
whose conscience is stained with deceit, and whose action is
not clear of deceit and tricks, resorts to flight and conceals 15
himself in a hiding-place, lest trial make evident his wickedness, and bring to light the bitterness of his fruits. And he is
like a foul-smelling thing which is hidden in the heart of the
earth, such as (114) dead bodies; for when they are freed from
the earth, they give out a putrid odour. And if I had been 20
accused justly, as envious men say, I should not have remained
in the King's gate; and if my soul were stained and my mind
polluted, it would not be able to give birth to bold and upright
words, or to make a defence; because wickedness would have
blinded its eye-balls, and deceit would have darkened the eyes 25
of its discernment. Because I doubt not that I have been
wronged by these envious men, I ask the victorious King to
make public this matter of which I have been accused. And
when the fact of my innocence is shown to him, he will account
me worthy of great honour, and make me sit on the lofty 30
throne of the innocent and upright, and ride on the neck of
all my enemies and haters; and by the confidence that I shall
get, I will cover all my calumniators with shame of face. One
request do I make of our victorious and very valiant King,
(namely) that the account of my defence of myself be not 35
kept from him; lest the truth be hidden from him, and he
be incriminated by the wiles of others. Nor let them keep
back those honest witnesses whom I shall openly produce in
my defence; perhaps they will be concealed and hidden. And

know, O victorious King and lover of good principles, that it is
not by reason (of any command) of God that the time of my
decease approaches or that I have arrived at the close of my
life. But it is by the band of these men who envy good
5 things (115) and suppress excellent things, that I lose this my
temporal life, injured and oppressed that I am. And if, which
God forbid! my uprigbt king, who is separate from all wickod-
ness and far from all oppression, cease to care for me, and I
remain like a feeble lamb in the hands of deceitful wolves,
10 thirsty for my righteous blood, I shall be as one who has no
help from anywhere, and like one who belongs to the house
of the dead, already slain within the tomb. But why do I say
'without help,' since there is God who will recompense every
man according to his works? Now it has been said by a wise
15 man, and excellently said, that when a man believes what ought
to be denied and denies what ought to be believed, there
happens to him what happened to the woman when she gave
herself to her servant, so that he disgraced her good character
and uncovered her nakedness, while she believed and credited
20 his idle tales.

The Lion. How runs the story about her?

Dimnah. There was a woman called 'Gate of pearls,' in
a region in Kashmîr - - - - - - and in that city was a certain
merchant called Pkizib, having a wife whose outward appearance
25 was beautiful, but her inward form hideous, who sold her good
character and wronged her husband. And in her neighbourhood was a certain painter, a worker in pictures, who was a
lover of this woman and an enemy of his Creator. It is related
that one day this woman who sold her honour and defiled her
30 purity, said to him: 'If by this your handicraft, you can make
(116) the likeness of something, so that when you visit me, you
can effect your coming to me without (speaking) a word and
without the cognizance of anyone, (do so). Because my heart
is filled with a great fear of others, lest perchance they observe
35 me, and I become ridiculous aud a laughing-stock.' Like that
which was said, (namely) 'They loved the praise of men more
than the praise of God.' The painter replied: 'I will make
something fine aud large, such as your soul will like; for lo! I
will paint a garment or cloak, and will make if of two colours,

one white and the other black. When the white side of it is
seen at night, it will look like the day, and when its black side
is seen in the day time, it will look like the night. So when I
come to you at night dressed in it, its whiteness will inform
you of my coming; and when I am dressed in it in the day- 5
time, its blackness: there being no voice or messenger (com-
municating) between us.' The woman rejoiced when she heard
this from him. And when she perceived him coming to her
house, by the sight of the cloak in which he was dressed, she
used to rejoice and exult that no one knew of this trick, and 10
her fear of her poor, injured husband was taken away from her.
But one day, one of the slaves of this woman's husband took
note and saw this cloak, and observed too that painter, clad
in the garment and entering in to his mistress. Now the
painter had a concubine, (117) who was a paramour of the 15
slave. One night the slave said to the painter's concubine:
'Give me the garment which your master puts on, that I may
show it to some one; and I will return it immediately.' And
the woman took the garment and gave it to the slave: who,
putting it on at night-time, came to his mistress, the merchant's 20
wife. The wretched woman, thinking that her deceitful paramour had come to her, went to him quickly according to her
evil custom, and gave herself to the slave, and polluted her
good character and disgraced herself. Then he returned the
garment, and gave it to the handmaid. At the end of the night 25
the painter, evil in tricks, came from a feast at which he had
been, and put on the garment and came to the woman. When
she saw him, she wondered at him and came to him hurriedly,
saying: 'Wherefore have you returned? Did I not serve your
wish at the beginning of the night?' When he heard it, he 30
repented within himself, saying: 'Some trick has befallen in
the meanwhile.' And he returned ashamed to his handmaid,
whom he seized and smote severely, until she informed him
about the garment. Then the painter repented that he had
transgressed the law, tore the garment in pieces, and turned 35
back from his evil way.

This parable I have related to you, my Lord the King, free
from all stain, [to show you] that not everything that babblers and
envious men say is true and fit to be believed. And you, O King,

mighty (118) in strength, are profound in thought, versed in knowledge and skilled in understanding, prudent and remote from
stain, adorned with justice and extolled for truth. Your soul
takes no pleasure in deceit, nor do your feet run to evil; your
5 hands delight not in bloodstains, nor does your goodness conceal
the truth for the speech of liars; you do not grant petitions to
the envious, or destroy the pure because of the deceit of the insolent; nor do you believe babblers, chase away the pure, or
incline your ear to the voice of guilty men. And you will not
10 satisfy the desire of my calumniators, poor and lonely, troubled
and distressed that I am. He whose soul longs for my slaughter,
and whose eyes look for the destruction of my life, let him know
that he gathers inexpiable sin for himself into his garners, and
brings endless sighing on himself, and that his eyes will see an
15 evil retribution. And you, O King, who love uprightness, have
seen with your own pure eyes, and heard with your own chaste
ears, and with your holy hands have touched what that forgettor
of the King's benefits was about to do when God the Merciful
brought his deceit on his own head, and exacted vengeance from
20 him for the victorious King (119), and made him like dust, a foot-
stool for his feet, and put him out of this life, and wiped out
his name from under heaven. He who informed you of this, O
victorious King, is worthy of gratitude and a reward of good
things, of large presents and great honours; and not of con-
25 tumely and disgrace. And if the coming of that deceitful confidant, who lived on grass and fed on roots, to the lion, the
king of all beasts, mighty in strength and glorious in victory—
if he had come in the manner of warriors and enemies, and
you had (actually) seen a personage bent on mischief, would
30 then such a miserable suspicion as this, which these envious
men have uttered against me, have been believed concerning
your poor servant, pure in mind and free from stain, rooted in
your love and harnessed to the yoke of your obedience, one in
whom you have never seen deceit, and whom avarice has never
35 overcome, who has never withheld what was due to you or
from the first day that he appeared before you defrauded you
of any of your rights, and never opened his mouth to ask for
presents and honours, as do the King's confidants, or molested
one of the king's courtiers? I have not rehearsed all these

things before you, O valiant King, because I am afraid to die; nor do I wish to remain in this world any longer with these men who are remote from the truth—even were I not anxious for your welfare (120)—except in order to manifest to your Excellency the wickedness of the envious, and make apparent 5 before your eyes the deceitfulness of the avaricious, and show to your Majesty the craftiness of the abominable, and drive these insolent men from your presence, and take away these clamorous men from your Majesty, and wipe out from your mind these accusations with which they have accused me, pure 10 (though I be) and innocent, sincere and without stain, a [true] friend and remote from wickedness. But if the soul of our King, mighty in power, doth acquiesce in the destruction of my life and the killing of my person, and it is desired by him that I go out of this world in the middle of my days, I doubt not 15 that though I be deprived of the pleasures of this world, God the Merciful will gladden me with those of the world to come. Because it has been said by the wise that he who delivers his soul to slaughter, when clear of iniquity, remote from evil, and free from stain, is worthy in this world of honours and presents, 20 gifts and rewards, liberation from evils and freedom from servitude, and in the world to come of great delights, (and) of a kingdom which has no like, and shares the banquet of the righteous and the seat of the martyrs and confessors.

O good and righteous King, you are acquainted with the 25 smallness of my stature and the insignificance of my person; and I have no help from anywhere, (121) and am unable to get assistance from anyone, but only from the justice and goodness of our victorious King. Nor when I was the King's confidant, did I aspire to reach things which were too high for 30 me, or to attain to the rank of the mighty, or to reap wealth from the King, or to amass possessions, lest perchance these might exalt me in my own eyes and I should attempt high things not befitting me. And had I an hundred lives and were to deliver them (all) to death for the King's welfare and 35 happiness, this would be a very slight matter in my eyes; because I do not doubt that whether I remain in the life that is here, or by death or slaughter depart to the world that is yonder, my honour and my merits will not be forgotten by the

King, or be blotted from his heart. If I remain in this life, my
Lord the King will know that I was wronged by my fellows and
oppressed, pure and without stain. And if after my death he
recalls my achievements, and recognizes the arduousness of my
5 labours, he will not neglect my heir or repulse my family from
him, or debar my brethren and near friends from his benefits.
These are not words wherewith I may flatter our victorious
King, in order that he may remove his justice from me, but (I
speak them) that if it seem good to the King, he may not hurry
10 punishment upon me or grant to wicked men their desire
concerning me, until he place me in the furnace of trial and
with the fire of investigation examine all my actions. And let
not a number of insolent men impel you to (122) defile your
pure hands with the shedding of my blood, innocent that I am;
15 because God has restrained you from all evil deeds, and filled all
your treasuries with righteousness and justice, even truth and
uprightness. And it has been said by the wise that the good
things of a man multiply and abound, and all his affairs progress,
and all bad things depart from him, when he restrains himself
20 from killing the innocent and does not destroy the life of the upright for the talk of babblers and envious men.

When the crafty Dimnah had ensnared the lion's heart with
these words, and was cooling the indignation of the king and
working a change on his thoughts, one of the king's magnates
25 rose up and said to Dimnah: 'You are wheedling and flattering
the king with these words, not because you are zealous for the
king's welfare, but in order that the severity of the punishment
decreed upon you and the sentence of justice for your evil
deeds and bitter requitals may be alleviated.'

30   *Dimnah.* Although I may be far from the truth, as you say,
(yet) no blame attaches to me, or censure or sin or punishment,
for defending the truth which has been stained by your lying,
and my integrity which has been brought in question by your
envy and calumny. And everyone who speaks out in his own
35 defence, and strives with all his might to rise out of the deep
pit which insolent men like you have digged, is praiseworthy and
without blame. And you, wretch that you are and enemy of
your own welfare and a provoker (123) of your Creator, have
gotten many woes for yourself, prepared for yourself endless sigh-

ing, and brought immeasurable losses into your garners; for you
have shown to all your hatred, and revealed to the righteous king
the plots and tricks which are in your heart; because you have
not kept the former things, nor held to the things which are present, nor waited for the latter things, but have been false to 5
love, forgotten friendship, not remembered salt, been a disgrace
among your companions, and to sum up, have departed from
God. It has been said by the wise, and excellently said,
that out of the overflowings of the - - heart of the cunning
and perverse do their lips speak falsehoods. Again it has been 10
said that he who rejoices in the misfortune of his companion is
not far from destruction and downfall. And you, O miserable
man, have not satisfied the king by your speech, nor his
magnates by your cunning : but have revealed your wickedness
and made known your villainy. Think not, madman, that since 15
you have done these things, all of them will not revile you,
banish you from their friendship, and debar you from their
society. Because just as you have not abided in love towards
another, so too you will not abide (in love) towards them ; and
just as you have not observed mercy or remembered friendship 20
between two, so too you will not keep faith with others.

When that speaker heard these words, he held his peace,
nor opened his mouth again to answer back.

Then said (124) the lion's mother to Dimnah : 'Woe to
you, insolent man ! How brazen-faced and how shameless 25
you are ! Nor does your disgrace put you to silence; for your
wickedness has been openly demonstrated, and your tricks and
cruel deceits proclaimed on the house-top. This temerity calls
for great wonder and astonishment.'

Dimnah. Wherefore, O mother of the just and upright 30
king, do you look with one eye, and listen with one ear ?. This
shows me that through my ill-fortune all men have strayed
from the way of truth, forsaken justice, and concealed the fear
of God ; and everyone speaks according to his own will, and not
according to the right which is due from him ; since they have 35
stopped their ears to that voice which says: 'For every idle
word that men shall speak, they shall give an account in the
day of judgment.' Again, another saying is that 'out of your
own words you shall be justified.' Now of all such as have

K. F.   .   G

departed from the fear of God, everyone is smitten with some temptation. One is smitten with deceitfulness; another with envy, and he delights in setting many at variance; another with quarrelsomeness and talebearing, and he is continually corrupt-
5 ing the minds of honest men; and another is smitten with slanderousness, and continually without cessation bites the weak with the teeth of his wickedness. To sum up, I do not think that there is any honesty abiding among men, and specially so at this evil time.

10   (125) *The Lion's Mother.* Woe to you, who stir up evils and traffic in trouble, disturber of the peace and remote from the truth! How remote from blame you represent yourself, and how innocent and pure you make yourself out, though you are defiled with corruption, and polluted by frauds and deceit, and
15 smitten with all kinds of insolence.

Dimnah. There are five kinds of men who act without knowledge. One is he who casts ashes on his land instead of dung; another is he who, when his vices are hidden from men, reveals and publishes them through the deceitfulness of his
20 tongue; another is the man who puts on a woman's dress and the woman who clothes herself in a man's dress; another is he who - - in a house which does not belong to him; and the other is he who speaks a great deal, but is not advantaged by his speaking and does not profit from it at all, but (only) brings
25 loss on others, bears no small sin for it, and reaps great disgrace, especially when he speaks of his own accord, no one having asked him to speak.

The Lion's Mother. O ill-starred one and shameless, your cunning and deceit does not silence you, and you know not that
30 you are about to fall into the (very) pit which you have digged (yourself); (126) from the retribution of severe judgment you shall not escape.

Dimnah. Ill-starred is he who cannot distinguish between good and evil, or discern between the things that shall be
35 rewarded and the things that shall be punished, and does not take to heart that which was spoken by the chief of the wise, (namely) 'Let no hateful word proceed from out of your mouth,' and that which is like it, namely 'Thou shalt not bear false witness.'

The Lion's Mother. Think you, miserable fellow, to flatter the king with these words so that he will cause judgment to pass from you and allow your insolence to escape punishment, draw near to your society, and believe your lying words afresh? Know, madman, that all those things are forbidden 5 to your evil nature, and that your greed has parted you from them, and the greatness of your avarice banished you from them; because you put away the fear of God from before your eyes, and, like a ravenous wolf, attacked a man faultless and prudent, intelligent and full of knowledge, and for no fault 10 or offence shed his blood like water in the midst of the king's palace.

Dimnah. He who inherits for himself eternal hell, and plunges himself into the deep abyss of despair, makes his whole man a stranger to the new and undying life and the heavenly 15 pleasures that pass not away and the joys that never end; he, namely, who incites the valiant King to evil, and encourages and counsels and helps him to stain his hand with shedding the innocent blood of the weak (127) and injured, oppressed and without help. In all these things I commit my judgment to 20 God, and to Him I call at this evil time, and concerning His justice I do not doubt.

The Lion's Mother. O insolent and deceitful fellow, turbulent and shameless, if I considered your wickedness and the shame and disgrace which you are reaping by this your baneful 25 transaction, I should not use parables or make a single utterance by word of mouth, because this wickedness of yours outweighs the wickedness of many, and is without equal.

Dimnah. A liar against the truth is he who renders evil things in return for good things, instead of speaking honestly is 30 an accepter of persons, and instead of putting a guard upon his tongue bears false witness. But I, poor one, have kept the truth, rendered what was due, given upright testimony, and not withheld the debt.

The Lion's Mother. And what is this truth, and these dues 35 and debts you speak of, since you are full of deceit and envy, and bereft of all goodness?

Dimnah. Our valiant King knows that if I were false and deceitful, according to the witness of liars, I should not dare to

speak before him or make a defence, and wipe out the truth
from before him. But because I am innocent of the charges
which these babblers and envious men, enemies of justice, have
uttered against me, he will listen gladly to these my words
5 which shall be spoken at the right time, and in the balance of
justice and intelligence mingled with the fear of God he will
weigh every utterance, and find that my honesty, (128) poor
and injured that I am, outweighs all the words that are spoken
before him, by friends as well as strangers, those that are far off
10 as well as those that are near.

Then that valiant one and mighty in power held his peace.

Then the lion's mother did not again open her mouth to
speak at that time, and made no answer, but held her peace ;
especially as she saw that the king inclined his gaze and
15 listened complacently to the speech of Dimnah. And she
feared that perhaps the king, when trying his words and being
captivated by their smoothness and believing them, would
neglect (to inflict) the punishment that was decreed upon him.
Whereupon, she opened her mouth and began to say to the
20 lion: 'He who is silent before his adversary at the time when
he makes his defence before him, acknowledges his truthfulness,
acquits him, and frees him from punishment.' And she rose up
from before him, vexed and angry.

And the lion commanded that Dimnah should be bound in
25 the prison-house until his case should be tried. When Dimnah
had been removed from his presence, the lion's mother said to
her son : 'All your courtiers, my Lord the King, both small
and great, the wise as well as the foolish, are murmuring and
wondering at the matter of this Dimnah, cursed that he is and of
30 evil life, crafty and deceitful, false and vicious. If you did not
doubt concerning the report of him, and were convinced of his
deceitfulness, I should not say a word about his affair, by night
or by day. But since he is versed in smooth words, (words) empty
and false, with which he ensnares the understanding of those
35 who hear them, you are neglecting to take vengeance on him,
(129) delaying to punish him, deferring his chastisement, and
hesitating to destroy him. Especially (do I speak thus), because
he has lost you a counsellor of excellent things, an upright confidant and a true friend, an obedient servant and an admirable

administrator of your kingdom, filling up all your breaches by
means of his intelligence, Shanzabeh the injured and envied.
There never was a time, O my son, when I did not recognise
the wickedness and cunning of this child of perdition. O beloved
of my soul and light of my eyes, staff of my old age and sup- 5
porter of my weakness, a statement has been made to me and
clear information lodged with me—after I had heard that first
report—by one of your courtiers, whose whole man is full of
truth, whose soul is cleansed from all filth, whose purity is free
from all dregs of iniquity, whose person is adorned with all 10
beauties, and who is equal to Shauzabeh in the nobleness of his
disposition and the excellence of his conduct. Therefore, O
valiant King, and blessed in everything, do not delay the matter,
or fear to destroy him, or incline your ear again to hear his
babblings, or lower your gaze to look upon his person, hideous 15
in appearance and filthy of smell, bitter of fruits and hateful in
deeds. For if you listen to his lying words, and he ensnare your
good sense with his flattery, and you neglect to pass judgment
upon him, and encourage his polluted mind, he will return to
his former bad ways and go back to his cunning and deceitful- 20
ness, will corrupt the heart of all your subjects, incite all your
enemies against you, and be able to corrupt the whole of (130)
your army by means of his subtlo plans and deep devices.
Therefore, O my lord, do not doubt in your mind, nor let your
thoughts be divided, nor let your goodness overpower you, nor 25
bring contempt on the nobleness of it: for 'there is no peace to
the wicked, saith the Lord.' And command, my Lord the victorious King, that the destruction of this insolent fellow take
place without investigation and without defence, according to
the sentence which he has reaped for his soul, bitter of fruits. 30

The Lion. It is customary for kings, the objects of men's
praise as well as of their abuse, not to give presents and rewards
without investigation to those who praise them, nor again to
bring down punishment and chastisement without trial on those
who abuse them. And because I know that Dimnah is skilled, 35
and extolled for his knowledge, and energetic in all his ways,
able in time of suffering to console, in time of trouble and
distress to relieve, and in time of anger to appease, and since I
see that these many people counsel his destruction and are

longing for his slaughter, and that all of them as one man are
thirsting for his blood, on this account I am afraid to take away
his life. Perhaps he is innocent and free from all stain and
crime, and by fulfilling the desire of these men I may bring loss
5 upon myself. Besides all these reasons, my conscience pricks
me very much and keeps me from killing and destroying him
without trial, since two honest and faithful witnesses have not
testified (131) to his wickedness, as the divine law requires,
namely that 'At the mouth of two or three witnesses, shall be
10 that is worthy of death be put to death; but at the mouth of
one witness he shall not be put to death.' But now I yield to
your persuasion. Tell me the name of that informant who is
believed by you, that we may consider his testimony and know
about his honesty, that we may pronounce rightful judgment
15 against Dimnah and may exact punishment according to law.

When the lion's mother heard these words, anger got the
better of her and fear excited her, and she said with indignation:
'My Lord the King, my informant was the upright and truthful
leopard, who is faithful and honest with you, righteous and
20 upright.'

The Lion. Calm your feelings, and quiet your emotions, let
your heart rejoice and your soul be glad; because the deceit of
this Dimnah of cursed life appears certain to me and I am convinced of it.

25 The lion having commanded that Dimnah should be bound
in the prison-house, his mother was satisfied and went to her
house glad and rejoicing. The king too rested on his couch.

When the middle of the night was come, Kalilah heard that
Dimnah had been remanded to the prison-house. And he went
30 to him quietly, when he knew that everyone was asleep. At
that time, on seeing him in the distress of the prison-house, and
perceiving the horrible odour that exhaled from those that were
bound there, natural affection waxed warm in his heart and he
sighed for him bitterly. His eyes poured forth sore weeping
35 and his tears coursed down his cheeks with sighing, when he
saw his brother face to face. And he began to say to him (132)
reproachfully: 'Oh my brother, you who have sold your freedom
through your avarice and destroyed yourself wilfully, have
reached the end of your journey and attained to all that you

hoped for, have gathered these bitter fruits from that vineyard
of your own planting which bears husks, and reaped from those
tares which you sowed these stalks void of all life-sustaining
grain. On this account I speak to you angrily, and with in-
vective reproach your madness. For I am in a state of great 5
astonishment and filled with unspeakable wonder when I remember those counsels that I used to give you; for I did not
neglect to correct you, or relax aught of my efforts to admonish
you. But you did not hearken to my words, receive my counsels, or eat of the fruits of my teaching, but continued and per- 10
sisted in your crafty ways, in your perverseness and crookedness
of mind proceeded along a road not clear but full of thorns, and
by your perverse disposition lost all your good principles. Woe
to your knowledge and training which are lost together with
your life, and are wasted. It has been said by the wise, and 15
well said: 'Flee impudence of face lest you be driven out from
the fold, eschew perverseness of disposition lest you be plunged
into the deep abyss, and be not overcome of avarice lest you
depart from life in the midst of your days.' But when I see
you suffering these torments and afflicted with these hardships 20
and distresses, death is much pleasanter than they, and to dwell
in the heart (133) of the earth more endurable than these
buffetings, and pleasanter than this sighing. Especially sweet
and desirable would be to escape from disgrace. But now too
will your own discernment show you that you are knocking at 25
death's door.

Dimnah. From your earliest days, brother, have I
known you speak the truth, and a counsellor of good things
have you been to me from the (first) day that I could discern
good from evil. But I, ill-fated one, have been overcome of 30
avarice, greediness has smitten me, and haughtiness of spirit
has made me fall into the snare of disobedience, so that I
received not your excellent counsels, nor hearkened to your
pleasant words, nor inclined to your righteous commands. But
now that I have come near despair and suicide, I will employ 35
artifices and contend by means of tricks, and fix the words of
the upright like spear-points in my heart. As one who swims
in the sea, am I buffeted hither and thither; (yet) perhaps I shall
find an escape from this punishment which I have brought upon

myself. It has been said by the wise that no one reaps such
dismay, stores such sighing in his barns, or fills his treasuries
with such distresses, as he who receives not the counsel of good
men and of those who fear an evil end. Lo, the bitter fruits of
5 disobedience have filled my mouth with aloes, and I have clearly
received the destruction of my life and the killing of my person,
and am bringing many calamities on myself. For wherefore did
avarice overcome me and greediness destroy me, so that I made
light of my good character, departed from the Creator and made
10 use of deceit, by tricks (134) and devices put an end to friendship, by talebearing corrupted peaceable minds, and through
envy destroyed the poor guiltless ox? What fruit have I
gathered from these things, and what profits have I stored in
my garners? I know not, except it be dismay and distress,
15 shame of face and sighing, the destruction of all my knowledge
and the loss of all my wisdom, and finally, a death of shame and
ignominy, and a wasting death in the middle of my days. As
a sick man, when recovering from an illness, is overcome by
desire for some food which does not suit his illness, and, on taking
20 it, relapses into a (second) illness worse than the first one, so I,
wretched one, have been overcome of avarice and have stumbled
by greediness, and the eyes of my discernment have been made
blind to knowledge; since bitter envy gained possession of me,
so that I became stripped of all that I possessed. These cala-
25 mities and trials in which I am plunged are the fruits of those
tares which I sowed; because it has been said by the wise that
seeds, though hidden in the heart of the earth, must of necessity
at some time or another spring up and be manifested to men.
And now, O beloved and honourable brother, all my knowledge
30 is lost to me, all my wisdom has departed from me, and all my
intelligence has been removed from me. But see; if your wisdom
can attain to some plan wherewith you may help your brother,
lost that he is, oppressed in spirit and despairing, (then) try it,
and help with counsels and stratagems, and neglect not (the
35 matter); because trials from every side have surrounded me,
(135) afflictions and sighs like a cloak have covered me, and
sharp arrows and spear-points have been fixed in my heart.
But nothing is so grievous to me, or dismisses my soul from life
with such sighing and pain, as two things. One is the shame

that I have reaped from the vine of my planting, and the abuse
and mockery which will proceed from all your friends and kinsmen on my account when I am dead. The other, which is worse
to me than all, is that you will reveal all my crimes and show to
everyone the bitter fruits of my tricks, and they will believe 5
you, and continually abuse me, when I am in the grave, wretched
that I am.

Kalilah. The matter is as you have said; because nothing
is equal to life, since it is excellently extolled by men who are
wise and of good conduct. And it has been said by the wise 10
that he whoso mind's eye is blind through fear, by reason of
wrongs that he has done, and whose intellect is confused on
account of wickedness that he has committed, should ask of one
whose mind is pure and the eye of whose understanding is full of
light, whose intellect is clear and pure, and his soul not stained 15
by sins nor his hands implicated in deceit, and as seems good to
that excellent man, so will he counsel. But now all the plans
have come to an end and all the tricks have failed, and the end
is near and despair has arrived. I have tarried long beside you,
and lo my soul is full of alarm, and my reins tremble with fear, 20
and I am about to depart from you, before any one in the
prison-house awakes, and becomes aware of my coming to you,
and I too be made a partner in the punishment decreed on you.
(136) So I give you these two words of counsel which will be of
use to you in this life, and in your latter end clear you of sinful- 25
ness, (namely) that you confess here your wrong and acknowledge your wickedness, and reveal to the king your crime, and
ask pardon of him, and beg all his companions to become inter-
cessors for you. For if they deal kindly with you and accept
your repentance, you will escape punishment, and appear as a 30
penitent in the sight of God. And if they do not accept your
repentance here, nor listen to your supplications, but decree the
death sentence upon you, and put you out of this life by killing
(you), you will go out of the world like one of the penitent,
without fault. 35

Dimnah. I firmly believe these words of yours, brother,
and acknowledge their rightness, and believe in their profitable-
ness; but to put them into practice and perform them, as you
advise, is very difficult for me. Lo I behold and see how

unanimous is the wish of those who investigate my actions, and
how can I refute their words or - - - - - - - .

And Kalilah went out thence, and returned to his house with
a troubled spirit and a sorrowful mind, and a sad heart and
5 perturbed thoughts, on account of three things. The first was
natural sorrow and grief at his brother's decease; the second,
the possibility that his coming to Dimnah might become known
to one of his accusers, who might make him partner with him
(137) in the indictment, that is, in the punishment; and the
10 third, the possibility that Dimnah, when convicted by the truth,
and when all his arguments failed and his tricks came to an
end and all his hope was cut off, might associate his brother with
him in a little of his guilt, so that he might make defence for
both of them, and moderate a little of the intensity of his burn-
15 ing, and retard too the immediate accomplishment of his execution.

While Kalilah was sunk in these anxious thoughts, there
attacked him a severe pain which took hold of his heart and
grasped his breast, and made his belly flow like a flood let
20 loose, and that same night he departed from this life, and with
suffering and distress was his exit from this world by means of
a violent and sudden death.

Now that night there was bound with Dimnah for some
offence one of the king's relatives, who was awake at the hour
25 when these words passed between Kalilah and Dimnah. And
he made as if he were sunk in sleep, and listened to everything
that they said to one another - - - - - - - - and Dimnah
could not deny one of them or contradict them to his brother,
but confessed them all. And the king's relative kept all these
30 words in his heart and revealed them to no one.

The lion's mother, expecting the fulfilment of her son's promise, and craving and longing for Dimnah's destruction, rose up
early in the morning, went in to the king, and said to him:
'Oh valiant King and beloved son, supporter of your mother's
35 old age (138) and answerer of your parent's questions, do you
remember what you resolved in your mind concerning Dimnah
the cursed and ill-starred, hater of the truth and remote from
justice? By his being put to death, great satisfaction will
result to the King, to his forces, and to his subjects. I remem-

ber from your conversation, victorious King, with your companions, that the wise say: "Do good as much as ever you can,
and depart from evil with all your might." O my beloved son,
the light of my eyes and the staff of my weakness, I see that
there is no good thing so abundantly rewarded by God or so 5
laudable in the eyes of men, as the destruction of him who de-
serves destruction. It has been said too by the wise that he who
neglects to punish offenders and severely chastise the insolent,
when he is prince over them, will be partner with them at
the resurrection day in sins and small offences.'   10

Then the lion ordered the judges to try the report about
Dimnah, that the truth about his deeds might be investigated,
while he called God to witness concerning them, lest they should
decline from the path of justice, and divert justice, for a bribe,
or through partiality, or in order to further the wish of others, 15
but that they should judge righteously and investigate uprightly, and make a copy of all the defence that he might make
for himself each day, and bring (it) up to him at even-time.

And the judge assembled all the king's forces and the
captains of his troops, and commanded, and Dimnah was 20
brought into the midst. When they had set him before them,
(139) the leopard lifted up his voice and said: 'You have seen
with your own eyes, O wings and arms of the victorious king,
what sorrow and dismay has come upon the king through the
killing of Shanzabeh. He fears lest Dimnah through envy 25
calumniated him, and stirred up the king, valiant in strength,
to kill him. And the king desires to try his matter; for if he
was justly killed, and punished according to his deserts, Dimnah
is free from punishment on his account, and remote from all
blame for his death. But if Dimnah destroyed him by deceit, 30
and brought about his death by talebearing and slander, on
Dimnah's head his revenge shall fall, and his blood shall be
required of him. Therefore let everyone of you who is acquainted with aught of these two things, disclose it and speak
honestly, and not depart from the truth nor suppress integrity 35
nor withhold what is due, nor turn aside to partiality, nor
again be overcome of hatred, and speak falsely and bear false
witness, for according to the word of your mouth shall judgment
be passed on Dimnah : and the king and the judges shall be

free from his sins. Therefore let everyone of you be in fear of
the swift judgment of the Lord, and say nothing except according to what his eyes have seen or his ears have heard.'

The Judge. You have heard what has been said to you.
5 Therefore let not one of you withhold what is due from him.
For there are three things which this trial will produce. (140)
One is truthfulness of speech, that as we hear from you, so we
may judge: so put not great things in place of small things.
No one is so praiseworthy and great in the sight of God, and so
10 laudable in the eyes of men, as he who reveals hidden things
and manifests secret matters, and reproves and delivers the
wicked and false to punishment and eternal destruction. He
who conceals them when they are evident to him and manifested
before his eyes, let such an one know that he is participator in
15 his sins. The second is that the stripes inflicted on the offender
bring two advantages, (namely) that many will be turned back
from their wickedness, and that the king and his subjects
will be at rest. And the third is that when the whole earth is
cleared of bad and foolish men, the world will abide in peace,
20 and the king be adorned with victory and extolled for valour,
and all the humble live in exaltation and till their land in gladness, and in delight of heart make double their gifts and fruits,
sacrifice praise to the Lord without ceasing, and offer worship
to the Highest at all times. Therefore let everyone of you set
25 God before him, and open his mouth and speak as if you were
standing and speaking before the terrible tribunal of His
Greatness.

Then they all held their peace, and each one (141) looked
down on the ground in silence. When Dimnah perceived that
30 they were all silent, he said boldly: 'Wherefore are you all
silent, and why do you not mention anything that you believe
of the report about me, poor that I am and tormented, troubled
and oppressed in spirit, wronged and envied and without offence.
It is certain too that for every offence there is a pardon, (but)
35 my sin is not pardoned, and this my offence is [- -]; because
I am delivered up to slaughter and death and destruction before
the appointed time. And it is certain that to everyone who
speaks without having seen, bears witness without having
heard, or affirms without being certain, happens what happened

to the physician who was not skilful in his treatment nor wise
in his profession and practice, and began to visit the sick without having been taught the art of healing.

The Judge. Tell us the story about him, and inform us
what he did. 5

Dimnah. In one of the maritime towns in the country of
the Æthiopians was a certain skilful physician, by whose hands
God used to work complete healing, and by his means give
health to many sick persons. He was extolled by all his
countrymen on account of his skill, and honoured by kings. 10
When his end was come, and he departed to his Lord, there
arose in his place a certain ignorant physician, who knew
nothing of the methods of healing. Now the king of that region
had (142) one only daughter, whom he loved exceedingly: and
she was the wife of one of the king's relatives. When she had 15
conceived, and the time of her delivery was come, she was
attacked by pains, and her pangs were severe. So her father
sent and assembled a number of physicians, and said to them:
'Choose me one of you who is skilful and learned in his profession, and ancient of days.' When this physician had been 20
chosen, he directed that a preparation of a certain drug called
zamharān mixed with wine and – – – – that is, shūshān, should
be made for her. And the king directed that a skilful physician
should come and mix the draught. That foolish and ignorant
physician came and said to them: 'I am acquainted with all the 25
roots, and wise too in numbers of drugs.' So the king directed
that all the drugs of that wise physician who had departed from
mortal life should be brought to him, that he might take of
them and prepare the draught. And that ignorant physician
put forth his hand and found a bag containing deadly poison; 30
and not knowing what it was, he said within himself: 'I have
done very foolishly and behaved dishonestly, and placed myself
in a position which does not suit me; for I am very far from the
knowledge and understanding of these drugs. But now what
shall I do? For I am sore afraid of the punishment which I 35
shall receive (143) instead of the gifts and honours which I am
getting (now). For if I delay the matter and say that I am not
acquainted with drugs – – – – – – – and I shall also bring
upon myself disgrace before the king and my brethren.' Now

to confess to ignorance and acknowledge the truth is far easier
and more laudable than recklessly to draw near to slaughter
for want of understanding and knowledge. So he approached
recklessly, and audaciously prepared the draught from the poison,
5 mixed it hastily, and put it in a vessel. When the king perceived his diligence and despatch, he commanded that a costly
robe from the royal wardrobe should be cast round his body,
and that he should be honoured with many presents. On the
following morning he brought the preparation in which he had
10 mixed poison with wine and zamharān and shūshān, and gave
it to the young woman. The moment it entered her mouth,
her spirit went out of her body. And the king commanded
that that wretched physician should drink of the poison: and
the moment it entered his mouth, he too departed this life,
15 through his folly and audacity. This parable I have narrated
to you in order that you may know that if a man says anything
without being assured of the truth of it, bears witness though
his eyes have not seen, and speaks though his ears have not
heard, God who searches the hidden things of hearts will bring
20 upon him what befel that ignorant physician. And it has been
said by the ancients that every one receives a reward according
to his work. And lo I call the Lord to witness concerning
you, and I put you in fear of (144) just retribution.

Then the king's butler, to further the wish of the lion's
25 mother, and being reliant on his familiarity with the king and
on his eloquence and renown, called out with a loud voice: 'I beg
you to look into that which I shall speak before you, with a pure
and candid mind. For the wise have said long ago, that from
the appearance of a man the secrets of his heart are recognised,
30 and his actions revealed, whether they be good or evil. And
you, the forces of the king mighty in power, because that God
the Adorable has filled your heart with wisdom and illumined
your minds with philosophy, must needs try the wickedness
of this crafty liar, and distinguish between what is bad and
35 what is good in him. First (you may do so) from the hideous
appearance of his countenance; next, from the confused talk
of his tongue; still plainer and more evident is the fearful
appearance of his eyes, the proximity of his eyebrows, and the
terrible trembling of his lips, which things are true witnesses to

his cruelty and deceit; and to conclude, the unanimity of many
in hating him. While these hearts of honest men have agreed
together about his case, and all their minds borne witness to his
perversity and depravity, so too have all their senses witnessed
to the sincerity and uprightness of Shanzabeh. Therefore these 5
are true witnesses against this crafty, depraved, and deceitful
shedder of innocent blood.

(145) And one of those present said to the king's chief
baker and butler, peaceably and quietly, gently and not angrily:
'We are not sure, nor do we acknowledge that a man is proved 10
guilty by appearance of face, change of exterior, or hurriedness
of language, or that he is proved innocent by handsomeness of
body. Therefore if you are acquainted with these things, inform
us about them.'

The butler replied with a loud voice: 'Wise men, teachers, 15
and philosophers say that he whose left eye is small and inces-
santly flowing, his gaze extended, and his nose bent towards
the right side, and who is narrow between the eyebrows, and
the locks of whose hair are tangled, who, when he walks, looks
down on the ground and glances hither and thither—when 20
these things appear in any one, he is remote from purity, and
polluted with all wickedness and deceit. Now we see that all
these things are combined in this ill-starred one.'

Then was Dimnah stricken with amazement and stood
wondering. And he opened his mouth and said: ' This calls 25
for weeping and for ridicule. For weeping, because the truth
has been hidden from the whole world, and every man has put
away the justice of God from before him : and on the other
hand for ridicule, because weak men and feeble, are audacious
enough to say that they know that the Most High makes 30
His creatures bad, enjoin false witness, and speak vain words,
running in the way of self-gratification, (146) and walking
in the footsteps of those who are anxious to accomplish their
wish to destroy me, thinking that they are helpers of those
who thirst for my blood, poor that I am, that they may be 35
honoured by them and be rewarded with a thank-offering from
them. But they know not, poor wretches, that they will be
reviled and buffeted by those very persons, since they know
that they have witnessed without having seen, and are speaking

without having heard, and have related without sure knowledge.
Now if it seem good to your Excellencies, O honoured and
blessed assembly, hear what I have to say and listen to my
defence, and in justice and truth judge between me and this
5 speaker of swelling things, and utterer of falsehoods, whether
these things which have been related by this rebel who has
lifted up his heel against his Maker, have been thus ordered by
the wise Creator. Why, if men do not require witnesses in
their dealings with one another, wherefore does God ordain by
10 the mouth of His prophets, saying: "In the mouth of two or
three witnesses, and so forth"? But if instead of this He said:
"Lo I have set you certain marks in offenders, so that everyone
in whom such-and-such marks appear is convicted of such-and-
such offences without investigation, trial, or witnesses; and so
15 too those who are worthy of honours and goodly rewards, when
such-and-such appearances present themselves in them are
worthy of such-and-such honours," then how did He ordain and
admonish, saying: "Judge righteously and investigate uprightly"?
And again : "With judgment (147) and moderation, and so
20 forth." And if, which God forbid, I have done and practised
the crimes of which these insolent and godless men accuse me,
and have committed these bad deeds, still I am not worthy of
blame and reproof, because He who formed me and called me
into existence by His nod, and brought me into this world as it
25 pleased Him, made also these features in my person, and sub-
jected me to these evils. Therefore that I should accomplish His
will and fulfil what He has worked in me is much more proper
and fitting than that I should rebel against Him and not perform
and fulfil everything that He has ordained and set within me.
30 And if I have fulfilled what He has set in my nature and fixed
in my person, I am worthy of honour, and not of ignominy and
punishment : since these marks (date) from my mother's womb,
for they were born with me, and to escape from them I am not
able. And discerning and wise men, when they come to a
35 certain age and these marks are set in them and appear in their
faces, ought to be punished; though they would certainly be
wronged and injured, by the Creator first, and then by His
creatures; for so it pleased Him to bring (them) into existence.
And these signs He placed in some whoever they be, and pre-

pared these stripes for others whom He so created, and delivered
them into the hand of the avengers. But away with such a
thought concerning that good and just One, upright and righteous, that thus He should act and ordain. By these ill-ordered
and shameful things which you have uttered is your madness 5
made known, and the disorder of your mind shown to every man.
(148) Because you have heard something, and not known how
to tell it, and in what manner to say it, and because you have
dared to make yourself out to be wiser than all these prudent
men who are present, your case is like (that of) the man who 10
said to his wife: 'Look, O ill-starred woman, at your own
shameful state first, and afterwards look at your companion's.'

They said to Dimnah: How runs the story about him?

Dimnah. A certain town called Burzgin was taken possession of by an enemy who killed many persons in it and took 15
captive many of its inhabitants. And they divided this spoil
among them. And there fell to one of them a certain peasant
and his two wives with him. Now their lord was sore distressed
by hunger and nakedness; and when the cold compelled him to
go out with his wives into the fields to gather sticks, one of them 20
took a rag, and with it covered her loins. The other woman
said to her husband: 'Do you not see this shameful woman
walking naked?' Her husband said to her: 'O luckless
woman, look first at your own shame and the exposure of your
own loins, and cover the nakedness of your body like her, and 25
then you may speak.

But because, O foolish and worthless fellow, your character
is hidden from the victorious king and from his righteous and
intelligent companions, you dare to approach the table of your
lord; (149) since you are polluted and impure, though you are 30
considered in your own eyes polished and adorned, pure and
smooth, cleansed from all pollutions. Nor is it I alone who am
acquainted with your stench and foulness; but all these present
are acquainted like me. I did not like to manifest your
shame and disclose your hideousness before to-day, because 35
I observed friendship with you; and I did not wish to make
your foulness manifest until all your companions should be
assembled. But now that you have revealed the hatred of your
heart and shown the hidden and disordered things that lurk

within you, and that you have accused me without being acquainted with one of my affairs, I will now speak against you in
justice, and with righteousness and integrity reveal all your foul
spots, that you may not dare to approach the table of the victo-
5 rious king again, or look on his pure and glorious face.

The chief baker.   Of what can you accuse me, O ill-starred
and shame-faced one ?   .

Dimnah.   God forbid that I should say against you anything
of which you are innocent, or accuse you falsely, or through
10 hatred cast a slur upon you, or charge you deceitfully.   But
with uprightness and truth do I show to every man your foulness by the plague spot of leprosy which is between your eyes,
and something hateful besides which I do not wish to mention
by name at this time.

15   When the butler heard (this), he held his peace, and from
the dire suffering of his heart the tears began to course down
his cheeks and he received them in his hands.

Dimnah on seeing his tears and the suffering which tortured
him, (150) said to him : 'Think not, O madman who in-
20 jures himself, that the victorious king will admit you to his
presence, or that you will approach his pure table after this;
nay, but your tongue has banished you from his good things and
named you abominable among your companions.'

Now in the assembled crowd was a certain one named Shah-
25 rah who was upright before the king and faithful, and had been
ordered too by him to be present in the assembly, and to report
all that he heard.   So when the assembly broke up on that day,
and the judges and scribes concluded their sitting, after writing
out fully all that had been spoken among them, Shahrah ap-
30 proached the king and reported first the account of the chief
baker and butler, and then the account of Dimnah   When the
king heard these things, he immediately commanded that his
butler should be dismissed from his office and should not appear
again before him.   When Dimnah had stood before them about
35 six hours, the king commanded concerning him, and they took
him back to the prison.   And the judge wrote out a full
account of him, and reported it to the king.

Now there was a certain jackal who was surnamed Rözbeh.
He was in high estimation with the lion, and dear to him, and

honourable. And he loved Kalilah exceedingly, and was very grieved at his decease. And he went in to Dimnah, and informed him (151) that his brother Kalilah had departed this life and been conducted to his Lord by a violent death, due to his anxiety and sorrow concerning his brother. Dimnah, on hearing (it), groaned 5 heavily, and wept bitterly, and beat sorrowfully on his breast, and said: 'What does life profit mo after that my own brother, pure and beloved, the supporter of my infirmity and rearer of my youth, wisest of philosophers and renowned among the prudent, pure from all stains and remote from all defects, free of 10 all greed and extolled for all excellencies, [has died]? It has been said that when a man is tried by means of affliction, misfortunes from every side press upon him, and the gates of trouble open before him. Oh dear brother, your decease has sore grieved me and your death has made me comfortless. All 15 my defects were supplied by the wealth of your knowledge, and all my pains were healed by the multitude of your utterances, and all my degradation was taken away by your honour, and my fall was recovered through your strength, and my breaches filled up by your might. But now may the Lord give you rest 20 and bring you to bliss, and grant a good end to your journey.'

And he began to say to Rōzbeh: 'Although our sainted brother has departed from me, and left me bereaved and troubled, yet now I have hope and confidence in your Fraternity, that you will be a brother to me in his stead, that in you my 25 loins will be strengthened, that I shall lean upon your love as upon a trusty staff, (152) and that through your care I shall not be disappointed. Now I and he had a few darics in such-and-such a place. If it is convenient to you to go and bring them to me, (do so).' When Rōzbeh had gone and brought the 30 darics, Dimnah took and divided them into two portions, one of which he gave to Rōzbeh, saying: 'This, the portion of my brother Kalilah, take you, who are a brother to me in his stead. But think not that I have given you a bribe, that you may be partial on my behalf, but only a compliment due to your Great- 35 ness.' The other portion Dimnah took for his own use and for his expenses in the prison. And he said to Rōzbeh, when he had accepted the dinars from him: 'When you go in before the king and mention of me is made, I should like you to inform me

7—2

in what terms I am spoken of before him, and what the lion's
mother says, and what the lion answers her.' Rözbeh promised
to do so, and left him.

The day after came the judge and the leopard and all the
5 scribes and all the host of the king's forces, and entered and
stood before the king. And they placed before him what they
had written out of the words of Dimnah and his defence and
the words of the others, his accusers. The king examined all
that both sides had said, and saw that the force of Dimnah's
10 words outweighed them all. And he ordered all the scribes to
copy out those words in two copies, of which one should be
left with him, and the other should remain with the scribes.
Having ordered (153) that Dimnah should be questioned again,
he sent and called for his mother, and read before her the
15 speeches of both sides; and she saw that the words of Dimnah
prevailed over those of his fellows.

Then she exclaimed with a loud voice and said to the king
out of all the indignation of her heart and her hatred for Dimnah :
'If I speak impetuously before you, my Lord the King, suffer
20 it. For I know that you do not discern between what benefits you and what harms you, and between what is for your
peace and what for your vexation. The evil done by Dimnah
outweighs all evils and exceeds all bounds, being more bitter
than aloes of Socotra, and more nauseous than wormwood. And
25 not a thing of to-day is his wickedness and craftiness, but of
times and days and years of long ago. For he has blinded the
eyes of many with these smooth words, and ensnared the hearts
of his hearers by his falseness. With them too would he assuage
the King's wrath and alleviate the punishment due to his
30 wickedness and cunning.' And she went out from the king
wrathful and indignant, vexed and complaining.

During this time, the jackal, surnamed Rözbeh, was sitting
in the king's presence, and saw and heard everything. And he
went to Dimnah and related to him the whole story. While
35 they were yet talking together, Dimnah was summoned to the
midst of the assembly. And he entered and stood before the
judges, that they might consider his case.

And the leopard began to say to Dimnah : 'We have tried
your case, and made an investigation of your deeds, and found

that your craftiness and deceit (154) and wicked works are
as evident as the sun. We have no need of other witnesses after
to-day, because that witness who witnessed against you, is
honest and truthful and remote from iniquity. It has been
said by a wise man that God the Worshipful has (so) constituted 5
actions that the children of this world may be known by them
to those who are kept in the other. We have abundantly tried
your deeds, and all your deceit has been proved to us, and
all your crimes have been manifested to us in the polished
mirror of justice, by truthful and upright men. But because 10
our victorious king is upright and righteous, compassionate and
peace-loving, just and remote from iniquity, he desires that your
words be heard again. He has commanded that they be tried
with uprightness and without delay, and that these things be
done honestly.'   15

    Dimnah. To God glory, and to our king, valiant in strength,
praise and gratitude are due at all times. For God, who loves
the children of men, is acquainted with my uprightness and
knows my oppression ; and the king's heart is in the hands of
God, who leads him as He pleases, nor is anything of the truth 20
about my deeds hidden from our peace-loving king. On this
account he will burn with the fire of his perfection all the forest
of envious and perverse men, even depraved and froward, who
witness lies and utter vain words, and will silence the storms of
their wickedness with the gentle voice of his pleasantness, and 25
put to shame their defiant mind with the balance of his justice. As for you, O leopard, (155) I see that your soul does
not incline to the truth, nor your mind love the investigation of
the upright ; but you are very desirous for the destruction of
upright men, (and) the longing of your soul is for the slaughter 30
of the oppressed, because you are assisting others, and walking
after the will of haters, remote from God, and after the words of
those who run in error and love disorder and confusion. For
you have placed honest men before you like a target, in which
you may fix arrows of partiality and words full of blood, and 35
lying stories and false testimonies; since the dishonesty of sinful
men has been revealed, and the guilelessness of the oppressed
has been manifested. But what shall I say to you ? That in
you is fulfilled that which the chief of the wise said, (namely):

'Woe to those who put bitter for sweet, and so forth.' And
you have dared to say that you have searched my whole case
and have learned all the hidden things thereof, while as yet you
have only been three days at this matter. How can you know the
5 end of my affair, oppressed that I am ? For, though you please
to search into it all the days of your life, you will not attain to
the end of it, arrive at the truth of it, or grasp but a small part
of its magnitude. And it has been said by the wise, that he
who is not furnished with purity of thought (and) character
10 himself, cannot stain the purity of others.

The judge said (156) to Dimnah: 'We find it said in books
that the just judge is he who punishes offenders according to
their offence, and rewards the good according to their goodness.
Therefore I say to you that you will have no rest or happiness
15 in dwelling among these men, whose feelings are so bitter
against you. But I counsel you one thing which is very pleasing
to God, and extolled too and in favour among men, (namely) to
confess the truth and acknowledge your offence, and make supplication for it, and ask pardon of your adversary. Be not afraid
20 of disgrace, nor succumb to chastisement for the truth's sake;
because it has been said by the wise that to speak the truth
and the right, although somewhat bitter now, in the end produces fruits of peace and restores to confidence. But know, O
thou whose soul is distressed and whose cup is bitter, that you
25 are mortal whatever happens, and if you do receive sentence of
death for an offence of which you have repented and made confession, you will have great gain, and your eyes will see au
excellent end, and it will place you with the penitent who have
been accepted, and deliver you from the intensity of torments. It
30 has been said by the wise that to die after a good manner is
better and more comely and beautiful and blessed than a life of
shame and distress.'

Dimnah. You have spoken, O Judge, the words of the
wise and upright, and counselled me as (157) good men coun-
35 sel, and I am grateful to God and to your Verity; but I remember too the words of the wise who say that he whose destiny is
good makes a defence for his life and does not throw it away,
when pure and innocent, while he who charges himself with a
crime, puts an end to it. Again it has been said that he who

hopes that his eyes will see a good end, and that he will be
furnished with a good provision, and despises and rejects things
which are pleasant but destructive, will display the truth with
all his might, establish right and justice with all his ability,
expose deceit and iniquity, and repel it from him as much as he 5
is able. Although he does not heed falsehoods or the words
of liars or the clamour of fools, yet fitness demands that he
should be absolved of the accusations made against him, and
that he should cast them behind him, and not defile his purity
and stain his good character by consenting to the wicked. 10
When a man's innocence is clearly wronged, although ho be
chastised by them and by others, they are a source of praise
and glory to him, and a crown of innocence and a diadem of
righteousness do they place upon his head. What loss have I,
or what ignominy attaches to me, if I am punished for the 15
truth, except suffering for a little while? Then, just as a precious pearl, which the mire or foul clay does not affect, (158)
and which, though it be much besmeared, is not diminished in
beauty or value,—because when it is washed in pure water, all
the foul clay falls to the ground,—so too as to these punishments 20
and threats, when the end comes and the creature is renewed,
the oppressed and injured one appears as a pure image and a
stamp of brightness, while the accuser is revealed as a barbarous
and hideous appearance. I, by the power of God and the assistance of his goodness, many years ago and a long time since 25
despised the things that are seen and departed from all things
transient, and my soul wearied of the satisfaction they gave;
and I grasped the things that abide, and after them do I pursue,
and to fulfil and accomplish them do I strive unweariedly. If,
O Judge, you command me to assent to the words of liars and 30
confess to what I am not conscious of, no evil having been committed by me, and no harm done by me, I shall be like the man
who took a sword and with it pierced himself. And it has been
said by the wise that when a man has not committed a fault, and
acknowledges and confesses to an offence of which he is not 35
guilty, through fear of a prince or by force of persuasion, his
chastisers are freed from punishment on his account, and are not
responsible for his wrongs, but his blood is on his own head,
because his destruction proceeded from the word of his own

mouth. But if any one of you acquiesces in my slaughter, poor wretch that I am, while he absolves me from these accusations and from all delinquencies, this is not reckoned death in my eyes, but only a short sleep, (159) which it pleases and gratifies 5 the chiefs of the people and the king's magnates and the judges of the law (to impose). If indeed I do perish violently at your hands, be it known to you that the just Judge delights not in oppression, nor neglects the oppressed, nor aids the oppressor, nor omits to exact punishment and vengeance from him. And 10 lo I [declare] to all here present without exception, what exact reckonings will be required of you in the judgment to come, and what defence each one of you will have to make for a single word unjustly spoken, and I warn you of that disgrace and shame which oppressors shall inherit, even deceivers and 15 calumniators of the upright, and of those sighs and pains which infidels and adversaries shall bring upon themselves, and of that weeping and gnashing of teeth which shall take possession of the whole army of the wicked, and of those that oppress the weak without a cause. You know all of you that you came into the 20 world naked, and naked you will go out of it; and none of its wealth will accompany you, nor will its possessions moderate the intensity of your torments. Nothing will assist or advantage any one of you except the provisions that accompany you from here, of which the chiefest and most glorious is truthfulness of 25 speech and belief in the living God, and justice and perfect love, and purity and chastity of conduct. For children cannot lessen the weight of your sins, nor can friends and neighbours (160) help you. And all those things which are seen shall cease, and all the adversaries be ashamed. And it has been said by the 30 wise that to the man who testifies to what he has not seen and relates what he has not heard, there happens what happened to the bird-trainer when he made a false and iniquitous accusation against his master's wife.

The Judge. What did he do and what happened to 35 him?

Dimnah. It is said that in a certain town called Mâzârp was a certain honest man, a prefect. And he had a wife called Nahdûbah, who was prudent in mind, beautiful in appearance, and modest in conduct. He had also a servant called Neq', who

was very skilful in the training and management of hawks, and
very valuable to his master. Now this deceitful servant studied
how he might do with his mistress what was not seemly. But
she, honourable woman, had cast over her limbs a chastity like
that of Joseph, and though he made many plans and dealt cun- 5
ningly in his deceitful and lascivious ways, he was unable to
rob the sincerity of her purity. When he perceived that his
hope remained unfulfilled and that his intention was not realised,
it gave birth to an evil thought, and he laid a trap for her by
means of two parrots. For, keeping them apart, he taught one of 10
them to say, 'I will say nothing,' [and the other to say, 'I saw
the prefect's wife with the porter doing what is very horrible to
name.'] The two (161) parrots learned what they were taught,
and he practised them in it for six months. When this servant
of accursed life knew that these two birds had attained a perfect 15
knowledge of the evil lesson, he brought and placed them before
his master while sitting with his wife on their comely and
honourable couch. When the two gave voice, the prefect
wondered at them, and was exceedingly pleased, although he
did not know what they said, because the tone of their words 20
resembled that of the inhabitants of the city of Balikh, while it
bore no resemblance to the tone of the inhabitants of that place.
Then he honoured their teacher and gave him presents and gifts
in consideration of his diligence and care on their account. And
he bade his wife take charge of those birds, and she did accord- 25
ing to his bidding. After a time there came some famous and
honourable men from the city of Balikh. And the prefect prepared for them a great and splendid feast, and furnished it with
many viands. When they had feasted and gladdened themselves
with wine and feasting, the prefect ordered those two parrots 30
to be brought before them. And when they had been placed
before them, they gave voice as usual. And these men of Balikh
who were present understood what the birds said, and were all
ashamed, and blushed, and looked down on the ground. And
one of them began to say to the prefect: 'Do you know what 35
they say?' The prefect replied: 'By your life I do not know;
(162) but their tones are very sweet.' The other said: 'We
know what they say, because they speak in the language of
the inhabitants of our country.' Then the prefect asked
them what they had said. But they were ashamed to tell

him. When he had pressed them many times, one of them
said to him: 'What they say is very abominable and hateful.
But if you will not be vexed or alarmed, we will tell you.'
He swore to them by God that he would not be vexed,
5 and they said to him: 'The language of these parrots is the
language of the inhabitants of Balīkh, and one of them says:
"I saw the prefect's wife with the porter doing what is very
horrible to name:" and the other says: "I will not say anything."
We will not remain in a house where such au abominable thing
10 has been done, nor taste food or drink there, for this is the
custom of our country.' When the bird-trainer heard what the
birds said, he too said, while standing outside: 'I also can bear
the same testimony as they.' And those men heard what was
said by that false witness speaking lies and telling falsehoods.
15 Whereupon the prefect commanded that his just and injured
wife should be put to death. The poor wife said: 'To put me
to death without having seen me do this thing with your own
eyes, or without having known the truth of it from two just and
upright witnesses fearing the justice of God, would be unjust.
20 (163) But if it please you, investigate and try this matter, and
perchance you will arrive at the truth of it. And its investigation is very easy; ask these parrots to say something else in the
language in which they have been taught. If they can say
something else in that language, then this testimony which
25 they have borne is true; but if they cannot say anything except
these two sentences which they have been taught, both you and
these present will know that there is some trickery in this
matter.' Then the prefect summoned the bird-trainer, who had
not heard anything that the woman had said. And he had on
30 his hand a young hawk which he was teaching. Then his mistress said to him from behind: 'O enemy of righteousness and
of your own soul, you did [not] see me doing this disgraceful
thing, and yet have borne witness against me. The Lord judge
between me and you.' Then that cursed one said: 'I have
35 testified to what I have seen.' Whereupon the young hawk
made a dart and plucked out both his eyes before the whole
assembled company. Then the prefect's wife said: 'Glory be to
Thee, O God, who in Thy righteousness and uprightness hast
brought punishment on the liar.'

This fable I have told you that you may know that he who
bears witness to what his eyes have not seen, and relates
what his ears have not heard, will suffer a similar punishment
in this world, (164) and a never-ending hell in the world to
come.   5

This was part of what Dimnah said on the third day. And
the scribes copied out and sealed up the proceedings. And
Dimnah was remanded to prison, where he was bound for seven
days longer, while defending himself.

Then the lion's mother entered her son's presence, and said: 10
'Oh my son, your infirm old mother is sore afraid of Dimnah's
crafty ways. Perhaps he is making some plan for your own destruction; or he will incite your whole army against you and create
a tumult and corrupt the hearts of your companions. And this
present anxiety exceeds the former one. If you leave Dimnah 15
alive, and he does not receive the punishment due to his offence,
then straightway the wickedness of the wicked will abound, and
your kingdom will be rent with a lamentable rent. Nor will
you be able to convict one of them, seeing that you have not
taken vengeance on this deceitful man and shedder of innocent 20
and excellent blood. The upright will abhor your throne, and
not one of them will care again to pay any of your dues, or to
report to you any rumour which may be of use to you and tend
to the stability of your kingdom.'

And she went out from his presence angry, and sent for the 25
leopard and summoned him, and said to him: 'Your position is
very exalted with the lion, and he believes all your words; and
it is incumbent on you, and your bounden duty, to make known
to him all the truth which has come to your ears. Urge him
to exact vengeance for the oppressed, and not to neglect (165) 30
the rights of the poor. It has been said by the wise that
he who denies what is due to a dead person, his due shall be
withheld from him, and he shall call to God in his trouble, but
He will not answer him, and at the last day he shall stand in
shame of face before all.'   35

When she had incited him with these words, he went with
her, and bore testimony before the lion to what he had heard of
the conversation of Dimnah and Kalilah.

That night, when it was heard that the leopard had borne

witness to these things before the king, that relative of the
king who had been imprisoned sent and informed the lion's
mother, saying: 'I am in possession of some evidence, so take
me out before you, and listen to what I have to tell you.' So
5 the lion sent for him, and listened to what he had overheard
of the conversation of Dimnah and Kalilah, on that night when
Dimnah confessed to Kalilah that he had destroyed Shanzabeh
by deceit and trickery. The lion said to him: 'Why did you
withhold this evidence from us?'

10   He replied: 'Because I knew that my evidence alone would
not be received; until at length I heard that another had borne
witness.'

Since two witnesses agreed together concerning Dimnah, the
king sent and they brought him out of prison, and the leopard
15 and the king's relative bore witness against him to his face; and
he was put to shame by the truth, and confounded. Then the
lion commanded that he should be carefully bound and that
they should add to his chains, and that he should be imprisoned
in a narrow place, and should be without nourishment, whether
20 to eat (166) or to drink. And he died in prison in this torment.

The story of Kalilah and Dimnah is ended.

STORY OF THE RING-DOVE.

THE king said to the philosopher: I have heard the
story of the envious and deceitful man who brought about the
corruption of friendly minds and dissension among pleasant
dispositions. Now show me how a man is received into inti- 5
macy by his fellow, and how strangers of alien race win love.

The philosopher replied: He whose intellect is clear, and his
mind sound, and the eye of whose discernment is bright, will
not sell the love of brethren for a great price. For nothing is
equal in value to brotherhood; for a multitude of brethren help 10
to good things and assist in the acquisition of excellent things,
and fill up breaches in times of trouble, and get consolation
in times of distress and rescue from hidden snares and evil
enemies. And their similitude is like that of the crow, the
mouse, the gazelle and the tortoise. 15

The king said: What did they do? The philosopher replied: It is said that in a certain region called Dakshināpatha
in the neighbourhood of a town called Mahilāropya was a fen
abounding in grass and dense with herbage. And there were
many fowlers there. In that region was a certain mighty tree 20
(167) with many branches and abundant foliage. And there
were crows in it. One day a certain old and knowing crow saw
in the distance a man of hateful appearance and gloomy countenance, clothed in rags, carrying a net over his shoulder and
holding a staff in his hand, approaching little by little until he 25
reached the tree. The crow was sore afraid of him, and said
within himself: 'This fellow is not creeping hither except to do
some evil deed, either to me or to some one else. But for the
present I will abide where I am, that I may see what he is
about to do.' And the fowler fixed his net and hid it in the 30
ground, and, having sprinkled a few safflower seeds above it, lay
in wait in a certain place. When he had waited for a little.

while, lo a certain dove called 'ringdove,' and with her many
other doves her companions. And this ring-dove was their chief.
When she saw these safflower seeds, without observing the net,
she was overcome by greediness and alighted with her com-
5 panions, and they were all taken in the net. And the fowler
began to come towards them little by little, slowly and deliberately. Whereupon each one of these doves studied how she
might free herself. The ring-dove said to them: 'Let not each
one of you doves, strive for her companions by herself. But
10 (168) hearken, my sisters, to my advice, and do all of you make
a united effort, and perhaps we shall be able to pluck this net
from its place, and fly with it all together to some place where
we may manage to escape from it.' And they all took her advice
and obeyed her direction, and pulled hard at the net, and
15 plucked it up, and flew away with it, with the senseless fowler
pursuing after them. For the wretched man thought that as
they were entangled in the net, they would only be able to fly a
little way and then fall. Then the crow said to himself: 'I will
go after them and see what becomes of them, and of the fowler
20 and the net.' And the ring-dove saw the fowler coming after
them. She said to her companions: 'As long as we fly over the
open country, the fowler will not despair of us, but will keep
running after us. But let us all fly among the houses, so that
the way may appear intricate to him, and he may despair of us
25 and turn back in shame and disappointment.' And they all did
as the ring-dove advised. And as they flew among the houses,
the pursuit of them became too difficult for the fowler, who
failed to see them again. Then the ring-dove brought them to
a certain hole in which was a mouse, a friend of hers. And the
30 crow flew with them. When they arrived in view of the hole,
the ring-dove said to them: 'Let us alight here.' (169) So they
all alighted in that place. Now the mouse, the ring-dove's
friend, was called Zírak. Then the ring-dove lifted up her voice
and called him by name; and she looked, and lo about a hundred
35 holes were situated at the entrance of his burrow, being required
for sudden alarms. The mouse, on hearing the voice of his
friend, recognised her, and answered her from his hole, saying:
'Who are you?' The ring-dove replied: 'I am so-and-so, your
friend.'

Then he came out to her. When he saw her lying in the net entangled in it together with her companions, he said to her: 'Who made you fall into this distress?'

She replied: 'Do you not know, O Zirak, my friend, that everything that happens to a man is decreed upon him by God? 5 So that these decrees closed our eyes and blinded the eye of our discernment to the snare and the sight of the net. These decrees too showed us these seeds. Do not be astonished or wonder at this, for lo the sun and moon suffer change in their light owing to accidents that befall (170) them, although not 10 set or constituted in their nature. And fishes are caught out of the water and birds in the air. It is that too which causes the weak to succeed when he seeks what he needs, or again deprives the powerful and understanding man of all his knowledge and estranges him from it and strips him of it.' 15

Then Zirak, her friend, began to sever the meshes which held his friend the ring-dove.

The ring-dove said to him: 'First of all, brother Zirak, begin and sever the meshes which hold my companions; and when you have done with them all, then sever mine too.' 20

But Zirak the mouse did not hearken to her nor listen to her words. When she had told him many times, he said to her: 'How excellent you are in not caring for yourself or being anxious for your own deliverance.'

She replied: 'Do not blame me, brother, for what you heard 25 me say, because I have placed my poor self in the position of chief and leader of these doves, and I owe them no small debt, because they are very obedient to me. Also it is my duty to care for them, for by reason of their obedience toward me, God has saved us from the hands of the fowler; and I feared that 30 perhaps when you had severed the meshes by which I am bound, you might neglect to attend to the others.'

The mouse. This only makes me love you all the more, and eager for your friendship, (171) and attracts me to your society.

Then Zirak began to sever the meshes in which all the rest 35 were bound. Last of all she came to the ring-dove, and severed her meshes too. Having congratulated one another on having all escaped, the doves took to flight and returned to their places, and the mouse went into his hole again.

Then the crow said to himself: 'How knowest thou, my soul, that perchance some misfortune will not befall thee, as it befell these doves? Thou needest a brother who will help thee as the mouse helped these doves.' So he approached the door of the
5 mouse, and began to call him by name, 'Zîrak!'

The mouse. Who are you? Give an account of yourself.

The crow. I am one who saw the warmth of your love to the doves, and I too have desired to become familiar with you.

The mouse. You and I have no cause or resemblance to one
10 another that we should approach one another. And he whoso judgment is sound and who is intelligent, does not seek for things except those which correspond to one another, and it is not good that he should desire for things which exceed his strength; for otherwise he is called a madman, just as he
15 who seeks to travel on land in a ship, or in a carriage on the water. How can there be concord between us, seeing that you devour us and that we are food for you?

(172) *The crow.* I am exceedingly astonished at your intelligence, and wonder greatly at your discernment. And although
20 you are fit to be my food, O Zîrak, yet your affection and your society are more attractive to me than all kinds of food; because food is only of use for a short time, and when it passes away from the palate, loses its taste, while brotherhood and intimacy with you would remain for ever. So do not refuse me your
25 friendship, nor repulse me from you, nor forbid me to become your brother, nor drive me away from your society. For the odour of your love has been wafted to me, even though you are concealed from me; as the odour of musk which is hidden and sealed up is wafted, for its natural property does not leave
30 it, until it has delighted many by its fragrance. And it is due to the soundness of your judgment that you should not refuse me your affection.

The mouse. Enmity exists among precious stones, because when they are mixed up together, jacinths, let me say, and
35 emeralds, and others that are like these, they get chipped and suffer damage by this chipping. But when they all remain separate, they remain as they were, without being chipped, and are not injured by the edges. There is enmity too between an elephant and a lion, and sometimes a lion kills an elephant [or

an elephant a lion]. And there is enmity between me and the
cat, and again between (173) me and thee. And this enmity is
without equal, because you are the ones who kill us, while we
cannot harm you at all. Nor is it proper that when a man is
aware of his enemy, he should approach him; because water 5
though boiling hot, [when applied] to fire, is not prevented by its
heat from extinguishing (it), when they come into contact with
one another. An enemy again resembles a snake; for though it
be tamed by the charmer so that he can put it in his garment,
yet a time comes when he does not escape from its bites.   10

The crow. I understand all that you say, but I ask you with
your subtle knowledge and great understanding to try my
words, and to weigh all my utterances in the balance of justice,
and to incline to me the shoulder of obedience, and not to
repulse me from your love ; for my soul craves and longs and 15
thirsts and pants for it. Pray devise for me an easy and peaceful entrance to familiarity with you. For the intelligent and
excellent in knowledge do not repulse the weak from their
society; but they earnestly desire and study how they may
draw many to them. And affection between good men lasts a 20
long time, and is not severed in a moment, while it is formed in
a twinkling. It is like a vessel of gold, which cannot be broken
in a moment, and when it is broken, is repaired and put to
rights in a moment. But affection between bad men is like a
pot-sherd, which is destroyed and rendered useless and good for 25
nothing by the least thing. But he whose intellect is exalted,
and his mind remote (174) from avarice, tests many words by a
single one, though they may not reach his pure ear, while the
proud and ignorant man endeavours (to do so) by many, but is
not profited a whit. And know, brother, that I will not stir 30
from your door, or taste food, until I see your face, salute you,
and enjoy fearless intercourse with you.

The mouse. I have hearkened to your entreaty, and consented to your love. And in order that no-one should ever
make me ashamed about these words which I have exchanged 35
with you, I desired to set - - - between me and you, and take
the Witness to witness; so that if there is a change on your
part, you may not think that this mouse was weak in knowledge
and void of understanding, or that he inclined to the word of

K. F.   8

his enemy because he was remote from discernment, or that his
fall into the snares of deceit and smooth words was so very
deep.

Then the mouse came out of his hole and stood in the
5 doorway.

The crow. What prevents you from coming out? I think
that your mind is not free from the suspicion of treachery.

The mouse. There are two kinds of friendship among the
dwellers in this world. One is the friendship of the soul, and
10 the other the friendship of the hands. And those who possess
spiritual love, which is the genuine love, remote from all deceit
and iniquity and change, [they are the sincere ones]. On the
other hand, those who are bound by carnal and material love,
(175) or seek (for it), those are they who desire, each one of
15 them, to effect some robbery, and what is more than this, for
sordid and transient gains. Now those who seek for carnal love
resemble the fowler who sprinkled a few safflower seeds over the
net so as to catch the birds with them, and sought his own
advantage and not that of the birds to whom he threw the bait.
20 But he who seeks for spiritual love, though he be far from his
fellow, yet is planted in his soul and fixed in his heart by the
influence of his love. And lo I am convinced of that which is in
your soul, and I believe in the truth and sincerity of it; and do
you too have the same faith and assurance. So doubt not, nor
25 let your mind make light (of it), nor say within your soul that
I am far from loving you. Because I know that you have companions of the same species as yourself; and an intense enmity
exists between us and them, as for example the enmity existing
between me and the cat. I fear lest one of them see me with
30 you and kill me.

The crow. It is usual for every friend to be a friend to his
friend's friend, and an enemy to his friend's enemy. And now
everyone that does not seek your society and love as I do, is
debarred from my love, and deprived of my friendship; like the
35 sower of sweet basil, for when it sprouts and grows there
springs up with it something else the smell of which is disgusting
and foul, and the sower at once sets (176) to gather it and burns
it with fire.

Then the mouse came out to him, and they embraced and

kissed each other, and each one rejoiced over his fellow with
great joy.

One day the crow said: 'This dwelling of yours stands by
the road-side, and I fear lest some enemy may pass by you, or
some ill-hap befall you; but I know a certain fen, far from the 5
habitations of men and hidden from the gaze of the multitude,
where I have a friend, a tortoise. And there are many fishes
there of which you may partake, and for me also much nourishment. I counsel you, take my advice and let us dwell near
him, and end our days in peace.   10

The mouse. I too am tired of this place, and am prepared to
go with you. And I have reason to tell you both a story when
we have reached our friend, the third one.

Then the crow took hold of the mouse's tail, took to flight,
and conveyed him to the fen in which the tortoise dwelt. 15
When the tortoise saw the crow, holding the mouse by his tail,
he was exceedingly astonished, and alarmed as well, not knowing
that this crow was his friend. So he hid himself in the water.
Then the crow deposited the mouse at the water's edge, flew
(177) into the air, alighted on a tree, and called to him from 20
within the tree on which he had alighted. When she heard his
voice, she recognized it, and raised her head out of the water;
and they spoke with one another. And the tortoise rejoiced
that the crow had come, and asked him whence he came. So
he related to her his whole story, as well as the story of the 25
mouse with the doves. The tortoise, on hearing the story of the
mouse, wondered at his intelligence as well as the sincerity of
his love for these doves. So she came to them out of the water,
and they saluted each other. And the tortoise said to him:
'How have you fared, and how did you come to this region?' 30
And they conversed with one another pleasantly.

The crow said to the mouse: 'Now relate what you said you
wished to tell us when we should be together; because the
love of this tortoise towards you is like mine.'

The mouse. The first place of abode that I had was in the 35
town of Mahilāröpya, in the house of a certain ascetic. Now he
had no one in the house with him. And every day a basket of
meat and other things was sent to him by one of his friends.
He used to dine from that basket all by himself; and whatever

8—2

remained over he used to take into the house and shut down the
lid. And when he was gone out, I used to jump (178) into the
midst where the basket was, and have an excellent meal from
it; and what remained I used to give to the other mice that
5 were in the house. And the ascetic made all sorts of plans to
shut the basket so that I could not open it, but he was not able.
One night a traveller came to him. When they had supped
together and the table had been taken away, they began to converse with one another. And the ascetic said to the traveller:
10 'From what place have you come, and whither do you intend to
go, and for what reason did you enter this town?' Now the
traveller had gone the round of many towns, and had seen great
and wonderful things; and he began to tell the ascetic one
thing after another of what he had seen in each country. And
15 the ascetic would sometimes listen and wonder, and sometimes
clap his hands so as to scare the mice, lest they should come
near the basket. And the traveller was vexed, and said to him:
'You have asked me to tell you my history, and now that I
begin to tell it you, it seems as if you were mocking me. Why
20 then did you ask me?' Whereupon the ascetic immediately
made apology, saying: 'I have erred in what I have done, but
my story is very extraordinary and worthy of wonder. For
there is a mouse in my house that does not leave me anything
that I do not eat.'
25   The traveller replied: 'Is it one mouse or many?' The
ascetic answered: 'My opinion is that there are many of them,
but that one of them is very wily (179) and cunning, so that I
am not a match for him.' The traveller said: 'There is something here which reminds me of the man who said: "That
30 woman did not change those peeled sesame pods for unpeeled
ones, except for some reason".'
     The ascetic said: 'How runs the story about her?'
     The traveller replied: 'I once lodged in the house of a
certain man in such and such a city. When I and the man had
35 supped, he prepared a bed for me, and I rested from the
weariness of the journey. And he went to bed, he and his wife
with him. Now between me and them was a lattice or plait-
work of reeds. And I heard the man say to his wife: 'I want
to invite my companions, that is, my friends and relations.'

His wife replied : ' How can you invite your companions, while you have nothing superfluous by you, and do not get in anything except what is needed for your household?'

The man answered : 'Let not your heart be disturbed, nor your mind be anxious as to what we possess. Perhaps others 5 would eat it up, and there might befall you what befell a certain wolf.'

The woman said : 'And what befell him ?'

The man said : 'It is related that a certain archer went out one day with his arrows placed in his breast. And he began 10 to shoot and enjoy himself, and killed a gazelle. When he sought to return to his house, there met him on the road a wild boar. And he put down the gazelle that he was carrying, drew his bow, and pierced the boar with a barbed arrow, (180) so that it passed through him owing to the sharpness of the 15 point. The boar, rushing at the man, wounded him with his tusk, and they both fell dead. And there passed by them a certain silly wolf, who, seeing the man, the boar, and the gazelle, lying on the ground, thought that he was about to get plenty of food from them, and said within himself : "I must carry and 20 gather as much of them as I am able and strong enough to; because not praiseworthy is he who despises to gather, and much to be blamed is he who does [not] do so." So he approached the bow, endeavouring to eat first the string attached to it, and to keep the rest for many other occasions; and the string 25 parted from the bow, and struck the wolf severely in a vital part, and he fell dead. This fable I have told you that you may know that he who hoards and amasses comes swiftly to ruin.'

The woman said : ' You have well spoken. We have some 30 sesame pods and some rice by us, sufficient for six or seven persons; see, I will get up early and prepare what is necessary in the morning. So invite to your feast whoever you wish.'

When day dawned, the woman took the sesame pods, peeled them, and placed them in the sun, saying to her husband: 35 ' Watch them (181) and drive off the dogs and birds from them, until they are parched.' And the woman went away to prepare something else, when a dog came and began to eat some of them. The woman, on perceiving it, shrank from the idea

of eating them, and would not cook any of them, but sent them
to the market and exchanged them for unpeeled sesame pods,
measure for measure. I was in the market at the moment, and
heard some people saying : 'This woman did not exchange the
5 sesame-pods that were peeled for unpeeled ones, except for some
reason.' So too I say about this mouse, there must be some
reason why he is so much more powerful than all his fellows and
jumps on the basket. Therefore bring me an axe, that I may
search out his place and know the reason of it. Perhaps there
10 is something hid in the house, which strengthens him and
makes his reins fat." So the ascetic brought him an axe. And I,
during the time that they were speaking with one another, was
in another hole, and not in the one in which I generally lived.
Now I had in that hole a thousand good darics; but I knew not
15 who had put them there. On entering that hole, I used to spread
them out underneath me, and sleep on them, while my heart
was glad and merry, and my soul exulted, my strength was
fortified, and my might strengthened, and my intellect exalted.
When this traveller had digged and reached those darics and
20 taken them, he said to the ascetic: 'These are the things that
have worked on the mouse and made him strong enough to leap
(182) on to your basket; because wealth strengthens the weak,
and gets prudence as well, and increases knowledge. Now you
wish that he may not again be able to leap on to your basket as
25 before, nor be exalted above his fellows.' When I heard what
he said to the ascetic, I knew that it was true, and became
aware of my own weakness, and all my strength melted away,
and the joy of my heart ceased. And I saw the traveller take
the dinars from my hole, and divide them into two portions, one
30 of which he took himself, and the other he gave to the ascetic.
And what fell to the ascetic, he placed under his head and slept
on it. But the traveller from gladness of heart could not get to
sleep. Then I made a plan for the ascetic, namely that I would
not come into his sight, thinking that when he was asleep
35 I should be able to steal the half that had fallen to him, from
under his head, and that a little of my strength would return to
me. So I crept slowly forward until I reached the traveller;
but when I got near the ascetic, the other raised a stick that
was in his hand, and smote me with it so that I felt as if I was

dying. And I crept slowly and entered the hole, with my soul
oppressed and sad. When the pain of the blow had subsided,
avarice overcame me, and greediness impelled me, and I returned afresh, thinking that perhaps both of them would be
asleep, and I should discover some plan.   So I crept again 5
slowly, but when I got to the ascetic, (183) that audacious
traveller who had stolen riches that did not belong to him, and
fattened on wealth which he had not amassed by his own labour,
was lying in wait for me, and smote me a second time with
another blow more painful than the first one.   I fell down 10
as dead, and was seized with a quivering in all my limbs.
And I returned and hid myself in the hole, having renounced
wealth and all that pertains to it.   And I extolled poverty and
all its ways, and my soul eschewed all the material things of
this world.   On the morrow all the mice that used to be 15
nourished by what I threw to them from the ascetic's basket,
were gathered to me according to their former custom.   And
they said to me: 'We are sore distressed and in want; and we
have no one to care for us besides God except you.   Therefore
come with us, and make plans according to your former custom, 20
that we may live and not die.'   So I went with them to the
place whence I used to jump on to the basket, and strove
with all my might to jump as I had been accustomed to do
before, but I was not able.   And all my companions perceived
the change that had come over me, and all those who had been 25
nourished by me held aloof from me; and I saw the insult put
upon me, and how they turned their backs upon me before my
very eyes.   When I saw that they mocked and insulted me,
I said to myself: 'You have no one to honour you or help you,
no brother or servant or friend or neighbour, except when your 30
purse is full, and your good things are plentiful.   And I see that
no love (184) in this temporal state endures or is acquired
except by abundance of gifts.'   And I saw that he who is
deficient in these is cast out, like water in a pool, which is
honoured in summer-time, but when the rain descends and the 35
wells abound, no one takes the water that is in that delicious
pool, and it remains where it is until the earth absorbs it and
gradually consumes it, there being no one to bring water from
another place and cast it in.   And I saw that he who has no

brother or friend is not esteemed among men and his mind not
sound. And he whose mind is not sound nor his profession
of faith in God sincere, does not enjoy a peaceful end either in
this world or in the next. And when a man who is despised
5 and contemned, reckless and unrestrained, loses his wealth, he
is compelled by necessity to make plans for his need and that of
his household, by means of something that destroys him and
breaks down the wall of his faith; and he estranges himself from
God. Among the trials of this world there is nothing more
10 bitter than the loss of property and poverty and deficiency
of nourishment. For the tree which is planted in the earth,
and the interior of which is consumed by rottenness, and its
fruit more bitter than aloes of Socotra, is better than a poor man
who looks and hopes for something that is in the hands of other
15 men. For poverty is the chief of all evils, (155) and destroys,
too, a man's good character, and takes away modesty from him
and gives him a brazen face. To sum up, poverty is the cause
of ruin in both worlds; because want makes a man a cheat and
a liar, crafty and deceitful, an outcast from men and ashamed,
20 deficient in prudence and void of wisdom. When a man is
afflicted with all these things, lucky strokes will not remove
him from trials, or from the evils into which they make him
fall, but (only) cause men to regard him as a shuffler, underhand
and a schemer. In return for his friendship, prudence, and
25 affection, they call him a tale-bearer, crafty and quarrelsome,
wicked and unjust. Then his understanding perishes, his knowledge fades away, and his skill turns to madness. And the loss
of his intelligence and wisdom is worse than the loss of his
goods and possessions. And there is nothing worse than this,
30 that while to the wealthy they are a source of exultation, a
splendid diadem and a glorious crown, to the poor they are
a source of shame, disgrace, and confusion. For when a man
whom poverty has affected is prudent, quiet, and humble, they
make him out a - - - - and call him a deceiver and a schemer.
35 When he is eloquent, they style him a babbler, and when he is
quiet and silent they style him deaf. (156) Since all these
things result to him who is deficient in sustenance, I saw that
death is much better for him than life such as this. And
when he looks to men who are not furnished with good things,

and in whom a noble disposition is not implanted, they increase
the anguish of his heart. Now it has been said that he who
falls into an incurable sickness, while his intimates and relations
are far from him, and is come to a strange place the inhabitants
of which he does not know, and is without hope of escape from 5
the Gehenna of trial, is dead although he seems to live, and
death is to him a source of joy and exultation. Sometimes too
want and poverty befall a man, and he is inclined to put out his
hand to some one, but is ashamed to ask for anything to supply
his need; and so he is induced to thieve, which is the cause of 10
his ruin. For when he thieves, he resorts to lying; and when
he lies, he employs oaths; and when he swears, he departs from
God. And it has been said that enchantment is better than
falsehood, and want better than wealth amassed in an unlawful
manner. I saw too how many misfortunes men bring upon 15
themselves when avarice overpowers them and greediness gets
the better of them, so that they love to amass wealth, which
does not abide with them, accompany them to the next
world, nor save them from the punishment of the judgment.
I saw that they (187) who love it, are smitten by three plagues 20
or evil passions. One of them makes them eager to take what
is not theirs, and thus engenders in them narrowness of mind
and confusion of thought; and another is perverseness of disposition; and another sourness of temper and smallness of soul.
I saw too that the very tranquil and peaceful is he who is 25
satisfied with what he has and lives on his pay. And it
has been said by the wise that there is no understanding
except by searching out matters, nor fear of God except by
departing from avarice, nor renown except by excellence of character, nor perfect happiness except in purity of conduct with 30
others and pleasantness of speech with every man. It has been
said too that there is nothing more praiseworthy and honourable
with God than care for the poor. And to pacify the mind is the
commencement of love, and the beginning of wisdom is the fear
of the Lord, which is gotten by the knowledge of a sound un- 35
derstanding. Then I remained as long as I was able, and
having departed from the ascetic's house, I dwelt in a desert
place remote from the high road. Now I had a friend among
the doves, who gained for me the love and brotherhood of this

crow, and this crow induced me to seek your society, saying
that he wished that we might journey to you, dwell in your
neighbourhood, and feed in your fold. And with him I accomplished my journey to you, because I was tired (188) of solitude,
5 and saw that there is nothing in this world so pleasant and
desirable as brothers and the associating with many, and no
suffering more bitter than solitude and absence of friends. And
I have seen by experience that there is nothing which keeps
him who has it in such peace, and makes him who pursues after
10 it so happy, as moderation of appetite, and a mind devoid of
greed, and that a man should not run and rush after what is
beyond his bare necessity, as his daily food which sustains his
life, and clothing for his body wherewith to cover his nakedness,
and a lodging which is large enough for his stature. And if he
15 has amassed all the good things of this world except those
which we have enumerated -
- - - - - - - and enjoys the sight of them as others who see
them enjoy (it). Now I desire to make you my brother, and
long to associate with you; and I have approached you as I
20 would approach the noble and wise. Do you therefore set me
in your heart and fix me in your mind, just as you are set and
fixed in my heart.'

Whereupon the tortoise answered him quietly and thought-
fully, and began to say to him: 'I hear what you say and under-
25 stand your answers, and see that everything which you have
related is very excellent. However your speech shows that you
are in suffering and oppressed in mind, since you remember
these things which have occasioned you trouble. And although I
have confidence in the excellence of your disposition, since you
30 are possessed of (189) prudence, yet you must not relate finely
without acting finely. For one of the wise has said: 'Count
him a truly wise man, who does a thousand things and teaches
(only) one;' because when a sick man is acquainted with the
drug which would benefit his sickness and cure his disease, and
35 does not make use of it, his knowledge of the drug does not
profit him a whit; for many drugs have a disgusting smell
and a bitter taste. Therefore, brother, let your understanding be the guide of your knowledge, and let your knowledge
teach you to act, and not only to speak. And do not be afraid

on account of the fewness of your goods and possessions; because
the good and patient, the intelligent namely and prudent, are
honoured by kings not for abundance of possessions, but for
plenteousness of understanding and purity of conduct. Just as
all are afraid of a lion, even when he is asleep on the ground; 5
while a reckless man and one without understanding is despised,
although he has much wealth, being like the dog who is continually barking, but terrifies no one. Therefore let not your
soul be afraid, nor your mind be troubled on account of your
being a stranger. Because the intelligent and wise man never 10
comes to the condition of a stranger, because his intelligence and
subtlety of knowledge guide him to the affections of others, and
bring him near to many. Nor does he depart to any place except his intelligence be with him; like the lion, who does not
depart to a place except (100) his strength be with him, with 15
which he terrifies many and overcomes inaccessible fortresses.
[Be true to yourself; when you have done this, good will
come to you, as naturally as water runs downwards. Now
advantage is (only) obtainable by the prudent man, who looks
into things: while the lazy, vacillating man fails to obtain it; 20
just as the society of a decrepit old man does not suit a
young woman. Now it has been said concerning [five] things
that they have no continuance or permanence; (namely) the
shadow of summer clouds, the friendship of the bad, the love of
women, a building without a foundation, and great wealth. And 25
the wise man does not grieve over a small amount of it, for a
wise man's wealth is his understanding, and the good deeds
which he has sent on before him; for he is sure that what he
has done cannot be taken away from him, and that he cannot
be punished for what he has not done. Nor must he neglect 30
the matter of his latter end; for death will certainly come on a
sudden, having no certain time. Now you, with the wisdom
which you possess, can well dispense with any admonition from
me. But I mean to grant you what is due to you from us;
because you are our brother, and what counsel we have shall be 35
given you.'

When the crow heard what the tortoise said to the mouse,
and how she answered him and dealt kindly with him, he
was glad of it and said: 'You have made me glad and conferred

a favour upon me; and you are worthy of being made glad yourself with the like of that wherewith you have gladdened me. Now of all the people in the world, that man has most happiness, whose dwelling never ceases to be inhabited by his
5 brethren and friends who are good, and who has continually with him a number of them, whom he gladdens himself and who make him glad. For he looks out for their interests.

Now when a noble man stumbles, it is only the noble who take hold of his hand (to assist him); just as when an elephant
10 sinks into the mud, only elephants pull him out.'

While the crow was talking, lo a gazelle came running towards them. The tortoise, being afraid at him, dived into the water, while the mouse went away to his burrow, and the crow took to flight and perched on a tree. Then the crow hovered
15 in the air to see whether anyone was hunting the gazelle, and looked, but saw nothing. So he called to the mouse and the tortoise, and they came out. The tortoise, seeing that the gazelle was searching for water, said to him:] I'my hearken to my words, and let my consolation be pleasant (to you), let your
20 soul rejoice, and your mind be merry, and promise your soul good. And though I depart from you, do not fear the terror of anyone, and draw near freely and gladly, and drink your fill of water if you are thirsty.'

When the gazelle heard the words of the tortoise, his alarm
25 abated and his soul rejoiced, and he approached them timidly. And they began to coax him saying: 'What is your history, and whence have you come?'

The gazelle. I used to be in a desert place, and the hunters gathered together against me, and pursued me from place to
30 place One day I saw an old man, the appearance of whose face was very altered, and his eyes terrible. And I was in great anguish and sorrow, and my soul was anxious lest he should take away my life. So I fled and came hither trembling.

The tortoise. Fear not, brother; because through the power
35 of God we have never seen any evil hap in this place, and no hunter has ever entered this region. We will care for you, and you shall be as one of us. And there is plenty of pasture round us. Therefore, if you like, remain with us and be as one of us.

After this, the gazelle (191) found pleasure in their society, and remained with them.

Now their custom was to meet together every day, and to enjoy each other's society, after that each of them had taken some food.   5

One day the tortoise, the mouse, and the crow, were met together, but the gazelle had not come. When he had been absent from them for some time, they became afraid that some misfortune had befallen him.

The tortoise said to the crow: 'The only one of us who can 10 find out what has happened to our friend is yourself. So fly away, brother, and soar in the air and descend and find out what has happened to him, and let us know. So the crow flew swiftly and beheld and lo the gazelle was lying in a hunter's net. And he descended to him, and said: 'Brother, who has caused you to 15 fall into this net?'

The gazelle answered : 'Is it not the hour of death ? But if you have some plan, try (it).'

And the crow flew swiftly to the tortoise and the mouse, and informed them that their brother had fallen into the toils 20 of death. Then they said to the mouse: 'The only one of us who can deliver our brother from the snare into which he has fallen is yourself.' So the mouse set out, and on reaching the gazelle, said to him: 'Brother, what caused you to fall into this distress? For you are intelligent.'   25

The gazelle replied: 'What avails intelligence and knowledge against destiny which is from above, as men say?'

While they were yet talking together, lo the tortoise came up to them.

The gazelle said [to the tortoise]: ' What troubles me most 30 is that *you* have come here: because (192) if this hunter reaches us, and the mouse cuts through all the meshes of the net for me, I can run swiftly away, and the crow can fly rapidly off, and the mouse can hide craftily in some hole : but you, our older brother, who calm us when we are alarmed, and console 35 us when we are sad, what can *you* do?'

The tortoise answered: 'What does life profit when brothers are separated from one another, and friends from their brothers ? There is nothing that profits more, more rejoices troubled hearts,

relieves afflicted minds, and frees the understanding from a
multitude of anxious thoughts, than that a brother should visit
his brother in his sickness, devise a cure for him in the time of
his infirmity, and restore his understanding to him in the time
5 of his fall, so as to bring him up out of the pit and raise him up
from his fall. For if some accident happens to their friendship
and a trial befalls their love, and something destroys their
familiarity, gladness perishes through the misery of their
hearts.'

10   While they were yet talking together, lo the hunter drew
near to them. But the meshes of the net were severed, and the
gazelle sprang up and ran swiftly away, the crow flew off and
ascended rapidly into the air, and the mouse hid himself
craftily; but the tortoise remained alone. When the hunter
15 saw (193) that he was baffled and found nothing except only
the tortoise, he bound him with a cord and carried him over his
shoulder. As he went slowly along, the gazelle, the crow and
the mouse, being distressed and sorrowful for their brother the
tortoise, that counsellor of excellent things, gathered together,
20 saying: 'How can we manage to rescue our brother, prudent
and intelligent that he is?'

The mouse, being sorrowful and oppressed, said to them: 'I
see that I never put an end to one hardship, but I fall into something that is worse than the first. He spoke truly who said: "As
25 long as a man does not stumble - - - - - - - his progress is
good, but when once he stumbles - - - - - , he keeps on
stumbling with it, and cannot avoid the stones, whether he go
slowly or quickly, and whether the road be smooth or rough."
Was it not my evil destiny which parted me from all my
30 possessions, and removed me from all my neighbours, and made
me a stranger too and remote from all the members of my
household and the children that I brought up? And now a
second time does it bereave me, and deprive me of the society
of this excellent friend and beloved brother, and from his
35 sincere love, and has put me far from him whose love was
warmer and inflamed my heart more than the love of children,
and was more sincere too than that of my blood relations; a
love remote from deceit, and a love clear of guile, and a love
that knew no greed, a love that was perfectly harmonious, a

love that was perfected in the fear of (194) God, a love that only death can sever, a love not to be sold for (all) the gold of the world or jacinths of the sea. Woe to this body which trials cleave to and sufferings enwrap; for its joys cannot be ensured, nor its pleasures secured, and its distress and misfortunes 5 cease not, and it is continually being turned aside from meritorious things to bad things, from its joys to miseries and distresses, and from tranquillity and peace to trouble and sadness. And the separation of brothers is like an ulcer on a man, which, when he has not arrived at complete health and is 10 still weak, by some little thing which happens to him is intensified, and a number of plagues succeed to the first one. My former sicknesses which I have enumerated to you were not sufficient for me, but I must have this sickness added to me, the pain of which is more severe and its affliction more bitter than 15 all my (former) sicknesses; for it is a plague that cannot be healed, and a suffering that will not cease, a distress without consolation, (even) the fall of our excellent friend and innocent associate and praiseworthy brother and the beloved of our soul, and one precious for his intelligence, the tortoise all free from 20 pollution and remote from all wickedness, by the hand of this audacious pitiless hunter.'

The gazelle and the crow replied: 'These words will not avail the tortoise anything; but try, brother, your subtle devices, and employ your healthful remedies, until you draw up 25 our brother out of (195) the pit into which he has fallen. Because it has been said, and well said, that by the furnace of misfortunes the strong man is distinguished from the coward, the vigorous man from the lazy one, and the clever man from the stupid one. Again, the upright man is distinguished 30 from the unjust one by means of giving and taking, and children and their mother are tried in times of poverty, and brethren and friends are known in trial.'

The mouse replied: 'It seems to me, brother gazelle, that you should go and lie down where the eyes of that evil hunter 35 will see you, as if you had received a severe wound from some audacious man, and let this crow come and settle upon you, as if to lick your wound: and when this hunter of wretched mind sees you, he will let go the tortoise and run after what he will

not catch. Whereupon I will manage to release the tortoise from his bonds; and when the hunter gets to you, jump up from the place and retire slowly, that he may have an opportunity of pursuing you, and that I too may be able to sever the
5 meshes in which our dear friend and beloved brother, the tortoise, is entangled.' And the gazelle and the crow did as the mouse had told them. And when the hunter saw them, he let go the tortoise out of his hands, and ran after the gazelle. Whereupon the mouse drew near (19G) and severed the meshes in which
10 the tortoise was entangled, and they were all saved. When he saw that he was disappointed of all of them, he was ashamed, and feared too with a great fear, and left that region and went to another. And the gazelle, the tortoise, the mouse, and the crow, approached one another with great joy, and embraced and
15 kissed each other. And they ended their lives in joy and peace abundant.

When I beheld and saw them all, O my brethren and friends, and considered the smallness of their stature and their insignificance, while each of them could deliver his companions,
20 I wondered exceedingly and said to myself and to all intelligent persons as well : 'How much more should each one of us be smitten with this love, perfect namely and pure, and seek friendship with many, and receive into friendship those that are far off.'

25 End of the Chapter of the Ring-dove, which shows the love and friendship existing between those who are remote (from each other).

STORY OF THE OWLS AND THE CROWS.

THE king said to the philosopher: I have heard the fable about brothers, and how they make friends with one another. Their concord is beautiful in my eyes. Now give me an example of an enemy whom no one should approach, even though 5 he show him a friendly face.

The philosopher answered: When a man believes a cunning foe, there befalls him what befell the owls at the hand of the crows.

The king said: What befell them, and how runs (197) the 10 story about them?

The philosopher answered: It is said that in a certain mountain was a large wood, full of big trees and abounding with pasturage. And there was a large rookery there in which were a thousand crows; and one of them was their king. 15 In that wood too were a thousand owls, one of whom was their king. One night the king of the owls went forth with his army, and fell upon the king of the crows and his army, and killed many of them, and tore and wounded those that were left. When day dawned, the king's herald proclaimed and assembled 20 all the crows to him, and he said to them: 'Do you not see what has happened to us at the hand of this king of the owls, and how many of you have perished, and how many a one is wounded or has had a wing broken? There is nothing more bitter than this calamity, or worse than this, namely that these 25 insolent ones have got to know your abode, and recognised your weakness, and learned your number. I am very much afraid of them, lest they constantly lie in ambush for us, until they take away our lives. Now gather all your wits together, and take thoughtful counsel with one another, and see what device we 30 may frame for each other's benefit, so that we may be delivered from their wickedness.'

K. F.   9

Now in the whole camp of the crows there were only five
(198) who were prudent in their understanding, and skilled in
their knowledge, and who filled up the king's breaches by means
of their counsels, and supplied the deficiencies of their com-
5 panions by their plans.

The king said to one of them: 'What do you think we ought
to do, brother?'

The first one said : ' Wise men and teachers said long ago
that the only thing (to do) in the case of an enemy when he is
10 powerful, is to remove far from him.'

The king said to the second one: ' What do you think
advisable?'

He replied : ' I do not think it a good thing that we should
fly from where we are, and satisfy the wish of our enemies, and
15 become a source of mockery and ridicule.   But I think that we
should all assemble together, prepare ourselves to do battle with
them, and choose us a number of men who shall surround our
camp day and night, and if they perceive the enemy approaching us, let us know (it), that we may all be prepared to fight
20 and contend with them.   And if they are going to contend with
us, we will place each of our men opposite one of theirs. If God
gives us the victory over them, how good and excellent (that
will be); and if, which God forbid, we find ourselves vanquished,
we shall be blameless, because we shall have fought for our
25 lives. If again it is possible for us gradually to treat with them,
until we get deliverance, or to put some plan into operation, or
to deal craftily, (good and well).'

(199) The king said to the third: ' And you, what do you
think we ought to do?'

30   He replied : ' I do not think we should act on the two
counsels which our companions have given, but that we should
select some prudent and intelligent persons, well-instructed and
peaceable, that they may mediate between us and them, and
ascertain how they feel towards us, and see whether perhaps
35 they would like to make peace with us. And if they are inclined to take tribute from us year by year, let us not disdain or
be ashamed to give it; because kings when they behold their
enemies and see that they are mightier than themselves in
strength, incline to peace, and do not destroy their forces, or

amass gold and silver, which profit not without peace and the
security of their subjects.'

The king said to the fourth : 'And you, what do *you* think
about this peace which your colleague has counselled ? Shall we
incline to it or not ?'   5

The fourth answered: 'I do not think that this is commend-
able, because the wise and noble, sound in mind and skilled in
knowledge, do not incline the neck and bend the knee to foes,
lest they lose their dignity, fall from their glory, and reach a low
estate. But I think we should submit and bear hardships and 10
drink bitter draughts, and put up with scarcity of food and drink,
and be watchful and not asleep, and not disgrace our good character. For I am sufficiently acquainted with these enemies to know
that even if we treat them in a conciliatory way, and attempt
to make peace with them as he said, (200) they will neverthe- 15
less deal greedily with us and demand large concessions from us.
It has been said, and well said: "Only conciliate your enemy to
a small extent, so that you may try his disposition and search
out his intentions, without his knowing the secrets of your heart
or the - - - of your mind, lest you appear small in his eyes. 20
Nor again must you vaunt yourself before him, so that perhaps when you incline the shoulder to him, he may immediately consent and incline to peace. But if you deliver yourself
wholly into his hands, he will be angry with you, and your
power will be small in his eyes, and he may refuse to take small 25
concessions from you ; like a post which is fixed between you
and the sun, for if you put it but a short distance from you, you
will perceive how very long is its shadow, but if you put it close
to you, it will not show any at all." And this enemy, as my mind
testifies to me, will not take small concessions from us, but will 30
demand high and large things from us, more so than at the
time when he fell upon us, and got to know the size of our army,
and spied out all our strength. Nay but we must submit to
him, and if his wickedness overcomes him, and he wishes to
make war with us, we must get our arms ready.'   35

The king said to the fifth : 'And you, what do *you* think
advisable ? Shall we make war with him or bring about peace ?'

He replied : 'I do not think that we should make war with
one whose nature is higher than ours. Because he who does

9—2

not know himself and is not acquainted with his own size, and
advances against his foe, and is willing to make war with him,
without knowing how weak he is, this man deceives himself,
(201) and is not reckoned among the wise. I am very much
5 afraid of these owls, and I do not advise a battle with them; because my reins were in sore trembling even before we sustained
this defeat at their hands. For he who is intelligent, prudent
and skilled in knowledge, shrinks from his enemy and does not
trust or believe in his deceitful ways. And although he see
10 him incline his look towards the ground, let him fear lest perchance he be about to lay an ambush. And no one is more
praiseworthy, excellent, and intelligent, than he who shuns fighting, because fighting causes no small loss both in the way of
expenses and of lives which cannot return in this temporal state,
15 but only after the regenemtion. So let not a battle with the
owls occur to your mind or be imagined in your thoughts; because he who approaches an elephant flies away at the very
breath of his mouth.'

[The king said: 'If we do not make war, what ought we to
20 do?']

His counsellor replied: 'Let us consider and see; because he
who takes counsel does not fall, since he asks such things as
these of the prudent and wise, but is able to attain to what
cannot be acquired by force and might. And since he gathers
25 his confidants from the excellent that are in his kingdom, these
open to him doors that are shut, and these are able to fill up
breaches by the subtlety of their intelligence and their depth of
thought. For he does nothing beyond (202) what becomes
subtle intelligence, and nothing is incomprehensible to him,
30 since he considers it with a sound mind. Because he weighs in
the balance of his intelligence and tries in the furnace of his
discernment the helpers that are in his camp and the warriors
that go forth with him to battle, and fortifies the armour and
apparatus which are suitable for war, whether he wishes to
35 advance or whether it behoves him to retreat. He who conducts
his affairs thus, never makes a mistake, and degradation never
comes upon him, and he cannot fall. But he who neglects the
trial of these things and their investigations, although he may
conquer in war for a short time because strength from above is

with him, is not praiseworthy or well instructed, and his affairs
will not succeed, for at some time or other, when he has got a
trifling victory over his enemies without looking out into the
future, an ambush of his enemies falls upon him from behind,
and he falls into the snare of punishment from the enemy with 5
whom he is fighting and the ambushes that fall upon him from
behind, and between the two he perishes. And you, O victorious King, are valiant in strength, adorned with all knowledge,
skilled in all useful things, and acquainted with the whole
management of the kingdom. And some of these matters it 10
behoves us to speak openly and some of them in secret. Since
you demand my counsel, namely that which may be openly
stated, it is this: while (203) I am afraid of war, at the same
time I do not like or advise inactivity, from which would result eternal disgrace. For the wise and intelligent man who 15
knows the truth must expect death, and not that he will remain
in opulence and ease, since sadness and sighs surround him.
And I think that we ought not to remain in a state of negligence
or keep delaying or be guilty of remissness, else we shall be
abased and fall into the pit of destruction; because from remiss- 20
ness and abasement springs corruption, and from corruption
punishment befalls (a man). And that which it behoves us to
speak in secret should be concealed and hidden in the heart of
the earth, and ought not to be heard except by four ears. For
it has been said that kings do not attain to the things which 25
they need, or subdue their enemies, except by secret meditation
and subtle investigation. And the secrets and confidences of
kings are only divulged by stupid fellows who are in his army,
and by unwise men who are his confidants, and by dull-witted
messengers and puzzle-headed scribes. But if the king has an 30
intelligent confidant and a wise counsellor, sometimes he conquers
in two things. One is that he overtakes his enemies, or that
he is delivered from shame and confusion. And he who secretly
meditates doing something cannot dispense with an excellent
confidant and counsellor and a statesman (204) remote from all 35
avarice and skilled in all truth. Although he who takes counsel
may be prudent and sound in mind, yet he derives assistance
from his counsellor, and reaps knowledge and learns plans (from
him) which perhaps would not be found with him (otherwise);

like fire which burns the brighter in proportion as · · · assist.
And when the man who takes counsel does not doubt concerning the word of his counsellor, his affair is crowned with success;
and (even) if it happens that he gives counsel which does not
5 completely restore peace, the one who asks counsel should not
reprove him; like the enchanter who, when he begins to divine,
coaxes and flatters the demon into doing some evil to a man, for
when he is become skilful in his craft, he should not be blamed,
even if his attempt does not turn out well.   And although our
10 King is valiant in strength, skilled in knowledge, and exalted
in conduct, yet a secret which is between two should not be
between three.   And some things are confounded by many
counsellors, and some things are only to be heard by two
speakers, and such is this matter of yours.'
15   The king, on hearing these things, rose hastily from his
place and sat apart, and called the counsellor to him alone, and
they two sat together.
       (205) The king said to the crow: ['You have seen and
heard many things. Do you know how enmity arose between
20 the owls and us?'
       The crow.] Yes, my Lord, I know.
       The king. What happened that their hatred waxed so
strong?
       The crow. (It arose) from something said by a certain crow
25 who was deficient in good sense.
       The king. What was it that he said?
       The crow. It is related that all the birds were gathered
together, and seeing that they had no king, they considered
and took counsel together, and settled and agreed to set up as
30 king over them one of the owls. As they were gathered together, there entered among them a certain silly crow and took
his seat with them. They said to one another: 'This crow is
prudent and wise in knowledge, and full of tricks as well; come
let us take counsel with him and see what he says.' So they
35 approached him and asked his advice.
       The crow said: 'If all the birds were gathered together, and
the peacock, the crane, the goose, and the dove (were missing).
it would behove you rather to remain without a king than that
an owl should reign over you. For he has a bad nature, keeping

his anger and hateful in appearance, of shameful life, deficient in intelligence, lacking in sense, foolish of understanding, (206) greedy and vaunting, and what is worse than all these, hating cultivated land and loving ruined places, hard to hear and a flitting spectre. He can conceal nothing in his heart, but 5 shameful words proceed unceasingly from his mouth. Remote from all love, a stranger to all fear of God, bereft of all good principles, destitute of all comely things, void of all good qualities (is he). In the day-time he does not see much, and at night he does not fly well. If your good nature compels you, and you 10 are overcome by liking for him, then only allow him to be king in name, and do you yourselves conduct the government of the kingdom but - - - - - - - - - - as the hare did, when she said that the moon was her king.'

The birds said: 'How runs the story about her?'   15

The crow. It is said that a certain place abounded with elephants, but lacked water, for a lake that had been there had disappeared, and its springs had dried up. Suffering from severe thirst, the elephants assembled together and complained to their king; who, thereupon, sent his confidants and the secretaries 20 that were in his camp to explore the land and seek for water. One of his messengers returned and said to him: 'I have found in such-and-such a place a mighty lake in which there is clear and pleasant water, and it is called the Lake of the Moon.' So the elephant brought all his camp to the lake to drink water from 25 it. (207) Now the king of the hares was there, and all the host of them with him. And the elephants, coming at night, trampled on a number of hares and killed them. When day dawned, those of the hares that remained gathered to their king and said: 'You know, O King, valiant in strength, how many of 30 our companions have perished, and how many of our brothers and kinsmen have died through these audacious and pitiless elephants. Pray now frame some plan for us which shall deliver us from their wickedness, that they may not return to this district and destroy this little remnant of us which is left.'   35

The king answered: 'Let all the faithful, prudent, and wise counsellors that are among you be gathered together.' When they were all assembled, they selected one called Pērōz, with whom the king was acquainted, knowing his intelligence and

the subtlety of his knowledge. This Pēróz said to the king: 'If it seems good to our victorious King, let him send me to this king of the elephants and send (with me) a man who is trusted by our victorious King, that he may hear my words and see what 5 I do with the elephants, and report to the King what he hears with his ears and sees with his eyes.'

The king said to Pēróz: 'You are my trusted one and honest. Go to the elephants and say to them as you think fit; because a messenger, when he is wise and intelligent, (208) does as 10 he himself sees fit. But as far as you can, accomplish your work in a gentle way, and perform your business with understanding.'

And Pēróz set out one moonlight night, and fearing to approach them lest perchance they might trample him with their feet, went and stood on a height which looked down on the 15 elephants, and lifted up his voice and said: 'O king of the elephants, puffed up by your strength and treading on ground that is not yours, hear what the moon says to you; and be not offended at the words of messengers, because a messenger is not to be blamed for what he is ordered to say, for as he hears so 20 does he repeat the message, and though what is spoken may be unpleasant, the unpleasantness of it must be charged on the sender and not on the bearer.'

The king of the elephants replied: 'What you say is true. Speak now as you have heard from the person who sent you, 25 and fear not.' Pēróz answered: 'The moon says to you: "When one is puffed up by his strength, and makes boast of his might against the weak, his strength will be a source of harm to him and the cause of his fall. Because you have trusted in your strength, come to my pool, disturbed it with your host, and drunk 30 water wrongfully and not lawfully, insolently and not rightly, lo I witness against you that if you return again and come near this pool, I will darken the light of your eyeballs, and take away the life of you and of all your companions." And if, O king, you doubt about the truth of my words, come with me to the 35 pool, that you may see the matter plainly.'

So the king of the elephants set out (209) with Pēróz, and they arrived at the pool and saw in it the reflection of the moon.

Pēróz said to the king: 'Take some of this water into your mouth and wash your face and mouth well, and then you shall

speak with the moon, first making obeisance to him.' When
the elephant had lowered his trunk and put his mouth into the
pool, he drew it up hastily, saying to Pĕrōz in alarm: 'How is it
that I see the moon trembling? perhaps he is vexed that I have
put my mouth into the pool of water.'   5

Pĕrōz replied: 'Even so, truly he is vexed.'

Then the king of the elephants speedily made obeisance to
the moon and began to make apology for his offence, saying: 'I
will not do this thing again, nor will I return to the pool.'

Besides these things which you have now related, the chief 10
of the owls is set on the destruction of the noble, and smitten
with perversity of mind and frowardness of disposition. And
there is nothing worse or more grievous than kings when they
rule their subjects with deceit and frowardness and flattering
speeches which are smoother than oil but more bitter in their 15
stings than barbs smeared with deadly poison, and induce the
simple by means of such words as these to approach them, and
then bring them to ruin, as happened to the hare and the
sparrow when they referred their dispute to the cat, who, when
they had taken his counsels (210) and believed his words when 20
he told them that he was an ascetic, killed them both.

The birds said: 'How runs the story about them?'

The crow. I had a neighbour, a sparrow, whose hole was
under the tree in which my nest was. I constantly enjoyed his
society because of our nearness to one another. After that, I 25
lost sight of him for a long time, and thought that some mishap
had befallen him and cost him his life. Then came a certain
hare and dwelt in the place in which the sparrow had dwelt,
and I did not hurt him or prevent him from living there, because
I despaired of the sparrow, [But after a time, the sparrow re- 30
turned] and came thither. Finding the hare there, he said to
her: 'This place has been mine for a long time past; therefore
depart from it that I may dwell in it.'

The hare. The place is in my possession; you are only a
beggar.   35

The sparrow. The place is mine and I have an upright
witness (thereto).

The hare. First seek out a judge, and then get ready your
honest witness.

The sparrow. There is here a place in which dwells a certain old cat, who fasts and prays, does not injure a creature or stain his hands with bloodshed, whose (only) food is porridge and rain-water. Come, let us go to him, that he may be judge
5 between you and me.

So the two proceeded to the cat, who, when he perceived them coming, stood on his feet to pray. When the hare saw him, she wondered at him, and marvelled. And they approached him, trembling (211) at his majesty and quaking at his gran-
10 deur. And they begged him to be judge between them; but he answered them nothing, but made long prayers and supplications. Again they supplicated him, saying: ' For the sake of God hearken to our story and settle our quarrel, because God has praised the peace-makers and magnified the wisdom of those
15 who reconcile brothers more than that of those who are always praying.'

Then he turned to them saying: 'Relate your affair to me, and have regard for the truth.'

When they had related the whole of their story, he said to
20 them: 'Because old age has come upon me and labours have weakened me, and my body is burdensome to me through fasting by day and watching by night, I do not hear readily what is related to me at a distance; if you please, come near me to relate your story. Above all [banish] falsehood from among
25 you, and let neither of you tell his story unless he be mingled with the fear of God and remote from all deceit and separate from iniquity, that we may find a physician who will cure your malady with ease.'

So they came near him and related their story to him. He
30 answered them : ' Now I understand what you have narrated. Listen now my brethren to my words and receive my counsel, and with a clear heart remote from iniquity, and with a mind strained from the dregs of wickedness, hear my commands, and get glory and a good name rather than all perishing wealth;
35 because it has been said by the wise that (212) a good name is better and more praiseworthy than good oil. And let each of you seek only for truth and uprightness; because he who seeks for uprightness and righteousness void of deceit, succeeds and becomes great. And although his rights be withheld from him,

and he be wrongfully deprived of his due through the wickedness of an iniquitous judge, yet he who does the wrong will be
put to shame and confounded, even though he be praised and
favoured unjustly by the iniquitous judge who does not fear
God &c.   And he who lives in this world has no wealth or pro- 5
perty or brethren or relations that will cleave to him so long, or
grant him such a safe ending in the next world, as the perform-
ance of good works, the sweet and pleasant fruits that are sent
on before him, and the good provision with which he is provided
in the way wherein he is about to travel, even with kings 10
and commoners, the rich as well as the poor.   He who considers
these things and the change which comes upon the things of
this world, despises all his temporal comforts, and does not
weary himself to get what is beyond his (bare) necessity.   And
he who pursues after amassing what is destined for others 15
- - - - - - - - - - - - - - - - - For gold which is placed in the
heart of the earth is [only regarded] by the faithful and those
that fear the justice of God, as a stone which sometimes falls on
him who bears it and destroys him, while sometimes he falls
upon it and breaks his limbs, or again as (213) the love of a 20
woman, the stings of which are like a viper's.   And each of you
should feel towards his fellow just as he himself likes others to
feel towards him, and should seek to please him just as he seeks
to be pleased and honoured by others.'

    By saying many such things as these, he ensnared the hearts 25
of the hare and the sparrow, so that they both took their staud
before him, when, leaping on them, he killed them both.

    The crow replied to his first narrative, saying: 'All these
things that you have related and more besides are to be found
with the owls; therefore let not this fellow reign over you.' And 30
all the birds believed what the crow said and took his counsel,
and drove away the owl, after they had promised and agreed
that he should reign over them.

    The owl who had been chosen king and (then) driven away
said to the crow deficient in knowledge: ' You have sinned against 35
me exceedingly and completely ruined me, though I do not remember ever having sinned against you or against one of your
companions in anything, whether small or great. Why have you
acted towards me thus? But know, O man of false love, that

by axe and hatchet great trees may be cut, and yet afterwards
bear fruit and grow, and that swords may cut men's flesh, and
yet afterwards it may be healed by drugs and restored to health;
but what is cut by the tongue and severed by the lips can never
5 (214) grow again, nor can a wound inflicted by them be cured.
And an arrow-head fixed to an arrow, when it parts from it and
buries itself in a man's flesh, can be taken out and its place
healed up; but a word when it enters the heart cannot come out
again. And fire when it blazes forth and mounts up and burns
10 can be extinguished with water; and the intensity and malignity
of deadly poison abates under the influence of the oil of oxen
and the milk of mountain goats; and patience allays the intensity of griefs, and the word of consolation drives away distresses.
But the fire of anger cannot be extinguished, nor the bitterness
15 of wrath turned to sweetness. Now be it known to all the race
of crows that you have sowed bitter seeds in the field of the
owls, and when they grow up, their fruits will be manifest.'
And he departed and went out angry and threatening.
    Then the crow perceived his folly and was sorry for the
20 foolishness of what he had said, and he chided himself saying:
'I have been very foolish and more than very foolish in what I
have done. For I have established enmity between us and the
whole race of owls. Specially - - - my foolish self, because I
doubt not that among the birds assembled was someone more
25 prudent than I, and far more discreet and more skilled in knowledge and more furnished with good counsel and more profound
in mind than I. Wherefore did I dare, foolish and stupid that
I am, to open my mouth and speak before them all, and get this
enmity for myself and bring (215) this sighing upon myself and
30 my companions? For a man is not praiseworthy when he makes
an enemy, and glory and praise is due, not to him who knows
how to speak (only), but to him who knows how to act first and
then how to speak and teach. And although disgrace may come
upon him for a time, yet when he reaches the end, he reaps
35 glory. But he who knows how to teach and speak, [and not how
to act,] although what he says may be pleasant to him who hears
it, yet when he - - - the end, he is indeed reviled and inherits
shame. And I am one who knows how to speak and not how
to act. I have not obtained a good result, because my wretched-

ness and evil destiny induced me to speak that which does not incline to peace and is remote from all friendship; since I took counsel of no man, nor did the speech of any one incite me to what my lips uttered and stammered out. He who does not take counsel of the intelligent and prudent, speedily falls into 5 the pit as I have fallen now. Wherefore did I need this damaging transaction, bequeathing sorrows and troubles, even anxiety and sighing of heart.'

With these words and more also did the crow chide himself and rebuke the feebleness of his knowledge. (216) Then he 10 went his way, sorrowful and sad.

This, O King, is the cause of the enmity which exists between us and the king of the owls.

The king. Now that you have finished your speech, tell me what is profitable for us to do, that we may deliver ourselves 15 from the wickedness of these enemies; for anxiety about them oppresses my soul.

The crow. That we should do battle and wage war with them does not commend itself to me, and that we should humble ourselves before them my soul abhors exceedingly. Long 20 ago I said, when I began speaking, that sometimes schemes and tricks may reach him whom arms and warfare cannot reach. So let us now frame plans and deal craftily, and perchance we shall find an escape from this affliction; because it was by schemes and tricks that the fat sheep was taken from the hermit or 25 ascetic.

The king. How runs the story about him?

The crow. It is said that a certain ascetic bought a fat ram to offer as a sacrifice. As he was leading it home, there met him three rogues who laid in wait for him at three (different) 30 places. [The first one said to him: 'What are you going to do with that dog, which you are leading along by a cord? The next one] said to him: 'Do you want to hunt game, O ascetic, with that dog?' And the third one met him and said to him: 'Ascetics and hermits truly do not use dogs; so this man is no 35 ascetic.' When the poor ascetic heard these words from those rogues, he let go (217) the sheep and left it in their hands, saying within himself: 'Perhaps those who sold me this sheep bewitched my eyes, and instead of a sheep gave me a dog.'

Now, O King valiant in strength, I have told you these things because I am about to play a trick from which I expect that we shall reap victory and get glory. I think, O King, that a report should go forth through all the camp that the victorious
5 King has been angry against such-and-such a crow, his confidant and counsellor. And let your Majesty command that I be smitten with blows and my wings plucked and my body beaten until the blood flows, and let them cast me beside one of the trees, and let the King leave this district and go to such-and-
10 such a place until the matter is published and the idea succeeds, by the power of the one good God and the good fortune of our King.

And the king commanded that they should do to the crow as he had said; whereupon the king departed with all his
15 forces. That very night came the king of the owls with his whole army to that place, and he found no crows there. And that cunning crow, fearing lest they should not perceive where he was and all his cunning should be wasted, began to creep from place to place until they perceived him; and when they
20 saw him they recognized him and brought him to the king. The king commanded them to ask him (218) for an account of himself and where all his companions were. When they had asked him, he said to them: 'I am so-and-so, the son of so-and-so. And the valiant King has commanded me to inform him
25 where my companions are. The appearance of my countenance shows that the crows have banished me from their society and driven me away.'

The king. This fellow is the confidant and counsellor of the king of the crows. Pray what was his offence that he has re-
30 ceived this punishment at their hands?

And the king asked the crow for his story and what offence he had committed in his counsels.

The crow. I gave a certain piece of advice, but all my companions turned against me and slandered me to the king. And
35 by the king's command they inflicted these blows upon me and made me swallow these bitter morsels.

The king. And what was the piece of advice?

The crow. When your Majesty made that mighty breach in the camp of the crows, the king assembled all his confidants,

counsellors, and secretaries that were in his kingdom, and said
to them: 'How do you think we ought to deal with the king of
the owls?' Now my position was exalted with the king and I
was superior to all my fellows, and the king had more confidence
in my words than in those of all the (other) members of his 5
camp. And many of them counselled the king to make war
with you. And when the king asked my advice, saying: 'And
you, what do you think advisable?' I replied: 'I do not think
that the King should make war with one who is greater in body
than we and superior (219) in strength, but I think that we 10
should study to make peace with them and pursue after friendship with them. Though they may impose on us some tribute
year by year, let us endure (it), and let us treat with them, so
that perchance we may escape from their onslaught and be
delivered from their attack. And if they will not consent to 15
make peace with us, let us remove from this place, because we
cannot contend with them, but must incline to them the
shoulder of obedience.' And I told them a parable.

The king. What was the parable?

The crow. I said to them: 'When an enemy is powerful and 20
warlike, his malignity can only be overcome and his enmity
removed, when his fellow who is weaker than he submits to him,
whereupon his wrath is assuaged, and the intensity of his fury
abates, and the bitterness of his anger is diminished. Let us
consider a seed as it sprouts and grows; when the wind drags it 25
away, it cannot withstand it, but wherever it chases it, does it
fly along with it, and turns about with it as it likes.' When the
crows, my companions, heard this my advice, they all withstood
me, and said with one voice: 'We are all ready to fight and will
not become a laughing-stock for your silly words, or cause the 30
kingdom to be abased. You, our companion, are giving us this
advice through deceit, because you have received some bribe
from (230) the king of the owls, and you are serving his pur-
poses and following his desire, and wish to make our king as
dust beneath his feet.' And all the foolish ones among them 35
assembled together against me, since they had heard these
things from the wise among them, and incited the king against
me, and heaped these evils upon me, and put these insults and
indignities upon my honourable person.

When the crow had done speaking, the king said to those present before him: 'What do the wise men among you think we ought to do with this crow?'

One of them who was very wise answered and said: 'He 5 ought to be put to death, because he is one of the king's mighty men, and of those who know his secrets and have acquaintance with affairs. By killing him we shall make a large breach in the camp of the crows, and be delivered too from his wiles; and when the crows hear of his being killed, we shall bring upon 10 them sorrow without end. For it has been said that he who attains to what is very difficult of attainment and then relinquishes it, should know that he suffers a great loss; and if he strives to attain something, and misses his opportunity, he reaps for himself dismay and sighing.'

15   The king said to another: 'What do you think advisable?'

The second replied: 'I do not think that he should be killed, because when an enemy is abased and weakness comes upon him, he ought to be treated with compassion. For sometimes (221) he is a source of advantage, like the advantage which a 20 certain merchant derived from a robber who entered his house, the merchant being grateful to him.'

The king. How runs the story about him?

The counsellor replied: 'It is said that there was a certain wealthy merchant of large property, who had a wife of beautiful 25 appearance. And she disliked him very much, while he, her husband, was captivated with love for her. And though he had studied how he might have pleasure with her, yet she would not give him so much as her hand. It happened one night that a robber came upon them in the house in which they were both 30 sleeping. When the woman perceived the thief, out of fear she arose hastily from where she was, and ran to her husband, and embraced him. And when her husband awoke and perceived that she was embracing him, he wondered exceedingly and marvelled, saying within himself: 'How did this happen last 35 night?' On lifting up his eyes, he saw the thief and said to him: 'Friend, take from my house whatever you wish, in peace and with a tranquil heart, and go in peace; because I am very grateful to you for having turned the heart of my wife to me.'

The king said to the third: 'And you, what do you think advisable?'

He answered: 'I think that he should be honoured by you, O king, and well received, that perchance we may reap advantage from him. For he who is prudent in his intelligence does 5 not forget the good that is done to him, and a change of feeling results on his part, as between the ascetic and the robber.'

The king. What did they do?

The third replied: "It is said (222) that a certain ascetic found a milch cow and led it by its horn to take it to his house. 10 A certain robber, seeing him, desired to take it away from him, and, to find means to do so, quietly followed him. And Satan, coming in the semblance of a man, said to the robber: 'Who are you, and what do you want from this man?' The robber said: 'Scheme against this hermit, so that I may take the cow from 15 him.' Satan answered: 'When men are sleeping, I will try to trouble his understanding and scatter his thoughts.' And they agreed together concerning this matter. When the ascetic had reached his house, he brought in the cow; and the two wicked ones came in after him. And he shut his door and went to 20 sleep. When Satan sought to approach the ascetic and accomplish his desire upon him, the robber was afraid lest he should awake before he could pull away the cow and get it outside. And the man went up to Satan and said to him: 'Leave alone for a little: give me time to get the cow out from the door, lest 25 perhaps when you approach him he may awake.' Satan answered: 'I fear that when the cow goes out at the door he will hear her voice; pray wait until I accomplish my desire upon him.' And they both fell to quarrelling with one another. And the robber drew near and awoke the master of the house, 30 saying: 'Arise, for Satan is here and seeking to destroy you.' And Satan said: 'Here is the robber, seeking to take your cow from you.' So the ascetic rose from his sleep, and they both went out (223) disappointed."

When the first counsellor heard these things, he was filled 35 with indignation and anger and said: 'I perceive that this crow is ensnaring your hearts with deceit and craftiness. If you do not consent to my advice, you will certainly perish by means of his evil plots. Let not the understanding of all of you be en-

anared, and do not deny what your eyes behold, or believe what
is hateful, or we shall be in the end like the carpenter who
denied what his eyes had seen, and believed lies and falsehoods.'
   The king. How runs the story about him?
5   *The counsellor.* It is said that there was a certain carpenter
in such-and-such a place who had a wife of beautiful appearance.
And she had a paramour. And one of the members of the
carpenter's household perceived them, and told the carpenter
that such-and-such things had been done in his house. One
10 day, the carpenter, wishing to test (the truth of) the matter
which he had heard, said to his faithless partner: 'I wish to
travel to such-and-such a place for a certain purpose, and I shall
tarry there many days; pray now keep to yourself, and see how
you conduct yourself in your house, and take care of every-
15 thing that is in it.' And by some artifice he entered and hid
himself under the bedstead on which was placed [the bed. She,
thinking that the carpenter has gone away, sent a message to
her lover, saying: 'My husband has gone away on some business, and will not be back for some time; so come quickly.' So
20 he came, and eat and drank with the carpenter's wife, and they
both made merry together. When night came, they got up
and lay down on] the carpenter's bed; he having seen and
heard everything. (224) And the carpenter being overcome by
drowsiness fell asleep, with his foot projecting from under the
25 bedstead. When his wife saw it, she recognized his foot. And
she fell to meditating, and began to frame a plan and weave a
thread of deceit. Then she said to her lover: "Ask me and say
to me: 'Do you love me or your husband and rightful partner?'"
And the luscivious man asked her as the base woman had told
30 him. She answered, saying: 'My husband is as precious to me
as my eyes, for there is nothing in the whole of the body more
precious than the eyes, because they are [the lamp of] the body,
and my husband is the light of my eyes, the diadem of my head,
the supporter of my weakness, the coverer of my shame, and the
35 fructifier of my breast, according to the command of his Maker.
But love for you only abides for a short time; for we only care
to have enjoyment with you, and when we have had enough of
it, what have we to do with you? The husband is regarded by
us as a father and more than a natural brother. And so has

God, the Maker of all, commanded that a man should leave his blood relations and cleave to his wife. Shame on the woman whose husband is not more precious to her than herself!' When the carpenter heard these words, he was ensnared by her, and the wretched man thought that his wife had spoken them sin- 5 cerely. When day dawned, that lascivious man went out and departed to his house. And the man rose from where he was, and sat on the bedstead (225) by his wife's head. When she awoke from her sleep, her husband said to her: 'Except for the love and respect that you have for me, I should have killed that 10 audacious and unjust despoiler of my bed; but because of the respect you have for me, I let him go.'

This fable I have told to you all here assembled, lest you be like that thoughtless carpenter who disbelieved what he saw, and believed the idle tales that were spoken in flattering and lying. 15

Now do not, O my brethren, believe the crow nor trust his false talk, and remember all of you the parable which with wisdom and investigation I have told you. And know, O our valiant king, that there are some enemies who, when they are not a match for the strength of their enemies at a distance, make 20 plans for their destruction at close quarters. For I never feared a crow so much in my life as I have feared this one from the very first day that I heard him speak and looked upon him, and saw too that your hearts were being led away after his words.

But the king did not hearken to his counsellor, but com- 25 manded concerning the crow that his wounds should be healed with drugs, and that he should be indulged with pleasant meats, that his wants should be supplied with great care and his needs attended to without delay.

That counsellor said to them again: 'If you do not listen to 30 my words and destroy this cunning crow, let him then be guarded among you as an enemy, but let him not be as (226) a friend, to explore your secrets and get to know your affairs; lest he do something treacherous to you. For a crow, wherever he is, is a source of evil. And this fellow, as all my feelings 35 bear me witness, has only left his king and parted from the members of his household and come to us, in order that he may get rich at our expense.'

But the king did not listen to what he said, and they did

10—2

not neglect to do honour to the crow; so that his wounds healed
and his wings grew, and they exalted him continually before the
king, and he used to talk pleasantly with him and craftily
ensnare by his conversation the king and all the men of his
5 army. When he perceived by the honour put upon him that
he was more honoured than all the king's companions and magnified in the eyes of the king and of his magnates, he said to
the king's courtiers: 'I wish to ask you for something which is
very easy for you (to give), and for which my soul desires and
10 longs.' They said to him: 'What is the thing?' The crow
replied: 'I wish you to persuade the king on my behalf to command you to burn me with fire, that I may ask of God and He
may renovate me afresh, and make me like one of you, that I
may exact vengeance from my enemies, and be avenged on all
15 those crows who counselled their king to treat me thus, so that
they brought me down from the dignity which I had before to
this ignominious condition. (227) Lo my heart is hot against
them as coals of fire, and longs for their destruction. And I see
that as long as I bear them resemblance, I cannot do them any
20 harm as I wish; and I have heard the wise say that he who
[gives] his soul to God on behalf of the truth is extolled and
exalted, and everything that he asks of God, He gives to him.
And I expect that when the valiant king has thus commanded
that I be dealt with, I shall ask of God and He will renew me
25 as one of you, and I shall be avenged on all my enemies.'
    That counsellor who had counselled the king to kill him,
said to him: 'How excellent (you are) when you begin anything, but how hateful when you finish it; and you resemble
clear wine in which deadly poison is mixed. Tell me, O crafty
30 one, if you are - - - by the fire according to your word and
desire, can your foul smell and disgusting flesh be changed from
their badness and foulness, and acquire a pleasant smell and a
good taste? Nay but you resemble the mouse, O wretched
one, when she desired that the sun should be her husband, and
35 the moon and the cloud and the mountain, and afterwards
relinquished them all and joined herself to a mouse like herself.'
    They said to him: 'And how runs the story about her?'
    The counsellor replied: "It is said that a certain ascetic was
very God-fearing, and walked (228) according to all his com-

mandments. And everything that he asked of God, He granted him. As he was walking one day along the bank of a river, he saw a young hawk flying upwards with a mouse hanging from his foot. And the mouse fell from it to the ground. The ascetic took it up, wrapped it in a leaf and took it home, and asked 5 .God to change it and make it into a girl. And God heard the voice of his supplication and changed His creature and made it into a female of beautiful appearance and handsome figure. Then said the ascetic to his wife: 'This is my daughter and the beloved of my soul; so care for her to the best of your ability, 10 and everything that you do for your own daughter, do for this one.' The woman did as her partner bade her. When the girl was grown up and come to years, the ascetic said: 'I must deal kindly with this my daughter, according as generous fathers do with their children; so I will seek her a suitable partner who 15 will supply her deficiencies, protect her purity, and preserve her good character from the pollution of evil suspicions. For it has been said and well said: 'Good fortune has he who does not leave his daughter in the house when the manner of women comes upon her, but gives her to a husband.' Then he said to 20 his daughter; 'You have reached the age for marrying, (220) for you ought to have a husband. Tell me now, whom do you wish to be your husband?'

She replied: 'I desire a mighty man whom defeat shall never overtake, intelligent and unaffected by foolishness, a man who 25 will not succumb to an enemy, a lamp the oil of whose brightness is never lacking.'

He said to her: 'Perhaps you desire the sun.'

She answered: 'Yes.'

Whereupon the ascetic drew near to the sun, saying: 'This 30 my daughter is of beautiful appearance and a handsome figure. Let her be your wife.'

The sun answered: 'I will direct you to some one who is mightier than I, namely one who can hide my light by means of his thunders.' 35

He said to him: 'Who is he?'

The sun answered: 'He is the cloud.'

So the ascetic drew near to the cloud, and said to him according to what he had said to the sun.

The cloud answered: 'There is one who is mightier than I,
namely he who can carry me whithersoever he pleases.'

He said to him: 'Who is he?'

He answered: 'The wind.'

5   So he drew near to the wind, and said to him as he had said
to the former ones.

But the wind answered: 'The mountain is mightier than I,
for he can hide me by means of his loftiness.'

So he drew near to the mountain and said to him in like
10 manner.

The mountain answered : ' The mouse is mightier than I, for
he has dug a hole and a burrow in me, and I cannot make him
depart from me.'

So the ascetic went to the mouse (230), and said to him what
15 he had said to the rest.

[The mouse answered]: ' It is impossible that this girl should
be my wife, because she is taller and greater in stature than I;
she could not go into my burrow with me.'

And the ascetic told his daughter his whole story. Then
20 she begged her father to ask God to make her into a mouse,
so that she might be able to marry the mouse. And the
ascetic asked of God, and He changed his daughter to her first
nature."

But the king did not incline to any of these words, but
25 commanded that the honour put upon the crow should be increased and his necessities abundantly supplied. And the crow
began to ensnare their hearts by his devices, so that he learned
all their ways, looked into all their secrets, and got to know all
their affairs. Then he flew away and came to his companions,
30 and said to the king of the crows: 'O our valiant king, I have
now laid the foundation, but you must complete the building.
And if I say anything and you do not do (it), I am absolved
from your punishment ; because the king of the owls is ready to
do something worse than the former thing.'

35   The king and all his companions, the crows, answered with
one voice : ' Lo we are ready to do anything that you tell us.'

The crow. The whole camp of the owls with their king
dwell in such-and-such a place by day, (231) and at night they
have a certain great hole into which they all enter. Therefore

command all the crows that everyone of them bring in his
mouth a piece of dry wood, and put it at the entrance of that
hole in which they live. And let one of the crows bring a
spark of fire and put it in the wood, whereupon let the crows
fly aloft that the fire may be fanned and burn the wood well, 5
and if anyone of the owls come out, the fire will burn him, and
if he remain inside he will die of the heat and the breath of the
fire and the fumes of the smoke.

And the crows did as he said, and burned all the owls by
means of the crow's advice. And all the crows returned vic- 10
torious to their place, exulting and rejoicing and hopping.

Then the king asked the crow (saying) 'How did you continue all that time with the owls? Because the good do not
continue with the bad, and the wise say that it is easier for the
good to be burned with fire than to dwell one hour with the 15
wicked.'

The crow answered: 'The matter is as the king says; but
it has been said that everyone the eye of whose intelligence is
bright, when something befalls him which is very grievous and
he fears the destruction of himself and of his companions, his 20
endurance opens a door to him and he vanquishes the evil
which is coming upon him. Besides aloes of Socotra are very
bitter and nauseous, but because (232) they procure health for
the sick, they endure their bitterness and many are cured by
them. And when fear comes upon a prince, he employs artifice, 25
so that he will change his dress for a woman's attire until his
design is realised and his plan crowned with success.

The king. How did you find the intelligence of the owls
and their skill and prudence?

The crow. I found no one among them more intelligent and 30
subtle in knowledge and clear in thought than he who advised
them to kill me. The others among them were without intelligence, for had there been intelligence among them, they
would not have been ensnared by my words, but would have
taken the advice of their intelligent one and the chief of their 35
camp, when he said to them: 'The crows are very crafty and
deceitful, and this one only left his king and relative and came
here, to prepare some fraud, and fulfil his desire upon us and
injure us, and put our whole camp to shame.' It has been said

by the wise that when a man goes to an enemy and is honoured by him, his enemies should guard against him as men guard against a snake so long as it dwells in the house, and as a dove in a nest (233), when she nests or builds for herself in 5 the banyan tree, guards against the silk-cotton tree, lest it fall on the banyan tree and destroy what she has constructed in it. And I attained to all their learning so that they did not conceal their secrets from me. And it has been said by the wise that a king seeks to be cautious with his words that they be not 10 known to any man, and specially in such a matter as this should the king be watchful. Let him consider first his dress, and next his food and drink, as well as the bedding on which he sleeps. Concerning these and similar things should he be keenly watchful, lest by reason of his inattention, his destruc-15 tion come to pass.

The king. No one killed the king of the owls but his confidants and counsellors. For their discernment was not clear, nor their knowledge sound.

The crow. You have spoken truly, for who ever attained to 20 any single thing and his mind was not lifted up? Who was ever ensnared by the love of women, and his discernment was not perverted? Who ever ate greedily, and did not suddenly fall ill? What man whose confidants and counsellors were stupid and ignorant, did not slip and fall on his back? And it 25 has been said that a proud haughty man must not expect the praise of the multitude, nor again a dissolute unwise man seek (234) to sit with kings, nor a crafty and deceitful man desire the affection of associates distinguished for the fear of God, nor he who does not repent of his sins crave for kingly power, 30 nor he who does not love good things or shrink from evil things expect to escape from trial, and that he whose hand is not stretched out to give gifts nor his - - - replenished with alms for the poor is not worthy of liberation from sufferings. And he who casts behind him the advice of his confidants 35 who speak with knowledge and counsel in the fear of God, will finish his life in sighing, and his troubles will be many, and his joys will leave him. It has been said that fire, when it has been lit in dry wood, burns without pity: so too when anxiety and solicitude affect the heart, the burning of its

life, that is its own destruction, takes place speedily and without delay.

The king. I think that you must have been in a state of great fear, when you humbled yourself before the owls.

The crow. The matter was even so, but because I was lay- 5 ing plans for their destruction and expecting an escape from their wickedness, nothing was burdensome to me; just as an enemy is not burdensome to a man when he falls into his hand, but he carries him on his shoulder and bears him to his friends and lovers that they may rejoice in their friend's victory and 10 also make sport of the enemy who has been caught in the trap. And their case resembles (that of) the black snake who carried the frog (235), and put him on his back.

The king. And how runs the story about him ?

The crow. It is said that a certain black snake, when he was 15 advanced in years and his strength had become feeble and his body thin, was unable to catch anything wherewith to nourish himself. And he crept slowly along until he arrived at a certain pool in which was much water, and in this water he found frogs without number. When he saw them, he lay mourning, with a 20 down-cast face and his appearance changed. And one of the frogs said to him: "What is the matter with you that you are so down-cast and distressed in mind?" The snake said to the frog: "Who should be more sad and distressed than I ? For my life used to be sustained by frogs, but misfortune has befallen 25 me, so that I have made a compact between myself and God and confirmed it with mighty oaths and decreed an ordinance upon myself that I would not again deal unjustly with them or taste them wrongfully, so that although they all come to me of their own accord, I cannot look at them nor hurt them in any single 30 thing." And all the frogs went to their king exulting with joy, and related what the snake had told them, namely that all his former strength had been taken from him. And the king of the frogs sent and called the snake to him. When he saw him, he said to him, "What is your story?" The snake answered: "One 35 (236) night I was creeping after a frog. And I entered a certain dark house in which was a hermit, or ascetic, who feared God and kept his commandments. He had a little son of beautiful appearance and comely form, who trod upon me with his heel;

and I, thinking he was a frog, hit him severely so that he died. And the ascetic went out oppressed in spirit and sorrowful in mind, and prayed to God and made supplication before him that as I had taken away the life of his son, He would take away all 5 my strength and humble me and make me a seat for frogs. And he said to me: 'You shall not partake of any frogs but only what may be given to you by them out of kindness.' And now I have come to you. If it appear good in your eyes, make me into a seat for your Majesty." The king said within himself: 10 "With a snake for my seat I shall get glory, and all the comp of frogs will gaze at me with great awe." So the king came near to the snake, and rode upon him many days. Then said the snake to the king: "My Lord the King, I should like you to do me a favour; (namely) to order a little food for me, since I have 15 become weak through hunger. When I eat, my body looks well; (and) when my Lord the King rides upon me, lo many will gaze at his comeliness and the comeliness of his seat, and extol the King." (237) The king said : " You certainly must have food." And he ordered his stewards to give the snake two frogs for his 20 nourishment, and the snake received them and fed upon them. So his humility did him no harm, nor did his submission diminish from his lineal rank.

Thus too was my continuance with the owls, while hoping for this deliverance from them which God worked for me, and 25 by which he saved me from their wickedness and boasting.

The king. I have found that humility and gentleness are better than arrogance and haughtiness of spirit ; because fire, in spite of its heat and great intensity, can only burn those trees which - - - - - - - - - - - - - - - - branches and fine boughs, 30 but water, in spite of its gentleness, tears them out by the roots. Thus too was your labour with the owls, for you destroyed them quietly and patiently, and won life for us, and for yourself a fair and excellent name and an exalted rank. It has been said that there are four things which we ought not to neglect, neither 35 despising the great ones among them nor scorning the little ones. The first one and the foundation as well as completion of the whole edifice, is a man's faith in God, that it be sound ; fire, (238) lest from a small beginning it work a great destruction ; an enemy when he is stronger than his opponent, for if he can-

not be overcome by stratagem, (mere) force will not affect him; and disease when it affects the body, for unless a skilful physician with divine medicine heals it, the patient is sure to die.

The crow. Any advantage that we have reaped, and any victory that we have gained, has been by the goodness of our 5 victorious King, the soundness of his faith in God, the purity of his heart, the clearness of his mind, and finally by his exalted destiny which is bound up in the Ear, and enclosed in that Bucket which, void of all dregs of iniquity, descends to the lowest parts of men's hearts, and ascends thence full of living 10 water; while the former is sown solitary and despised, and falls dying into the heart of the earth, but afterwards springs up and grows, laden with nourishment for all men. So too have we attained to all these things by the good fortune of our King of many virtues; since I have found that he keeps 15 secrets and hearkens to counsel, conceals stratagems and bides thoughts, and specially since you are one who repays with justice, distributes gifts lavishly and with a good will, and awards chastisement according as right demands. Your mind also has awaked out of the sleep of inattention. You are careful 20 for the nourishment of those of your kind, for you love the peace of all your camp. You are distinguished (239) for lack of greed and remote from all avarice.

The king. Since your mind was clear of enmity, you loved with all your heart to establish our kingdom and desired the 25 tranquillity of all the camp, and divine aid assisted you; because subtle thought and patient endurance attain to difficult things which abundance of power does not attain to, and is like a man who holds in his hand a small axe, and keeps ou striking a mighty tree, and little by little cuts it through. But nothing is 30 more wonderful to me than the manner in which the owls did not make you indignant by their bold language, and did not move the tower of your patience or break through the wall of your long-suffering.

The crow. All these things were done by means of your 35 Lordship's command, and by your good destiny did we attain to them, and by the fear of God which adorns you. Every shut door through you has been opened, and every impregnable fortress through you has been subdued.

The king. Everything that you have done, you have done
with intelligence. And your speech is remote from falsehood.
No helper was with you either to counsel or to act. And it
has been said that he who has no helper in word or (240) in
5 deed, though he be intelligent and prudent, is not accounted
perfect; because when there are two or three persons, they do
not fall; like a cord, which, when it is twisted with two or three
strands, is not quickly severed. And I do not find that your
joy outweighs mine in this thing that I have attained to, because
10 although it is counted your victory and your horn is lifted up
and your gifts are made great and your honours are many, my
joy and boasting exceed yours; because you are my wing, and
with the strength that you draw from my body do you fly.
And it has been said that a sick man does not enjoy sleep until
15 his body attains perfect health, and a ruler does not have pleasure
in his dominion or rejoice in his subjects until he gets deliverance from his enemies, and in victory tramples them under his
foot. All these things happened through you, and through your
means were accomplished. And it is said that when a fever has
20 left a man, his soul gets rest; that he who puts down a burden
which is on his shoulder, frees all his senses from toil; and that
when a man takes hold of his enemies, his mind is cleared and
his intellect restored to health.

Then the crow blessed the king, saying: 'I ask of Him
25 who by His nod brought all things into being, without toil or
tarrying put everything in order, and by His mighty bidding
has destroyed all those that hate you, and by the strength of
His power has destroyed all your enemies (241) before you,
that He will cause you to rejoice in all your kingdom, lift you
30 up over all the nations that surround you, level the hill before
you, direct your ways into the paths which conduct to dominion, establish in your hands the javelin of power, guide you in
the direction of your kingdom, gladden you with the peace of
your subjects, and rejoice your familiar friends with the pros-
35 perity of your affairs. Because when a kingdom is troubled,
all the king's subjects are doomed to destruction.'

The king. Of what sort were the ways of the king of the
owls with his army?

[*The crow.* He was overbearing, foolish, and careless. His

counsellors too, except the one who was my enemy, were stupid
and bad.

The king. What character did you find him to possess?]

The crow. I saw in him two admirable things. One of
them was that he took no pleasure in words of flattery remote 5
from the truth, as spoken by many who live among kings, but
counselled with sincerity and spoke with sound intelligence.
The other was that he did not incline to one of my words like
many of his companions who were snared by empty talking,
but counselled them to kill me and forewarned them that if 10
they did not spill my blood on the ground, none of them would
be far from destruction. And because he was exceedingly
excellent in his ways, he quietly and intelligently counselled
his king, while employing parables - - - - - - - - - - - - - - - -
- - - - - - - - - - - - - - - - by reason (242) of neglect are 15
rents made, and through inattention are doors of trouble opened
upon the king. And he was continually stirring up the king,
and quietly urging him to awake from the sleep of inattention,
to be watchful in the establishing of his affairs, to look continually to the right and to the left, and to extend his gaze 20
before him and direct his thoughts behind him, lest his sighs
should be many and his enjoyment and peace be taken from
him, and not to delay and trample on his noble character, lest
the fear he caused should be like the fear caused by an ape;
because it is said that the apo perishes like a shadow, and 25
strikes like a drunken man. And he who is not grateful for
services done him and blessings granted him is like a basilisk.
May the Lord destroy all the king's enemies, and as chaff is
scattered by the wind so may all those who hate him perish, and
may the king have exultation, gladness, and satisfaction all the 30
days of his life, and may his right hand terrify all the nations
that delight in war. And let the king rejoice in God, and let
everyone who makes the Lord his refuge boast himself, and let
the mouth of liars be speedily stopped.

The story of the owls and the crows is ended.   35

(243)   Another tale, (namely) one about the man who amasses (something), and does not know how to take care of it.

The king said to the philosopher : I have heard the parable of deceitful enemies, and how one ought to guard against
5 them.   Now tell me a parable of the man who amasses (something), and does not know how to take care of it.

The teacher said: 'To amass something is easier than to keep it.   And he who amasses something and does not know how to manage it is like the tortoise and the ape.   For the
10 tortoise got the ape into his grasp to a certain extent, being in hopes of him, but as he did not know how to take care of him, the ape slipped from his grasp, and he got disappointment instead.'

The king.   What did he do?
15 The philosopher.   It is said that in one of the islands of the ocean was a land, the whole of which was full of apes.   And their king was a certain old one who was very infirm, and his name was Pardin.   Now a certain young ape who was a near neighbour and kinsman of the king desired to (usurp) his
20 sovereignty.   So the young ape began to flatter all the renowned and notable men in the king's army till they were all led away by him.   And thinking to make him king over them, they all assembled together and drove out the old king. Whereupon (244) the old ape crept along little by little until
25 he arrived at a certain pond by which were many trees and fruits of every kind.   And the ape remained in a certain large fig-tree which was planted by that pond, and ate of the figs which fell from it.   As the ape was eating, there fell from him some figs into the water; and he heard the sound that they
30 made, and it gave him pleasure.   One day, he looked and saw a tortoise taking the figs out of the water and eating them. And the tortoise, thinking that the ape was throwing figs into the water for his benefit, wished to become his friend.   So the tortoise called him, and the ape answered him; and the

twn became familiar with one another, and rejoiced the one in
the other.   And each of them left his kith and kin; and they
clave to one another, and enjoyed each one the society of his
fellow.   Now the tortoise was absent from his wife for a very
long time, she not remembering such a long absence on his part 5
(before).   Being sore troubled, she complained to one of her
friends and companions, saying: ' My husband has been absent
from me a long while this time.'

Her friend answered: ' Be not troubled on account of his
delay, for I have heard that he fares well.   However, he has 10
become attached to a certain ape who lives in that region, and
has been led away after him, and has left off loving you and the
rest of his family.   Since he has thus neglected you, do you
too in the same manner account him despised and contemned.
And if it lies in your power to destroy that (245) ape, do so ; 15
for when the ape departs this life, your husband will speedily
return to you.   And I, as far as I am able, will help you in
this thing.'

And these two devised the following plan.   The wife of the
tortoise wrote a letter to him, saying: ' I am ill with a grievous 20
sickness; therefore baste to come to me speedily, before I depart
this life and all your property be lost.'

Then the tortoise read the letter to the ape, and they were
both sore troubled.   And the ape said to the tortoise: ' You
ought, O brother, to hasten to her and visit her and seek drugs 25
for her from the doctors and physicians, to the end that God
may command and grant recovery.'

So the tortoise went to his wife, who, when she saw him
in the distance, lay down on her back as if she were very weak
from illness, and not able to speak.   30

The tortoise said: ' Tell me about your illness.'   But she
gave him no answer.   Notwithstanding, her friend conversed
with him.

The tortoise said to her friend : ' Tell me about this illness,
for she does not even give me an answer.'   35

Her friend replied: ' How can a sick person speak, over
whose heart sickness is spread, while he knows the medicine
that is suitable for his sickness and is unable to get it ?'

The tortoise said : ' And what is this medicine which is so

difficult to get? Tell me, for if it is my own life, for love of
her I will give her my life.'

She answered: 'One must go (246) far to find it, and the
search for it is very arduous ; for we women know the medicine
5 which is suitable for her sickness. Now this sickness proceeds
from a disease of the womb, and the only medicine for it,
according to the prescription of physicians, is an ape's heart,
which, when roasted over a fire together with other things,
can cure this sickness.'

10   The tortoise said : 'And whence can we get an ape's heart?'

His wife's friend answered: 'On this account does distress
encompass your wife's heart, because her medicine is difficult
to get.'

The tortoise, on hearing this, was greatly troubled on
15 account of his wife, and began to weave plots and devise
stratagems, and conceived the idea of destroying his friend the
ape by treachery. And he turned to his soul and said : 'Oh my
soul, how canst thou destroy a loving and beloved brother, whose
brotherhood thou hast gained by great labour, and whom thou
20 hast found an honest brother, remote from all stain and a
stranger to all avarice, who fills up the breaches of his friends
and supplies the deficiencies of his lovers? Besides, I am
afraid to be false to the promises which I made to him. But
when I remember my wife, I am very much alarmed at the
25 thought of leaving her without medicine, because she is the
source of progeny, and heirs are born of her, and the fear of
God is perfected in her. And I cannot gather everything into
my barns nor can my affairs arrive at absolute perfection, unless
(247) I relinquish some trifle. And if this brother perish to-day
30 and my partner recovers health, it is no great matter; because
if this brother perish to-day, another can be taken instead of
him. Also the chief of the wise men commanded and admonished
that "a man should leave everything and cleave to his wife."
So he made himself ready to go to his friend the ape to catch
35 him by fraud, in order to put him to death and take his heart
from him. And early in the morning he set out with the
knife of deceit forged in his mind. And he formed the project
of bringing the ape as far as the island where his wife dwelt,
and of leaving him there without food until he died of hunger,

and then taking his heart out of him and giving it to his wife.
The ape, on seeing him, was very pleased at his coming and
said to him: 'Wherefore have you delayed all this time and
left me lonely and sad, and how did you leave our sister your
wife ?'   5

The tortoise. What kept me so long from you, brother,
in spite of my longing to see you and my desire for your
society, was modesty on your account, because of the inability
of my poor self to repay the debts which are due to you; since
your loving-kindness has been very great to me. And I left to 10
my wife knocking at the door of the tomb, and am come to
you that you may comfort me a little in my sorrow, and that
I may repay (248) a little of what is due from me.

The ape. Speak not so, brother, and shrink not from being
my brother, for your services are very acceptable to me; and 15
be not reserved towards me in any of your affairs. For that
which makes me eager to be your brother is your perfect love
for God, which is remote from all deceit; and you too in the
same manner (desire to be mine). And know, O brother, that
if, when I departed from my family, I had gone to you and 20
enjoyed your society, the many troubles of my heart would
through you have been removed.

The tortoise. [The love of friends is increased by three
things : the first is that a friend should go to his friend's house ;
the second, that he should see his wife and children; and the 25
third, that he should eat and drink in his house. But as yet
you have not entered my house, nor eaten and drunk with me,
nor seen my wife and children.]

The ape. It is needful for a friend to seek and require of
his friend that he care for his soul, and to try his love and 30
thoroughly examine his brotherly feeling. And when he finds
that he is remote from deceit and perfect in all the fear of God,
he should win him and leave other things. Because we see
that many approach one another in eating and drinking; just
as robbers who eat and drink together do not approach one 35
another because of the fear of God, but in order to rob people.
We see (249) too that the mule and the ass eat at the same
trough, though they are very far from being brothers. Let no
man be accounted by you a true brother except he loves the

K. P.   11

good of others as he loves his own good; as the chief of the wise
men said : ['Therefore all things whatsoever ye would that men
should do unto you, do ye even so to them.']

The tortoise. You have spoken the truth, brother; because
5 he who has perfect love is independent of eating and drinking,
which like a dream of the night pass away and are no more.
And like the vapour which ascends from a pot and vanishes in
the air and is no more, so passes away from many the love which
is dependent on eating and drinking. And it has been said that
10 a brother should not ask his brother to do what may perhaps be
grievous to him, or he will repulse him from his brotherhood, as
the cow drives away her calf, when it sucks too long at her udder.
And because I have confidence in your love, I am emboldened
to ask you to grant me a kindness and to double my joy,
15 namely to go with your servant to the region where my family
dwells. For it is an excellent region, in which are dense forests
and cool waters and everything that is suitable for your Fraternity, that all my race may rejoice in you, and my children
may be your children and appear submissive before you, and
20 that my wife may recover from her sickness by your coming.

The ape on hearing these things, (250) lusted after the fruit
of the trees and the service which he was to get from the children of the tortoise. So he said to the tortoise: 'I will do so,
25 and peace be with you.'

And the ape rode on the back of the tortoise, who began to
swim through the water to convey him to the region where he
lived. After traversing a short distance, the tortoise stopped
swimming. The ape, perceiving that some change had come
30 upon the tortoise, repented within himself and began to meditate, saying: 'I have sinned against my soul exceedingly in
having delivered it into the hand of this tortoise, for I think
he is preparing some evil against me. It has been said that
gold is tried in the fire, the faithfulness of a man in mutual
35 dealing, and the strength of a horse by swift running while he
carries a heavy burden.' And the ape's mind was troubled when
he saw that the tortoise delayed in his swimming. 'Nothing,'
said he [to himself], 'is so easily affected as a heart which is
troubled by some trifle. The intelligent man ought to manage

it with prudence, and from time to time and hour to hour ascertain by subtle thought how his friends feel (towards him).' [Then he said to the tortoise:] 'What is the matter with you, brother tortoise, that I see you delaying in your swimming? Perhaps I am too heavy for your back, brother.'   5

The tortoise answered: 'Forbid it that this should be or that it ever should have been. But a thought has occurred to me about my wife, and suggested that since she lies in a grievous sickness, there is no one to care for our need and to order our affairs as befits your Fraternity.'   10

The ape said: 'I (251) have no doubt of your love, and let not the fear of these things or anxiety about them disturb your mind. Be not anxious about the sickness of your wife, for anxiety profits nothing and distress (of mind) does not bring relief. But manage to get what the doctor prescribes, for I   15 expect that thereby she will recover. For it has been said that gold and silver are needed for two things. One is the maintenance of the poor and the relief of the distressed; and these are the fruits which bring one near to the other world. And the other is the getting near to princes, and the adornment   20 of women for him who loves carnal gratification.'

Whereupon the tortoise swam a little further and then halted. And the ape's mind was troubled, and he began to say to the tortoise: 'Wherefore do I see you halting, and oppressed in spirit and troubled in mind?'   25

The tortoise. On account of my wife's illness, for the physician has prescribed a medicine for her which is very difficult to get.

The ape. What is it?

The tortoise. The heart of an ape.   30

When the ape heard this, he perceived within himself that evil had come. Then he began to say to himself: 'These are the fruits of greediness, for every one who is not satisfied with his pay plunges himself into the deep abyss. This I have brought upon me in my old age, and it has made me an object   35 of laughter and ridicule, mockery and derision, to all that know me. Thus it happens to those who attempt to get superfluities which are over and above (252) the necessity and sustenance of their bodies, when they are greedy and fall into the pit of

11—2

temptations. But now I see a narrow egress for myself from
this broad land of trial into which I have entered.'

Then he said to the tortoise: 'It has been said by the wise
that a man who follows after the fear of God ought not to with-
5 hold his questions from ascetics, since they can bring him near
to God; nor again withhold from princes anything that may
help them to fight against their enemies and bring them to
rest and the peace of their army; nor withhold from his friend
anything that may console his trouble and relieve his distress.
10 Also I am persuaded that this your partner is very precious to
you, and I cannot deny you this medicine which is suitable
for her sickness; and our women too are attacked by a disease
similar to this one, and we give them our hearts and they partake of them and recover. And we are not injured except that
15 pain comes upon us for a little while, after which we are restored to health again. If we had remembered this before you
had set out from that place, I would have brought my heart
with me. For I left it there for the reason that it is a disturber
of the body, because thoughts are born of it, and it continually
20 vexes the body. So because I wished to be merry with you on
this our journey and to make you merry (too), I did not wish
to have it with me, lest perhaps when we should be glad and
merry with one another, it might pour out upon us disturbing
thoughts. (253) And it is customary for the whole race of apes,
25 when invited to a feast or banquet, to leave their hearts at
home, and not to carry them with them, lest they disturb their
feast; and our joy with our friends is not complete unless our
hearts are kept away from us. Now I am afraid that your wife
will be troubled at the very thing which is our joy. For when
30 I reach her without my heart, she will entertain the wretched
suspicion concerning me that it was because I do not desire her
recovery that I left my heart in that tree in which I used to
delight. But I think as we are near to the place whence we
started, we should return and take her medicine with us, that
35 our joy may be complete through her recovery, and that she too
may attend to our welfare and serve us.'

When the foolish tortoise heard this, his soul rejoiced, his
mind was tranquillized, and his thoughts had rest, and he gladly
brought back the ape to his place. And the ape mounted the

tree iu which he lived. Then the tortoise began to urge him to
come down from it, while the ape laughed at him, reviled his
folly, and abused his want of good faith, saying: 'O false-loving
brother, think not that I am like the ass of whom the fox said
to the lion that he had no heart.'   5

    The tortoise. How runs the story about him?

    The ape. It is said that in a certain place was a forest iu
which was a lion whose body had become scabby. And all his
strength had departed from him, and he was unable to catch
prey. (254) Now with him was a certain fox who served him 10
and fed on his leavings.

    The fox said to the lion: 'O glory of all beasts, beloved of
my soul and supporter of my weakness, is there no medicine for
this scab?'

    The lion answered: 'There is, but it is not easy to get it.'   15

    The fox. What is it?

    The lion. The ear and heart of an ass.

    The fox. What hinders (you) from (getting) them?

    The lion. I am ashamed to go out and seek one, for men
will see that the colour of my body is thus spoiled, and the race 20
of beasts will see me too and mock and insult me.

    The fox. I will bring you an ass, and leave him with you
in this place.

    The lion. If you do this for me, it will be a deed that can-
not be repaid.   25

    The fox. There is a pond here containing clear water, and
a certain fuller goes there every day with his stuffs loaded on a
certain ass. When he takes the stuffs off him, he leaves him to
feed by the side of that pond. Now when he comes there, I
will coax the ass until I bring him to you. But I ask of you to 30
make a compact with me that you will not take anything from
him except his ears and heart only.

    And the lion made this compact with him, as he asked of
him. And the cunning fox went to the ass, (255) and found
him alone feeding. He went up to him and said: 'Wherefore 35
do I see you weak in strength and thin in body? and why too
are you covered with sores?'

    The ass. I belong to a man that is a fuller, who works me
very hard and does not provide for my need, except that when

he takes down the burden from me, he leaves me in this field,
where I feed on the roots and herbs and drink of this water,
until he wishes to load these stuffs upon me again.

The fox. Wherefore do you stay with him?

5   *The ass.* But what am I to do?

The fox. If you will listen to what I say and be persuaded
by my advice, I will take you to a certain swamp in which there
is herbage of every kind, and in the midst of it a certain she-ass
of beautiful appearance and fat in body. There you shall live
10 with her, eat of that pleasant pasture and drink clear and pleasant water, and be joined to that she-ass and have children, and
your heart shall rejoice in them.

When that greedy ass heard these things, he consented to
the fox and immediately left the place where he was and came
15 after him. And he began to say to him: 'If I derive nothing
from the place which you have mentioned, your love alone
suffices me.'

When they reached the lion and he saw the ass, he made
haste and sprang upon him, but dealt him such a feeble blow
20 that he escaped from him and departed hastily and returned to
the place where he had pastured at first.

(256) The fox, having come to the lion, said to him: 'Wherefore have you become so weak, and mocked me as well and
made me a derision and a mockery to all that see me? For all
25 my acquaintances say that this king of beasts was no match for
the strength of a feeble ass.'

The lion, not wishing him to make it known that this had
happened through his weakness, said to the fox: 'Not everything
that kings do in their affairs should inferiors make known;
30 because the actions of kings are subtle, and profoundly wise
are their meditations. Pray cease this, nor ask concerning
things which are above you, nor advance beyond your station.
But now, if you wish your energy to be known, the soundness
of your love tested, and your obedience tried, return to the ass
35 and prepare your plans and spread your wiles before him, and
when you bring him to me, I will count you worthy of great
gifts and it will be a kindness that I cannot repay you.'

[*The fox.* - - - - - - -] And lo I will go to him in reliance
upon God.

When the fox came and reached the ass, the ass was indignant at him and began to say to him: 'Wherefore then did
you deceive me? And why too did you invite me to my slayer
and make me fall into the hand of a pitiless enemy?'

The fox answered: 'O you who hate your own advantages 5
and fly too from your own pleasures, I did not think this of
you, that you did not (257) know what would free you from
your trouble. This which the she-ass did to you was through
her gladness on your account. Do you not know that when a
male ass approaches a female, she bites him with her mouth 10
and smites him with her feet? This was not through enmity
but through her delight.'

As this foolish ass had never seen a lion before that day,
the greedy creature thought that the fox had told him the
truth, and his desire for the she-ass waxed strong and he re- 15
turned and came with the fox.

As he drew near to the lion, the lion lay in ambush behind
him, sprang upon him and killed him. When he had killed
him, he said to the fox: 'Remain you here while I go and
wash my body from the ass's blood.' When he was gone, that 20
crafty fox began to eat the ears and heart of the ass. So when
the lion came (back), he asked him about the heart of the ass
and his ears. The fox answered: 'How extraordinary are your
ways, O King. If this ass had had ears to hear with and a
heart to distinguish between good and evil, he would not have 25
erred twice, or yielded to my words after seeing what you did
the first time, my Lord the King.'

The ape said to the tortoise: 'This parable I have narrated
to you, O tortoise, because you have not kept your promises
nor continued in the fear of God, nor remembered mutual love, 30
nor set the statutes of the Lord before your eyes, but have
wrought deceitfully. And just as you led away (258) my simplicity
with lying words and robbed me of my good sense by your
lying speeches, so likewise have I dealt with you, until I broke
through your snares, severed the meshes of your nets, and 35
made you trust in the wind. The wise say that the foe of
every trial is intelligence. And by the fear [of God] and by
sound intelligence have I delivered myself from your snares.'

The tortoise. You have spoken the truth, brother; and I

have sinned and cannot deny it, and to forget your love I am
unable, and I am not free from blame.   However, one thing at
least comforts me, (namely) that it has been said by the wise
that he who confesses his sin and acknowledges his fall, offers
5 up repentance for his fault, makes his eyes run (with tears) for
his offences, and buffets his body for his delinquencies, is accepted by the Beholder of secrets, and all his wickedness is
wiped away from him by the Searcher of hearts and of reins.
In like manner let my fault be regarded by you, and abolish,
10 wipe out, and forgive me my offence.   Remember that from
earth we were formed, that into earth we shall be changed,
that from earth we are nourished, that to earth we shall return
again, and that from earth too we shall be renewed.

The ape.   Since then you have thus confessed your sin and
15 repented of your fault, I too will accept your repentance and
not remember the former things.   Now if it seem good to you
to remain (259) with me as aforetime, I will assuredly not
repulse you, but will grant you increased nourishment.   But
if you desire to go to your house and the house of your family,
20 go in peace; and when the time comes and you think to return
to me, your coming shall be blessed.

Then the tortoise, when he heard these things, through the
great shame that had come upon him for his fault, fell down
and worshipped him, and left him and went to his house
25 ashamed.

The end.

The king said to the philosopher: I have heard this parable and believe your words; you have demonstrated excellently and illustrated aptly. Now show me, if you please, and tell me a parable of the man who does things too soon, and does them before he examines them and (considers) how the end 5 will be.

The teacher answered: When a man does not search into matters or direct his gaze into the future, and is hasty a thousand times and once (only) takes advice before he decides, there happens to him what happened to the ascetic when 10 he killed the weasel without investigation or examination, and brought upon himself dismay and sighing.

The king. How runs the story about him?

The teacher. It is said that in a country called Jurjān was an ascetic who had a wife of beautiful appearance and whom 15 he loved very much. And she bore him a son of beautiful appearance and comely (260) form. Now this son was born to them after they had despaired of offspring for a long time. And before he was born to them, the boy's father used to say to his mother: 'Now you are going to bear a male child whose 20 appearance will be such-and-such, and I will teach him such-and-such things.'

His wife answered: 'It is very extraordinary of you, O man, to speak such untimely words which will profit you nothing. How do you know whether it will be a male child 25 or a female, and whether it will be born or not born, and whether it will be alive or not alive? Nay but commit your affairs to God, and everything that is desirable in His sight and in accordance with His will shall come to pass. For he who is intelligent and perfect in the fear of God commits all 30 his affairs into God's hand, and they proceed according to His will. But if a man does things too soon and does them before he examines them, there happens to him what happened to the ascetic when he lost his honey and oil.'

The man said to his wife: 'How runs the story about him?'
His wife answered: 'It is said that an ascetic derived his
nourishment from a king, that is, the governor of a town, every
day so much oil and so much honey. And whatever he had
5 remaining, he used to pour into an earthenware vessel which he
hung on a peg above the bedstead on which he slept. One
(261) day while sleeping on the bedstead, with the earthenware
vessel full of oil and honey, he began to say within himself:
'If I sold this honey and oil, I might sell it for a dínār and
10 with the dínār I might buy ten she-goats, and after five months
they would have young, and after a lapse of five years these
would have young and their number would become very large,
and I should buy two yoke of oxen and a cow, and I should
sow my fields and reap much corn and amass much oil, and
15 I should buy a certain number of servants and maid-servants,
and when I had taken to myself a wife of beautiful appearance
and she had borne me a handsome son, I should instruct him
and he would be secretary to the king.' Now in his hand was
a staff, and while he was saying these things, he kept brandish-
20 ing the staff with his hand, and struck the earthenware vessel
with it and broke it, whereupon the oil and honey ran down on
his head as he slept. So all his plans came to naught, and he
was confounded.'

The woman said: 'This parable I have related, that you
25 too may not be hasty and do things too soon.'

When the ascetic heard these things, he held his peace.
After a little while, she bore him a son as he had hoped; and
he remained continually with him. One day his wife said to
him: 'I am going upon one of your affairs, so keep a watch
30 over the boy.' But when the woman had gone, a messenger
from one of the chiefs of the town came for him and (262)
could not wait. So he left the boy and departed. Now they
had in the house a weasel who used to help them in all their
affairs, and did not leave a single mouse in the house without
35 killing him. And he left him with the boy and went with the
messenger. Whereupon there came forth a powerful snake
and sought to kill the boy. And the weasel fought with the
snake until he killed him and bit him into several pieces, and
the body of the weasel was stained with the snake's blood.

When the ascetic returned from the man who had sent for him
and saw the weasel with his body stained with blood, he thought
that the boy had been killed, and without searching into the
matter, sprang on the weasel and killed him. When he had
killed him, he looked and saw and lo the boy was alive. And 5
he repented and was ashamed and brought upon himself grief
and sighing, and he began to - - - - himself for mortification,
saying to himself: 'Would that this boy had not been born,
for then I had not been guilty of this murder.' And the
woman returned and - - - him, saying: 'Did I not tell you 10
not to be hasty and do things too soon before you had tried
them, lest you should reap a bad end?'

The king said : ' I have heard your parable, which you have told very aptly. Now tell me a parable of the man who, though his enemies are many and approach him from all sides, (263) yet manages to escape from them.'

5   *The teacher.* Not every tyranny and not every enmity is abiding. For sometimes love changes to enmity instead, and sometimes enmity ceases and love reigns in its place. Now when change comes over things and matters utter and the mind is troubled, hatred which is hidden in the heart certainly be-
10 comes manifest, yet sometimes too necessity invites to love and (banishes) fear and makes friendly those that are remote (from one another), so that they approach one another, as happened to the mouse with the cat; when they made alliance for a common object, framed a plan, and delivered themselves from
15 the hand of their enemies.

The king. How runs the story about them ?

The teacher. It is said that in one of the provinces was a banyan tree. And under it was the burrow of a mouse named Perídûn, and near that place was the hole of a cat called Rûmî.
20 Now it was customary for hunters to come to that tree and hunt every kind of animal that was found there. And when one of the hunters had laid his net and had concealed it in the ground, the cat came out of his hole to seek something that he needed, and hunger blinded his eyes, and he came and fell into
25 the net that was hidden. (264) And he despaired of life be-cause he had no helper to look up to. The mouse coming out at one of his holes, saw the cat lying in the net. And he looked to one side, and lo a weasel on his right hand lying in wait to destroy him. And he lifted up his eyes towards the tree, and
30 lo an owl sitting in it seeking to snatch [him.] Then was the mouse afraid that, if he turned back, the weasel would kill him, that if he mounted the tree, the owl would snatch him, and that if he remained where he was, the cat would perceive some way of escape from the trap in which he lay, and kill him. So

he was left in a state of despair. Then the mouse began to
reason with himself, saying, ' Why are you cast in doubt ? Nay
but let me spy out some plan and deliver my life before
calamity overtake me. Though I have no helper, guide or
counsellor, except my own strength, yet I ought not to remain 5
in idleness, because through idleness destruction befalls (a
man). But now I will search into matters and explore them ;
because he who explores the ocean may certainly by means
of subtle intelligence sometimes fathom its depths. And it is
impossible that intelligence when sound should not find out 10
the secrets of things, even though they be very profound and
mysterious. (For) just as it is not difficult to fathom the ocean
for the divers (265) who descend and seek pearls in it, so too it
is not difficult for sound intelligence to bring up good ideas like
good pearls. And now there is nothing so advisable for me 15
in this great strait as to make friends with this cat, who has
fallen into a grievous pit, and is very perplexed and longing to
get out of it. Now he cannot be delivered from this not except
by me. I will now approach him, appease the wrath of his
heart with gentle words, wheedle it by means of subtle intelli- 20
gence, and heal the ulcer of enmity by the soothing medicine
of a love remote from deceit; as oil and wax, when mixed together, alleviate swollen and grievous ulcers.'

So the mouse approached the cat and said to him: 'How are
you, brother ? '   25

The cat.   As you see me. Lo I lie in a snare and am
knocking at death's door and am far from temporal life and
pleasures, because I have no helper except God.

The mouse.   The matter is as you have said, and although
before to-day I was desirous of your destruction and would have 30
been glad at your ruin because of the enmities that are fixed
between our nature and yours, yet I too am knocking at death's
door and surrounded by waves of trouble. And when I considered, I saw that there was no escape for me or deliverance
from these miseries that surround me except through you, and 35
that for you too there was no liberation from this prison-house
in which you are bound except (266) through me. When you
search with your intelligence into this matter that I tell you of,
you will know that it is true and remote from all deceit, free

from all cunning and removed from all lying; because you see
my enemies who surround me, the weasel on my right and the
owl above my head. Although I have called them my enemies,
yet they are yours equally. I have looked out for my de-
5 liverance and for yours and I have only found one thing, and
that must be done between us.

The cat. What is it?

The mouse. That you make a sincere compact with me,
give me the right hand of truth, and take to witness between
10 me and you the Witness who searches into the secret things of
the heart that you will not harm me when I approach you, and
sever the meshes of this net in which you lie, and free you
from this prison-house in which you are bound. And I too
shall get deliverance and liberation from those enemies who
15 surround me. And know, O my beloved, that no one is more
blind in mind and more ill-starred than two persons who are in
one prison-house and know that when they make alliance together, they will get liberation for themselves, and neglect to do
so. Now, brother, consider what I have said to you, weigh my
20 words in the balance of intelligence, and prove them with love
remote from deceit, and their uprightness will outweigh - - - -
- - - - - - - - - - - - - - . Let us imitate those who ride on
the sea (267) in a ship, who, when the sea runs high against
them and the waves set the whole ship in commotion and
25 miseries and distresses surround them on all sides, all with
one voice and with one cry cry out to God, and out of one
troubled and miserable heart call to Him. For the Adorable
One, because He knows the purity of their conscience, does
not despise their petition, but immediately allays the angry
30 sea, His command restrains its waves, and there is a great
calm. In the same manner let us also act towards one another.

The cat, on hearing these words from the mouse, and seeing
that he had spoken them sincerely, answered: 'I see that what
you say is sincere and very remote from deceit, and I believe all
35 your words, and I think that God has provided for me and you
a deliverance from these waves which surround us.'

Then the cat made a compact with the mouse and took God
to witness for him concerning himself that he would not break
his promises.

The mouse. I will first approach that we may salute one
another, so that the weasel and the owl may despair of us and
return disappointed, and that our strength, which has departed
through fear of them, may return to us, so that we may be able
to sever the meshes of the net.   5

The cat. Brother, let it be as you wish.

Whereupon, the mouse approached the cat, and they embraced one another, and each asked how the other fared, and
they rejoiced each in his fellow. The owl and the weasel, seeing
it, wondered (268) at them and marvelled, and departed and 10
returned from beside them astonished. And the mouse began
to sever the meshes of the net slowly and not diligently. [The
cat perceiving it, said to him: 'My friend, why were you so eager
in your own interest, while you are luke-warm in mine?] Perhaps now that you are aware that you have been liberated from 15
the wickedness of these enemies that surrounded you, you have
inclined to treachery and are about to enter in at the door of
deceit. But this is not worthy of wise men or of those who
fear God or of the noble. For you have reaped for yourself
many advantages by approaching me and deliverance from 20
enemies, and for this you ought to make a grateful return to me
who sowed in your mind fruits of peace. And now is energy
required of you, and the duty which is due from your Nobility is
to strive to deliver me from this snare in which I lie. And let
not any of those former things enter your mind, because he who 25
has drawn us to brotherhood with one another has shown you
my whole-heartedness towards you. And you know very well
what a joyful end the fulfilment of a promise brings about,
especially when the beginning of the matter is peaceable and

- - - - - - - - - - - - - 30

you know, too, O my beloved, what a bad end and what a deep
pit (269) deceit digs for him who employs it. For all the wise
acknowledge and say that there is no blow harder than the blow
of deceit; for it is without cure, and without remedy is the
injury to him who receives it. And have you not heard, O 35
brother, that if a man's brother makes a slip in anything or is
the cause of some error in one of his affairs, and asks pardon of
his brother, while confessing his sin and acknowledging his
transgression, and his brother does not accept his repentance or

grant him pardon out of a heart sincere and clear of all wickedness, neither will God forgive him any of his transgressions?'

The mouse. He who is eager to make an end is he who
5 studies the welfare of both sides, and takes care lest either of them fall into the snares of the evil one. Now one whose submission is steadfast lays down his life for his brother, according to the word of the chief of the wise who says: *   *   *   * and not from any necessity which compels him. But if he to
10 whom it falls to do this, does not abide by his friend in perfect steadfast love, but draws near to him on account of some necessity which compels him, it comes to pass that when they quarrel, he departs from him by reason of his angry feelings, and it is found that he is not perfect in the fear of God, (270) but con-
15 forms to the love of worldlings. For [among these] no one approaches his fellow except to rob him of his gains, after which he departs from him. Lo I come near to sever the meshes of the net, but I shall leave one of the threads, reserved for the time of distress.

20   Then the mouse drew near and severed the meshes of the net, and left one thread only. But on seeing the hunter, who had crept up little by little and got close to them, when he was about three paces distant from them he drew near and severed the thread and hasted and entered a burrow in front of him,
25 which he had prepared before he severed the last thread; the cat sprang and mounted the tree; and the hunter drew near them, but seeing that the threads of the net had been severed, turned back in disappointment.

After a little, the mouse came out to see what had become
30 of the hunter. The cat, seeing him from the tree, said to him: 'Brother, you are worthy of great gratitude; wherefore do you shrink from us and are frightened? Let not your heart be anxious nor your mind hesitate.' For the love which we have for one another sword cannot sever, nor fire burn, nor can anything
35 also in the way of gold or pearls of this world work a change in it. Therefore believe my words and come out to me, that we may enjoy one another's society, because the kindness that you have done me cannot be - - - and the obligation that rests upon me cannot be discharged. As long as I live in this world,

everything that I amass (271) of wealth will I place before you;
so fear not nor hesitate concerning the truth of my words.'

Then the mouse answered him, saying: 'There is an enmity
hidden in the heart, which makes it appear outwardly that the
heart of him who bears it is laden with love, but the wound 5
inflicted by it is more painful than that inflicted by the enmity
which is manifest. To him who does not guard against it, there
happens the like of what happened to a man who was riding on
an elephant's back, and who, being overcome by sleep, fell in
front of the elephant's feet, so that he trampled on him and 10
killed him. Now the thing which is named brotherhood between
brothers, and drawing near to the distant, or friendship with
strangers, is in proportion to the assistance which a man gets
from his companion. And in the same manner as a cloud, when
it rains, produces darkness and sometimes pours down rain, and 15
afterwards is dissipated, and fine weather comes and the sun
shines, so too love sometimes exists between many, and sometimes removes from them, and a change comes upon them.
And to everything there is both a limit and a cause. There is
a love which is implanted in the nature, like that of a father 20
for his children. In the same manner, there is an enmity which
is the result of a change in mutual dealing, and this is not so
serious by far as that which is implanted in the nature. Now
our enmity towards one another is implanted in the nature, and
not caused by any action, in the same way as our love towards 25
one another is caused by a chance occurrence. You know that
water is an enemy to the nature of fire, and that when they are
mixed with one another, and [the water] is warmed by the fire,
(272) it is not prevented from extinguishing the fire, when
thrown upon it; so an enemy who knows that his foe is stronger 30
and mightier than he, ought not to go near him. For we have
approached one another through a chance necessity. And now
that God has granted liberation to each of us and deliverance
to both sides, let each of us remain in his hole. Lo I bid you
farewell, and depart from beside you. Be safe and sound all the 35
days of your life, while remote from sins and separate from all
deceit and wickedness. And be not afraid, brother, of this
peace at a distance, because I, like you - - - - .

This is a parable of enemies who become friendly and
familiar with one another, and afterwards part.

The king. You have made an excellent simile and a wise
parable. Now tell me a parable of those who live in one house,
and how each of them ought to guard against the wickedness of
his fellow.

5   *The teacher.* It is said that one of the kings in Kashmir,
called Brahmadatta, had a bird whose name was Pinzih, and
who could talk and was very clever. Now this bird had (273)
a young one. And the king bade one of his wives, the one who
was dearer to him than all her fellows, to take this bird with
10 its young one, and care for them. It came to pass that the
king's wife bore a son after a long period during which he had
had no children; and when the boy had grown a little, he
consorted with the bird, and the two began to grow up together. And Pinzih used every day to go out to a hill, and
15 bring from the trees that were there two fruits that were
unknown to the inhabitants of that town, and place them, one
in the mouth of the king's son, and the other in the mouth of
her young one. And they became very strong through this
food. This thing came to the ears of the king; who was pleased
20 at it, for it was very beautiful in his eyes; and the pleasure of
the king and his wife in Pinzih and in her young one increased.
One day, when Pinzih had gone to the hill as usual, her young
one hopped from the lap of the king's son and perched on
the breast of one of the (other) boys. The king's son, being
25 angry (at it,) took the young bird, dashed him to the ground,
and killed him.

When the bird came back from the hill, bringing with her
two fruits as usual, and beheld and saw that her young one
was killed, she was very grieved, and wept over him, and began
30 to utter woeful lamentations. Then she said, being sorrowful
and distressed: 'Woe, woe on friendship with kings, who observe not love nor perform obligations, (274) who love not
their familiar friends nor remember how they were brought
up together -

for they honour no man, neither him whose wickedness they
fear, nor him who fills up their breaches. When these things
are done to them, they repulse those who do them from beside
them, while breaking their covenant and not keeping their
promises, because they are destitute of all fear of God. But 5
God do so unto me and more also, if I do not exact vengeance
for my son from his murderer and from this wicked, audacious,
and shameless brother of his, who did not spare the innocence
of my son.'

Having said these words, she darted at the eyes of the 10
king's son, and tore them both out with her claws, and left him
in agony; whereupon she flew away and perched on a high
place where the hand of man could not reach her.

When the king heard (it), he mounted his beast oppressed
in spirit and sad of soul, and went to her, thinking that he 15
would certainly catch her by deceit, and take her life away in
return for having blinded the eyes of his son. When he looked
and saw that she was perched in that place, he said to her:
'Fear not for what you have done, because we first sinned
against you, and rightfully have you taken vengeance upon us.' 20

Pinzih. O King who break your promises, O master who
oppress your servants, know that everyone who does not observe
his covenant (275) or keep his oath, who neither fears his Maker
nor stands in awe of the judgement of his Creator, has a bad
end. And although the punishment of the just Judge may be 25
delayed, while for a time, in the long-suffering of God, He
bears with him, yet certainly will justice require it (at last).
And though it may not require it of *him*, it will be required
of his children, even to three and four generations. For very
wonderful are the works of God, and his doings past finding 30
out. Sometimes, when a man sins, immediately he receives in
his own person the recompence due to his audacity, like that
which was done in the case of that robber who hid the forbidden thing, and was burned with fire, he and all his family;
while in the case of another, who coveted his neighbour's vine- 35
yard, He reserved his sentence for the children whom he begat.
And because this insolent son of yours has transgressed God's
decree and destroyed his unoffending brother, immediately has
God brought just and rightful punishment upon him.

The king. You have spoken the truth, and all the things which you have enumerated I understand, and from the truth you have not departed. The retribution due to the audacity of our son have you required of him; but now be not afraid 5 of us, nor depart from the old love, but consent to my words and incline to our entreaty, return to your office, and purge the store-house of your love. Lo, we will make you fresh promises and a sincere covenant (276), taking to witness between us and you the Witness who tries hearts and searches the garners of 10 the thoughts.

Pinzih. Say no more nor multiply your words, for your oath, like the first one, is of no value whatever. It has been said by the wise and intelligent that one should not make trial of a thing twice, and though the lips may utter words of flattery 15 and deceit, yet those words are very remote from the truth. For the wound inflicted by a wrathful man is worse than that of a basilisk. It has been said too that he who is intelligent and prudent gets many friends for his parents, makes friends with those who are far off, draws foreign peoples to his love, 20 and gets prudence for the foolish by means of what he says. And now, behold, I depart from beside you, and bid you fare-well at a distance.

The king. If we had not first sinned against you, by break-ing our promise to you and daring to kill your heir, you would 25 have had cause to be afraid of us; but (since the matter is otherwise,) doubt not concerning our love, be not afraid of our service, nor depart from beside us.

Pinzih. Wrath, when it reigns in the heart, leaves no place for harmony nor a foot-breadth for love, but continually en-30 genders calamities and produces troubles, stores up anger, dis-turbs the pure mind and confounds the reason. Now this is a witness on behalf of the tongue, as a sword is witness on behalf of the executioner, and as cessation of fire is witness on behalf of the rain. And my heart (277) does not testify to your tongue 35 for the truth of these your words, just as your heart does not witness to the truth of them, but testifies that they are spoken deceitfully.

The king. Do you not know very well that wrath and enmity exist in the hearts of all? But he whose intelligence

is sound, and who is eager to tear up the roots of deceit from his heart, and obliterate all wrath from his mind, will first draw near to his God, and his prayer will ascend out of a pure heart to Him who fashioned him, when all his excited feelings will subside, and all his perturbation be allayed.   5

Pinzih. The matter is as you have said. But a wise man ought not to trust a wrathful man, or believe a rogue, especially when he knows that ho has been false to him once. What is worse than this and compels me to fear, is that the King will see his son in a state of blindness; for this will stir up troubles 10 and lead him to employ deceit. - - - - - - - - - - - - - - - -
- .

The king. He whose mind is exalted, and the eye of whose discernment is bright, does not part with his brothern and kins-men, or throw away love which has been won with difficulty, 15 even though he may fear destruction for himself. And we see that this is the case with tho - - - , for they have dogs who are useful for many things, and sometimes they slaughter them and eat them, (278) and yet we see that those other dogs that remain with them are not hindered from hunting, nor cease to 20 dwell with them. We see too in the case of steeds and horses that neigh and save their riders from the hand of their enemies, while it happens too that many foes flee from before them, that sometimes they are slaughtered by their owners, and yet that the others who remain are not indignant, but submit 25 to the yoke of obedience, and are not afraid to remain with them.

Pinzih. Wrath is very terrible wherever it be, and there is nothing more terrible, or worse, or more alarming than the wrath which is in the hearts of kings; because these take their 30 revenge by force, judge men tyrannically, and wrongfully take vengeance on those who hate them. And he whose reason is sound does not believe their words, after having tried them and seen the frowardness of their mind. For they are like wine, the evil of which is hidden, but which, when once it is partaken of, 35 shows its virulence plainly. And the heart is not to be pacified as long as wrath is hidden in it. For when wood causes fire to burn, and it blazes up, the fire may be extinguished by much water and ashes without measure, after it has ruined many

things, and destroyed the property of rich and poor alike. In
the same manner, when wrath (279) stirs up the heart, it cannot
be extinguished by water nor smothered with ashes, until it has
wrought its slaughter. Again, when fire is hidden in iron as
5 wrath is hidden in the heart, if a man want a light, by means of
a stone which he strikes on the iron does it issue forth and
destroy; though sometimes it is of advantage and does not
destroy. So wrath is hidden in the heart, and when a man
wishes to injure his fellow, he brings it forth. Now I, my lord
10 the King, am weak and not one to fill up breaches or give
counsels. And you have no need of me; nor again am I able to
root out the wrath from your heart, for the injury which I have
done to your son is constantly depicted before your eyes.
Although it was a retribution upon him from us, yet the injury
15 that your son did to me is hidden from you, because the
murdered one is buried in the heart of the earth, while the blind
one sits on the roof and cries. And the deceit which I have
seen in you, and the audacity which your son was guilty of
towards my young one, forbids me to believe your words, or to
20 abide by your love, because I should be in a continual state of
fear and trembling before you, neither performing your services
nor supplying your wants. Nothing will profit me more than
to separate from you, and depart out of your sight. Lo I bid
you a last farewell.

25   *The king.* Do not be in a hurry; because a man may not
beget a child except by the will of God, and so too (280) this
misfortune between my son and yours, and the retribution which
followed, only occurred through the will of God. Therefore,
since the matter is so, neither side of those who sinned against
30 one another is blameworthy.

   Pingth. That which is determined by God is sure, and we
do not deny it; as, for example, a man's life, the beginning of
his existence, his conception in the womb, and his departure
from life by natural death; these are all determined by God,
35 and we acknowledge that it is so. However, death by murder
and abominable things are accomplished by the will of those who
commit them, and are not determined by God. If your son
took mine and killed him, and if I darted at your son's eyes and
blinded them, forbid it that I should say and profess that God

commanded us to do these things. However, O King, since
your soul longs and craves for my destruction, you are seeking
to catch me by these miserable arguments, while your mouth
professes what is far from your heart. It has been said, and
excellently said, that want is bitter and poverty horrible; but 5
not so bitter and horrible as to dwell with an enemy. The
parting of brethren from brethren is bitter, but not so exceeding bitter as the parting of the soul from the body. And no
man feels in his heart the sickness (281) of his fellow so much as
he who is affected by the same sickness. So I well know the 10
bitter suffering of your heart by the bitterness which is in my
heart on account of the parting of my dear and beloved one.
And just as the remembrance of my precious one does not
depart from my heart, so too the remembrance of the beauty of
your son's eyes will not depart from your heart. What is 15
determined in your mind I know very well. Therefore do not
trouble and weary yourself, and multiply words that will not
profit you a whit.

The king. He who cannot alter what is in his heart is not
reckoned among the wise. So if the matter is as you have said, 20
there is no more freedom of will. Therefore, how can we change
ourselves from evil to good, or subdue the passions which are
implanted in the nature? On the contrary, freedom of will
does rule over men; for when a man desires a woman who is
not his, his will withholds him from doing abomination with her. 25
And those who conquer passion, when it is roused in their
hearts, are extolled by God and man. But those who do not
subdue their passions are blamed by God, disgraced among men,
and chastised by the ruler.

Pinzih. When a man has a sore under his foot, it is very 30
difficult for him to put his foot down; and if he is obliged to
take a step, that step causes injury to his foot. And if a person
(282) with sound eye-sight looks at the light of the sun, it does
not hurt him at all; but if his eye-sight is weak, he cannot lift
up his eyes to the sun and look, and if he does take a look at 35
the sun-light, he gets hurt to his eyes. And he who loves this
life cannot dwell in the same house with his enemy or in the
same city, nor enjoy life wherever he may be. But if he does
dwell (thus), and does not pursue after safety, perhaps, through

what he eats, calamity will befall him; like a man who eats
some food, whatever it may be, thinking it to be sweet to his
palate and his stomach, for sometimes his food will stick in his
throat without descending lower or rising higher, and in a short
5 moment his life departs from him, and his soul leaves his body.
Sometimes too thirst parches his body, and he thinks that a
cup of cold water will cool the intensity of his heat, and through
a single mouthful of water his soul departs from his body, or
suffocating pains come upon him. And he who believes the
10 words of his follow [without] knowing the secrets of his heart,
mocks his own soul. A man ought to make an estimate of
himself first, and see to what extent he is in his own power and
- -. And he who is
prudent, wise and knowing, knows in what place to put him-
15 self; and I, in accordance with my feebleness, am well (283)
acquainted with myself, and know that I shall have no advantage from friendship with you, and that you will have no use
for me. Wherever I may put myself, I can find all that I
need, since I have put away greediness from me. When five
20 things accompany a man, he fares well, wherever he goes, and
ends the days of his life in gladness. The first of them is that
he should not injure or defraud any man : another is innocency
towards all : another is to flee from avarice : another is lack [of
greed and] perfection of conduct : and [the other] is holiness of
25 life. When a man is afraid of losing his life, the loss of his
wealth and the parting with his brethren is a light matter
to him ; and when a man renounces his goods, relinquishes all
his possessions, and possesses himself alone, the things that he
parts with here he sometimes gets in another place. Sometimes
30 the high heavenly One makes haste, and he departs from this
life wherever he is, and everything is abandoned to vanity and
vanity of vanities. And what profits wealth which does not
relieve others, or children when they are not obedient, or a wife
when she does not behave virtuously, or kings when they do
35 not keep their oaths and covenants, do not (284) abide by
their promises, discharge obligations, or procure peace for their
subjects ? Therefore know, O King, that I do not trust to
your oath nor credit your words, and will not remain beside
you, nor converse with you again, nor bid you another farewell.

So Pinzih left the king and took to flight, and the king returned, oppressed in soul, troubled in thought, and gloomy in mind, because that he had failed to catch her, and take revenge upon her for his son.

The story of Pinzih and the King is ended.   5

THE STORY OF THE LION AND THE JACKAL.

The king. I have heard your similitude, and highly extol
your wisdom. Now, if it please you, show me the similitude of
kings, and how they draw a man to friendship with them, and
5 put him over their affairs, and how they are angry with him for
a time, and how they restore him again.

The teacher. If the king, when he sins against him in anything, or attacks him wrongfully or on the strength of a false
accusation made (against him) by envious men, does not restore
10 him again to his office, (285) then the matter is very evil. And
especially in the case of educated and intelligent men, the king
ought first to search into the actions of such, look at them in
the polished mirror of sound intelligence and excellent discernment, and consider those who were guilty of some little error
15 in their service; and according to their skill and the greatness
of the king's need of them, so let him do to them, and receive
back him with whom he was angry before. And when he tries
him with his intelligence and weighs him in the balance of his
discernment, and finds that his former conduct was remote from
20 avarice and free from deceit, and that he is not smitten with
envy, does not run after vain talk, incline to bribery, or suppress
the truth through partiality, and, to sum up all these excellencies,
that he is a fearer of God and dreads an evil name—when the
king tries these things with the subtlety of his intelligence, and
25 finds in him one who loves the peace of his kingdom, is eager
for the safety of his whole army, can manage all his courtiers,
and conceals in the heart of the earth all his secrets—when the
king finds such men as this one, let him hold fast to them with
all his might, honour them more than any of his intimates, and
30 lavish his gifts upon them, that they may be freed from all
sadness, be made eager for his welfare, and contend for the
prosperity of his affairs. And if any deficiency be found on

their part through ignorance, let him reprove them gently (286) and not harshly, as those who have sinned unwittingly, and not as those who love evil. But if [the accusations] are due to envy and calumny, with patient and accurate investigation let him try the charge made against him. A king, too, when he 5 puts men over the management of his kingdom, ought continually to test their character and principles; because sometimes a change comes upon them, just as water may become changed, being at one time clear and pure, and at another thick and turbid. If, when he searches into them, they are found 10 clear and pure, let him increase their salaries, exalt their ranks, and raise their seat. But if he finds a deterioration in them, let him dismiss them in disgrace, that others may see and be terrified at deceit, and that the good may behold the gifts which the pure receive, may love uprightness, hold fast to 15 justice, and remove far from all avarice. For there is nothing worse for a king or a subject than avarice. And let not his similitude be that of the lion and the jackal.

The king. How runs the story about them?

The teacher. It is said that in the land of the Indians was a 20 certain jackal, who was an ascetic and a faster, and ate no flesh, (287) taking no part in slaughter and eschewing bloodshed. Now he dwelt with wolves and many other jackals; and since he took no part in anything that they used to do, but every evening used to partake of a few wild herbs and a little water 25 from the pools, and every day used to stand on his hind legs and pray, these animals began to quarrel with him, saying: ' Since you are one of us and belong to our race, we do not like you not to engage with us in hunting and eating of flesh. If you will not do this, begone from us and separate yourself 30 from us.'

The jackal answered them : ' My manner of life among you harms neither me nor you; but for me to act as you do would harm me very much, and not profit you a whit. If a man stay in a bad place, while his manner of life is good, that place does 35 not harm him. Nor, if a man stay in a good place, while his manner of life is ill ordered, does that place advantage him or profit him in any way whatever ; but on the contrary he incurs banishment from God. For if a man dwell in the house of

God and commit a murder, what profits him his dwelling in
the house (288) of God? (Nothing;) but, on the contrary,
his chastisement is made all the more severe. And what harms
him who dwells among beasts, and delivers afflicted souls from
5 slaughter? (Nothing ;) but, on the contrary, the benefit he
gets is great. So a man should not be reviled for dwelling
with sinful men, if his own manner of life is pure; nor again in
a man to be praised for living among the righteous, [if his
manner of life is impure]. And I, though I am with you in
10 body, yet in soul I am very far from you.'

Whereupon, the jackal was left to his asceticism, and continued in fasting and abstinence; and no one like him appeared
in his time. The fame of him came to the ears of a lion who
was in that region. And the lion wondered at him exceedingly,
15 and sent for him and saluted him, and exhorted him urgently
and begged him to become his steward. And he said to him:
'My kingdom is very mighty, and the affairs of my dominion
are extensive, and my soul longs for you because of these excellencies that I hear you possess. Now I wish you to consent
20 to my words, that I may make you intimate with me, honour
you, and make you sit above all your fellows.'

The jackal. It is [customary] for kings to select for themselves those that suit them; but they should also avoid forcing a
man against his will and compelling his inclination, for then
25 his working does not profit. Now I, my Lord, am afraid of the
service of princes, and unaccustomed to serve them, and not
skilled in their service; nor (289) will the King get any advantage from me, as he thinks concerning me. You, my Lord,
are king of beasts, and acquainted with every species among
30 them. There must be some among them who will be suited to
your service, and fitted for your affairs. If you command these,
they will obey, and every one of them will strive for your
service. And if you select many from them, every one of
them will strive on his own account to show the excellence of
35 his service.

The king. Cease these words, for I will never leave you.

The jackal. Only two kinds of men can do a king's business,
and I am not one of them. Either he must be a wicked,
deceitful, and crafty man who knows how to steal and eat,

and give many others to eat, lest they inform against him
and divulge his lies, and saves himself from their bad will by
blinding their eyes with bribery. Or he must be a bumble
simple man whom no one envies. And he who draws near to a
king should rid himself of avarice, and remove far from lying. 5
If he cannot (do so), he will not succeed. And he cannot be
with kings when two disadvantages combine against him.
One of them is the enmity which he gets with many, when he
debars them from the king's delights. The other is the wrath
of magnates, and the terror and fear that dominates him; for 10
he knows not when a flood of anger may burst upon him, (290)
and his life perish in a moment.

The king. Away with all the anxieties which you have
enumemted, because I will never believe a word which any
adversary may say against you. And as far as I can, I will 15
avoid showing you a vexed or angry face, but on the contrary
will exalt your seat, make you sit at the head of all your fellows,
and not debar you from anything.

The jackal. I am grateful to God and the king. But one
petition I make of him, namely that he will leave me to finish 20
my days as I am. For I have herbs to eat and water from the
pool to drink, and serve God with all my strength. I shall not fare
badly in living thus, and thus ending the brief span of my life.

The lion. There is no escape for you from my service, and
you must not doubt concerning what I promise you, nor be 25
in fear.

The jackal. If the King will make a compact with me, and
give me a promise, and take him to witness the immortal
Witness, and make an alliance with me which envy cannot
dissolve nor the wickedness of tale-bearers alter, that not one of 30
the false accusers shall corrupt his mind, nor his hand pursue
after bloodshed, until he has made trial of what has come to his
ears—if the King valiant in strength, will promise me this,
then will I put the yoke of service on my shoulder, and strive
with all my might for the king's interests, aided by heavenly 35
strength.

(291) *The king.* All these promises which you have mentioned, you shall have, and I take God to witness concerning
myself.

Then the king assigned him the stewardship of his house,
entrusted all his store-houses into his hands, and placed all
his wealth under his seal ring, and he was trusted by him.
And wisely did he rule over the king's household, and justly
5 and quietly did he command all his army. And all his affairs
progressed and advanced, because they were managed in the
fear of God. The king was very pleased with him, and every
day advanced him a step higher, and put some new honour upon
him, and the king did nothing except by his advice, and none of
10 his secrets were concealed from him. When the envious saw
all these things, their thoughts were troubled and their hearts
disturbed, and they began to dig a pit and lay snares for him.
   Failing to move his honesty, because he had cleansed himself from all avarice, they laid plans for him, and incited against
15 him many of the king's friends and of the soldiery to calumniate
him, and corrupt the king's opinion about him. And a great
synod or mighty gathering assembled together, and they made
plans among themselves, and weaved threads of deceit.
   Now one day, the fat flesh of some animal was placed before
20 the king, (292) who ate of it with relish. And he directed the
jackal to reserve some of it for his supper; so the jackal went
and gave the piece of flesh into the keeping of the chief cook.
And those envious men gathered together, and made a plan
and forged a plot with the king's head cook; and they gave
25 him money, and took the flesh, and sent and hid it in the
jackal's house, the jackal being unaware of it. When the lion
wished to sup, they sought for the flesh, but could not find it.
And the thing was grievous to the king, who said: 'If such
is the case with this wretched piece of flesh that I entrusted
30 to him, how is it with other things?' For the jackal was not
there at the time.
   And they came and gathered together, and dealt deceitfully and digged this pit, saying: 'Wherefore do we see the
victorious King agitated and all his companions troubled?'
35 And they all began to say: 'O victorious King, the obligation
which lies upon us towards you is too great to be discharged,
and your merits are ineffable. Everything which gives the
King satisfaction is lauded by us, and whatever disturbs his
mind is hateful in our eyes. Now we see that the victorious

King is agitated, and his forces troubled and alarmed, on account of a thing which is very slight in one way, but very grievous in another; slight on account of its triviality, but grievous,
because he who was entrusted with the King's treasures (293),
and in whose hand all his wealth had been placed, lusted after 5
this little and - - - thing.   How then can he manage other
things that are greater than these?'

Some of them said: 'We hear that the jackal has taken this
flesh to his own house.' Others said: 'Do not be sure of this,
until you have tested the end of the matter, nor act hastily and 10
do an injustice.' Others said: 'If this flesh is found in the
jackal's house, then everything that they say about him is
true.' Others said: 'Let no man be certain that his opinion
is right, because sometimes it happens that an opinion
is proved false.' Others said: 'And how can he be - - - by 15
these things, who has ensnared the heart of a prince by
fraud and lying and a false garb?' Others said: 'We have
known this fellow's deceitfulness and trickery ever since
the day when he began to say: "I never eat flesh, for I am
an ascetic." By these means he has ensnared the king's heart.' 20
Others said: 'If this hermit has done these things, it calls for
wonder and astonishment; for (then) not a man in the world
may any more be considered sincere, nor is a single human
being worthy of confidence.' Others said: 'If this flesh is really
found in the jackal's house, then all the disparaging things 25
which they say about him are true, and this fellow is an
unbeliever in God, because he has not repaid His goodness, observed justice, or walked in uprightness, or - - - to stand by the
rights of the valiant king, who lifted up (294) the low fellow to
be steward over all his property, and committed all his goods 30
and store-houses into his hands.' Others said: 'All of you our
brethren are upright.   Every one of you has discharged his obligations to the king, and every one of you has well shown his love
to the king, and not withheld any of his dues.   But now if this
flesh is sought for in the jackal's house and found there, the 35
truth of everything that they say about him is made manifest.'
Others said: 'If you wish that his house be searched, let it be
done quickly, lest he think of some stratagem, and hide it some-
where else.' Others said: 'The fellow only dared to do this,

because the king had confidence in his sound counsels with
which he ensnares the king's heart, so that he will neglect to
punish him.' Others said: 'This offence is not like other offences
the authors of which ought to be pardoned; because this person
5 had the nourishment of many put into his hands, and if in this
little trifling thing he be found false and faithless, then how was
he with other things?'

When they had continued this conversation a long time, the
lion became troubled and angry, sent in hot haste, and sum-
10 moned the jackal into his presence, and asked him, saying:
'Where is the flesh with which I charged you?' The jackal answered: 'I gave it into the keeping of such-and-such a man, the
chief cook.'

Now this chief cook, being one of those who had agreed upon
15 the jackal's destruction, wronged that he was, denied, saying:
'You did not give me anything.'

And the lion's mind was troubled, (295) and he commanded
that the jackal's house should be searched. A number of men
went immediately, sought for the flesh, and found it hidden
20 where it had been placed by those deceitful tale-bearers. They
brought it, and placed it before the king.

Then a certain wolf who had not spoken along with those
evil men who had calumniated him in wickedness, approached
the lion. But, though he concealed the fact, he was notwith-
25 standing a companion of theirs. And he said to the king, while
making it appear by a false countenance that he was a friend
of the jackal, and not of those who bore false witness: 'My Lord
the King, every one who is found with food, whether he be friend
or stranger, and whose theft is thus clearly manifested, should
30 not be suffered to live, but should speedily perish, lest he incite
numbers of others to do this evil thing which has been done in
the King's house. For, when the multitude hear about this
upright steward, in whose hands was placed all this treasure,
that he has polluted himself with this little thing, then will
35 many (others) be infected, and many will do such evil as this in
the King's camp.'

Then the king became angry, and ordered the jackal to be
taken out from his presence in disgrace and shame, and to be
strictly guarded. And they took him out ashamed and amazed

at this thing; but he was too abashed to say a single word of
defence for himself.

Then the king sent to him one of those who were present,
to question him; (296) but that messenger of accursed life came
and returned to the king a false answer which had not been 5
given to him.

[The lion, being angry at it, commanded that the jackal
should be put to death.

But the lion's mother, knowing that he had acted hastily
concerning him, sent word to those who had been ordered to kill 10
him, bidding them wait. Then she went in to her son, and said:
'My son, for what offence have you ordered the jackal to be put
to death?' So he told her about the matter. She replied: 'My
son, you have been too hasty. The wise man guards against
regret by avoiding haste, and by patience. For a hasty person 15
continually reaps the fruits of repentance, by reason of weakness
of mind. No one is more in need of firmness and patience than
a king. A woman needs her husband; a child, his father; a
pupil, his teacher; an army, its general; an ascetic, his religion;
the people need kings; kings need piety; piety requires under- 20
standing; understanding requires patience and deliberation; and
the chief of all is caution. Now for a king the most important
precaution is that he know his companions, assign to them
stations suited to their different characters, and watch carefully
between each man and his fellow; for if one of them finds means 25
to destroy another, he does so. Now, having tried the jackal
and tested his disposition, good-faith, and virtue, you used to
praise him continually, being pleased with him. The King
ought not to accuse him of treachery, after having been pleased
with him, and confided in him. Ever since he came, even till 30
now, no deceit has been found in him; on the contrary, (only)
purity and piety.] - - - - like this stain which they put upon
him by these accusations. Because your intelligence should
not lead you to make such accusations as these against an
intelligent and deep-thinking person, high-minded and of 35
enlightened discernment, clear in knowledge and remote from
avarice. For he was chosen and taken from a feeble estate and
exalted from a humble condition, and admitted to friendship
by the King, and his rank has been exalted, and his ser-

vices extolled, and abundant honour has been put upon him.
That he should dare to disgrace himself by this small and contemptible offence, neither pleasant to God nor bringing temporal
wealth, but only a mouthful of food which in one hour disap-
5 pears and is consumed, that he should bring himself to such
disgrace as this, I do not believe. Especially so, because many
have testified concerning him that for a long time he has not
partaken of flesh for food. It is necessary, O my son, that you
should make this investigation in your own person, lest perhaps
10 they have recourse to deceit, incline to bribery, or be guilty of
partiality, and put away the fear of God from before them and
change the truth into lies, and judicial sentence be precipitated,
and an innocent man perish from among us, and bequeath
dismay and sighing; resembling wine which is tried (297), and
15 its pleasantness and wholesome smell and clear colour recognized: because sometimes it gives a smell while its taste is
insipid, and sometimes its colour is clear while its smell is foul.
Just as a man who, having a disease in his eyes called 'sebel,'
thinks that a piece of hair is in his eyes, while to every one
20 else he seems [a fool; or as a simpleton who sees] the bright
reflection of stars at night-time, for the silly, ignorant fellow
thinks it to be the shining of fire, but when he comes near it
and finds that it is nothing, then he knows that he has made
a great mistake. O my son, your Wisdom must try this
25 matter yourself, and see with your intelligence and with your
mind's eye this mire which has been daubed on this pure and
innocent man by the many accusations of these insolent men.
And since he does not eat flesh - - - - - - - - - - - - - - - - -
investigate well and search into his affair carefully, examine
30 intelligently, and persevere in your efforts patiently; because
the foolish among men envy the wise, the dissolute hate the
abstemious, the lawless abuse ascetics, cowards find fault with
the valiant, (298) educated men and teachers are envied by the
ignorant, the good are insulted by the bad, and the knowing
35 are disparaged by the unlearned. For perchance when the case
of this poor man is searched into, he may be found innocent
and pure, and his accusers may find themselves disappointed.
For perhaps they sent this piece of flesh and put it in his house,
and these audacious men calumniated him with this talk which

they have uttered against him, through envy. Now this fruit of envy is implanted in every race, whether beasts or fowls or cattle or the whole race of birds. For when a bird has caught prey, a multitude of other birds will gather against her; and in the same way, when a dog finds a sinew or a bone, other 5 dogs, his companions, gather together against him. Besides, since these men have been dismissed from the King's service, and removed from his affairs, because of the evil of their deeds and their gluttony, while this ascetic has been found pure and sincere, they have invented these things, and wrought deceit- 10 fully against this man. It was not to please you that all these men gathered together, but every one of them wished to ac-complish his own desire, and every one of them wished to seize and longed to take the rank of steward for himself. But see, my son and beloved of my soul, what advantages you reaped 15 from the person whom you chose for the distribution of your good things, and how satisfied was your illustrious soul with all his ways. So hold fast to him, and let not the desire of others for his destruction be satisfied. For he who satisfies others (299) while he hurts himself, brings upon himself not one but 20 many distresses. One of them is the loss of an honest man. Another is a great sin by shedding the blood of an innocent man. Another is that you will deprive yourself of good ser-vants, and sincere subjects, and wise stewards, and excellent and praiseworthy men. And this man who nourished your 25 troops, and gave salaries to all your men-servants and maid-servants, was unjust to none of them, nor compelled one of them, nor injured anything in your store-house, but on the contrary, in his hands your goods became plentiful, and your possessions were preserved undiminished. Injustice he did to no man, nor 30 offered a bribe to any one, on account of his integrity; but these sinners have planned these stratagems and spun these threads of trickery and accused him falsely, while God forbid that he should be accused.'

The king, on hearing these things from his mother, began 35 to turn over the matter in his mind, and commanded that the jackal should be kept alive. And he said to his mother: 'O blessed mother and distinguished for noble character, I do not doubt concerning your words nor deny their sincerity, nor

am I inclined to do anything else, but shall abide therein; because I have tried all your ways, and found them like tried gold,
whose purity shines forth.'

While conversing thus with his mother, he commanded that
5 the jackal should come before him. The jackal, on hearing the
king say this, (300) opened his mouth boldly, and said: ' O
King valiant in strength, you have been in a great hurry to
destroy your servant. Nor have you acted towards me as
nature demands and the book directs. For nature testifies to
10 the injustice done me; for how should I lust after a piece of
flesh which is small in appearance and trifling in value? For
I am not even in the habit of eating it; and especially (it is
improbable) since I was directed by the King to take charge of
it. Did I then leave the King's treasure and wealth, without
15 stealing of it, and care to steal this trifling miserable thing?
But know, O King, that the book directs that witnesses who
give witness of their own accord, though the judge has not
asked them, nor the slandered persons caused them to give
evidence on their behalf—concerning these the book directs
20 that their testimonies are not to be received. I have many
more things against the King, but now is not the time for me
to tell them, because my mind is sore troubled at the change
that I have seen on the King's part. But to understand this
thing, if the victorious King likes, is very easy.

25   *The king.* And how is it possible (to do so)?

   The jackal. Let the King call one of these my accusers by
himself, and say to him: "I am persuaded that you are the
most upright of all these men, and I am about to make you my
secretary if you will show me the true facts of this case. And
30 I will make a compact with you that I will not do any harm
(301) to the man who has done this thing." On hearing the
truth from him, make a show of gratitude to him for a time,
and let his honour be distinguished. Then call a second one,
and coax him by the same and similar words, so that you may
35 hear the truth from two or three persons, when it will be easy
for you to find out the whole of this affair. After that, do as
your pure eyes may see fit. It was fitting, O victorious King,
that I should wonder at these things, (namely) how all these
persons conspired to speak against me, and how you believed

their words; since you have not found in me a single deficiency, nor even for a single day have you or any other person seen me eating flesh. Nor was it by day that I used to take food; but alone in the dead of night, like a wayfarer, did I partake of it. And I hope that He for whose sake I have borne these burdens, 5 and for whose pleasure I have endured these toils and labours, will not conceal from you the truth about me, but will speedily make manifest to you, and to all your companions with you, the integrity of my conduct towards you and the honesty of my dealings with you.   10

The king, on hearing these things, was sore distressed, as well as pleased. He was distressed, because the jackal had reviled his want of wisdom, denounced by his words his lack of education, and abused the scantiness of his knowledge. Then he was glad, for he had opened to him a door by which he could obtain 15 what he sought for. Then the king summoned one of them, an old man, ancient of days and honourable, and said to him as the jackal (302) had already put into his mouth (to say), adding other words besides. And the person, whoever he was, on hearing (what he said), inclined to the truth and confessed his 20 offence, and that of all his companions; since he heard the king say that any man who was knocking at death's door and whose last days had come, when the gray hairs showed themselves upon him, [ought to tell the truth]; and besides he wished to get the presents which the king had promised to him, 25 and the office which he was to entrust into his hand. The king, on hearing him say these things, honoured and magnified him for a time. And it came to the ears of his companions that he had been magnified in this way, because he had spoken the truth. And the king sent and summoned another. In this 30 manner he entrapped them, so that they confessed to the truth, and absolved the poor jackal from blame. So these audacious men bemired their own persons and accused themselves.

When this matter had been made public, the lion's mother said to her son : ' O my son, blessed be God who has restrained 35 you, O beloved of my soul and staff of my old age, from the shedding of innocent blood, and delivered you from (inflicting) unjust punishment, and has not distressed both you and me with the loss of an upright and innocent steward. Now, as for these

lying, crafty, and audacious fellows, do not observe the compact
with them, nor the promise to them, nor let them live any
longer.   For they are liars, children of a lying father and
wicked calumniator ; because peace is not observed by them, nor
5 love established with them.   For (303) they have grieved the
King's mind and disturbed his thoughts, troubled all his friends,
and invented deceit and set traps.   May God bring down their
iniquity on their own heads.   And now exert yourself diligently,
O my son, that this zealous and injured steward may return to
10 his office, pure that he is and without stain, and that the work
of the stewardship may be committed to his hands.   Be not
ashamed or afraid because of the wrath which enflamed you on
his account, or because of the punishment which you decreed
upon him.   For thus it happens to kings, that when they put
15 abundant honour upon men who for a time have been rebuked
by them, they are honoured by all with whom they come in
contact.   Much advantage too do those derive for themselves
who for a time are removed from the height of their dignity, so
that they may not look at the eminence of it and become
20 unrestrained and fall through pride into the snare of Satan, and
depart altogether from the fold of humility.   Besides all this,
the jackal is intelligent and subtle in knowledge, and anger
will not overcome him, nor will pride over his victory cause
him to leave your fold, or be disobedient to your commands, or
25 disdain to serve you.   Nor do I think that his good character
will be affected by these restraints which you have put upon
him for a short time.   But shun, O beloved of my soul, those
who have not feared the retribution of justice, nor been afraid
of disgrace, nor torrified at (304) the punishment and torment
30 reserved for the wicked.   And repulse from you those who
are stricken with avarice and noted for greed, and enslaved
by drink, who speak with double tongues, whose god is their
belly, who eat gluttonously and drink deeply, who engage in
amassing wealth unjustly and fill their storehouses with bribes,
35 who signify wickedness with their eyes shamefully, and give
counsel deceitfully.   Draw near to you, O my son, and put in
charge of your storehouses, those who are satisfied with their
pay, who drink water out of one fountain, who sleep on one
bed who speak with one tongue, who are ashamed to wink

with the eyes, who are far from evil, who never slander, who love peace with all, who live together in perpetual harmony.'

When the king heard these words from his mother, he knew that the jackal had been found innocent and pure and spotless, 5 and come out of the furnace of trial like pure gold. And he sent for the jackal and caused him to stand before him, and began to apologise for what he had done, and raised him to an exalted position, and honoured him in the presence of all with prudent and gentle converse, saying to him : 'Know, O brother, 10 that this thing has magnified you exceedingly in my eyes, (305) and the honour which I am about to place upon you is un- equalled by anything; in a word, I will magnify your seat above all my courtiers, give you dominion over all that hate you, and entrust you with all my house. So continue in your steward- 15 ship, and undertake all your duties as in the former days.'

Whereupon the jackal made obeisance before the king, and said to him : 'O King live for ever! I have something to say to you, my Lord the King: hear it from me, and shrink not from it, nor be angry at it. Though it be a little grievous, yet do 20 not disdain it; because a man ought to listen to the defence which his fellow makes for himself. For you too, O victorious King, through your goodness and greatness, purity of heart, enlightened discernment, and sincere love, thought me just and far from iniquity. These things have taken place without any 25 change of kindness on *your* part. For they were clearly de- picted before my eyes, when I was found to be righteous and a lover of righteousness, in this age which is destitute of just men, deprived of the upright, and void of the god-fearing, (an age) in which Kings are swallowed up with iniquity,- - - - - - 30 - - - - - - - - - - - - - - have left off caring for their subjects, freely indulged in fleshly lusts, and corrupted their purity by their lasciviousness. In their case is indeed come to pass (306) that which was spoken : 'That which dieth let it die, and that which perisheth let it perish, and let that which is left eat the 35 flesh of the rest.' When this character is found in kings, all who follow after them are corrupted : and if with difficulty there be found one person who delights in the fear of God he spends the days of his life without pleasure, for many are

his enemies and his adversaries abound, they set many traps for
him, and utter lies against him and speak falsehoods about
him, for they are all smitten with [envy]. And when the
victorious King had forced me against my will, I inclined to
5 him the shoulder of obedience, after that he had considered
and tried me, and knew all my ways, how that for a long time
past I had loved to live alone and fed on herbs out of all the
good things of God. Therefore your Majesty was weak and
your discernment feeble, that you should be false to your
10 promises and put away your pleasantness for the bite of a
wretched goat; since I had made no breach in your kingdom,
nor despoiled your treasury, but through some miserable insignificant thing, pierced my feeble body with sharp arrows and
barbs smeared with deadly poison. But this was not your
15 doing, O King, but of the children of this your generation who
have been put in charge of your service, who eat and give
others to eat, whose lovers and false witnesses are more
numerous than they who abuse and oppose them (307). If,
O king, I had eaten of your wealth and given others to eat,
20 and squandered your possessions and wasted your goods, I too
should have had many friends and many to praise me to you.
But because I observed righteousness and feared the judgment
of the Highest, and stood in awe of the punishment of hell, I
performed my duty to the King throughout my conduct, and
25 discharged obligations, and departed from earthly friends who
pursue (only) after things which will advantage them, and relinquished pleasures, and cast behind my back the praise of the
multitude. Yet in one instant I lost my life, and by one foul
mouthful I disgraced my good name; though I was not punished
30 or chastised, except through the scorching wind (of calumny)
which has been roused, and only through the viper of envy
was sentence of death [passed] upon me. But God, whom I
have served in sincerity and whose commandments I have kept
according to my strength, has not neglected me, but has
35 chosen to show that there are fruits of peace and a good end for
him who practises righteousness, and that a man cannot be
robbed of the reward of his labour. And though the good and
bad alike shall receive their recompense in the world to come,
yet here too, before the eyes of many, is their innocence made

manifest. And now, O victorious King, my mind is troubled. These promises of yours, like the former ones, are not worthy of trust; because I served before the King in righteousness and honesty, and was never accused of stealing from him jacinths or emeralds, or gold and silver, to enrich myself with them, (308) 5 and thus did I continually abase myself, and relinquished all material good, [and yet you believed the slander against me]. Add to this that the whole nature of created things is subject to change, and that evil desire is implanted in them, and that they are liable to aberration. Perhaps they have been over- 10 come of desire and partaken of that foul piece of meat which, immediately it passes from the teeth, dissolves and turns into dung. So deal kindly with these men, for that perhaps they were overcome by the force of nature, but not overcome - - - - - - - - - - . What too profits it to approach the king ? For it 15 has been said by the wisest of the wise : - And now, O King, wash your hands of me, and abolish from your mind the idea that I am going to serve you. Considering too all that has been heard throughout your camp to the effect 20 that such and such a one, the steward, has been accused of so and so many things, been dismissed from his employment, and condemned to death, how can he return afresh to his steward- ship ? These things would cause many to mock and deride you, saying, 'Wherefore was the king so hasty; and wherefore did 25 he investigate concerning the steward, and how could he submit to disgrace, since he has become a laughingstock throughout the king's - - - - ? If he goes back to this fellow, he is devoid of intelligence, and must be considered destitute of education.' Now may the King, and his friends and companions, have 30 abundant peace concerning his stewardship, even as he believed their words.'

The king. How excellent is all that you have said, but hard to listen to, and grievous to those who bear (you). (309) But I must needs bear them, because we have sinned against 35 you.

The jackal. My Lord the King, let not the truth be grievous to you, and be not offended at straightforwardness, nor let lying speech rejoice your heart, nor calumny gladden your

mind. Think not that I have dared to say these things to
the victorious King through ignorance or pride or fear; but it
was on account of two things that I said these things. One of
them is that if a man, on being falsely accused or wronged,
5 speaks the truth before the world, and his good character is tried
and found genuine, many will love honesty, and depart from
iniquity. I sought too that no anger should remain in the
heart of him who had been accused formerly, and that he should
declare his whole mind, so that he should not say (afterwards) :
10 'Thus I was treated, and thus I ought to have spoken,' and
some hatred remain in his heart and a lingering spite. Then,
[if] the King gets angry at what he has heard, and orders either
that he be put to death or chastised, every one will know that
it was for the defence which he made for himself that he was
15 chastised or put to death, and not because he committed an
offence and was ashamed and unable to open his mouth and
say a word for himself. But in spite of all this, I do [not]
quite despair of your kindness, nor do I think you altogether
so devoid of justice as to refuse to listen to truthful words,
20 though they be a little grievous, for in the end they will bear
fruits of peace. Pray, my Lord, be not offended at them.

The king. Have I not inclined my gaze upon you with
gentleness, and listened to the defence, (310) and borne the
grievousness of your words, and hastened to act in accordance
25 with them ?

The jackal. By the king I have been condemned to death,
but through his blessed mother do I faintly hope for life.

The king. Did you not say that when a man confesses his
fault and acknowledges his offence, his confession should be
30 accepted of him ? Then how is it that after we have acknowledged your integrity, and made confession before you like a
guilty one, you do not accept it of me, but your mind keeps
brooding over it ? Do not speak excellently without acting
excellently ; because it has been said that he who acts first and
35 [then] teaches is called great.

The jackal. I have not said these things, O my Lord the
King, in order to show the King that he has acted badly towards
me, and commanded unjustly concerning me ; because I am the
king's servant, and if I live, it is for him that I live, and if I

die, it is to him that I am lost. Nay, but I wished to make
the King and all his companions see how serious is the matter
of liars, that they may remove the talebearers from his court,
and that he may purge his army of all froward men; for I
doubt not that they will now find the door open whereby false 5
accusers may approach the victorious King and corrupt his
mind.

The king. But how can they now dare to do so ?

The jackal. They can now say : ' Because the jackal's mind
is corrupted by the accusation which we made against him, and 10
by that with which the King charged him, he thus uttered (311)
words fraught with offence and enmity and destruction.'

The king. To-day you are no longer accounted by me as
one of those against whom I would accept what men say, now
that the fact of your righteousness has been demonstrated in 15
the furnace of trial, but are like tried gold and stainless pearls
and spotless jacinths. Now let no thought occur to you which
may corrupt your mind, but decide to remain with us, abide
in your office and return to your employment: believe what we
say and trust to our promises : and wash away this filth from 20
your heart, even as it is washed away from mine.

And the king caused proclamation to be made in his camp
that the steward had been found pure and upright and spotless. He returned also to his stewardship, and was honoured by
all his fellows.   25

The story of the lion and the jackal is ended.

THE STORY OF THE TRAVELLER AND THE GOLDSMITH.

The king. I have heard what [you have narrated,] and excellently and well do your words agree and suit. Now show
5 me to whom out of the whole number of men ought the king
to do a benefit.

The philosopher. It is excellent for kings to do benefits to
every man, and right that all should have enjoyment from their
wealth, but it is not right that they should have confidence in
10 every one. (312) Especially should benefits be conferred upon
him who is grateful for what is done to him. And they should
not consider their near friends and intimates only : or the rich
and powerful, without putting them into the furnace of trial ;
nor again the weak and needy whose case has not been searched
15 into, nor their character and disposition tested, lest in spite of
their weakness they be perverse and froward, even crafty and
crooked in their ways ; but both sides should first be tested, the
rich as well as the poor, both the mighty and the weak. And
he among them who is found to be a fearer of God, his mouth
20 full of gratitude, his mind clear of iniquity, and his soul free
from avarice and remote from greed - - - - - - - - - - - - - -
and then let everyone of them be done to him, and let him be
rewarded as the innocence of his conduct and the integrity of
his ways dictate. For a skilful physician, in giving directions
25 for the sick, or prescribing medicine for the wounded, does not
merely look at their exteriors, but feels the pulse and looks at
the water every day, and then looks at their faces, as to whether
they are downcast or cheerful, and treats them accordingly with
medicine suitable for their complaints. And if there be found
30 a man who is destitute of the wealth of this passing fleeting
world, but rich in God and wise in spiritual things (313) and
perfect in all those things which are exalted, he ought to be

befriended by the king, aud honoured by him and magnified;
lest he have need of him, and when he wants him, he be not at
hand. Among beasts too and birds and fowls there are some
who ought to be sa kept; for there is no avoiding the events
which happen and the things which occur and the necessities 5
which affect (us), and sometimes it happens that there is fear of
human beings, and a man has recourse to animals; as when a
man has found a weasel and kept it in his house, or a young
hawk and carries it on his hand, [and when it has caught anything, he profits by it and gives it him to eat of it. Aud it has 10
been said that an intelligent man ought not to despise any one,
whether small or great, man or beast; but that he should first
test them, and (then) act towards them according to what he
finds in them. This is illustrated by a fable which one of the
wise has related.]   15
    The king.   And what is it?
    The teacher.   Some men dug a pit in which to catch ani-
mals, and it chanced that a certain goldsmith passed by, and
full into it. And [a tiger] passed by, and fell into the pit. An
ape also passed by, and a snake, and they in like manner fell in. 20
It chanced that a certain traveller passed by; and seeing
them, he had pity on them, saying within himself: 'Nothing
will bring me so near to God as to draw up these unfortunates
out of this pit into which they are sunk. Especially ought I to
draw up this man who is cast among these beasts. So he took 25
a rope and threw it down, [and the ape took hold of it and was .
drawn up. And he threw it down again], and the tiger took
hold of it and was drawn up. He threw it down again, and the
snake took hold of it and was drawn up. Whereupon, these
animals began to thank (314) the traveller, and said to him: 30
'Do not draw up the man out of this pit, because there is
nothing in all creation worse than he.' But he did not take
their advice, for he was sorry for him. When he had thrown him
the rope and drawn him up by it, each one of them said to him:
'How can I show you gratitude for this your solicitude on our 35
behalf?' And the animals said: 'We live in such and such a
district, and should occasion call you to our neighbourhood, we
will discharge the duty that lies upon us.' And they left, and
departed from him. Then the goldsmith too said to him: 'I

dwell in this town, and if you come to us, I will render you the
reward which you deserve, and not be ungrateful for your kindness to us.' And the man too departed from him. After some
time it happened that the traveller passed through that dis-
5 trict; and the ape met him and received him gladly, and went
to the mountain and brought of all the fruits of the trees that
were there, and placed them before him, and he ate of them
and thanked him.

And he departed from the ape, and after traversing a short
10 distance, he saw the tiger, who received him gladly and said
to him : ' Blessed is your coming ! I do not possess anything,
but wait for me here a little while, and I will manage to
repay what I owe you.' So he went to the king's daughter
and killed her, and took her trinkets, and brought (315) them
15 to the traveller, saying : 'Take these, wherewith to supply your
needs.' But the traveller knew not whence he had brought
them.

Straightway the traveller said within himself : ' If these who
are but dumb animals have discharged their obligations so well,
20 how then ought a human being to repay them ? I will arise and
go to the goldsmith and deliver those trinkets into his hands,
and he shall sell them and give some of their price to the
poor and take a little for himself, and I will take a little and
get relief from my poverty.' So he arose and went to the
25 goldsmith's house. When he saw him, he received him gladly,
especially when he beheld the gold (which he had) with him.
And the goldsmith, recognising the gold as belonging to the
king's daughter, took it and went to the king's gate, and said
to the porter : ' I have some business with the king, which will
30 advantage him.' So the porter went in to the king hastily,
and let him know. And he admitted him to the king. The
goldsmith showed him the gold belonging to his daughter,
saying : ' The man who killed your daughter and took this gold
from her, is staying with me.' The king commanded, and they
35 brought the traveller. When he saw him and saw his daughter's gold, he commanded that he should be scourged and taken
all round the city, with a herald in front of him proclaiming
and saying : ' This is the man who killed the king's daughter !'
and then crucified. When they had done so to him, and had

crucified him, he began to weep and say to himself: 'If (316)
I had hearkened to the advice of those animals, and left this
man in the pit, this evil had not befallen me.' The snake,
hearing his voice, came out of his hole. And when he saw
him hanging on a cross, it grieved him exceedingly. And he 5
devised means for his deliverance, and crept little [by little], and
stung the king's son. The king, hearing of it, assembled the
enchanters and wizards; and they divined, but he was not profited a whit, but his pain became worse. And it was revealed
to the king's son in a dream that if this traveller did not come 10
and put his hand on his wound, he would not be cured; because that this traveller had been unjustly condemned. The
king, on hearing it, commanded, and they took him down from
the cross, and he said to him: 'I wish you to tell me your circumstances, and to give me an account of yourself, and (tell me) 15
why you came to this city.' The traveller then told him his
story from beginning to end. And the king said: 'Grant recovery to my son from the bite of the snake, that everything
you have said may be confirmed.' The traveller, not knowing
what to say to him, lifted up his eyes to heaven, and said: 'O 20
Lord God, if I have told the truth to the king, without falsi-
fying any thing, grant recovery to this boy, and let the king
and those present know that I have told the truth.' Immediately the boy was cured of the snake's bite. And the king
and all who were with him wondered. And the king com- 25
manded, and they honoured the traveller, and gave him great
presents. He also commanded concerning the goldsmith, and
they scourged him (317) severely, and afterwards crucified him
justly; because that dumb animals had paid what they owed
and discharged obligations, while a rational human being had 30
been ungrateful and false.

The story of the traveller and the goldsmith is ended.

THE STORY OF THE KING'S SON AND HIS COMPANIONS.

The king. I have heard and understood how that a king ought to choose (some), and repulse (others) from him. Now
5 tell me the reason why the position of a contentious foolish man may be exalted, and his honour distinguished, and his good things made plentiful, while the temporal affairs of a wise man, bold and God-fearing, may be impeded, and the evils which affect him may be many.

10 *The teacher.* Just as a man does not see except with his eyes, nor hear except with his ears, so knowledge and wisdom cannot come except by intelligence and patience, and instruction from teachers. And some have said about this that these things are ordained by God and decreed [on] each man - - - - - - -
15 those which are decreed of God vanquish a man's nature and overcome all things. Now it is related that four persons were in company, and wrote on the gate of a certain city (318) that perfection of beauty, and of strength, and of devices, is decreed by God.

20 *The king.* How runs the story about them?

The teacher. It is related that a king's son, a merchant's son, a nobleman's son of handsome appearance, and a husband-man's son, set out upon a journey. And they were all weary with the fatigue of travelling, and in great distress and want.
25 As they were going along together, the king's son said to his companions: 'All things are decreed by God upon men, whether wealth, or poverty, or other things which are similar to these.' The merchant's son said: 'And wealth is gotten by intelligence.' The one who was handsome and well-born said: 'Wealth is
30 gotten through beauty.' The husbandman's son said: 'Wealth is gotten by labour and toil.'

They said to the husbandman's son : 'Go in advance of us,
and by your strength manage to get for us what will satisfy our
hunger, because we are very hungry and our soul is distressed.'
So the husbandman's son went and entered the city, and asked
what he could find to do there in order to satisfy the hunger 5
of four persons. He was told that there was wood in the
neighbourhood, distant about a parasang's journey, and that
if a man went and fetched some of it, he could sell (it), and
get food with the price of it. And the husbandman went out
to the place, which was distant from the city about ten stadia, 10
(319) and gathered wood, brought it to the market-place of
the city, and sold it for half a zūz, with which he bought
bread and vegetables. These he brought to his companions.
When they had eaten, he wrote on the gate of the city : 'The
work of a whole day has profited half a zūz.'   15

The next day they said to the man of handsome appearance :
'Manage to get for us what will be of use to us.' So he
went and entered [the city], and sat in the market-place, not
knowing what to do. And there passed by him the wife of
a certain rich man who had goods and possessions. When 20
the foolish woman saw him, she was captivated by his beauty,
sent her handmaid after him, and brought him into her
house. * * * And when she had given him all kinds of
meats to eat and wines to drink, and perfumed him with divers
perfumes, and it were towards evening, he told her that he had 25
companions who were expecting him. And she gave him five
hundred darics. And he went to his companions, and told
them all that he had done, and wrote on the gate of the town :
'Beauty has procured the delights of a whole day, and five
hundred dīnārs (besides).'   30

On the morrow they said to the merchant's son : 'Go
forth, and see what you can do with your trading.' [So he went
off and entered the town.] And he heard that a large ship had
arrived from the ocean, laden with all kinds of merchandise.
And the merchants of the town went out to buy the goods 35
with which it was laden. The merchant's son, on seeing them,
joined himself to them, without their knowing whence he was.
When they reached the ship, they said (320) to one another :
'Let us go back, and come (again) tomorrow, so that the

K. V.   14

owner of the vessel may not ask too high a price.' And the
merchant's son bought all that was in it for an hundred thousand
darics, and gave the owner his pledge. And the merchants,
hearing (of it), came to the merchant's son, and gave him
5 an hundred thousand dínárs as profit, and took the ship.
Then he went to his companions, and told them all that had
happened to him, and wrote on the gate of the city: 'The
trading of a day has profited an hundred thousand dínárs.'
   The next day they said to the king's son: 'Do you go forth,
10 and see what you can do.' So he went forth and sat at the
gate of the city. Now it happened that day that the king of
the city died, without leaving behind him either son or brother
to claim the kingdom. And as they carried the king's bier
and brought it past the gate, this king's son did not move
15 from his place or go away, and the report of the king's death
did not move him, nor did he accompany the bier. One of
those who were with the king's bier came up to him and said:
'Who are you, that you should be so bold as not to rise up
from your place and accompany the king's bier?' But he
20 made no answer. The other forthwith reviled him and drove
him from the gate. But when they had put the king into the
heart of the earth and were returning, he found him again
sitting in the same place. So he seized him, saying: 'Did
I not (321) command you not to sit here?' and sent him away
25 and had him bound in the prison-house. Now when they were
assembled together to choose them a king, they could not find
one person in all the palace who was fit for or could claim the
kingdom. As they were considering with one another, the
man who had bound the king's son said to them: 'I saw a
30 certain young man, who did so and so many things; perhaps
he would be suitable for this thing, and fit to reign over us.'
And he sent to the prison house and had him brought, and
asked him to give an account of himself. Then he related to
them his whole story, and said: 'I am the son of such and
35 such a king, from such and such a city. When my father died,
my younger brother robbed me of the kingdom and took it for
himself, and I, fearing lest I should lose my life, left him everything and come here.' When those present heard (this), they
perceived that he had told them the truth, and they agreed to

make the young man king over them. So they sent heralds
to the public places of the city, and assembled all the magnates
and nobles of the city, a great gathering, and made the youth
king over them. Now they had a custom, when they set up
a king over them, of mounting him on a certain celebrated 5
elephant, and conducting him all round the town, while heralds
proclaimed before him: 'This is the king of our country.'
And when he reached the gate, he saw what his companions
had written on it. And the king commanded, [and they wrote:]
'Labour and beauty and traffic and intelligence have not 10
profited so much as that which God the Merciful has given,
He who has brought me (322) to this exalted position, and
lifted up my horn, and raised my seat, and clothed me with the
robe of royalty.'

And as he sat on his judgment-seat, he sent for his com- 15
panions and called them to him, and enriched them with many
presents, and said to his courtiers: 'These are my companions,
each of whom placed his confidence in some one thing. One
relied on his strength, and one on the beauty of his appearance,
and one on his intelligence. I, lonely one, despaired of happiness, 20
and after that my brother wronged me and robbed me of the
kingdom which had fallen to my lot, I believed that I should
pass all my life in misfortune and distress. But God in his
mercy did not neglect me, but in his goodness decreed for me
this kingdom; because I know that there are men in this place 25
who are better instructed and more intelligent than I, and more
fitted for this thing. However, things are not gained by
strength, or by beauty, or by intelligence. I now render thanks
to God and to you, O nobles and sons of honoured lineage, that
this has seemed good in your eyes, and that you have not dis- 30
liked me for being a stranger.'

When he had spoken these words, there arose a traveller in
the midst of the assembly, and said to him before all present: 'O
King, you have spoken excellently and intelligently, and inter-
preted aright, and have been grateful to God wisely. Now, our 35
joy in you is increased, and our spirit is uplifted (323) through
your reigning over us, because we know that you have observed
right and told the truth. On account of this, God [has] rightly
[taken pity] upon you, and rewarded you as you deserved. There

is no man whose fortune is so good and to whom we ought to
render such kindness as you, nor whose joy should be so abundant as yours. Lo, God has fulfilled to us through you all our
desire, and we render thanks to him who made you king over
5 us. May our Lord establish the sceptre of your kingdom, and
terrify with your sword all the enemies of the truth, and may
your right-hand overtake all that hate you.'

When he had done speaking, another traveller rose up in the
midst, and opened his mouth, and glorified God, and [rendered]
10 thanks, saying: "Hear from me, O glorious King, two words; for
they are very wonderful, and will incite every man to do right
things. [When] I was a youth, I joined myself to a great and
renowned man, who was rich in all temporal things; and I
served him with all my strength, in all integrity. One day, I
15 considered and said to myself: 'Lo, my days are spent in idleness, and I am employed in doing what will not save me from
the Judge, or bring a peaceful end.' And I desired to be
an ascetic and serve God. So I said to the man: 'See, give me
all the pay that you owe me, because I desire other service.'
20 And he gave me two dinārs. Having taken them, I wished to
give one of them to the poor, and to keep the other for my own
necessities. As I was (324) pondering these thoughts, I saw in
the market-place a fowler with two doves. I said to myself:
'There is nothing so profitable as to release souls.' So I said
25 to the fowler: 'How much money do you want from me for
these doves?' He answered: 'Two dinārs.' I tried to make
him take (only) one from me, and leave me the other for my
expenses, but he would not; and to take the one, and leave the
other, did not please me; for I said: 'Perhaps they are a pair,
30 and then how can I separate them from one another? Or perhaps they are brothers, and it will grieve them if they are
parted from one another.' Then I gave both the dinārs to the
fowler, and took the doves from him. And I thought to leave
them in the house, but I feared they might get hungry and
35 thirsty, and long for food, and then be caught. So I took them
to the open field, and threw them seeds and water. Having
eaten the seeds and drunk the water, they flew away and
perched on a tree. And when I sought to return, the doves
said to one another: 'How can we leave this man without a

recompense, and without returning thanks? For his kindness
has been very great to us, for he has brought us together,
and delivered us from distress.' Then they beckoned to me,
and I drew near to them, and they said to me: 'We cannot
repay your kindness, but now we will do to you as much as we 5
can. Dig under this tree on which we are, and take (325)
whatever you find, because a jar full of darics has been placed
there.' So I digged and took them. Then I knew that nothing
remains unrequited. Whereupon, I said to the doves: 'Since
you are so wise, how is it that you can fall into the fowler's 10
snare?' The doves answered: 'Why, do you not know, O fearer
of God, that everything which is decreed by Him, overrides all
manner of wisdom?'"

The story of the king's son and his companions is ended.

STORY OF THE LIONESS AND THE JACKAL.

The king. I have understood the similitude which you
have used, and excellently have you spoken. Now tell me what
is profitable for a man whom want affects, and who encounters
5 trials and bears them without entangling others in them, or
studying how he may place them on everybody else; in order
that their intensity may abate, and their severity be diminished.

The teacher. He who desires the affliction and injury of
other men is foolish and ignorant and a denier of God, that is,
10 shameless and without modesty, having no intelligence, and is
remote from [the fear of] God's retribution, and a stranger to
shame before men, and (only) fears this world's punishment.
But if a man is delivered from the malevolence of his fellow, it
is by a chance that he is delivered, or because, being in hopes of
15 robbing (326) him of something, he delays the mischief which
is set in his heart, lest it become manifest, and not for fear of
the punishment of hell. Such a man illustrates the story of the
horseman, the lioness, and the jackal.

The king. How runs the story about them?

20   *The teacher.* It is related that in a wood was a certain
lioness who had two whelps. When she had gone out (one
day), there passed by them a man shooting with a bow, called
an 'iswār,' who shot arrows at them, and killed them. Having
stripped them of their skins, he threw away their flesh into the
25 wood, but took their hides. When the lioness came (back) and
saw them, she lifted up her voice in weeping and bitter lamentations and woeful plaints. A neighbour of hers, called by a
name which some say means 'jackal,' hearing her, approached
her, saying: 'What is this mishap which has befallen you? Let
30 me know, that I may sympathize with you.'

The lioness. I had two children, that is whelps, who were
the delight of my eyes. But an armed horseman passed by

them, and shot arrows at them, and killed them, and stripped off their skins and took (them) with him, and threw away their flesh.

The jackal. Do not complain, but condemn your own self, and know that this man has only done you this injury, because 5 you have injured others (327) as he has (you). Nor would this grief have agonised your heart unless you in like manner had caused grief to others; because it has been said: 'With what measure (ye mete, it shall be measured to you;') and again: 'As a man sows, so shall he reap;' and again: 'Every man shall be 10 recompensed according to his work;' and finally: 'As ye would that men should do unto you, so do ye also to them.'

The liouess. Explain to me what you have said, and make it clear, so that I may know the truth of it.

The jackal. How old are you?   15

Lioness. An hundred years.

Jackal. On what have you been feeding all these years?

Lioness. On the flesh of animals of all kinds.

Jackal. What enabled you to eat them?

Lioness. My own self.   20

Jackal. Had they not mothers, who grieved for them?

Lioness. Yes.

Jackal. And wherefore did you not hearken to *their* cry, if your own feelings have been (so) stirred by this that has happened to yourself? As you have done (to others), so have others 25 done to you. Because you did not consider the end of your way and the result of your deeds, or the pain of heart of your companions, and their wounded feelings, God has visited you, and rewarded you as your transgression deserved.

The lioness, when she heard these words, knew that he had 30 told her the truth, and that she had been the first (328) to sin, and understood that he who does a thing wrongfully, and presumes on a multitude of things which do not belong to him, receives such a punishment as this. Then she left off hunting and eating flesh, and entered the state of an ascetic or hermit, 35 and began to eat fruit in the field and the fruits of the trees on the mountain; so that the fruit of the trees was diminished. Now there was a certain jackal, who used to feed on the fruit of the trees, and when he saw that it was diminished, he thought

that the trees had ceased to bear fruit. But when he behold
one day and saw the lioness eating it, he knew that the blessing
had been taken from it, since violence had entered in ; because
the lioness had left the use of her nature, and joined herself to
5 something which did not belong to her, wrongfully and not
justly, oppressively and not lawfully. And he began to say :
" Woe to the trees and to those who get food from them, since
the violence of another has overtaken them, and they are
doomed to perish. But neither will these oppressors attain to
10 a peaceful end, since oppression and violence has been wrought.
And he said excellently, who said : 'Woe to the oppressed from
the oppressor, but woe to the oppressor from God!'"

The End.

(329) STORY OF THE HERMIT AND THE TRAVELLER:

A chapter which shows that he who understands something and leaves it and takes to something else, forgets the first without learning the second.

The king. 1 understand what you say, and excellently 5 have you investigated, and well have you illustrated. Now show me the similitude of a craftsman who leaves his craft and takes to another, and forgets the first without prospering in the second.

The teacher. It is related that in a certain region lived a 10 devout hermit. Once upon a time a traveller came to him, and presented him with a little fruit. When the two began to eat, the traveller said: 'How sweet and pleasant this fruit is! Would that in our country there were palm-trees like these! However, though we have not palm-trees, we have other trees of 15 all kinds, fig-trees and many others, which a man may enjoy, and which benefit the body more than fruits which cause wind.'

The hermit. He is not accounted lucky, who has need of what he cannot get, and casts longing looks at it, who longs for it and does not resign himself to being without it: but his 20 troubles abound, and his sighs are increased to him. But you, O beloved of my soul, have good fortune and a sound mind and a clear (330) intellect; for you have abided in that which God prepared, without casting longing looks at something else which is far from you.   25

The traveller. You have spoken justly, and investigated with wisdom. Now I hear you speak a language which is very pleasant and desired by the prudent, and my soul is very desirous to learn from you how to speak as you do. Oh that you would therefore grant me the favour, and teach me some 30 of it!

The hermit. You are not far from a transgression, for if you relinquish the language to which you are used, and practise another, there will happen to you what happened to the crow.

The traveller. How runs the story about him, and what 5 happened to him?

The hermit. It is related that a certain crow, seeing a hen strutting as she walked, sought to walk [like her], and began to try and step as she did. But he did not succeed, and forgot his former paces besides; for he kept continually stumbling, 10 besides losing what he possessed before. I have told you this, because I fear for you, lest in practising a language to which you are not accustomed, you forget the one to which you are accustomed, and men reckon you foolish and without knowledge and intelligence, for practising what neither you nor your parents 15 before you were brought up to.

The story of the traveller and the hermit is ended.

(331) THE STORY OF THE WISE BILĀR.

THE king said to the philosopher: I have heard what you
have said, but now tell me whereby a king is honoured by his
subjects, and by what thing he can make peace to reign in his
army, and overcome the malevolence of his generals, and prevent
his kingdom from being rent and given to others; whether by
patience and longsuffering and abundance of gifts and kindly
behaviour, or by harshness and cruelty, evil dealing and bitterness of soul.

The teacher replied: There is nothing which makes a king
so honourable in the eyes of all men, and sets his whole kingdom
in such peace and tranquillity, and so terrifies his enemies and
alarms all the evil-doers as patience, or longsuffering. Now
longsuffering is only acquired by wisdom; and wisdom cannot
be grasped except by the fear of God, according as the book has
said and as nature dictates; and the fear of God can only be
grounded by continual meditation with books, and by disputation
with teachers versed in knowledge, remote from pride, and separate from avarice, who do not aim at amassing wealth, are not
smitten with greed, love not empty glory, consent not to foolish
thoughts, are not addicted to deceit, nor envy the workers of
good, (332) nor calumniate a man in secret. All these excellent qualities which we have enumemted, are profitable to a
king; and an additional help would be a good wife, and confidants and counsellors. But if a man be found quarrelsome, and not
possessed of long-suffering, while his counsellors are feeble in
knowledge, his fall will be speedy; because, since he is not
possessed of long-suffering, and his counsellor is not versed in
affairs, but does things with heat and impetuosity, great dismay
will come upon him, and no little trouble and sighing without
measure will he bring upon himself, and he will become a
mockery and a derision among his fellows, and a laughing-stock

and a sport to all his acquaintances. And though he succeed in
some one of his affairs through help and strength from on high,
it is only for a short time that he succeeds, and not long is the
duration of his prosperity. But when a king is pure in mind
5 and far from iniquity, devoid of impurity and cleansed from
lasciviousness, and finally has a soul unsmitten with greed, and
far from envy, and counsellors who are God-fearing, who love the
prosperity of his subjects, are zealous for the tranquillity of his
army, and bury his secrets in the heart of the earth, this king
10 attains to all things, spends the days of his life with all satisfaction, overcomes all oppositions, and subdues all fortified places;
and whenever that king is minded to do a thing, he accomplishes
his desire in whatever matter it may be, while taking advice of
his counsellors, (333) men remote from fraud, and full of love
15 and faith. And there will happen to him what happened to
Dēvaçarman, king of India, concerning Ilār his wife and Bilār
his confidant.

The king said : And what happened to them?

The teacher. I have been told that Bilār was an ascetic,
20 subtle and wise and prudent, of an excellent disposition and
praiseworthy in his conduct, gentle in all his affairs, and patient
in all that appertained to him. The king of India in whose time
he lived, was very fond of him, and used to extol his wisdom,
and he was more honourable in his eyes than any of his courtiers.
25 It came to pass one day, when the king was asleep in an
upper room where cushions had been laid for him, that he saw
eight different dreams, each of which woke him up from his sleep.
He was much alarmed by them and distressed. At the end of
them he woke up with a trembling heart, and the colour of his
30 face was altered. And he sent and called all his interpreters of
dreams and diviners, related to them the dreams which he had
seen, and demanded of them the interpretation of them. The
interpreters answered: 'Very wonderful are your dreams, O
valiant King, and terrible and alarming; and the like of them
35 we have never heard before. Now, O King, glorious in victory,
if it seem good to your Greatness, give us a little time, that we
may consider them well, and look for some device, that perchance we may be able to take away this (334) evil from you:
and let this space of time be for seven days.' The king believed

them, and gave them a delay of seven days. Then those unjust
men and dèniers of God sat and hatched an evil design among
them, saying to one another: "Now has the king revealed to us
all the secrets of his heart. Come, let us bring upon him endless woes, and prepare him distresses that shall not pass away, 5
and prevent him living in his kingdom (any longer), that his life
may depart before the time. And let us say to him all together
and with one voice: 'This is the interpretation of your dreams; ·
that unless you deliver into our hands the eleven persons in
your kingdom whom you love, for us to put to death as shall 10
seem good to us, and unless we mix their blood in a cauldron, and
you sit on that cauldron, while we stand over your head and
utter incantations, and then plunge you in water mixed with
sweet basil, which we shall have in addition,—if you do not consent to this, your kingdom will be rent from you, and another 15
will snatch it out of your hands, and make you waste away in
all kinds of torture, and heap many afflictions upon you'." One
of them said: "When the king asks us: 'Who are those persons
that are as dear to me as my soul?' we will answer: 'Ilār, the
queen and mother of Gōbar your son, who is dearer to you than 20
all your (other) wives, and Gōbar your son, whom you love more
than all your (other) sons, and Kayîl your secretary, who is your
mouth-piece, and Bilār your confidant (335) and counsellor, and
the horse called Gōd, who can overtake the gazelle by his swift-
ness, and the sword whose like cannot be found, and the white 25
elephant that does battle, and the female elephants that go out
to battle with him, and the Bactrian camel that carries like an
elephant, and the wise Qintūrōn'. When we have done all this
to him, we shall be avenged upon him for all our city. And if
he is afraid to do these things, or disdains them, we will say to 30
him: 'Let these go for you, and your kingdom shall be established for ever, and in place of these, you can get many others
like them; and we too will procure you consolation, that your
heart may be relieved of distress on their account'."

So they all agreed together concerning this, and went in to 35
the king, and said to him: 'Our Lord the King, live for ever, we
have a secret matter to tell the valiant King, which must be told
in secret; because we have discovered the interpretations of your
dreams.'

Then the king commanded all who were in his presence to
go out, and the king and the interpreters went into a private
chamber. And they put out all the king's servants who were
standing in attendance on him, and they were left alone with
5 the king.

Then they began all of them with one voice to say: 'O victorious King, we have tried by all manner of means, and striven
in every way, (336) until we have comprehended the interpretations of your dreams. Lo, if you listen to what we shall say
10 to you, you will save yourself from many evils, and remain in
your kingdom unmoved; but if you will not hearken to our
words, we shall be without blame for the loss of your kingdom.'

The king said: 'And what ought I to do?'

They told him according as they had made ready and coun-
15 selled together.

The king replied: 'Death is much pleasanter to me than
life, if I must destroy those who are the light of my eyes, the
delight of my heart, and the sum of all my joy. Perhaps I
might have a short time to live after them, but in distress with-
20 out measure should I spend it. Therefore what profits me life
after these have been put to death, since every one of them is
as dear to me as myself?'

Those interpreters, remote from God and from all truth,
answered: 'If your Majesty will not be vexed, let us tell you
25 that you have not considered well, nor given answer intelligently, nor spoken justly; because if you put others in your own
stead, though they perish to-day, there are many to rise up in
place of them. But if, which God forbid, a hair of your head
perish—for we will not be so audacious as to say, if you yourself
30 perish—you will lose the whole of your kingdom and wealth,
and all your familiar friends and all your property will go to
ruin, and all your children and wives and servants and maid-
servants will be led away captive by enemies. And finally, if
(337) you do lose all your wives and children and secretaries
35 and counsellors and horses and carriages and all that your
Majesty possesses, you can soon find substitutes for them, and
others better than they. But if your soul departs from your
body, which God avert and forbid, to replace it will be impossible.
So, pray, hearken and listen to our counsels, and doubt not

concerning the sincerity of our love, because we too are bound
up with you; and do you bring near those whom we have named
to you, and make their loss a substitute for all the evils which
threaten you.   For the sorrow on their account will last (only)
for a short time, and the distress at parting with them in a little 5
while will be forgotten, and substitutes for them may be found
in a twinkling.   Preserve yourself, and have a care for your
subjects, and a regard for the continuance of your kingdom.
And know, O valiant King, that wise and faithful men do not
put something great as a substitute for what is small, but the 10
small they put in the earth, and the great they seat on a
throne.   Know too, our Lord the King, that this place in which
you sit was gotten with great [labour] and difficulty, while
these others were gotten with ease.   Therefore shrink not from
these honest words of ours, but haste to put these persons to 15
death, that this calamity may be averted from you, and consider
that a natural death has released these persons from life, or that
some accident has befallen them, as the accidents of this world
are accustomed to do.   (338) Therefore banish distress from
your heart, and consider your towns and cities.'   20
    When the king heard these words, he was sore distressed,
and he struggled in his mind.   And, having ordered that no
man should go in to him, he began to turn over his thoughts,
saying to himself: 'O my soul, wherein wilt thou have enjoyment,
if these perish?' And he fell on his face, and began to weep 25
and groan and turn over from side to side, while sleep fled from
his eyes, and he tasted no food as he was used to do.   At one
time he would be in torment and speak to himself in thought,
while at another he would encourage his mind.   And he said to
himself: 'If I hearken to the advice of these interpreters, and 30
destroy those whom my soul loves, and put to death those who
are the light of my eyes, my sighs will abound, and my distresses
will be increased; and if I do not hearken to their counsels,
and the interpretations of the dreams are as they say, I shall
immediately lose my life and my kingdom will be torn asunder, 35
and my body destroyed, and what will profit me those friends
of mine who survive me, or whom others carry off to enjoy their
beauties, or to destroy the weak among them?'
    Being sore distressed by these thoughts, he said again to

himself: 'If I consent to the will of these interpreters, how can
I live without seeing the beauty of the mother of Gōbar and
enjoying her society, or without embracing my dear son Gōbar
and kissing his sweet mouth? And how (330) can my kingdom
5 be established without Bilār my counsellor? Who shall be my
mouth-piece when Kayīl the secretary has been put to death?
Who shall deliver [me] in battle from my enemies, when the
horse Gōd, strong and swift to go, has been slaughtered? How
shall I kill the lion when he meets me, when that sword which
10 has no equal has been broken? How shall I vaunt myself over
my fellow-kings, when the white elephant, swift as a bird, has
been killed, with the two female elephants, his companions, who
are reckoned equal to two victories, when we make war with
enemies? Whereupon shall we load the heavy burdens and the
15 weight that is with us, when we have slaughtered the Bactrian
camel? Who shall gladden me when I have sorrow, whatever
it may be, when the wise Qintārōn, who is perfect in all his
conduct, is no more in the army?'

When Bilār saw that the king was cast in anxiety and dis-
20 tress, his soul too was distressed, and his mind perturbed, and
he said to himself: 'My soul, you must manage to learn what
ails the king, and wherefore he is gloomy and disturbed. But it
is indispensable that I should approach the mother of Gōbar,
for she is the dearest of all his wives, and ask her to go in to
25 the king, and learn the cause of this distress and wherefore it
has come about; because I know that he will not conceal it
from her, since she is a wise woman, and very precious (340) in
his sight.'

So he arose and went to the mother of Gōbar, and said to
30 her: 'O wise and intelligent woman, and extolled among the
noble, hear what your servant has to say before you. [Ever since]
I was joined to this blessed king, he has never hidden anything
from me, or failed to consult me about anything that he wished
to do; because I used to counsel him in the fear of God and
35 with a pure mind, and with a subtle intelligence used to resolve
all the perplexities of his heart; and he used to single me out for
special honour among all his servants, and I used also to go in
and out of his Majesty's palace as I chose. And lo now for
these seven days has the king taken counsel with these wizards,

and, as it seems to me, revealed to them something which is in
his heart, and they have given him some advice which troubles
him sorely; but to me he has not revealed (it), nor has he
admitted me to his presence. I fear that these insolents have
counselled him to do something evil, and I am afraid that he 5
will do it. Now there is no one who is so honourable in his
sight as you. If you please, go in to him, and ask of him quietly
to reveal to you what is in his heart, and what is the fear which
has come upon him. Perhaps these insolents have counselled
him to put to death one of his friends and loved ones, and on 10
this account he is oppressed and gloomy; or they have counselled
him to commit some sin, and he in his goodness hesitates to do
it.'

She answered : 'If then the matter is thus, I do not think
fit (341) to go in to him now, because he has spoken very little 15
to me, and now that he is angry, I will not approach him.'

Bilâr said : "Do not fly into a passion on account of a
wretched thing like this, and let not this matter be delayed.
Peradventure dismay will overtake us, and we shall fail to track
out the thing before it be actually done; and dismay will not 20
profit us when lives have been lost. For at such a time as this,
no one else can go in to him. Besides, I have often heard the
king say : 'Though anxiety and much distress has come upon
me, yet now that I see the mother of Gôbar, all the distress and
anxiety is turned to gladness.' Pray, arise now, thou door of 25
good deeds and most honoured of all queens, and go in to the
king and raise him up from the distress in which he lies, and
speak to him as befits your wisdom, and whatever you do and
(whatever) you hear the king say, let me know."

When he had encouraged her with such words as these, she 30
went in to the king, whom she found lying on the ground,
weeping and groaning, and sad and sorrowful in soul. Sitting
down by his head, she said to him : 'My Lord the King, live for
ever, and may your enemies perish under your feet. Tell to
your handmaid why you are sorrowful and why your soul is 35
oppressed, and what the wizards said to you (342). If you have
good reason to be sorrowful and just cause to be oppressed, I
will share in your grief as I share in your joy, and will lighten
your heart, my Lord the King, of a little part of what is buried

K. F.   15

in it ; because the King's happiness is my heart's exultation,
and his distress and sufferings are my life's destruction.'

The king. O woman, do not add distress to distress, and
ask me not concerning what makes my heart sad ; for (to tell
5 you) would not profit me anything or diminish from my suffering.

The queen. My Lord, is then this calamity so grievous and
so bitter that you must hide it from me ? Have you in all your
life found deceit in me, or am I indifferent to your happiness,
10 or do you esteem my love insincere ?

The king. God forbid that I should have such an opinion of
you, (or consider you) other than wise and upright, just and true.

The queen. Then, my Lord the King, reveal (it) to your
handmaid. Peradventure she will be able to help her lord
15 by some little word. For sometimes help comes from a person
who is a simpleton and not esteemed. And it is customary
for valiant kings, when they are embarrassed, to employ the
counsel of some humble person in whose affection they have
reliance, and whose sincerity they do not doubt, and who is able
20 to lighten their suffering a little, so that they are restored to
their happiness. And you, O my Lord the King, have upright
confidants and sound counsellors ; take counsel with them, and
I have confidence in (343) God that they will be able to lighten
these your troubles a little.

25 *The king.* O noble woman and of excellent character,
what are you profited when you hear the news of your own
death, and of my destruction after you through the groans and
distresses in which I shall end my life ? The reason of my
distress is this : I dreamed dreams eight times in one night,
30 and when I asked these interpreters for the explanation of
them, they told me that the interpretation of them is the
putting to death of the mother of Gôbar, and of Gôbar her son,
and of all those who are the light of my eyes and the up-
holders of my kingdom. I think that no man was ever tried
35 by such a trial as this, or smitten with such a grievous blow.

When the wise woman heard these words, she restrained
herself patiently, gathered her wits together wisely, and answered the king intelligently and replied cheerfully, saying to
him boldly : 'My Lord the King, live for ever ! (Live) a life

long and pleasant, far from griefs and separate from distresses,
free from sorrows and void of trials. Be not afraid, my Lord, of
this; because I would cheerfully and gladly give myself up to
a violent death, that the King might have a single day's pleasure. What profits me life or the riches of the whole world, 5
when my Lord the King, the diadem of my head, the pride of
my soul, the joy of my heart, is troubled in mind (344) and
distressed in soul? For though you lose me, and the sight of
my face be taken away from your eyes, you have in your zeuṅna
many other wives, who are fairer than I, and more excellent 10
in all their conduct; and if you are sad on account of your
son Gōbar, you have many other sons like him, and many even
better than he. Rejoice and take pleasure in these twelve
thousand wives that you possess, for they will bear you many
more sons like Gōbar. But one request do I make of my Lord 15
the King, before I part from him; for there is something which
will profit the King all the days of his life; because although
I be deprived of you, my Lord the King, and in the middle of
my days take up my abode in the tomb among the dead, I am
very zealous for your happiness. Place no more confidence in 20
these interpreters after this time, and believe not nor credit their
lying interpretations, nor make haste to listen to them, before
you have investigated everything that they say; lest dismay
overtake you. For [if] the victorious King put to death him
who is dear to him, he cannot see him again; therefore he 25
ought first to investigate the matter, whatever it be, lest in the
end he repent and it profit him nothing; just as with a pearl
or emerald, men do not throw it away, until they have shown
it to one who is acquainted with its value. And you, O (345)
diadem of my head, cannot know your enemies and those who 30
delight in the trouble of your heart and the hurt of your soul,
until you make them enter the furnace of trial and test them
in the fire of investigation. If you do this, the truth will be
clearly revealed to you, and [you will be able to dislodge] these
interpreters from the ambush of that enmity and wickedness 35
which lurks in their minds that they may put your Majesty to
shame. But let not this their desire come to pass nor be realised;
for they have wished that you should put to death everyone in
whom your soul rejoices, and who fills up the breaches in your

kingdom, and then be oppressed in soul and sorrowful in mind,
and deprived of skilful secretaries and honest counsellors, that
so they may get an opportunity of enjoying your kingdom.
You know, O my lord, that the wise Qīntārōn is adorned with
5 the fear of God and profound in thought, that the eye of his
discernment is clear and his ideas exalted, and that he is free
from all avarice, and remote from all wickedness and fraud. If
it seem good to the victorious King, let him go to him and
rehearse his dreams to him, and see what answer he gives him,
10 and how he counsels him. As he tells the valiant King, so let
him do, and if he counsel according to the counsel (346) of
these interpreters. let the King perform it without delay or fear,
and not shrink or be hindered from this.'

When the king heard her say these words, the perturbation
15 of his soul abated, and he hearkened to her counsel joyfully,
and hastily mounting his beast, came to the house of the wise
Qīntārōn, one who had not been mixed up with the deeds of
the other insolent fellows. When he appeared before him, the
king did obeisance to the earth and bowed his head to the
20 ground and saluted him. Qīntārōn said to him : ' What is the
reason of your coming, and wherefore is the appearance of your
face changed, and for what cause is your countenance gloomy,
and the diadem not set on your head nor the royal crown (placed)
upon it ? '

25 *The king.* Being asleep one day on the roof of the palace,
I heard seven terrifying and alarming sounds (proceed) from
the ground, and I awoke for fear. Again I slept and saw eight
dreams in eight different fashions. On awaking, I summoned
the interpreters and related my dreams to them. They inter-
30 preted them to me as signifying trouble and bitterness and
destruction, and I am sore afraid that the destruction of my life
is at hand.

Qīntārōn answered : ' Relate these dreams to me.' The king
having related them to him one after the other. Qīntārōn said
35 to him : ' May the King live for ever ! Fear not, my Lord, nor
let your mind be troubled, nor your heart afraid ; for the interpretations of your dreams are full of many benefits, and not as
these men, remote from wisdom, have told you. Nay but let
your heart rejoice (347) and your soul exult, and your mind

be joyful; for there shall not happen to the victorious King a single distressful thing, according to the [true] interpretation of these dreams. Now the interpretations of your dreams, my Lord, are these: The two red fishes which you saw standing erect on their tails, (mean that) there will come to your Majesty, 5 a messenger from Nehamtûr, the king of Slûhr, sent to you with two splendid chains in his hands, adorned with gold and precious pearls, and beautified with emeralds and priceless jacinths, and containing about four hundred thousand talents weight of pure gold. They shall he placed before you, standing 10 like the fishes on their tails. The two geese that you saw flying from behind you and coming in front of you, (mean that) there will come to your Majesty a messenger of the king of Blīkh, having with him two chariots or carriages unequalled in all your kingdom. The serpent which you saw creeping up to you 15 and crawling on to your left foot, (means that) a messenger will reach you from Sidraā, the king of Gūnzādī, bringing you a sword made of pure metal, unequalled in all your kingdom. The blood which you saw smeared on your body, (means that) there shall come to you a messenger from Tarsūr, the king of 20 Galsiyūn, having with him a wonderful and gorgeous robe called 'guldon', (348) the beauty of which shall shine in the dark night like the light [of the sun]. The water in which you saw yourself swimming (means that) a messenger shall be sent to you by Rāz, the king of Mūrgshah, bringing you garments the like 25 of which you never saw in your kingdom. Your seeing yourself seated on a white mountain (means that) a messenger shall come to you from Watlûn, the king of Pūrish, bringing you a swift white elephant which a race-horse cannot overtake. The fire which you saw blazing above your head (means that) a 30 messenger shall reach you from Dadrā, the king of Arman, having with him a diadem of pure gold, which shall shine in the darkness of night. (The meaning of) the white bird which you saw approach your head and peck it with her mouth, it is not seasonable that I should interpret; but be not afraid of 35 it, because the little trouble which it portends will not come from strangers but from intimate friends. Therefore my Lord the King, now that you have seen the interpretations of your dreams, and heard how excellent are the things which they

really signify, banish sorrow from your heart, drive distress
from your mind, and put away trouble from your thoughts.
And that you saw them three times (means that) within seven
days the messengers shall reach you, being assembled together
5 three days.'

When the king heard these words from Qintārōn, his mind
rejoiced and his heart was glad, and his face lightened, and he
rose in haste and did obeisance before him, (349) and returned
to his house in gladness of mind.   On the eighth day it came
10 to pass that all the messengers arrived, according to the word
of Qintārōn.   That day the king adorned himself with all sorts
of beautiful ornaments and garments of all colours, placed
the diadem of royalty on his head, and sat on his judgment-
seat, and summoned all the chieftains and generals.   As they
15 were all standing before him, the messengers and chieftains of
his fellow kings came in, and all his magnates were brought in
with them.   On seeing that everything had come to pass
according to the word of Qintārōn, he rejoiced with great joy,
and glorified God for everything that had been done to him,
20 and said before his magnates: 'Instead of keeping to myself
the dream which I saw, or relating it to the wise Qintārōn,
who is excellent in all his conduct and adorned with the fear
of God, glorious for knowledge and versed in wisdom, far from
all avarice and a stranger to greed, perfect and complete in
25 all excellent qualities, I related it to these insolent and iniquitous men, who are far from the truth, enemies of God
and the king, avaricious and envious, crafty and full of deceit, crooked and perverse, servants of Satan and children of
the devil.   These counselled me to do a thing which, had
30 not the mercy of God overtaken me and the counsels of
Qintārōn saved me, would have cost me my life, and with the
beasts of the field I should have ended my days, in sorrow and
sighing, weeping and anguish.   (350) The person who opened
before me this door, and [persuaded me to] go to him and
35 consult him, is my consort, glorious and splendid, wise and
intelligent, noble and full of virtues, the mother of Gōbar; may
the blessing of God rest upon him and his parents, for not
badly did they beget, and not badly did they rear.   By the
mercy of God she drew me out of the deep pit, and raised

me out of the mire of destruction. Therefore everyone who
is wise ought first to take counsel and approach his near ones
according to the flesh, for they will pity their own flesh; like
the mother of Gōbar, excellent queen and faithful consort.'

The king having thus spoken, called for Gōbar his son, and 5
for his counsellor, and his secretary, and his confidant, and said
to them : 'We must not put any of these shining things into
our treasury, but do you divide them among yourselves; since
they are in return for your willingness to sacrifice yourselves.
Specially [is a reward due] to the mother of Gōbar, by whose 10
good and sound advice we have been delivered from this.'

They answered : 'Let not the victorious King be astonished
that the King's servants offered to die for their Lord. For
though the King has power over the lives of his servants, yet
on account of his goodness did he delay doing what the enemies 15
advised, and did not haste to put his servants to death. God
who knew the pure inclination of the King has let him realise
his wish, and has made his servants debtors in very truth, and
clothed them with a coat of shame. So let not (351) our
victorious King praise his servants, the debtors to his love, for 20
having delivered up their souls to death for him; for everyone
who fails to do this, does not pay the debt which he owes, and
is not reckoned among the wise and obedient, or numbered
among familiar friends. Now as for us, the servants of the
King and of his consort the mother of Gōbar, it is not fitting 25
that we should take anything, for everything ought to belong
to the excellent queen and to the glorious branch which from
her has grown, Gōbar.'

The king. That an excellent report and a great deed may
be heard by all with regard to these precious things or honours 30
which have been sent by the kings, it is fitting that all of you
should partake of them. Therefore let everyone of you take
whatever he desires.

Bīlār. Let the King, mighty in strength, begin, and be the
first to take what is desirable and beautiful in his eyes. 35

The king began by taking the white elephant, giving to
Gōbar his son one of the chariots, to Bīlār the wonderful sword
of pure metal, to Klīk the secretary, a horse equal to Gōbar's
horse, while he sent to Qintārōn some of the royal garments,

saying that gold-embroidered garments and diadems are only
suitable for women. Having told the herald to carry the
diadem and the gold embroidered garments, and follow him
to the women's abode, he bade them call the mother of Gôbar
5 and her companions. When they were come, he said to Bilâr :
'Rise and take the garments and the golden diadem (352) to
the mother of Gôbar, that she may take which she likes.' When
the mother of Gôbar saw the golden diadem, she admired it
and wished to take it. So she looked to Bilâr round the corners
10 of her eyes, (meaning) that he should indicate which of them
was the best and most beautiful and excellent. He signified
to her by a wink that the garment was better than the diadem.
But the king was looking at him when he winked. When she
perceived that the king had seen Bilâr wink to her concerning
15 the garments, she feared lest the king should conceive some
miserable suspicion about her in connection with Bilâr. So
she passed by the golden dress, and took the diadem. Bilâr
lived for forty years after this time, and whenever he went in
to the king, he used to shut his eye, as the king had seen him
20 shut it when he winked to the mother of Gôbar. But for the
subtle intelligence of this man, and the great wisdom of the
woman in leaving the dress and taking the diadem, and the
wonderful knowledge of this man in making a habit of winking
his eyes all through these years, two persons would have lost
25 their lives, or been accused and banished from the king's presence.

     Now the king used to spend one night with the mother of
Gôbar, and one night with her companion Gûlpâh. Each day
that he came to one of them, she used to prepare him food.
One day, when (353) the preparation fell to the mother of
30 Gôbar, she made the food ready for him, and prepared the table
before him, and made a mixture of rice and honey. Having
put it on a golden plate, she brought it to place before the king,
being dressed and adorned, with the golden tiara placed on her
head. Now her companion Gûlpâh was very envious of her,
35 because she was far more beloved by the king than she herself.
So she made haste and put on the royal garment of gold, and
went in to the king, while the mother of Gôbar was standing
before him, bearing the plate on which was the rice. The
beauty of the garment shone like the light of the sun, the whole

house being illumined by the beauty of her garment. Very
beautiful too was Gūlpāh's own appearance. When the king
saw her, she was beautiful in his eyes; and he said to the
mother of Gōbar: 'You have acted very foolishly towards yourself in leaving this garment which has no equal in all my king- 5
dom, and taking this diadem instead. For lo there is much
gold in our treasury to make you one like it and better than it.'
When the mother of Gōbar perceived that he praised the other
and chided her, and called her foolish, she was very wroth and
vexed, and, lifting up the plate which she was bearing, struck it 10
against the king's head, and the [rice] flowed down on to his
head and beard. So the dream came true, which Qintārōn had
mentioned but not explained.

Then the king (354) was very vexed and angry, and, sum-
moning Bīlār, said to him: 'See you, O Bīlār, what this inso- 15
lent woman has done? And how she has insulted and abased
a royal person such as me? Pray take her forth at once, and
go, cut off her head quickly.'

On hearing these words, Bīlār took her, and went out sadly,
saying to himself: 'I must not put to death such a queen as 20
this; for though the king is angry now, yet I must wait until
the intensity of his indignation abates, and I see how he endures
without her, and how too he remembers her countenance.
Besides, she was the cause of our deliverance from the calamity
prepared for us, and great blessings have been obtained for us 25
from the king by her intervention. Peradventure too when the
intensity of the king's wrath abates, he will say to me: "Could
you not have delayed her execution for one day?" So I
think I shall keep her alive until I see how it goes with the
king. If I see that he repents of putting her to death, I shall 30
have gained for myself three excellent things which are very
high and exalted. The first of them will be my own escape from
destruction: the second, that the king will be without distress
and anxiety; and the third, that I shall have done a great
kindness to the king and to all his courtiers, because she loved 35
the welfare of all the subjects of the realm, (355) and was eager
to have benefits done to all the members of the army. But if
he does not remember her, or repent of having put her to death,
I will do to her according to his command.' So he took her

home and put her in a secret place, setting two of the king's
eunuchs to guard her, being those who were entrusted with the
charge of all the king's wives. And he bade his household pay
her exalted honours, until he should see how the king was
5 minded. Then Bilâr, having stained his sword with blood, went
in to the king with a mournful face and his appearance altered,
and said to him: 'O king, live for ever! Lo I have performed
your wish, according as you commanded.'

After a little time, when the king's indignation had sub-
10 sided and his wrath abated, he remembered the mother of
Gôbar, and her intelligence and prudence, and repented having
put her to death and began to groan, and pangs of sorrow smote
him. But he was ashamed to ask Bilâr whether she had really
been put to death; and on the other hand he was perplexed,
15 saying: 'Bilâr being a servant under orders, feared for his life,
and certainly accomplished what I told him.'

Bilâr, after looking at the king and weighing in the balances
of his knowledge what he saw in the king's face, began to say to
him: 'My Lord the King, let not your thoughts disturb you,
20 nor give way to sorrow, nor grieve at the loss of one ewe;
because grief and sorrow will not profit a whit now, but only
destroy your strength, enfeeble your body, (356) and make gladness to cease, cause your enemies to rejoice, and distress your
friends, and especially will make all your subjects wonder and
25 say: "Who ever saw the like of this?" For the king is troubled
for a thing that is done beyond recall; for that a dead man
should return is impossible. So now let this sorrow pass from
you, and wipe out the memory of her from your heart, and
grieve not for what you cannot see again. For a wise King
30 ought to search well into matters before he acts, and should
not be hasty.'

When the king heard these words, he feared lest in truth
the mother of Gôbar had been put to death, and his sorrow was
increased. He said to Bilâr angrily: 'On account of a single
35 fault that she committed, did you do the deed which I commanded you, and not delay the matter a single instant?'

Bilâr. He whose word cannot be changed is one.

The king. And who is he?

Bilâr. The glorious God who changes not.

The king. The killing of Gôbar's mother has made me very sad.

Bilâr. There are two persons who call for sorrow and justify grief: he who never did a good thing, and he who every-day imitates evil things; because the satisfaction and pleasure 5 which they give in this transitory life, is (only) for a time, while the torment which they cause in the world to come, is for ever.

The king. If I see the mother of Gôhar alive (again), I shall never be sad any more.

Bilâr. There are two persons (357) who need never be 10 sad; one is he who never did wrong, and (the other) is he who does good actions continually.

The king. Therefore I shall never see the mother of Gôbar.

Bilâr. There are two persons who do not see; a blind man who [cannot make use] of his eyes, and a fool who cannot discern 15 with his intelligence. As a blind man cannot behold the sun, so a fool without intelligence cannot discern good from evil, or what is ugly from what is beautiful.

The king. I should have great joy if I were to see the face of the mother of Gôbar.   20

Bilâr. There are two persons who should rejoice exceed-ingly; an intelligent, patient, and wise man, who discerns things before they happen, and advances in worldly circumstances, while (keeping) far from sins; and he who guides many to run in the way that leads to the kingdom of God, while he shows 25 them (the way) himself, and they follow after him, and who warns men and puts them in fear of that broad road that leads to hell, being one who acts first and then teaches, and not who teaches without acting.

The king. I never had enough of the sight of the mother 30 of Gôbar.

Bilâr. There are two persons who never have enough; he who loves money and is eager to amass possessions, and he who eats more than he needs and wants something more.

The king. We must depart from you, O Bilâr.   35

Bilâr. There are two persons from whom one should depart. One is he who says (358) that folly does not bring to want, that goodness profits not, that there is no retribution or justice, no resurrection and no judgment, no bliss and no torment; the

other is he who cannot overcome his lust, and does not cease to amass wealth, or stop his ears from hearing the slander of others, or purify his heart from any evil.

The king. It is useless to talk about the mother of Göbar.

5 *Bilár.* There are three things which are useless : a river in which there is no water—like a country in which there is no king; a woman who has no husband ; and a man who neglects to cultivate virtue, and does not believe that God will reward the righteous with bliss and chastise the wicked in hell.

10 *The king.* You have wrongfully destroyed my peace, O Bilár.

Bilár. There are three persons who destroy wrongfully : he who puts on a white garment and sits by a furnace ; a fuller who puts new sandals on his feet and stands in water ; and a 15 merchant who weds a wife of beautiful appearance.

The king. I think that your offence calls for severe stripes.

Bilár. There are three persons who are worthy of stripes : a fool when he reviles the good ; he who comes [to a feast] which is not his, no one having invited him ; and he who asks 20 his friends for something that they have not got, [and] when they tell him that it is not to be found with them, comes back again and demands it from them.

The king. It seems to me that you ought to be driven away (359) from me, and that I should not take your advice 25 again.

Bilár. There are three persons who ought to be driven away : a carpenter who makes a small house, and brings wood and fills the house with it, and when the dwelling is too narrow for his household, expels them from the house, and leaves the 30 wood in it ; he who shaves with a razor without knowing (how to shave), and injures the head of the person he is shaving ; and he who chooses to traffic in a place where there are robbers, and when misfortune comes, loses his life and his wealth too, and impoverishes his household, whose name is forgotten and his 35 history obliterated.

[*The king.*] You ought to have waited until the intensity of my anger had subsided.

Bilár. There are three persons who need to wait : he who ascends a high mountain ; he who eats fish ; and he who thinks

of doing something which defies his strength and exceeds his knowledge.

The king. I long to have but one glimpse of the mother of Gōhar's countenance.

Bilâr. There are three persons who should be derided: a man that says that he was in a battle and overcame many or killed them, while there is not a single mark on his body to show that he (ever) saw the battle, whether wound of sword, or prick of arrow, or bruise of stone; a man who says that he is an ascetic or hermit, while his body is fat and stout, his face merry, his countenance cheerful, and his mouth full of laughter, while his tongue utters mockery and his lips bubble over with fun ; (360) and a woman who says that she is a virgin, and is not modest.

The king. It is I who have brought this trouble upon myself.

Bilâr. There are three persons who bring trouble upon themselves : he who is eager for slaughter and longs to slay, and then engages in battle and is cowardly and lazy; he who is eager to get wealth and has no heir; and an old man who takes a young virgin to wife, for when she has been with him a short time, she hopes that he will die, that she may take a young husband, and makes plans too for his destruction.

The king. Very small am I in your eyes, O Bilâr, that you should be so audacious as [to say] such things against me.

Bilâr. There are three persons who are audacious : he who speaks foolish things when he gives counsel, and speaks of what he has not seen ; a servant whose master is deficient in wealth, while the servant is puffed up and boastful, and does not supply his master's needs ; and a servant and a maidservant who revile their masters and drag them before the ruler.

The king. You have got great impudence.

Bilâr. There are three persons who are very impudent : a fool who according to his ignorance makes replies to the wise and prudent, and though he knows that not two of them are believed, is not deterred, but returns to make more replies, however contemptible ; he who attaches himself to the scurrilous (361), who fall upon him and turn and calumniate him, and then goes to them again and becomes intimate with them,

though he sees with his eyes that he is ridiculed, and hears
with his ears how he is abused; and he who entrusts his secret
to untrustworthy persons, remote from the fear of God, who
make a mock of him and reveal his secret to everybody, and
5 make him a laughing-stock and a derision.

The king. Love abides no longer between me and you,
O Bilâr.

Bilâr. There are three persons with whom love does not
abide : a friend who never meets with his friend, or inquires
10 after him or remembers him, whether by (sending) a messenger
or a letter; he who is honoured by others and is not mindful
of them, and does not recompense them well, but simply makes
sport of them ; and a stranger who is honoured by others and
admitted to intimacy by everybody, and is not grateful even in
15 word.

The king. By putting to death the mother of Gôbar, you
have shown that your love is not perfect and your knowledge
incomplete.

Bilâr. There are three such persons: a liar whose words do
20 not agree with his deeds ; a wrathful man who cannot contain
his anger, so that his losses outnumber his satisfactions, and in
the end he brings upon himself dismay and sighing; and a king
who attempts great things without the advice (362) of the wise
and without deep thought.

25 *The king.* Had you observed what was right and walked
after the manner of friends and lovers, you would not have put
to death the mother of Gôbar.

Bilâr. There are four persons who observe what is right:
a man and a woman who study one another's good ; a cook or
30 baker who prepares the king's table and makes ready his repast,
(making it) elegant and excellent and clear of all insects; a man
who contains his wrath, and withholds his hand from striking,
and his tongue from slander and calumny ; and a king who
does not haste to battle alone, or set his troops in order for the
35 fight until he has taken counsel of men whose mind is pure
from iniquity, and who are far from all avarice and greed.

The king. O Bilâr, you are much to be feared.

Bilâr. There are four creatures who fear needlessly: a small
bird that lifts up her wing on high, and extends her feet up-

wards, saying: 'I am afraid lest the sky fall upon me, but if it fall, I will support it with my feet and my wings, that it may not fall upon my whole body;' a crane that stands on one leg and says: ' If I support the other leg, I shall cleave the ground and it will swallow me up;' the snake whoso food is the dust of the 5 earth, and who says: ' I am afraid (363) lest I consume all the dust and so be unable to get food;' and the bat, who is afraid to fly in the day time, and says: ' No bird is fairer than I; I fear lest men catch me.'

The king. Did you vow a vow that you would kill Ĭlãr, 10 O Bīlãr?

Bīlãr. There are four persons for whom a vow is necessary: he who constructs a chariot which is to save the king from tho hand of enemies in time of battle and defeat of his army; an ox for ploughing, that tills the farmer's land; a good and God- 15 fearing woman who loves her husband and preserves her chastity by good character, and an upright servant who serves and loves the prosperity of his master and of his wealth.

The king. I can find no equal to the mother of Gōhar.

Bīlãr. There are four persons whose equal cannot be found: 20 a haughty man who never takes counsel; a woman who remains and abides with one man; a man who has prepared falsity for his tongue, and is intoxicated with excess of riches; and a prince when he falls into doubt, for all his thoughts leave him and his power is taken from him. 25

The king. Would that this had been spoken before to-day, since now it profits not nor helps.

Bīlãr. There are four things which it is necessary to know about before doing them. (364) Before a general who is - - - - goes forth to battle, it is necessary for him to try his artillery. 30 lest he be defeated and become a laughing-stock. When a man is puffed up through his knowledge and boasts of his learning, seeks to speak before a number of persons and to expound in public, it is necessary for him to search well into his learning, lest there be in the assembly one who is more learned than he, 35 and more skilled in disputation, and he be shown up before every one. When a man goes to law with his fellow and seeks for an umpire to stand between him and his adversary, let him seek out a man who fears God, who is remote from avarice and

inclines not to bribes nor speaks with partiality, and who has been an umpire between others, and has judged between them with justice, and reproved the offender with uprightness. When a man invites to his house an eminent, distinguished, and
5 wealthy person, let him (first) prepare everything that is suitable for the person invited, and then bring him into his house; and if he cannot (do this), let him make excuse and invite him no more.

The king. None can make such sport of a man as you,
10 O Bilār.

Bilār. There are four persons whom it is not right to make sport of: a man renowned for the fear of God and distinguished for wisdom; a hermit or ascetic; a man of noble birth and good family; and a madman whose reason has left
15 him.

The king. After these words, we ought not to rely upon you (any more), or trust you and reveal to you the secrets of our heart.

Bilār. There are four creatures that cannot be relied upon
20 or trusted: a venomous, poisonous serpent; (365) wild beasts that dwell upon the mountains and - - - - - and eat flesh; wicked and iniquitous men; and those who are smitten with envy, because the fruits of envy are death.

The king. We must not consort with you (any more),
25 O Bilār.

Bilār. There are four things which do not consort with one another: night with day; sweet with bitter; a just and righteous man with a wicked and unrighteous man; and good with evil.

The king. When I see my twelve thousand wives, without
30 seeing Ilār among them, the troubles of my heart are more than its joys.

Bilār. There are four women for whom one should not be troubled: she who is not chaste and speaks foolish things and many; she whose hand is swift to strike; she who squanders the
35 wealth of her lord; and she who continually opposes what he says.

The king. There never befell us or afflicted us such a sorrow as this sorrow, such was the intelligence of the mother of Gōbar, and the good order of her conduct.

Bĩlãr. When one of five things is found in a woman, the loss of her calls for much sorrow. She who esteems her good reputation as more excellent than pure gold; she whose face is as bright (366) as the rays of the sun; she whose knowledge is as subtle as the wisdom of the serpent; she who seeks not wealth 5 and is not smitten with greed; and she who obeys the bidding of her lord with alacrity, and is contented with her sustenance; [the loss of such women calls for much sorrow.]

The king. To him who restores Ĩlãr to me alive, will I give wealth and gold as much as he wishes. 10

Bĩlãr. There are five persons who love wealth and property more than their own souls: he who goes to war without having an enemy, but offers his services in order to get money, and sometimes perishes without getting it; a merchantman who is continually looking out and hoping, and sailing on the ocean, in 15 order to amass wealth, and sometimes is drowned and loses his life and his wealth too; a man who pierces walls, for at any time they may fall upon him and he may perish; a jailor who is continually looking out and hoping for more prisoners and murderers to come into the prison, for the sake of the money 20 which he may get from them, and sometimes for some cause or other is killed by one of them; and a judge who perverts justice for the sake of a bribe, and departs from God and receives punishment and the retribution of hell and of the fire.

The king. You have corrupted your good character by 25 putting Ĩlãr to death.

Bĩlãr. There are seven persons who corrupt their good character and put away truth from their hearts; an accurate teacher and a true sage who withholds his knowledge instead of (367) making many happy with it, that they may profit by the 30 hearing of it, and be turned to the knowledge of the truth; a man who does [kindnesses indiscriminately], and a king who squanders his wealth and gives it to everybody, even to those who deny the goodness of their Creator and do not repay what they owe in return for the benefits which they receive; a slave 35 who has a bad master, and does not ask him to sell him; a mother who wheedles her son when he is an evil doer, and makes no mention of his offences, instead of reproving him that he may return to the way of God; he who trusts a crafty and

K. F. 16

deceitful man; he who is too hasty in blaming his friend, and puts an end to friendship with him; and he who does not desire to walk in the way of the just and good, that the Lord God may keep him.

5   *The king.* You have moved my heart and inflamed it with animosity towards you through the death of the mother of Gôbar.

Bilâr. There are four creatures in whose hearts (mutual) animosity is implanted: the wolf and the lamb; the cat and
10 the mouse; the young hawk and the hazel-hen; and the owl and the crow.

The king. Sleep has fled from my eyes through the killing of the mother of Gôbar.

Bilâr. There are six persons who sleep not: he who pre-
15 pares himself to kill another in the night; he who possesses much wealth but has not a wise steward; a seditious man who insults the noble, and continually (368) meditates abominable thoughts, how and in what way he may disturb the concord of the upright; he from whom a heavy tribute is required and has
20 not sufficient to pay it; a sick person who is needy and has no physician to visit him; and he who loves his friend and fears lest he may depart out of his sight.

The king. Why have you been destitute of pity and not spared me, that you should destroy the mother of my beloved
25 Gôbar?

Bilâr. There are five persons who are destitute of pity: an irascible king who spares not his servants and handmaidens; he who carries dead bodies and takes pay from their heirs; a rob-ber who waits for the dark night, that he may break through
30 bolts and bars, and rob houses which are none of his; he who urges the judges to take a bribe, and to exercise partiality in judging; and an audacious man who makes haste to steal another man's cloak, and does not know whether he may not be struck from behind, and his soul depart from his body, or
35 whether he may not smite the owner of the cloak and so bring himself to ruin.

The king. How grievous is this loss which you have inflicted on me, O Bilâr.

Bilâr. There are seven states which involve great loss:

(that of) an old man from whom the strength of youth has departed, who is no longer respected but despised by everyone; (that of) a wise man who becomes angry, for his wisdom forsakes him, and he is reckoned a madman; a disease which dissolves the structure of the body and loosens the joints; anxiety, when 5 it affects the heart, troubling the thoughts and misleading the understanding; hunger (369) and thirst which dry up the limbs; nakedness which puts to shame the noble; and last of all, death, which desolates houses, and makes women widows and children orphans.   10

The king. You have not left any confidence between us, that I should ever make use of your counsels again, or commit my affairs into your hands.

Bilâr. There are seven persons with whom we ought to have no dealing: he who takes counsel of one who is not 15 patient and versed in knowledge; a friend who is grieved at his fellow for no offence at all; he who is puffed up in his soul and whose spirit is exalted in his own eyes and who despises his near ones according to the flesh; a liar who is far from the truth; he who is possessed of much wealth and conceals it in the heart of 20 the earth and does not (even) relieve his own wants; he who does not care for the wants of his teacher and continually upbraids him; and he who constantly irritates his brothers and complains of them.

The king. Let what you have said suffice you, O Bilâr; be- 25 cause you have brought me into a state of great uncertainty.

Bilâr. There are ten things in which a man must be tried: a dauntless man (must be tried) in battle with an enemy; a husbandman in tilling his land; a servant in obedience to his master; a king in the time of his anger, as to how his long- 30 suffering may be shown; a merchant, as to how his integrity may be proved in his trafficking; brethren, as to how they can bear the unkindnesses of their brethren; the patient and intelligent, as to how they can support the trials which befall them; an ascetic or hermit, (370) in the perfection of his conduct; a 35 rich man, in the abundance of his giving; and a poor man and one lacking sustenance, as to how he can endure his wants without impatience and murmuring and blasphemy, and how he can ask his kinsmen to supply his need.

The king. Do you dare to speak in my presence again, now that I am angry?

Bilār. There are seven persons who are continually in a state of sadness : one is he who serves a passionate king, for 5 he is in a constant state of terror lest he suddenly make some mistake, and the king hastily order him to be put to death ; another is he from whom a word of consolation is required, and who in his folly - being rude in his knowledge; he who loves to be extolled by 10 every one - ; another is he who speaks among men with partiality, and seeks to please both sides ; another is he who is about to give a king poison to drink, and trembles lest his wickedness be discovered, and the poison return upon him and kill him ; another is 15 he who bears false witness, and is in continual fear lest it become known and his deceit be revealed ; another is he to whom a deposit has been entrusted, and who covets the deposit and spends it, and afterwards is sorry, (knowing) that when the owner of the deposit comes and asks it of him, he will be detected.

20   *The king.* You have wearied me sorely, (371) O Bilār, and yourself too.

Bilār. There are ten persons who weary themselves and others too: one of them is he who is not acquainted with affairs, and teaches men what he does not know; a rich man who is 25 puffed up by his wealth and remote from wisdom; a judge or decider of a matter, when - - - - - - - - - - ; he who seeks to attain to a seat with kings; he whose conduct is ill-ordered and who seeks to incriminate upright men, and sets himself to revile them, while the more he reviles them the greater do they be- 30 come; he who does lofty things which do not befit him; he who does a thing without taking the advice of his companions, when he has asked it of them; he who disputes with one who is better instructed than he and more skilled in debate, and does not accept the truth when he hears it; he who wearies kings by 35 importunity, and disturbs their minds; and he who is acquainted with what the king needs and conceals it from him.

Then Bilār held his peace, when he perceived the king's distress and the bitter trouble which kept agitating him, when he remembered the mother of Gōbar; and he said within him-

self: 'I have severely rebuked the king with my words and cen-
sured him beyond what was right, and ho has horne it. I must
now make him glad with the news that she is alive, and let him
see her countenance quickly. For although I have rightly
upbraided tho king and justly (372) blamed what he did so 5
hastily, he in spite of his royalty and lofty position has not been
wroth with me, but has inclined to me the shoulder of humility,
tasted my hitter words, endured the stabs of my barh-like utterances, shut his eyes to the severity of my countenance, and
stopped his cars to the heavy lead which I poured into them.' 10

Bilãr, having finished speaking thus (to himself), rose up and
made obeisance before tho king, saying: 'O King, live for ever!
Among kings there is none equal to you, either among those
who havo passed away or among those who reign now; because
that anger has not overcome you, nor has the severity of my 15
clumsy words moved the tower of your endumnce. You, in
spite of your royalty, have not been wroth with me, as might
befit your Excellency; because your soul is full of peace and
overflowing with tranquillity, versed in gentleness and adorned
with intelligence, girt about with integrity and far from oppres- 20
sion, perfect in goodness and not abhorring tho truth. You have
endured my words, acknowledged my defence, and forgotten tho
asperity of my answers; since you were rebuked and not pmised,
abused and not honoured. You were reviled and did not become
augry; you were abused and took no offence. Too weak is 25
thought to conceive your eulogies; too small the mouth and too
stammering the tongue to rehearse your praises; too tremulous
the hand to signify the magnitude of your goodness. All your
good qualities have been heaped on me. Now (373) let your
soul rejoice and your mind exult; let your emotions subside and 30
your perturbation cease; let your eye be bright and your heart
glad; for the mother of Gōbar has been kept alive.'

When the king heard that the mother of Gōbar was alive,
he rejoiced with exceeding great joy, and gave thanks to God,
and extolled Bilãr, saying: 'As for this vexation which you have 35
caused (me), O Bilãr, long ago I knew of the genuiuencss of
your disposition and the uprightness of your conduct, the wisdom
of your intelligence and the excellence of your character, the
sincerity of your love and the subtlety of your knowledge.

Besides all this, it is I who have offended, in that I was overcome by the bite of a wretched fly. You in your wisdom, had
you executed my order, would have done rightly; but now that
you have waited, you have shown the perfection of goodness.
5 For you wished to try the feeling of the king and see whether
he would be wroth with you for not having put to death the
mother of Gôbar, or would praise your long-suffering with her.
God forbid that I should not be grateful to you and prepare gifts
for you and make ready to honour you; for you shall receive
10 more than you hoped for. Rise up now quickly and bring the
mother of Gôbar.

So Bilâr went out in haste and told the mother of Gôbar to
make herself ready and deck herself with ornaments meet for
the king. Having done as he had told her, she went in to the
15 king and bowed herself before him. When the king beheld and
saw her, he said to her: 'O mother of Gôbar, are you alive?'
She answered him (374): 'May the Lord establish the King's
life for ever in tranquil peace and lasting prosperity, in joy and
exultation; because that by your goodness I am alive. For my
20 fault was heinous and my offence great, but the long-suffering
of Bilâr delivered me from death, and saved the soul of the
victorious King from distress.'

The king said to Bilâr: 'Great is your goodness to me, and
there is none equal to you in the whole kingdom, for you have
25 lengthened Ilâr's life for me. Behold I have given you power
over the whole of my kingdom; rule it as seems good to you.'

Bilâr. I am your servant, and by the goodness of God and
of yourself I am what I am. But one request I have to make
of God and of my Lord the King, namely that he be not hasty
30 in anything, for he who is too hasty brings upon himself only
sorrow and dismay.

The king. Let those garments which shine at night like
the light of the sun be given to the mother of Gôbar, together
with lands and many cities.

35   And he gave her authority over all his wives; and to Bilâr
he gave great gifts not a few; and those Brahmans and interpreters of dreams he commanded to be put to death. And the
king made merry with the mother of Gôbar and rendered thanks
to God.

The philosopher said to the king: My Lord the King, live a thousand years, and reign over the seven climes. May the Lord multiply your good things from above and your blessings from below. May you be glorified with all honours, may your right hand reach the neck of your enemies, may you be envied and 5 not envious, (375) and may you have a good end with the men of peace, for ever. Amen.

The story of the wise Bilār and Queen Ilār, (a story) full of worldly wisdom, is ended.

With God's help, we next write the history of Barzōi, the Indian
teacher, who diligently translated this book from Indian
into Arabic.

Barzōi narrated as follows :—My father belonged to a distinguished race, and my mother was descended from mighty chiefs
of the Magi. Through the great goodness of God to me, I was
dearer to my parents than all their other children, and they
5 cared more for my welfare and advantage than for that of all
my brothers. When I came to be seven years old, they sent
me to a school. Having learnt everything according to the
custom of our law, I was grateful to God and my parents for
the benefits which I had received from teachers, and the. learn-
10 ing I had gained from instructors. But when I examined all
the different beliefs, and considered the various professions, and
weighed everything with common sense, I conceived an ardent
desire to study medicine, and to this occupation I devoted
myself with all my might, and persevered in it, and made it
15 my object, until I acquired much wealth from it. After reaping from it a goodly harvest, I was anxious to visit the sick
and to relieve their distress. Then I said to myself : 'O (376)
my soul I choose thou one thing, either some of that which is
desired by kings and commoners, beloved by the freeman as
20 well as the slave, extolled by the rich as well as the poor,
(namely) worldly gains which pass away and vanish, and temporal pleasures which fade and perish, or heavenly joys which
shall never die, and glorious abodes which abide and cannot
be destroyed.' Having said this to myself, I continued : 'O
25 my soul! thou must choose one of these things in the freedom
of thine inward will, with the aid of thine enlightened mind
and subtle knowledge, either earthly possessions which many
run after, though in a twinkling they vanish from them and
become alienated from them, or an excellent character, and a
good name which you may leave behind you in this world

among men, and a recompense of good things which shall not
pass away, which you will inherit in the kingdom of heaven.'
Then did the pilot and captain of our bark bring me to pro-
secute the study of medicine; since I had found that it was
highly extolled among the prudent and wise, and I could not dis- 5
cover a single religion which condemned it And I read in books
of medicine that no one in this profession is greater and more
praiseworthy in the opinion of their authors than he who only
cares for the sick, and constantly visits the afflicted, and is
anxious to relieve the distressed, in hope of the recompense 10
which he shall receive from God in the world to come. So I
longed to attend to this profession with all my might, not that
I might get by it gold which perishes, or silver which may be
stolen, or to sell the things which are to come and shall abide
and are exalted and glorious (377) for a paltry price which is 15
like vapour from a pot, which evaporates in the air and vanishes
away. For I feared lest I might resemble the thoughtless merchant who sold a valuable pearl, from the price of which enor-
mous wealth might have been expected, for a paltry farthing or
a wretched mite.   20

I also found it written in ancient books that when a skilful
physician is anxious to get from his practice enduring wealth
and the inheritance of eternal life, all the things of this world
which human nature requires shall be added to him; and ho
resembles the husbandman who tills his land, and ploughs it, 25
and - - - - - it, that it may yield him a good crop, and not
that it may yield him weeds, though this does not prevent the
ground from bringing forth with the corn also weeds of all
kinds. Then I made the treatment of the sick my object, and
cared for all their wants, and never neglected to serve them, 30
whether those who I thought might recover, or those of whom
I despaired, so that those whom I expected to recover might
speedily be quit of their sicknesses, and that those of whose lives
I despaired might be relieved a little of their distress, until the
heavenly bidding should command them to depart to their Lord. 35
Those whom I could visit personally, I visited; and for those
whom I could not serve personally, I wrote directions and gave
medicines. And to the poor I gave money as well as medicine
(378). I did not ask one of them for the proper fee, or for

praise or gratitude; but only from the One who gives
abundantly and recompenses an hundredfold, according to
His promise, which cannot be broken. I neither envied nor
praised anyone who was occupied in this profession, whether he
5 was similar to myself, or more excellent than I, and wealthier
in goods and possessions; but only those who had excellence
of character, and were adorned with kindliness, in conduct
first and then in speech. And it never entered my head to
wish to attain to the degree of those among them who were
10 rich. When sometimes nature prompted and urged me to
amass money, and to get abundance of goods and possessions, I
used to rebuke myself, saying: " O my soul! why discernest
thou not between the things that profit thee and the things that
hurt thee ? Wherefore art thou absorbed in the things which
15 pass away, and desirous to get labour and toil, distress and
vexation ? What have vile possessions profited their owners ?
Have they not all been parted from their possessions, and left
them to their enemies behind them, while they left them and
departed with great dismay and unnumbered sighs? A minute
20 account of the way in which their wealth was amassed has
been sent on before them, and they must give a statement of it at
the judgement. O my soul! art thou not ashamed to join
thyself to men who lack knowledge, who care for these perishing things, and labour with their minds as well as their limbs
25 to get what they will have to part with ? For it will not save
them from death nor (379) go with them, that they may offer
it as a bribe to the righteous Judge. No wise and rational
man [desires] to acquire it, or is anxious for it, since he considers the bad end of it; but only those simple-minded ones, not
30 versed in prudence. Nay, turn thy gaze, my soul, from this
paltry thing, and incline and pursue after the things which abide
and satisfy, and get the things which can be retained and which
profit, and amass things which will remain and make glad.
These will delight thee in the end, and clear thee before the
35 Judge, save thee from the punishment of hell, set thee at the
right-hand, and deliver thee from the fire which shall never be
put out. Trust not to a vain hope which shall not avail nor
profit. Remember that this body, with which thou art clothed,
is a house of trial, full of every humour of evil. For all kinds of

evils cleave to it, which are opposed the one to the other, being
gathered from the four elements, and all combined in the rational being. When this soul departs from the body, all feelings
cease, and all the elements are dissolved, and they resemble a
wooden figure, the limbs of which are all independent and the 5
joints (artificially) bound together; for when the limbs hold
together, there is a bolt or peg holding it together, and when
this peg is taken out, the limbs (380) no longer cohere, but
go to pieces, and fall away in all directions. O my soul!
pursue not after brothers or friends, and kinsmen and relatives, 10
for they will not profit thee a whit; because a multitude of
kinsmen and brothers and friends brings with it more troubles
than joys, and the vexations they cause are more numerous
than the pleasures, and in time of death and the hour of
decease they bring grief and weeping, and sorrow and sighing 15
without measure, and resemble a wooden ladle which, when it
is whole, brings out of the pot cooked meat of all kinds, but
after it is broken, is burnt. O my soul! care not for wife and
children, for these would make you anxious to amass money by
unlawful means, money which would conduct you to perdition, 20
while these would enjoy it and be without blame; and you
would be like aloe-wood, whose sweet smell others enjoy, while
itself is burnt with fire. O my soul! look not at the wealth
of the rich, or at knotted bridal chambers and ornamented
harooms.   25

At the time of departure from this house of sojourning by
means of sudden death, they resemble the hair of the head
and face, which, as long as it grows on the body, is honoured
and anointed, but when it is shaved off, is abhorred and cast
away with the dung. O my soul! care for the sick, support 30
the weak, relieve the distressed. Be not tired of them, nor let
the wretched thought occur to you (381) that the medical profession requires great labour, and that the practice of it is very
arduous. Knowest thou not how great are its advantages, and
how many useful things are combined in it? Consider, O my 35
soul, and weigh with the intelligence of thy discernment, him
who relieves one distressed person, or looses one who is bound,
or visits one afflicted person, or supplies the wants of one needy
individual, or pulls up one who has sunk, how he is recom-

pensed by such a one, and how he is looked upon by them.
And if when a good deed is done to one single man, a great
recompense is certainly paid for it, how shall the physician be
forgotten when he cares for many sick people, both kings and
5 commoners, rich and poor, and relieves their distress, draws them
out of the pit into which they have fallen, moderates the intensity of their maladies, and restores them to rest and happiness,
and eating and drinking, * * *, to bodily as well as mental
enjoyment, so that they forget their pains and remember their
10 sicknesses no more? So doubt not, my soul, that thou wilt
reap many honours, inherit gains without measure, receive goods
and possessions not a few, that thou wilt leave among men a
good name, which is better than all manner of wealth, according
as the wise man has said, and receive from God a reward such
15 as cannot be imagined by the mind of man, (382) on behalf of
the poor and needy. O my soul! think not that the end is
distant from thee, nor imagine that there is yet a long time and
many years, nor care for those paltry things which pass away,
nor lose the lofty things which abide and perish not, and remain
20 and pass not away, for the things which are seen now, but
which like a dream of the night will soon cease and be no more,
and will be taken from you and given to others, whether friends
or foes, lest thou become like the carpenter whose house was full
of the finest and most precious aloe-wood, and who considered
25 within himself, saying, 'If I sell this, little by little, according
to weight, it will last me a long time,' and sold it in small
quantities [by guess-work] for a small price, and brought on
himself dismay and great distress."

Having reproved my soul with such words as these, I pointed
30 her to the way of truth, although a little narrow, and put her
in fear of the way of things desirable, although very broad, and
she perceived the truth and ceased from her burning desire.
So I cared for the sick in hope of the future recompense, and did
not leave that occupation until it had got me temporal wealth,
35 and I received many honours and presents from kings before
I got to India, and gathered into my barns more than I could
have hoped for. Now I searched all the books of medicine and
tried all the different theories but I could not find - - - - - - -
and found no medical book, however skilful and versed in

knowledge the writer might be, which would get complete
recovery for a sick man, (383) so that he should not again fall
ill, and might rely on continued health. For disease can[not]
be entirely expelled from a man's body, but a physician must
fear and tremble lest there befall those patients who recovered 5
long ago a disease worse than the first, yea, one which will reach
and exceed the limit of the power of medicine, until it brings
them to the very door of the tomb, consigns them to the heart
of the earth, takes them into the chambers of darkness, and
hinds them there.   10

When I considered these things, and weighed them in the
balance of intelligence, justice, and knowledge, I ceased from
my ardour and zeal for the medical profession, since it could not
give complete recovery free from all sufferings. Then I made
my soul labour in thought, and knocked at the door of mercy, 15
asking that the way of truth might be opened to me, that I
might travel in it and walk without fear. Immediately there
was shown me a way clear and free from all sorrow and suffering, which produces complete health, namely, the service of God
and the observance of all his commandments. Then I despised 20
medicine and wished to search into all the kinds of belief in
the true God, and to embrace that one among them which was
true, and therein serve God. But when I searched into them,
I found them to be many, and to contain many varieties. Nor
did I find in medical books anything that elucidated or con- 25
firmed one of the religions. Looking at the religion of men, I
saw that some of them had embraced religion by compulsion,
(384) that some merely walked in their parents' footsteps, and
that some of them wished for the rewards and possessions given
by kings, and so walked according to their religions. And 30
everyone of them said, ' I hold the truth.' So I asked a number of teachers belonging to all the different religions, to show
me, each one of them, the truth which - - - - - - - - - , that
I might follow it, and embrace the religion it taught. But I
found none among them except such as extolled his own reli- 35
gion - - - - - - - - - - - - -, and reviled the religion of his
fellow. Everyone of them said: ' He who does not embrace
my religion is damned, and is no believer in God, but walks
in darkness.' And I saw that there was a great difference

between the Creator and the creature, and that very difficult is
the comprehension of both the beginning and end of a thing.
Having tried what all the teachers and celebrated men in all
the religions had to say, I did not believe them, nor did it
5 please me to follow after something the truth of which was not
evident, or to acquiesce in the words or believe the utterances
of those who professed to be teachers. For each one of them
contradicted the other, which did not please me at all. And I
knew and perceived that all of them were pursuing after their
10 own inclination and making defence for it, and making such
statements as would confirm their religion. But not one did I
see who could roll away the veil of thick darkness from my
heart. And to believe a thing concerning the truth of which I
doubted, [did not please me]. For I feared lest there might
15 happen to me what happened to the thief (385) or robber who
trusted and believed, and then slipped and fell. For it is related that some robbers went out one night to rob the house of
a certain rich man. When they had mounted the roof of the
house, the master of the house woke up from his sleep, and
20 perceived that wicked men had ascended to the roof of his
house. So he awoke his wife, and said to her softly: 'I think
that there are some robbers on our roof, because he whose
errand is an honest one, does not walk on a roof at such a time
as this. Pray rouse me with a loud voice which may be heard
25 by these robbers and say to me : " Will not you tell me how you
amassed all this wealth and property which is gathered and
amassed in your storehouses ?" And when I refuse to tell you,
weary me by talking to me and questioning me about this thing.'
Whereupon the woman did as the man had bidden her. The man
30 said to his wife : 'Hold your peace, and eat what God has prepared for you, and do not try to find out what is secret, for if it
be revealed, evil will come upon us.' The woman replied: 'O
good husband, tell me the truth concerning what I have asked
from you, and be not afraid of me or of others ; for at this time
35 there is no one to hear or listen.' Then her husband said to
her : 'This wealth which you see, I amassed by thieving.' His
wife said to him : 'But how did you amass it by thieving, since
you (386) are accounted honest among men, and just and sincere ?'

The man replied, 'I found ont a certain piece of knowledge and attained to a clever device in the matter of thieving, and on this account the hills were levelled before me and doors opened to me, and I got courage and fortitude of mind, and no man was ever able to hurt me in any single way.'   The woman said, 5 'And what was this piece of knowledge?'   The man said, 'I used to go on moonlight nights, having companions or comrades with me, and as we ascended to the roof of the house which we wished to rob, I used to approach the window through which the light of the moon was shining by myself, and say seven 10 times the words which I am going to tell you, and embrace the moonbeams which were shining into the house, and descend through the window, and rob the whole house.'   The woman said: 'And what are these words which you used to repeat?' The man replied, 'I used to say: "Shulam, shulam," seven 15 times, and in descending into the house I used to repeat these words seven times (more), and nothing remained in that house but it was set before me, whether gold that had been hidden, or silver that had been buried in the earth, or precious pearls and vessels of all kinds; and I used to take of them whatever I 20 wanted, and pass them on to my companions through the window. After that, I used to repeat these words seven times more, and ascend through the window to (387) my comrades while embracing the light of the moon.   And everything that I had taken I loaded on the backs of my companions, and we went 25 away in peace.'   When the thieves heard these words, they rejoiced exceedingly, saying to one another, 'To-night we have found in this house what will benefit us more than all the gold and silver that is in it, this great and glorious piece of learning, which robs us of all fear and frees us from labour and trouble, 30 toil and anxiety.'   So the thieves waited a short time until they thought that the master of the house had gone to sleep and his wife with him.   Then the chief of the robbers went up to the window through which the light of the moon was shining into the man's house, joyful and merry, and said, 'Shulam, 35 shulam' seven times, and embraced the moonbeams which were shining in at the window, the fool thinking that he would descend into the house safely.   But he fell backwards into the middle of the house; whereupon the master of the house rose

up hastily and seized him, saying: 'Who are you, curse upon
you?' and beat him severely with a stout staff, until all his
strength left him.   Then he asked him whence he had come,
and what he was doing there.   The thief replied: 'I am one who
5 believed and trusted, and slipped and fell: this is the sweetness
of the fruit which was supposed to be sweet, but is more bitter
than aloes, and more nauseous than wormwood.'   Then I fell
to meditating, and great anxiety came upon me.   I was afraid
to attach myself to any (388) religion the truth of which had
10 not been made clear to me, lest it should plunge me into the
great abyss, and conduct me to eternal perdition.   So I wished
to search into matters again, and investigate the truth, and test
all [the religions] which I thought might roll away the veil of
darkness from my heart, and the truth of which would open the
15 eyes of mine understanding.   But I could not find such.   Then
I said to my soul: 'O my soul! since thou hast not found anything, as thou didst desire, and since the truth has not been
revealed to thee as thou didst hope, take thee the religion of
thy parents, the religion in which thou didst find them walking,
20 and therein abide.'

Then my mind conceived a reproving thought saying, 'Thou
fool! they whose parents worshipped idols and were magicians
and enchanters, what advantage did they reap for themselves
that their children should imitate them?   Are they not going to
25 inherit a burning hell for their denial of God?'   And I remembered what had been said by the glutton who, on being rebuked
for his gluttony, said: 'My parents used to eat in the same
manner.'   Not finding a religion which was evidently true and
made certainly manifest, so that I might embrace it, and not
30 being justified in continuing to walk in darkness, I wished again
to search into matters, and investigate the truth.   [Then] the
thought occurred to me, and the fear alarmed me, that perhaps
the time for dying was at hand, and the hour of departure hence
was near, and I was standing at the door of the tomb, (389) and
35 in a little moment should be placed in the bosom of the earth.
Then I left off investigating and searching, and cast myself on the
mercy of God, and then on the good deeds and excellent actions
which had gone before me, knowing that works produce fruits
which please the Creator and gratify the righteous Judge.   Then a

thought occurred to me, and I brought to mind that which was spoken by the divine Word: "Though ye do all manner of good, say 'we are unprofitable servants,'" and I was terrified by that which was spoken: 'Bind him hand and foot, and cast him into outer darkness.' Because of these threats, and by reason of these terrifying sayings, I wished again to investigate the truth of religions, and to embrace that one which was proved right, and therein abide. But there chanced to meet me a certain wise old man, ancient of days and skilled in learning, namely, 'Intelligence,' which is fixed in the brain, rebuking and saying: 'Fool! why weary thyself with labour, and (why) seek to comprehend what is too difficult for thee, and exceeds thy power? Perhaps the looser of thy bonds is knocking at the door, and in error of thought and trouble of mind the years of thy life will come to an end, and thou wilt be like the man who wronged himself and angered (390) his Creator, who in his insolence dared to spoil the bed of his fellow, by attaching himself to a woman who stained her good character and wronged her husband.' This wicked woman dug from the house of her poor husband a tunnel or exit, through which her paramour used to come in to her. Now, she had bored the tunnel behind a certain water-jar, and cunningly covered up the opening, so that when her lover came to her, no one should notice him. One day that foolish adulterer came and went in to the woman who behaved so unjustly to her husband, and while they were whispering lasciviously and dishonestly together, lo the poor injured husband began to knock at the outer door. Then that foolish woman said to her infamous paramour: 'Make haste at once, and get out through the tunnel which comes out behind the water-jar.' So that lascivious and infamous man made haste and sought to get out and save himself; but when he came to the mouth of the tunnel of which the base woman had spoken, he found that the water-jar had been taken away. So he returned to the woman who had sold her good character, and said to her: 'I did not find the water-jar in the place of which you told me.' The base woman answered: 'O unlucky fool, what have you to do with the water-jar? Wretched man, do you not know that I placed the jar so that you should recognize the spot, and know where to find the door of the tunnel through which you came in?'

That destroyer of his own good principles said to her: (391)
' As the water-jar was, not there, you need not have said anything about it, because it confused me and made me think that
I did not know, and delivered me into the hand of justice, which
5 will take vengeance on me for having done wrong.' That destroyer of her own good character answered: ' Cease from your
folly and answering back, and make haste and save yourself, lest
I be put to shame as well as you.' And while these mis-
creants were disputing with one another, and the one blaming
10 the other, the poor husband came in, and took hold of that
robber and beat him severely, smote his body and bruised him
with good right, and justly delivered him over to the officers,
and took lawful vengeance on him.

Not finding the truth, as I longed to do, nor attaining to a
15 religion uninfluenced by inclination, I remained in what I had
laboured and spent large sums to obtain, despised all hurtful
things, and relinquished everything which might anger the
Creator, and offend and vex the righteous Judge. I abhorred
murder, which leads to perdition; eschewed oppression, which
20 brings to poverty; put away envy, which confounds good
principles; departed from lying, which begets impudence;
from anger, which disturbs harmony and produces evils; from
railing, which bows the head in shame in the Judgement; and
from slander, which sends to hell. I became a stranger to
25 the seat of sinners, loved quietness, delighted in good things,
aspired to virtue, (392) chose me a seat with the excellent,
who stand in awe of death, tremble at the punishment of hell,
and shrink from ignominy, but do not tremble at any earthly
prince, they whom water cannot drown, nor fire burn, nor vipers
30 sting. I knew that to him who pursues after gratification,
speeds his days in pleasure and carnal delights, and sells for
short-lived enjoyments those things which are to come and will
not pass away, there will happen what happened to the borer of
pearls, when a certain rich man, as they say, agreed with him
35 that he should bore certain precious pearls for a hundred dīnārs
a day. For as the workman entered the merchant's house, he
saw a pleasant sounding cymbal, whereupon the merchant asked
him whether he knew how to play it. The workman said that he
did. The master of the house said to him: 'Then do as you like,

and act according to your own wish.' So he left the work which
he had stipulated with him to do, and spent the whole day in
amusement and fun, while the pearls remained unbored. When
evening came, the workman said to the master of the house:
'Lo, the day is over; give me the hundred dīnārs which you 5
agreed upon with me.' The master of the house answered:
'What have you done here that you should demand pay of me?
Have you not passed the whole day in wantonness and fun?'
The workman replied: 'Did I not first ask your permission
before (393) I took the cymbal?' The merchant replied: 10
'Did you not agree with me with a sound mind, a clear discernment, and a subtle knowledge, for a hundred dīnars of hard
gold, a sum of money which would relieve distress and satisfy
hunger? Wherefore, through a weak will, were you overcome
by the love of amusement, so as to spend the whole day in 15
vanity, which impoverishes, like the steam which ascends from
a pot and vanishes in the air, when its place is known no more?'
Then the hireling, or workman, went to his house ashamed,
empty and sad, in want and repentant.

When I perceived these miseries which attach to the 20
pleasures of the world and to the enjoyments which it affords,
[which] pass away like a dream in the night, my soul hated them,
and they were accounted in my eyes as dung. And I thought I
would be an ascetic, or hermit, for his occupation is excellent
and his portion good, his innocence is desirable and his ways are 25
without snares. As fathers educate their children from infancy
to youth, and from manhood to old age, so do the ways of the
ascetic progress from the elementary to the intermediate stage,
and from the intermediate stage to perfection. Asceticism is
the open door which introduces to the Kingdom him who walks 30
in purity and spends the short space of his sojourning in innocence of conduct, circumspect behaviour, and purity of thought.

Then (394) my mind, from the intelligence which is implanted in the nature and resides in the brain, brought to
remembrance what happens to him who guides his steps along 35
this way of ascetics, both bodily weakness which affects beings
made from dust, and the many trials, varied troubles, and
lurking enemies, who thirst for ruin, long for destruction, and
contend without ceasing; and then the fear lest this poor weak

person should not persevere, but be overcome by force of suffering and multitude of trials, turn back his face in defeat, and
become a laughing-stock among his brethren and the derision of
his friends, and I should lose all the excellent things which I
5 had amassed, and be no more found, but lost, and become like the
dog who, they relate, once passed by a pond with a bone in his
mouth, and, seeing in the pond the reflection of the bone which
he had in his mouth, thought that something else was in the
water, and, descending to the water, let fall the bone out of his
10 mouth, and got nothing but distress and want.

Then I gave up the idea of walking in the way of ascetics,
and prepared myself to abide by the occupation which I had taken
up at first. After having compared and weighed in the balance
of my mind that which an ascetic must endure in the way of
15 hardships, and what varied delights are enjoyed by (395) him who
is attached to pleasures, I perceived that those delights are as
unsavoury salt, and like tasteless food, with which a man cannot
fill his mouth, and that they resemble a bare bone, void of all
juiciness, which a dog takes that he may lick it; for as long as
20 he keeps hold of it, and grips it firmly with his teeth, his mouth
is filled with his own blood, and when he tastes the blood which
flows from his mouth he tightens his grasp and bites the bone
all the more firmly, and it hurts him severely. They resemble,
too, a mouthful of honey in which poison has been mixed, for if
25 a man tastes it, his palate has a sense of sweetness for the twinkling of an eye, and (then) his life departs from him for ever.
They resemble, too, a lamp destitute of oil, which gives light
for a short time only to those who rely on its light, and then
leaves them sitting in darkness. They resemble, too, a dream
30 of the night which a man dreams and believes, thinking that he
has found something and acquired it; for when he wakes from
his sleep, he finds his hands empty. They resemble, too, the
silk-worm, for as long as it weaves, it winds and twists the silk
round its own body.

35   Then my soul longed again for asceticism, (396) and I sought
to walk in that way of life, and therein abide, believing that it
would save me from all stumbling-blocks and deliver me, too,
from all faults, conduct me to the door of the Feast, delight me
with the bliss of the Kingdom, and make me innocent before

the just Judge. Then my conscience pricked me, and put me
in fear and trembling, and rebuked me, saying: 'O feeble
man, formed from - - - - - - - - - - - - - - - , and fashioned
out of opposing elements, in whom is hidden [that] which unceasingly stirs him up, first consider your weakness and examine 5
with your mind's eye the precise nature of an ascetic's way
of life, and, with clear bright thought, consider how scanty
his food is, how deficient his supplies are, how many are his
labours, how varied his troubles, and how severe his trials, and
be in fear lest you be vanquished by the sufferings, when they 10
befall you, and succumb to the trials, when they attack your weakness, and you stand in great shame before your brethren and
kinsmen, and become a laughing-stock to all your acquaintances.'

When I considered those lovers of pleasure, who spend their
days in carnal delights, and pass their lives in unprofitable 15
labours, and what dismay they reap at the end of their doings,
and what distress and sighing they bear at the time of their
departure, and what fruitless provisions they take for their
journey, and considered, too, (397) how many hardships ascetics
bear, then I relinquished the idea of either of them, and knew 20
not which emblem to adopt, or in which way to run. I was
like the judge to whom two suitors applied about the same
matter and with the same object and contention; for when the
first had told him his story - - - - - - - , he pronounced him
innocent and his opponent guilty and confuted; but after the 25
other had told him his story, he condemned the first, who had
been acquitted before, and acquitted the one who had been
pronounced guilty, because of the difference between the two
accounts.

Then I laboured in thought, and projected my gaze into 30
the future; and I perceived that for him who is addicted to
carnal pleasures, who departs from this world in the midst of
luxurious ease, and sells the bliss to come for dishonest pleasures,
very evil things are reserved, namely, the terrible merciless
Judgement, the ceaseless weeping and gnashing of teeth, and the 35
fire which feeds not on wood and cannot be quenched, the
worm that dies not, and the shame which passes not away. I
considered, too, those things which wear out the ascetic in this
present life, namely, scantiness of food, and want of necessaries,

and found that the ascetic who gets the victory in them all
reaps never-dying happiness, and obtains unchanging bliss,
while his soul rejoices among the good, and departs without
sorrow or fear to his Lord, and leaves his body while exulting
5 and praising (398). I saw, too, with what sorrow the soul of
the wanton departs to its Maker, and with what sighing it
puts off its clothing, with what distress it leaves its partner,
and with what dismay and sadness it parts with its wealth
which it amassed unjustly and gathered into its storehouse
10 unlawfully, and insolently refused to use for the advantage
of the distressed, and wickedly neglected to employ so as to
please the righteous Judge; and, to sum up, I saw that it had
wrongly defiled itself with every kind of sin. So I said to
my soul: 'O soul! imagine that thou wilt continue in this
15 world an hundred years, that every day some distress will afflict
thee, some trial befall thee, and some bitter cup be given thee
to drink; yet to all these a limit is set, for they will assuredly
cease when death releases thee from this prison-house, and thou
art freed from all sorrows, relieved from all evils, and liberated
20 from all miseries and distresses, and without anxiety and fear
shalt thou stand in the Judgement to come.' Then the estate
of an ascetic seemed fair in my eyes, and the condition of a
hermit pleased me, although the way of it is narrow, and to
walk in it difficult. And I considered that every kind of
25 creeping thing, and bird, and beast, and fowl, who continue
in ease and distress, in joy and sorrow, are not liable to the
punishment of hell, and are without anxiety or (399) fear. I
compared, too, the beginning of the formation of man, [who]
comes into being in distress and hardship, and in sorrow and
30 sighing issues from the womb. I found in one of the medical
books, that the seed from which the man is formed, when it
falls into the womb of the woman, is mixed with her seed and
her blood, and when it gets thick and curdles a little, the spirit
moves it, and it turns about like liquid cheese, and after that
35 becomes solid, and its arteries are formed, its limbs constructed,
and its joints distinguished. If he is a male, his face is placed
towards his mother's back, and if a female, towards her mother's
belly. His hands are placed against his face, and he cries like
one being scourged, and his soul is sad and distressed, and he

resembles one whose limbs are all bound, while, in addition, a weight presses on him from above. His navel adheres to that of his mother, and thereby he sucks and is nourished by the strength of his mother's food and drink. He remains pent up in this dark and narrow chamber until the time of his birth. When that day comes, the heavenly bidding commands the spirit to trouble the womb, whereupon the infant struggles to be born, and begins to move and strike with its head against the opening, and from his distressed pent-up condition experiences what a thief does, when a ruler commands that his limbs be broken in pieces. Then, when he comes out thence, and falls on to the ground, and feels the air or the touch of people's hands, (400) he suffers as sore pain as a man who is being flayed. Besides all this, he endures different kinds of treatment, and his body is made sick by all of them, and he is not inclined to take meat or drink, and little by little be is reared by means of bands, unguents, swaddling clothes, and sleeping on his back, unable to turn to either side. On emerging from all these torments, he falls into that of school, is next attacked by illness, and worn out by hardships. On attaining to the age of manhood, he marries and begets children. In providing for these, he becomes desirous of amassing wealth unlawfully. Besides all these, there oppose him the four things which oppose one another, black bile and blood and phlegm and yellow bile. He has other enemies besides these, deadly poison, for instance, and dwelling with wild beasts, sojourning with the wicked, birds of prey, cold and heat, and trials of every kind; and, finally, the infirmity of old age, and death and departure. And though a man were freed from all these things which we have enumerated, a faithful surety standing in his stead, so that he should not be hurt by them all the days of his life, let him only remember the hour of his decease, when the swift executioner shall part him from brother and near kinsmen, (401) from wife and ill-gotten property, and let him but look into his evil qualities with a subtle intelligence, and let him tremble and be alarmed at the just Judgement, even the fire that will burn him amid great dismay and sighing, weeping and gnashing of teeth. So every rational being [ought] to hate the world and its pleasures, renounce its gratifications, and put away its

delights, [that] he may escape first from the trials of this life,
and finally be delivered from shame. Especially ought he to
do so in this our age, for it has grown old and is worn out, and
resembles dark clouds or the atmosphere which the north wind
5 disturbs; although God in His mercy created the world, by
His kindness filled it with the plenitude of his blessings, and
set up kings in it, and adorned them with victory, strengthened
them with might, extended their arms like a bow, and implanted
justice in them; yea, He filled his treasuries with good things,
10 that He might instruct princes as He wills. In His justice
He commits to the elders the severe punishment of fools, and
in His generosity He distributes gifts to the good, and grants
of His wealth to the noble. He punishes the abominable in
His severity. He is not weak in His discernment, or feeble in
15 His knowledge. He cares for His lambs, and neglects not His
sheep. He supplies the wants of His flock, and does not withhold from them what they need. He desires greatly for their
welfare, longs exceedingly for their happiness. We find, O my
honoured brethren (402) and distinguished teachers, that the
20 world is going backwards in this hard time of ours, and in this
our evil and vexatious generation, [especially in the days in
which it has seemed good to your Excellency that this book
should be brought to light and translated from Arabic into
Syriac. For we find that the truth on which the world is
25 founded, and on which [as] on solid adamant the Church of
Christ is built, has been specially hidden by the teachers of the
Church and the pastors of God. Yea, they have hidden in the
heart of the earth that love which is the perfecter of all virtues,
according to the testimony of the wise architect and zealous
30 treasurer and heavenly apostle. It is utterly taken from the
world, especially from the priests and from those who seek the
priestly office, and is laid in the dust of the earth.] Wickedness,
fearful and appalling, rears its head, and good is wholly taken
away from our midst. Deceit, calumny, and envy exult.
35 Insolence, mockery, and wantonness laugh aloud. Long-suffering and peacefulness wear a downcast face. Knowledge and
understanding are buried in a deep gulf. Churlishness and
pride cry aloud from the roofs. Cruelty, ill-will, and love
of money [- - -]. The amassers of evil hoards give orders

and are obeyed. Innocence of heart, sincerity of disposition,
and liberality in giving, have ceased and perished. The good
are no more respected, while shame is approved and extolled
among the wicked. Tricks and wiles pour forth like the Nile.
The givers of good counsel have been driven away and dis- 5
believed, (403) while falsehood has been uttered by every
mouth, that every man may accomplish his wish, and every
man perform his desire.

[Three lines are unintelligible.]

No man is contented with his pay, but his soul is eager to 10
seize the property of others. Tyrants spring up and flourish
like the cedars of Lebanon, and the humble and oppressed have
their faces defiled with dust. The ruler chooses the wicked, and
delights in those who counsel evil things. The judge drives
away the honest from his seat, and repulses those who pursue 15
after peace, who rebuke justly and give upright testimony, and
delights in false witnesses and in those who take bribes and love
vain glory. [Finally, the whole mass of mankind, especially the
sons of the Church, have put away the remembrance of the end
from before their eyes, and cast the fear of the Judge and of 20
His keen vengeance behind their backs.]
    When I had considered all these things, weighed them with
the balances of justice, and estimated them all with intelligent
discernment, great astonishment took hold of me, and put me
into a state of great amazement, because I saw that this being, 25
man, though more glorious than any other creature on account
of his reason, and more honoured (404) by his Maker than all
other beings, and though subtle in knowledge, a searcher of
matters by his discernment, and a revealer of secrets by his
knowledge, nevertheless loses the things which are to come and 30
change not, rejoice and do not grieve, are gentle and not perverse, for a little miserable pleasure which abides not and cannot be retained; namely, a little smelling; a little food, which,
immediately it passes from the palate, becomes hurtful and
emits a foul odour; sight, which when it is hidden from the 35
eyes, becomes like vapour ascending from an oven, which
evaporates in the air and is no more; [and] hearing, which, when

it passes from the ear, becomes like sounding brass or a clanging
cymbal. I studied to compare him with something which is
like him, or which illustrates his weak nature, and found for
him this similitude. Mankind is like a man who, in flying from
5 some terror, has lit upon a pit or deep hole, and, descending into
it to be concealed, has found a withered branch, and seized it
with his hand, lest he should fall to the bottom. On looking
into the bottom of the pit, he perceives a big dragon, with open
mouth, waiting to swallow him up. He lifts up his head
10 towards the branch to which he is clinging in hopes that it will
not let him fall down into the pit, (405) and lo two mice, one
black and the other white, gnawing at it. While cast in this
state of anxiety and torment, these storms and difficulties, he looks
and perceives a swarm of honey-bees near him. He stretches out
15 his hand, and tastes a little of the honey. Then he looks aside
and becomes wholly intent on the honey, and the fool forgets
that there are four beasts below him who mutually oppose one
another, so to speak, one of whom may raise his head and take
away his life. Nor, again, does the wretched man remember the
20 mice who are continually gnawing the branch, for if it be
severed, he must fall down into the pit, and the dragon with
the open mouth will swallow him up. But the wretched man
looks only at the honey, and all his anxiety is put away by its
sweetness until the branch is severed by the mice, and the
25 greedy glutton falls down the pit, and the dragon swallows him
up. Then I made a comparison and explained the pit or well
to mean this world, which is full of trials. The four beasts
I likened to the four humours which sustain the body, when
they exist in equal proportions; whereas if one of them prevails
30 over another, he becomes as one who has tasted deadly poison.
The black mouse I likened to night, and the white mouse to
day; for the two are constantly wearing life away, and con-
suming the years. The dragon I likened to death, from which
there is no escape. The honey I compared to those (406) little
35 sweet morsels which a man enjoys here in this life, even smell,
taste, sight, and hearing, which prevent and withhold him from
taking care to save his life.

Then, when I had made all these comparisons, and weighed
them with the balance of knowledge, I held to what I had

taken to at first, and laboured with all my might. - - - - - - - - -
- - - - - - - - - - - - - - - - - - without delay or tarrying,
in hopes that I should find salvation for my soul, and those who
would help me to a perfect religion. And I returned from India
to my own country, and copied out from the books of the
Indians this book, which is called by them (the book) of Kalilah
and Dimnah. The end.

By divine help is ended the book of Kalilah and Dimnah,
and the discourse of Barzöi. Let the reader pray for everyone
who participates in it. Amen.   10

NOTES AND CORRECTIONS.

I use a few abbreviations. They are as follows:

Add. and Corr. = Additions and Corrections, prefixed to Professor W. Wright's edition of the Syriac text of this book. See below under Syr. T.

Ar. V. = Arabic Version.

Benfey's Pantsch. = Pantschatontra: fünf Bücher indischer Fabeln, Märchen und Erzählungen. Aus dem Sanscrit übersetzt mit Einleitung und Anmerkungen von Theodor Benfey. In two parts. (Leipzig, 1859.)

Cal. é Dym. = Calila é Dymna, in the Biblioteca de Autores Españoles, desde la formacion del languajo hasta nuestros dias; escritores en prosa anteriores al siglo xv. recogidos é ilustrados por Don Pascual de Gayangos (Madrid, 1860); in the 52nd volume (the volumes are not numbered). This is the Old Spanish version made from the Arabic in the middle of the 13th century.

De Sacy = De Sacy's Calila et Dimna, ou Fables de Bidpai (Paris, 1816).

Derenbourg = Deux versions Hébraïques du livre de Kalîlâh et Dimnâh par Joseph Derenbourg (Paris, 1881). The first of these versions is the one made from the Arabic version. The other is worthless and modern, being a mere cento of Bible verses.

Glossary = Professor Wright's Glossary, prefixed to his edition of the Syriac text.

Guidi (Studii) = Studii sul testo Arabo del libro di Calila e Dimna per Ignazio Guidi (Roma, 1873). This book contains a number of extracts from three Arabic MSS., which Guidi names M, P, V respectively.

Kal. u. Dom. = Kalilag und Damnag, die Syrische Übersetzung des Indischen Fürstenspiegels. Text und German translation by Gustav Bickell. With an Introduction by Theodor Benfey (Leipzig, 1876). This is the old Syriac version made from the Pahlevi about A.D. 570. The pagination of the Introduction is in Roman, that of the rest in Arabic numerals. The translation is referred to as Kal. u. Dam. Transl.

O. Syr. (V.) = Old Syriac (Version).

Syr. T. = Syriac Text. The Book of Kalilah and Dimnah translated from Arabic into Syriac. Edited by W. Wright, LL.D. (London, Trübner and Co., 1884). The book is accompanied by an introduction, a glossary, and a list of Additions and Corrections.

P. 1, lines 1, 2. The heading may have been added by the Syriac translator, or by a subsequent scribe. ܩܨܐ is singular in agreement with ܟܬܒܐ ܕܟܠܝܠܗ in the sense of 'the book of K. and D.'

2. *Kalilah* (ܩܠܝܠܗ; Ar. V. كليلة'; O. Syr. ܩܠܝܠܐ')
represents the Sanscrit *Karataka*, a name which means 'crow'[1]. The change of Sanscrit *r* to *l* may be due to the fact that the Pehlevi signs for *r* and *l* are quite or almost identical[4]. The change of *t* to *l* is not so surprising when it is remembered that *t* contains a predominating *r* element[2]. Words which in Pehlevi end in *k* exhibit instead an *h* when they pass into modern Persian[6], and it appears that the Arabic translator was guided by the same habit of language here. Two of Guidi's manuscripts attest the pronunciation *Kulailah*[7]—a common diminutive form in Arabic—but the Sanscrit *Karataka* is against this vocalisation, and our modern Syriac translator certainly did not pronounce the word so, else he would have written ܩܠܝܠܐ.

Dimnah. (ܕܡܢܗ?, Ar. V. دمنة[9]; O. Syr. ܕܡܢܐ?') represents the Sanscrit *Damanaka*, a name which Benfey interprets to mean 'tamer'[10]. The change of Sanscrit *a* to *i* in the Ar. V. is attested by the Old Spanish (*Dymna*)[11], John of Capua (*Dimna*)[12], Raimund of Beziers (*Dina*)[13], as well as by our modern Syriac version. See too a note by Nöldeke in the Z. D. M. G. xxx. p. 752.

4. *Dabdahram.* The vocalisation is conjectural. That the name begins with ? is known by Syr. T. 95, 23. Possibly ܕܐܗܕܘ? is a corruption of ܕܐܗܪܡ? which might represent the دبشليم of De Sacy's Arabic text. But it is nearly certain that ܕܐܗܕܘ? is not a corrupt form, for it occurs again at Syr. T. 95, 24 and 96, 10. Besides the form دبشليم, Guidi has found ديسلم, ديشلم and ديلم[14]. The O. Syr. has ܕܐܗܪܡ[15]. This reflects a Pehlevi form which gave rise to a form دبشلم. The change of *r* to *l* has been explained in the note on the name *Kalilah*. The form ديسلم

[1] De Sacy, p. ٨٢, l. 2.	[9] Kal. u. Dam. p. 2, l. 6.
[2] Kal. u. Dam. p. 2, l. 5.	[10] Benfey's Pantsch. II. p. 8.
[3] Benfey's Pantsch. II. p. 8.	[11] Cal. é Dym. p. 20, a.
[4] Kal. u. Dam. p. lxxxv.	[12] Directorium, b. 5. r.
[5] Ib. p. xlix.	[13] Notices et Extraits des Manuscrits
[6] Ib. p. xlil.	Vol. x. Pt. 2, pp. 9, 11 etc.
[7] Guidi, Studii, p. 6.	[14] Guidi, Studii, p. 21.
[8] De Sacy, p. ٨٢, l. 2.	[15] Kal. u Dam. pp. 49, 61 and 81.

seems to be reflected in the Old Spanish *Dicelen*[16], Hebrew דיסלם[17], and Raimund's *Dizalen*[18]. John of Capua's *Dieles*[19] and Raimund's *Dysles*[20], *Dyzlex*, merely reflect a false reading דיסלם. What Sanscrit name is reflected by دبشلم or دبشلم is wholly unknown. The corresponding name in the Panchatantra is *Amaraçakti*[21]. Benfey conjectures *Devaçarman*[22], a name which occurs several times in that work[23], and means according to Benfey, ' Das Glück der Götter haltend ' or ' Von den Göttern beglückt '[24].

On دبشلم see further Benfey's *Pantsch.* i. p. 32, note 1.

Nadrab. Here and at Syr. T. 96, 9, the name is written نادرب. At Syr. T. 3, 11, it appears as نادرب. At Syr. T. 95, 24, نادرب is a mistake for نادرب. These forms must reflect Arabic نادرب which our translator vocalised *Nadrab.* But how Ibn el-Mokaffa' wrote the name is uncertain. The manuscripts give بيدبا[a], بيدنا[b], تندباد[c], and شربا[d]. Now the O. Syr. has صممي[e]. This agrees best with بيدبا, for the Pehlevi signs for *n* and *w* are the same, and the termination written *āk*, pronounced *āg*, becomes *ā* in modern Persian. Accordingly Nöldeke assumes a Pehlevi form like *Wēda-nāka*, *Wāla-wāka* or *Wēda-nāga*, which the O. Syr. translator rendered *Bēdawāg*[f]. But Benfey proposes a form *Vidyā-pati* meaning ' Herr der Wissenschaft '[g]. The corresponding name in the Panchatantra is *Vishnuçarman*[h]. For an explanation of the סנדבאר of the Hebrew version[i] (John of Capua's *Sendebar*[j]) see *Pantsch.* i. p. 13. Raimund's *Sendebat*[k] is merely a corruption of this. The forms *Bundobet*, *Barduben* or *Burduben*, *Bendubec*, of manuscripts of the Old Spanish[l], and *Bendobel*, *Bendubeh* of Raimund's

16 *Cal. é Dym.* p. 11, a.
17 Derenbourg, p. 17.
18 *Notices et Extraits des Manuscrits*, loc. cit. pp. 20, 29.
19 *Directorium*, b. 4. r; c. 5. v. etc.
20 *Notices et Extraits des Manuscrits*, loc. cit. p. 29.
21 Benfey's *Pantsch.* ii. p. 1.
22 *Ib.* i. p. 84.
23 *Ib.* ii. pp. 31, 141, 320.
24 *Ib.* ii. p. 320.
25 De Sacy, p. vᴀ, l. 9.
26 Guidi, *Studii*, p. 21.

27 *Kal. u. Dam.* p. 51, l. 3.
28 Nöldeke's *Mäusekönig*, p. 6, note 8.
29 *Kal. u. Dam.* p. xliv, note.
30 Benfey's *Pantsch.* ii. p. 3.
31 Derenbourg, pp. 17, 18, 61 etc.
32 *Directorium*, a. 4. r; b. 4. r.
33 *Notices et Extraits des Manuscrits*, loc. cit.
34 *Cal. é Dym.* p. 11, a, and note 8 which contains an error. *Bendubec* occurs, 1 think, at p. 19, a, where I would read 'Dijo el rey d Benalubce un filósofo.'

272   BOOK OF KALILAH AND DIMNAH.

Latin version⁵⁵, all point to a form whose first consonant was *b*, the third *d*, and the fourth *b*. See too *Pantsch.* 1. p. 32, note 2.

5. *The philosopher.* The original مَنَكِى (Add. and Corr. 3, 7) means 'one skilled in rhetoric and argument, an eloquent, persuasive person.' The word occurs again at Syr. T. 185, 21, where I render 'eloquent' (120, 35). Except in the passage before us, Nadrab is always called 'the philosopher' (ܦܝܠܘܣܘܦܐ), as also in the Ar. V. (فيلسوف). In the Panchatantra he is described as a Brahman, perfect in all sciences⁵⁶. The O. Syr. V. does not describe him in any way.

13. The Panchatantra has: 'In a province of the South lies a town called Mahilāropya, in which lived a merchant' &c.⁵⁷ This town is in the Deccan, the Sanscrit name of which is *Dakshināpatha*. No doubt this latter is reflected in the دسناباد of Guidi's manuscript F⁵⁸; for, changing ن into ك we get *Damabad*, a form very near indeed to *Dakshināpatha*. The Old Spanish has *Gurguen* in one manuscript, *Jurgen* in another⁵⁹. Similarly Raimund has *Jorgeni*⁶⁰. These reflect an Arabic جرجان (Georgia), which some scribe substituted for the unknown name which puzzled him. Compare the commencement of the chapter of the weasel and the ascetic, where in De Sacy's Arabic text جرجان has been inserted⁶¹, though no name is given at the corresponding place in the Panchatantra⁶².

22. *Provision for the world to come.* That is, good works sent on to the next world. So the Old Spanish: 'anteponer buenas obras para el otro siglo'⁶³. Compare p. 266, ll. 36—39.

P. 2, 4. (Syr. T. 4, 19.) Read ܠܒܣܐ and render: *despises wealth and cares not at all for it.*

8. (Syr. T. 4, 23.) *With ... steady attention.* ܠܡܝܣܒ is defined at Syr. T. 331, 14, to mean ܢܦܫ ܠܒܝܒܐ (patience, perseverance).

⁵⁵ *Notices et Extraits des Manuscrits,* loc. cit.
⁵⁶ Benfey's *Pantsch.* II. p. 8.
⁵⁷ *Ib.* II. p. 7.
⁵⁸ Guidi, *Studii,* p. 32.
⁵⁹ *Cal. é Dym.* p. 19, b.

⁶⁰ *Notices et Extraits des Manuscrits,* loc. cit. p. 34, l. 2.
⁶¹ De Sacy, p. ١١٩, l. 7.
⁶² Benfey's *Pantsch.* II. p. 326.
⁶³ *Cal. é Dym.* p. 19, b, l. 14.

9. *Eye-paint or kohl.* Lane in his *Modern Egyptians* (Vol. 1. p. 44) after speaking of the beautiful eyes of Egyptian women continues as follows: 'their charming effect is much heightened by the concealment of the other features (however pleasing the latter may be), and is rendered still more striking by a practice universal among the females of the higher and middle classes, and very common among those of the lower orders, which is that of blackening the edge of the eyelids, both above and below the eye, with a black powder called "kohl." This is a collyrium commonly composed of the smoke-black which is produced by burning a kind of "libán," an aromatic resin, a species of frankincense, used, I am told, in preference to the better kind of frankincense, as being cheaper, and equally good for this purpose. Kohl is also prepared of the smoke-black produced by burning the shells of almonds. Those two kinds, though believed to be beneficial to the eyes, are used merely for ornament; but there are several other kinds used for their real or supposed medical properties; particularly the powder of several kinds of lead ore (*kohl el-hagar*): to which are often added sarcocolla ('*anzaroot*), long pepper ('*ark ed-dahab*), sugar-candy, fine dust of a Venetian sequin, and sometimes powdered pearls. Antimony, it is said, was formerly used for painting the edges of the eyelids. The kohl is applied with a small probe, of wood, ivory, or silver, tapering towards the end, but blunt: this is moistened, sometimes with rose-water, then dipped in the powder, and drawn along the edges of the eyelids....The custom of thus ornamenting the eyes prevailed among both sexes in Egypt in very ancient times: this is shewn by the sculptures and paintings in the temples and tombs of this country....The same custom existed among the ancient Greek ladies, and among the Jewish women in early times. See 2 Kings ix. 30 (where, in our common version, we find the words "painted her face" for "pointed her eyes"), and Ezekiel iii. 40.'

22. *Tank.* ܡ̇ܚܶ means properly 'a stagnant pond,' or 'marshy lake.' The same word occurs at 3, 7, where I render 'fen'; 31, 13 ('pool'); 43, 35, and 48, 33 ('marsh'); 119, 34 ('pool,' a stagnant one is meant); 135, 17 ('lake'); 165, 26 ('pond'); 187, 26 ('pools') and 260, 6 ('pond'). The word is explained in the native lexicons by غَدِير and بِرْكَة (בְּרֵכָה).

274   BOOK OF KALILAH AND DIMNAH.

For the illustration compare Benfey's *Panschatantra*, II. p. 199,
Strophe 157.

32. *Energy.* لحَمُورَا conveys the notions of activity and
prosperity.

34. *Mathurá.* The Panchatantra has *Mathurá*, Ptolemy's Ma-
doupa, a town north of Agra, and still called by nearly the same
name" (spelt now *Muttra*). The name is well preserved in the O.
Syr. which has مَثُورَا". The Arabic manuscripts give variously
مَتُوتٍ, مَنُورٍ", and سَنُورٍ". Of these مَنُورٍ is the most
correct. For if we add a point and write it مَتُورٍ (Matûr) it is
brought into conformity with the Sanscrit, the O. Syr., and with
John of Capua who has *Mathor*". The *Mayon*" of the Old Spanish
reflects the form مَيُورٍ. Raimund wilfully alters to *Majorica*". Our
مَثُورَا should probably be referred to a form مَتُورَا (for مَتُرَا)".

37. *Shanzabeh.* The Panchatantra has *Sanjívaka*, a name
which Benfey interprets to mean 'der Zusammenlebende' or 'der
gesellig Lebende'". The O. Syr. has سَنْزِبَا"; and De Sacy's
Arabic text شَنْزَبَة", the termination *ka* being dropped, or at least
merely represented by a written *ه*. Compare *Kalilah* for *Karataka*.
Guidi's manuscripts exhibit corrupt forms".

Banzabeh. The Panchatantra has *Nandaka*, 'the gladdener'".
Analogy would lead one to expect in the Arabic a form like نَنْدَه
(Nandah), but the name has been assimilated to the other one, the
Arabic manuscripts and offshoots all agreeing in appending a
terminal *b*. De Sacy's text" and one of Guidi's manuscripts give
بَنْدَبَه". Of Guidi's other two manuscripts one has نَنْدَبَه (the
correct form), the other سَنْدَبَه". In this latter the first two letters
are ambiguous, having no dineritical points. Benfey seems to have
mistaken it for سَدْبَه (S d b h) and applied it to the wrong ox".

---

[a] Benfey's *Pantsch.* II. p. 6.
[b] *Kal. u. Dam.* p. I, l. 6.
[c] De Sacy, p. ٧٩, lin. ult.
[d] Guidi, *Studii*, p. 23.
[e] *Directorium*, b. 4, v.
[f] *Col. é Dym.* p. 19, b.
[g] *Notices et Extraits des Manuscrits,*
loc. cit. p. 34, l. 5.
[h] Prof. Wright's Preface to the Syr.

T. p. xvi.
[i] Benfey's *Pantsch.* II. p. 7.
[j] *Kal. u. Dam.* p. LXIV.
[k] De Sacy, p. ٨٠, l. 1.
[l] Guidi, *Studii*, p. 28.
[m] Benfey's *Pantsch.* II. p. 7
[n] De Sacy, p. ٨٠, l. 2.
[o] Guidi, *Studii*, p. 23.
[p] *Kal. u. Dam.* p. LXV.

Our Syriac translator must have had before him a form in which the name had been still further assimilated to that of the other ox, *d* having been changed to *z* (بنزيذ).

The Old Syriac renders ܚܨܘܗ, for an explanation of which see *Kal. u. Dam.* p. LXXXI. More probably as Nöldeke says (*Z. D. M. G.* xxx. p. 756, note 4), this should be read ܠܙܘܗ.

37. *Became weary.* ܐܥܠ occurs also at Syr. T. 38, 12, and 256, 2.

P. 3, 5. *The ox has died in yonder place.*

In the Arabic Version according to De Sacy's text (p. ٨٠) and Guidi's manuscript F (Guidi, *Studii*, p. 23) the hireling follows up his lie by a highly moral tale showing that death when it comes cannot be avoided by any amount of precaution.

'And he said to him : Man when his term is over and his fated end approaches, though he may strenuously avoid the things from which he fears destruction, is not thereby profited a whit, and often his very precautions and anxiety turn to his hurt. This is shown in a story they tell. A man was travelling through a desert place infested by wild beasts, he being acquainted with the difficulty and danger of the country. When he had proceeded a little distance, a very fierce and blood-thirsty wolf met him. Seeing that the wolf was making for him, he was afraid, and looked to the right and to the left for a place where he might take refuge from the wolf, but saw nothing but a town behind a stream. So he went hastily towards the town. When he reached the stream, he could see no bridge across it, but observing that the wolf had nearly overtaken him, he cast himself into the water, though unable to swim well, and came nigh to drowning. But some of the townsfolk saw him and rushed up to pull him out, which they did, he having almost died. When the man reached their place and knew that he was safe from the wolf's attack, he espied on the bank of the stream a house standing by itself, and said : I will enter this house and rest myself in it. On entering it, he found a band of robbers who had just committed a highway robbery on a merchant, dividing his wealth among themselves and intending to kill him. Whereupon he took fright and went off towards the town. And he leant his back against one of the walls therein to rest himself from the terror and

weariness which had come upon him, when the wall fell upon him and he died. The merchant replied: You are right. I have heard this story before.'

The story is given in John of Capua, where however an ox is the unfortunate party, and no mention is made of the robbers. In the Old Spanish it occurs, but is differently introduced (*Cal. ê Dym.* p. 19). There the unfortunate is represented as gathering herbs in the same meadow to which Shanzabeh, guided by his destiny, finds his way: the point of the story being that the same destiny which brought death on the man guided Shanzabeh to prosperity. Neither the O. Syr. nor any of the Sanscrit recensions contain it, but compare Benfey's *Pantsch.* II. p. 8, Str. 24: 'Wer unbeschützt, findet sich vom Geschick beschützt: was wohl beschützt, kommt vom Geschick geschlagen um; am Leben bleibt, der in dem Walde hülflos lag; trotz aller Mühe stirbt der im Haus Verpflegete.'

In the Old Spanish, as in the Directorium, no robbers are mentioned. As to John of Capua's ox see *Kal. u. Dam.* p. cvi.

7. *Fen.* See note on p. 2, 22.

12. *Pingalaka.* This is the name in the Panchatantra (Benfey's *Pantsch.* II. p. 8), and means 'the dark yellow.' Our version has ܐܠܟܠܗ (Aulklh), which no doubt rests on a misreading of an Arabic form reflecting *Pingalaka.* See Prof. Wright's Preface to his edition of the Syriac text (p. xvi.).

22. *Two jackals.* The Syr. T. gives three synonyms for 'jackals', viz. ܬܥܠܐ ܡܥܩܒܐ, ܬܥܠܐ ܝܪܘܪ, and ܬܥܠܐ ܟܘܦܐ. For the first see Prof. Wright's Glossary. The second is a common Syriac term. ܟܘܦܐ is simply the Pehlevi word *tûrek* (*Kal. u. Dam.* p. lxxxiii). The Arabic has اِبْنُ آوَىْ.

23. For the names *Kalílah* and *Dimnah* see note on p. 1, 2.

P. 4, 5. *Splitting.* Rather, *sawing*; and so in line 8. But the Ar. V. has *splitting*, شَقِّ (De Sacy, p. ٤٢, l. 10).

6. *Carriage.* ܩܪܘܩܐ is the Latin *carruca.* At p. 23, 1 the plural word occurs, meaning 'horses.'

7. (Syr. T. 8, 2.) *Wedge of wood.* In the text follow three words which I do not understand, viz, ܩܝܣܐ ܐܩܣܐ ܡܩܣܐ. This would seem to denote the kind of wood. In the Panchatantra the log is

said to be of *Anjana* wood, and the wedge of *Khadira* wood (Benfey's *Pantsch.* II. p. 9). It seems that *Anjana* survives in ـيٰٱ and *Khadira* in ﺣﺪﺭﺍ

13. *Tail.* The Syriac text has

مشتنبحوہ اوحا جنبحت حصوحوہ

14. The words in brackets are supplied from the Ar. V.

ونزع الوتد (De Sacy, p. ٨٢, l. antepenult.) Compare Benfey's *Pantsch.* II. p. 9.

33. *Fine spirit.* Or 'true manliness.' ﻗﻨﯩﻮﺗﺎ is equivalent to المروۃ.

P. 5, 7. (Syr. T. 9, 17.) *Coaxingly wagging his tail.* Perhaps read جمبوحوہ جبحوہ. Professor Theodor Noldeke of Strassburg, in a note which he was kind enough to send me on the root زمر, says that زمر, زمر, and its derived nouns زمورتا, etc., in all the instances he has noted, convey the notion of *sound*, and specially of *soothing, wheedling tones.* Thus زمر = *to sing to, to sing to sleep,* etc.; زمورتا = *lullabies* (Ephr. II. 424 D; III. 330E); also, *spells* or *charms* (Hoffmann, *Opusc. Nestor.* 94, 7).

Possibly زمر may have come to mean simply *to wheedle,* the notion of sound being dropped, so that 'to wheedle with the tail' would mean to wag it coaxingly. I think this theory will satisfactorily account for the meaning 'caudo motitationem' assigned to زمورتا by Castell (p. 564), on the authority of Bar Bahlul; for he couples it with 'blanditiae canum.' Professor Noldeke is inclined to think that either Bar Bahlul made a mistake, or that Castell misunderstood him, and that our Syriac translator was misled by Bar Bahlul; but it should be noted that the meanings 'to bark' and 'to wag the tail' are both assigned to another root by the lexicographers, namely to ﻧﺒﺢ. See Payne Smith's *Thesaurus Syriacus,* col. 1370.

There is still another possibility, namely that something has dropped out before جمبوہ. But to explain one corruption by supposing another is a dangerously easy method.

35. *Leave it for others that are too high for him.* More literally: 'go forth in search of what is too high for him.'

P. 6, 1. *Sharpening the wits.* More literally: 'stirring up, stimulating the senses.'

P. 7, 6. Four words are unintelligible to me.

7. *By novelty of situation.* Perhaps better: 'By being in a foreign or strange country.'

9—19. This passage corresponds to Guidi's extract 12 (p. 24).

18. *For another.* Kalilah means himself.

29. I have translated according to Syr. T. 13, note 2, but I suspect that for ܠܟܝܬܐ should be read ܡܟܐܬܐ ('a mean position,' compare Syr. T. 296, 9), and that for ܥܡܝܠܐ should be read ܥܒܝܕ ܥܡܝܠܐ ('and makes his bed ').

P. 8, 23. The words in brackets are supplied from De Sacy's Arabic text, p. ٨٦, l. 9.

30. (Syr. T. 15, 5.) I read ܡܟܬܝܢܐ

P. 9, 30. I read ܡܢܘ ܐܕܐ ܗܢ because it is the question to which the answer corresponds, and because the Ar. V. has من هذا (De Sacy, p. ٨٧, l. 12).

39. For ܥܒܡܐ instead of ܥܒܡܐ (Add. and Corr. 17, 5) see De Sacy's text, p. ٨٧, l. 15.

P. 10, 2—7. This passage is supplied by Guidi (p. 25, extract 13) but without mention of the little insect. De Sacy's text has simply: 'A piece of wood lying on the ground is often useful, so that a man takes it up, and it becomes an implement for him to use.'

20—11, 29. Supplied by Guidi (p. 25, extract 14), but in a curtailed form.

25. The words ܐܠܐ ܡܝܬܪܢ (Syr. T. 18, 8) seem entirely superfluous.

29. I would read ܡܟܬܝܢܐ (Syr. T. 18, 12). The judgment is surely meant. Compare Syr. T. 14, 6.

30. *Clarifier.* ܡܨܠܠܢܐ must mean some machine for testing the purity of honey.

38. *Weighs down the scale.* See Add. and Corr. 18, 22.

P. 11, 1. *Abundance of intellect.* For ܣܘܓܐܐ (Syr. T. 18, 24), read ܫܦܝܘܬܐ, and render 'clearness of intellect.' ܫܦܝܘܬ ܪܥܝܢܐ is a common phrase in this book. Compare Syr. T. 13, 18; 21, 5.

13. The Syriac might also be rendered: 'a man should not follow another who does not know his right hand from his left.' Neither rendering yields a satisfactory sense. The meaning is clear in Guidi's corresponding extract. His MS. F has يقال لا يصحب

الرجل صاحبا لا يعرف يمينه فضلا عن شماله (Guidi, p. ix, l. 5).

'It is said: Let not a man join company with one whose right hand he does not know, much less his left'; i.e. with a person whom he does not know in the least. The same caution is given at p. 34, 7.

35. *A shekel.* Perhaps read ܡܐܟܠܐ (Syr. T. 20, 9), and render 'it yields food.'

P. 12, 24—29. This passage corresponds to Guidi's extract 15 (p. 26).

P. 13, 6. Two words are unintelligible to me (Syr. T. 22, 9).

12—17. De Sacy's text of the Ar. V. has simply: 'He is like cool sandal-wood, which when it is rubbed hard, becomes hot and injurious' (p. ٤٩, l. penult.).

31—14, 5. Given by Guidi (p. 26, extract 15 bis) more fully than by De Sacy, and more according to the Syriac. But Guidi has misread السِّكَر *dam* (p. x, line 3). Compare Benfey's *Pantsch.* II. p. 20, Str. 115: 'Die Brücke wird vom Wasser gebrochen &c.' السِّكَر, *wine*, gives capital sense ('water ruins weak wine'), but is certainly wrong.

P. 14, 7. This story occurs in the Panchatantra (Benfey's *Pantsch.* II. p. 25), and is given by Guidi (p. 27, extract 16).

36. *Kinsfolk.* See Glossary.

P. 16, 16—19. Enlarged by Guidi (p. 27, extract 17); compare Benfey's *Pantsch.* II. 24, Strophes 138, 139.

18. *Carucans.* See Glossary under ܟܪܘ.

P. 18, 11. *At the expense of my own.* For ܟܕܣܝܬ I read ܟܕܢܣܝܬ (Syr. T. 29, 22).

16 ff. This story is related at great length in the Panchatantra (Benfey's *Pantsch.* II. 34 foll.), where it is called 'Drei Missgeschick' aus eigner Schuld.'

30. *Boldly.* For ܢܟܣܝܬܐ (Syr. T. 30, 15), read ܢܬܢܨܚ

and render 'until he was able to steal his garments wrongfully
(lit. thievingly).' ﺑﺼﺎﺋﻢ is generally used in a good sense.

P. 19, 4. The passage which I have left untranslated occurs
also in the Old Syriac Version, and is rendered into Latin on p. 9
of Bickell's translation of it. Knatchbull has retained it but with
alterations (p. 105). So too the Dominican fathers in the Mosul
edition (p. ١٢).

P. 20, 34. The text of the ascetic's address to the judge is not
complete. Either the modern scribe who wrote foll. 18 and 19
(Syr. T. 31, note 1) did not finish his work, or a leaf is missing,
for the next words ('to God and said: &c.') begin fol. 20 (Syr.
T. 34, 10).

P. 21, 3. I think that the words 'Then the ascetic said'
introduce a fresh speech by him. If so, something has been omitted.
Nöldeke comes to the same conclusion (Add. and Corr. 34, 17).

27. After ﻟﻰ insert ﺣﻢ (Syr. T. 35, 21).

P. 22, 1. The six damaging circumstances according to De Sacy's
text of the Ar. V. (p. ٩٩, l. 3) are misfortune (ﺍﻟﺤﺮﻣﺎﻥ), sedition

(ﺍﻟﻔﺘﻨﺔ), passion (ﺍﻟﻬﻮﻯ), cruelty (ﺍﻟﻔﻈﺎﻇﺔ), bad weather (ﺍﻟﺰﻣﺎﻥ),

and stupidity (ﺍﻟﺤﻤﻖ). Of these, two are not to be found in
our Syriac versions, viz. cruelty and stupidity. As to the latter, it
is easy to see that the Syriac translator read ﺍﻟﺤﺮﻳﻖ fire, instead
of ﺍﻟﺤﻤﻖ. The former is probably the right reading, for in
the O. Syr. (Kal. u. Dam. Transl. p. 11) there is no mention
of stupidity, but there is of fire. On the other hand cruelty ought
to have found a place, for not only is it mentioned in the O. Syr.
(l. c.) but it is dwelt upon a few lines lower down (29—33).

6. Extolled. The word (ﺑﻤﺸﻘﻠﺔ Syr. T. 36, 16) might
perhaps also be rendered 'taken away,' a translation which gives a
different turn to the sense. My rendering is, I think, supported by
the O. Syr. which runs thus: 'ferner, dass sie aus Zorn aufbrausende
Reden und eine bissige Zunge führen ; dann dass sie aus Thorheit
Unternehmungen gegen ihre Feinde wagen, während sie vielmehr
mit diesen in Frieden und nicht im Kriege leben sollten ; endlich,

dass sio Beschädigung erleiden durch Feuer oder Wasser, Ueberfluss oder Mangel an Regen, Hagel, Frost oder Hitze, Hungersnoth oder Pest' (*Kal. u. Dam.* Transl. pp. 11, 12). The first clause in this extract corresponds to the 'cruelty' (القسوة) of the Ar. V. The next one, I think, answers to the warlike policy in the Syriac, which is 'extolled by inconsiderate generals.'

14. After ܐܟܙܐ. insert ܩܕܡ (Syr. T. 36, 23). But perhaps it is unnecessary to do so, and we may render 'too large-minded for any greed.' For this construction compare Syr. T. 55, 18.

16—20. (Syr. T. 37, 1—5.) See Add. and Corr. The same confusion (ܒ with ܠ) occurs also at Syr. T. 65, 3, 4, 5; 176, 15; and 240, 2.

P. 23, 1. *Horses.* ܩܘܖܐ (carruca) in the sense of horses for carriages.

5. *Labours to get understanding.* ܢܩܦ ܠܟܐ ܚܟܡܐ (Syr. T. 38, 6).

15. *Standard.* ܢܝܫܐ means a mark, that is (*a*) a mark to aim at, an object, or (*b*) an emblem, sign, distinguishing mark, standard. The first of these two meanings must be the one intended here. Render 'with what object are you going to fight with him?' i.e. your fighting with him will surely be useless. The same remarks apply to p. 26, 27.

29. Read ܩܘܡܬܐ ܢܨܝܚܬܐ (Syr. T. 39, 3). Compare Syr. T. 46, 12.

P. 24, 1. *A jackal.* For the two synonyms given in the Syriac, see note on p. 3, 22.

18. Similar words to those supplied are contained in De Sacy's Arabic text (p. ١٠٠, l. penult.) and in the O. Syr. (*Kal. u. Dam.* Transl. p. 12), and they are necessary to complete the sense.

33—39. This passage corresponds to Guidi's extract 21 (p. 28).

P. 25, 36. The words in brackets are supplied from the Ar. V. (De Sacy, p. ١٠٢, l. 10). Compare Syr. T. 43, 4.

P. 26, 6. (Syr. T. 42, 16.) ܣܓܝ is used in this book of persons and in the plural construction. Compare Syr. T. 87, 26; 93, 10; 94, 27; 207, 3; 231, 8; 236, 12; 313, 12; 342, 20.

27. The note on p. 23, 15 applies here.

35. I read ܗܢܝܐ, without ܘ (Syr. T. 13, 15), because I think that

here begins the apodosis of the sentence commencing ܡܐ ܐܠܐܝܢܐ (Syr. T. 43, 12). ܡܐ generally introduces a fresh sentence.

P. 27, 12. (Syr. T. 44, 6.) *Bean-food.* ܠܚܡܘܗܝ, Ar. خروب and خرنوب. The fruit of the Ceratonia siliqua.

34. *Belongs to me.* ܐܝܬ ... ܠܚ ܗܘܐ ܠܝ (Syr. T. 45, 2, 3) is a translation of انا اولى بهذه الارض (De Sacy, p. ١٠١, l. penult.) = 'I have a better right to this country (than anybody else).' In English simply: 'I have *the* right to.'

P. 28, 30. (Syr. T. 46, 17.) The text is corrupt here, and I am not sure how to amend it. Perhaps read: ܠܐ ܡܛܠ ܣܓܝ ܠܗ ܐܠܐ ܠܡܫܡܥܢܐ, and render: 'When the utterance is profitable, the profit falls to the hearer. The speaker derives no advantage (from it), except to be reckoned upright and sincere by the hearer, and to be more firmly established in his friendship.' Similarly the Old Spanish version has: 'e el decidor ha y pro ninguna, salvo mostrar la verdat &c.' (*Cal. é Dym.* p. 26, a). For the whole passage compare the O. Syr. (*Kal. u. Dam.* Transl. p. 15), and Benfey's *Pantsch.* II. p. 68, Str. 269.

P. 29, 5. (Syr. T. 46, 24.) *Excellence.* Read ܫܦܝܘܬܐ, and render 'clearness.' See note on 11, 1.

13. The words in brackets are supplied conjecturally but are justified by the O. Syr. which has: 'Mein Herr nun ist weise, und wer aus Liebe ein Wort zu ihm redet, hat deshalb keinen Schaden zu befürchten' (*Kal. u. Dam.* Transl. p. 15, ll. 8—10).

28. *Miserable suspicion.* The same phrase occurs at Syr. T. 119, 11 ; 253, 8 ; and 352, 8.

32. *His disease from the physician.* The corresponding Arabic is supplied by Gnidi (extract 22, p. 29). By 'suffering' (l. 33) I think is meant sorrow. De Sacy's text (p. ١٠١, l. 6) has رأيه ('his counsel'), and the O. Syr. (*Kal. u. Dam.* Transl. p. 15) has a wholly different clause, viz. 'wer das Geheimniss der Weisen nicht bewahrt.' The Old Spanish (*Cal. é Dym.* p. 26, a) has: 'en el que encubre á su señor su buen consejo, et á los físicos su enfermedat, é á los abogados la verdat del pleito, et al confessor sus pecados, ó á sus amigos su facienda, á sí mesmo engaña.'

P. 30, 3. *Plans.* (Syr. T. 48, 10.) I read ܠܣܩܡܘܣܘܠܐܣ,
in accordance with De Sacy's text (p. ١٠٢, l. 9) which has مُكَيِّد.

22. *Sees.* See Add. and Corr. 49, 4.

27. (Syr. T. 49, 9.) For *stamp out* substitute 'arrest' or
'overtake.'

P. 31, 13. The story is in the O. Syr. (*Kal. u. Dam.* Transl.
p. 15), and in the Panchatantra it is told by the sandpiper's wife.
See Benfey's *Pantech.* Vol. I. p. 211 ; Vol. II. p. 91.

P. 32, 14—16. (Syr. T. 51, 23—25.) I read ܠܚܡܣܘ (l. 23) and
ܠܚܝܣ (l. 25). The use of ܣܘ in the second clause of line 24, and
in line 25, is not familiar to me. It would seem to mean *out of*
in the sense of *after, instead of.* Compare Syr. T. 143, 1, where I
render 'the punishment which I shall receive *instead of* the gifts...
I am getting (now)' : also Cureton's *Ancient Syriac Documents*
ܣܝܟ, line 19.

30. (Syr. T. 52, 13, 14.) I read ܟܩܢܝ and ܩܡܝ (participles).

32. A word is illegible here in the manuscript (Syr. T. 52,
16).

34. *Hard ulcers.* See Add. and Corr. 52, 19. I can see no
force or meaning in ܠܛܐܩ (internal).

P. 33, 11—13. (Syr. T. 53, 13—23.) Delete *reckless.* See
Add. and Corr. under 53, 13.

Here the Syriac translator has utterly obscured the sense of the
original Arabic, which agrees closely with the Old Syriac (*Kal. u.
Dam.* Transl. p. 16). De Sacy's text (p. ١٠٢, l. 10) runs thus :
'If a man made fire his pillow and serpents his bed, he might sleep
more soundly than if he knew that his companion had hostile
intentions towards him and yet relied upon him.'

The rest of this paragraph in the Syriac yields poor sense. The
Ar. V., agreeing substantially with the O. Syr. (loc. cit.) runs thus :
'The weakest of kings is the one who is most given to make light of
things, and who most neglects to consider the future of matters, and
who is most like an untrained elephant (more lit. 'a must-elephant')
that heeds nothing ; for if a thing vex him, he makes light of it, and
if he ruins the state, he charges it upon his colleagues' (De Sacy,
p. ١٠٢, l. 12).

P. 34, 4. *A plan.* Read 'plans.' See Add. and Corr., under 54, 22.

7—9. Compare 11, 12—14.

25. The note on p. 25, 36 applies here.

P. 35, 1, 2. Deuteronomy xxxii. 15.

7, 8. I read ܩܢ݂ܬ ܡܢܣܠܐ ܐܘ: not as in Add. and Corr. under 56, 13. For *strikes* substitute 'has struck.'

9. *Malady.* Lit. 'spirit.' Compare Luke xiii. 11 ('spirit of infirmity '), and 104, 18, where ' disease ' is a translation of ܟܐܒ.

11. (Syr. T. 56, 15, 16.) Either read ܡ without ܘ, or ܗܘܐ without ܘ

14. *Foul.* In support of my emendation (Add. and Corr. 56, 19) see *Kal. u. Dam.* p. cxxvi.

P. 36, 11, 12. Lit. *derides and mocks himself.*

20. (Syr. T. 58, 12.) I would delete ܒܨܚܘܐ ܐܘ. ܚܨܡ can only mean 'explore,' 'examine,' 'interrogate.'

P. 37, 27. A word is unintelligible to me here. See Add. and Corr. under 60, 2.

P. 38, 1. I have rendered according to De Sacy's Arabic text (p. ١١٤, l. 3).

For the objectionable expression 'a harlot' our Syriac translator has substituted 'the waves of the sea,' and ruined the sense.

3. (Syr. T. 60, 16.) Note ܠܡܐ in the sense of hearing.

5, 6. *Against myself.* That this is the correct rendering of ܣܩܘܒܠܐ is shown by the O. Syr. (*Kal. u. Dam.* Transl. p. 18, l. 40).

P. 39, 17 21. The Ar. V. is simpler. See De Sacy, p. ١١٠, lin. penult.

P. 40, 37—41, 29. Corresponds to Guidi's extract 24 (p. 30).

38. *Insolence.* My emendation (Add. and Corr. 65, 2) is in accordance with De Sacy's Arabic text (p. ١١٧, l. 6), and Guidi, p. xi, l. 12, which read بعض سكرات السلطان.

P. 41, 5—8. Compare 8, 29 foll.

P. 42, 2. *Says Dimnah &c.* These words should head a fresh paragraph.

26—29. Corresponds to Guidi's extract 25 (p. 31), De Sacy's

text, p. ١١٨, l. 4 ff., and to *Kal. u. Dam.* Transl. p. 20, ll. 33—36. Neither the Arabic version, nor the Old Syriac, mentions the loss of wings, but attributes the destruction of the bees to their remaining on the leaf till sunset, when it closes upon them; Guidi's text adding that it also sinks under water.

26. *Lotus-leaf.* See Add. and Corr. 67, 15.

35. Compare the Old Spanish (*Cal. é Dym.* p. 29, a), the Ar. V. (loc. cit.), and the O. Syr. (loc. cit.).

P. 44, 11. See Add. and Corr. 69, 26.

P. 45, 14. *Comes.* See Glossary under ‏أتى‏.

33—46, 31. This long passage I have supplied partly from De Sacy's Arabic text (p. ١٢١, l. 9—p. ١٢٢, l. 11), partly from Guidi's extract 25 bis. A leaf is wanting in the Syriac manuscript.

P. 46, 1—20. Corresponds to Guidi's extract 25 bis (p. 32).

P. 47, 26. *Evils.* Rather *vices.* Compare De Sacy's text (p. ١٢١, l. 2), which has: 'He who abstains from the unlawful.'

23—30. Corresponds to Guidi's extract 27 (p. 33).

38. (Syr. T. 74, 7.) *By fraud in some hiding place.* Perhaps we might also render: 'by fraud and ambush instead.' I have altered the punctuation in this passage. See Add. and Corr. 74, 7.

39. *Sandpiper.* See Glossary under ‏ܨܠܘܦܝܐ‏.

P. 48, 31. *Tortoise.* The second synonym in the Syr. T. (75, 14) is wholly unknown to me.

30. The insertion is required to complete the sense.

P. 49, 19. The words in brackets are those of the Ar. V. (De Sacy's text, p. ١٢٠, l. ult.). The corresponding words of the Syriac (76, 10) are hopelessly corrupt, but see the editor's note on the passage.

26—37. Corresponds to Guidi's extract 28 (p. 33).

P. 50, 9, 16, 17, 18. *The Sîmurg.* This is the Persian name for the fabulous King of birds: the Arabic name for the same being ‏العنقا‏ and the Sanscrit *Garuda.* See *Kal. u. Dam.* p. LXXII. The synonym given in the Syr. T. (77, 22 and 78, 7, 8, 9) ‏ܒܗܡܘܬ‏, rests perhaps on a false explanation of the Hebrew ‏בְּהֵמוֹת‏ (Job xl. 10), which is recorded by Bar-Hebraeus. (Bernst. *Chrest.* p. 207, cap. II. 10, 15.)

20. (Syr. T. 78, 10.) For ‎ܪܩܒܘ‎ I read ‎ܪܩܒܘ‎. But the O. Syr. (*Kal. u. Dam.* Syr. T. 25, 4 from bottom) has ‎ܐܙܠ‎ ‎ܩܠܝܠ‎ ('went quickly off'). Perhaps we should read ‎ܪܩܒܘ‎ ‎ܐܪܡܝ‎ ('restrained himself'). Compare Syr. T. 303, 15.

25. Delete 'I may.' See Add. and Corr. 78, 14.

29. (Syr. T. 78, 19.) After ‎ܕܠ‎ insert ‎ܥܠܝܗ‎ to complete the relative clause.

P. 51, 12—55, 29. Corresponds to Guidi's extract 29 (pp. 34—36). This sermonetto seems to have been sorely mangled by scribes and translators.

P. 54, 16. That ‎ܦܘܪܥܢܐ‎ should be read is certain because (1) ‎ܦܘܪܥܢܐ‎ ‎ܕܛܒܬܐ‎ is a common phrase, (2) the corresponding expression in Guidi's extract (p. xvi. l. 3 from bottom) is قصد *intention*, (3) *liberality* has already been dwelt on above.

30. *The four passions.* Compare 263, 24.

P. 55, 2—5. Compare 9, 1; 73, 4; and 155, 33. These passages led me to the emendations contained in Add. and Corr. 85, 7—9.

20. Before *arrogance* insert 'and', and delete *and* in line 22. See Add. and Corr. 86, 1.

P. 56, 7. Read: 'bows out of wood, &c.'

27. For ‎ܐܠܐ‎ in the sense of 'Nay, but' compare Syr. T. 200, 17; 222, 20; 260, 11; 281, 14; 337, 7. I do not think a ‎ܐܠܐ‎ need be inserted here.

P. 57, 3. (Syr. T. 88, 8.) *Cry out* (ܩܥܐ). Compare 326, 11 (ܩܥܘܬܐ), and see Glossary.

20—58, 8. Corresponds to Guidi's extract 30 (p. 37).

P. 59, 20. ‎ܣܓܝܐܐ‎. Compare ‎ܣܓܝܐܐ‎ (Syr. T. 159, 3).

32—60, 9. Corresponds to Guidi's extracts 33, 34 (p. 38), where the merchant's pretended assurance is given better.

P. 60, 8. *No* should be in square brackets. See Add. and Corr. 92, 26. But perhaps, without inserting anything, we might render interrogatively: 'Is it a wonder that &c.?'

15. See Add. and Corr. 93, 4. ‎ܓܝܘܪܐ‎ is found at Syr. T. 183, 13.

20. (Syr. T. 93, 10.) See note on 26, 6.

24—26. Corresponds to Guidi's extract 31 (p. 36).

25. See Add. and Corr. 93, 15. ܒܥܐ does not occur in the book: but ܒܠܥ is found at Syr. T. 158, 1; 209, 19; and 306, 19.

33—36. Corresponds to Guidi's extract 32 (p. 38).

P. 61, 24, 25. Substitute: 'Because he who is wise does not spare one whom he fears.' See Add. and Corr. 94, 26.

P. 62, 3—end. There is no trace of Dimnah's retribution in the O. Syr. or in the Panchatantra, the first book of which concludes as follows: 'Pingalaka, having been thus admonished by him (Dimnah), troubled himself no more about Sanjivaka (Shanzabeh), promoted Damanaka (Dimnah) to be minister, and reigned happily' (Benfey's *Pantsch.* II. p. 124).

P. 63. *Dimnah's Defence.* This chapter is wholly wanting both in the O. Syr. and in the Panchatantra. It is not of Indian origin at all, and was added by some one who was indignant at the notion that such rascality should meet with reward instead of punishment. See Benfey's *Pantsch.* Vol. I. pp. 297—299.

1. For the names *Dabdahram* and *Nadrab* see notes on p. 1, 4.

9. (Syr. T. 96, 7.) I omit ܐܠܐ.

16. (Syr. T. 96, 13.) I read ܡܚܣܢ ܠܟ ܐܠܐ ܕܝܠܗܘܢ.

26. (Syr. T. 96, 24.) I read ܗܝ.

P. 65, 23. (Syr. T. 99, 14.) I read ܡܠܐܘܗܝ ܟܡܐ.

P. 67, 18. (Syr. T. 102, 5.) Here and at Syr. T. 203, 15 I read ܟܣܘܡ for ܟܣܘܡܐ.

P. 68, 25. (Syr. T. 103, 23.) I have made no alteration in the text.

P. 69, 1. See Add. and Corr. 104, 11, 12. The sense seems to be: 'My word is sufficient. The additional testimony of a hundred unanimous witnesses would not make my story more credible.'

P. 71, 9. (Syr. T. 107, 17.) I read ܐܣܪ ܚܣܡܝܢܐ.

P. 72, 23. (Syr. T. 109, 14.) I read ܒܨܪܗ.

P. 73, 10. (Syr. T. 110, 16.) I read ܬܚܕܕܬܐ.

26. *Take.* A mere guess. See Syr. T. 111, 7 and note.

P. 74, 23. (Syr. T. 112, 17.) I read ܟܠܝܢܗ.

P. 76. 22—24. On these names see Prof. Wright's Preface to the Syriac text, p. XVII.

39. (Syr. T. 116, 9.) I read ܠܩܘ.

P. 78, 27. For other broken sentences see Syr. T. 145, 9—15 and 285, 9—20. See, on the whole passage, Add. and Corr. 119, 8—10.

32. (Syr. T. 119, 13.) I read ܟܚܣܩ not ܟܚܩܠ.

P. 79, 22. (Syr. T. 120, 18.) Read ܠܡܬܝܠܟ.

P. 80, 9. Read 'the just King.'

24. For *magnates* read 'household.' See Add. and Corr. 122, 11.

38. (Syr. T. 122, 25.) I read ܘܗܩܡܝܫ

P. 81, 6. *Salt.* The solemn pledge of hospitality.

P. 82, 19. (Syr. T. 125, 10.) Read ܩܚܡܣ ܠܩܟܟ and render: 'publishes them through the folly of his speech.'

P. 84, 19—25. Corresponds to Guidi's extract 36 (p. 42).

30, 31. (Syr. T. 128, 22, 23.) I read ܝܡܝܣ; but probably Nöldeke's reading (Add. and Corr.) is right, and we should render: 'If I doubted concerning the report of him, and were not convinced of his deceitfulness,......'

P. 85, 8. (Syr. T. 129, 12.) *Man* should be in square brackets. After ܐܚܠܩ I supply ܩܠܝܚܩ. Compare Syr. T. 126, 23.

P. 86, 28—90, 22. Corresponds to Guidi's extract 37 (pp. 12—44).

P. 88, 30. (Syr. T. 134, 21.) Read ܐܩܠ without ܡ.

P. 90, 27. (Syr. T. 137, 17.) I believe something has dropped out in the text.

P. 92, 35. (Syr. T. 141, 8.) I think that an adjective or participle has dropped out after ܚܠܡܡ.

P. 93, 6—97, 6. Corresponds to Guidi's extract 38 (pp. 44 46).

22. (Syr. T. 142, 8, 9.) Perhaps ܐܩܩܕܘ is made up of the beginning of one word and the end of the next, the first being a synonym of *shushân*, and the second ܐܩܝܠ ('or,' 'that is to say').

36. (Syr. T. 142, 22—143, 1.) For the use of ܠܩ here see note on p. 32, 14—16. But perhaps should be read ܠܡܩ ܡܩ ܩܠܝܫ.

38. I assume a lacuna in the manuscript.

P. 94, 3. The sentence ending at 'knowledge' seems to be parenthetical, and a mere reflection of the translator. If so, we need not suppose a gap after 'knowledge' (Add. and Corr. 143, 7).

38. For *proximity* read 'knitting.'

P. 95, 18. For *narrow* read 'wide.'

32. (Syr. T. 145, 25.) I would make no alteration in the text.

P. 96, 28. (Syr. T. 147, 9.) I read ܣܘ̈ܣܟܐ ܘܣܘ̈ܟܠ ܕܐܡܪ̈ܝ ܡܢ.

32, 33. (Syr. T. 147, 13.) I would make no alteration in the text.

34—38. (Syr. T. 147, 14—20.) My translation takes no account of ܕܪܘܗܝ (l. 16), or of ܐܘܢ ܠܝܐܬ ܕܡܐ (l. 17.) These words puzzle me. ܠܥܐܙܬ (l. 18) is a misprint for ܠܥܐܙܬ (Add. and Corr.).

P. 97, 14. For the proper name see Prof. Wright's Preface to the Syr. T. p. xvii. The name in the Hebrew version is in accordance with the Old Spanish, which has *Maruen* (*Cal. é Dym.* p. 39, a), and with John of Capua, who has *Merua.*

P. 98, 4. (Syr. T. 149, 14.) I would delete ܗ.

24, 38. For the proper names see Prof. Wright's Preface to the Syr. T. p. xvii.

39. (Syr. T. 150, 20, 21.) Render: 'He was dear to the lion, and highly esteemed by him, and honourable.' See Add. and Corr.

P. 99, 11. I would insert ܠܐܣܘ before ܠܘܝ̈ (Syr. T. 151, 5).

P. 101, 31. (Syr. T. 155, 4.) Possibly for ܠܝܪܘ̈ܝ should be read ܠܚܣܝܪ̈ ('the crafty').

34—36. (Syr. T. 155, 7—9.) This passage is corrupt. See Add. and Corr. My rendering cannot be maintained, because there is no authority for assuming that ܣܟܝܐ can mean 'target' in any other sense than that of 'shield.'

P. 102, 3. (Syr. T. 155, 15.) I read ܣܟܐܣܐܕܗ.

9. (Syr. T. 155, 21.) I read ܣܪܘܒܐܠ.

31. (Syr. T. 156, 21.) Delete *blessed* and substitute 'pleasant' (ܣܒܝܣܐ or ܣܒܝܐܬܘ).

33—104, 28. Corresponds to Guidi's extract 39 (p. 46).

P. 103, 17. (Syr. T. 157, 23.) For *or* read 'of.'

P. 104, 7. Rather: 'ye shall know that &c.'

36 ff. For the proper names in this story see Prof. Wright's Preface to the Syriac text, p. xvii.

P. 105, 11—13. Supplied from next page (l. 6). Compare De

K. F. 19

Sacy's Arabic text (p. ١٠٦, l. 1). But probably the omission is after ܠܡܢܐ? (Syr. T. 160, 22), and the two speeches should be inverted.

31—106, 39. Corresponds to Guidi's extract 40 (p. 47).

P 106, 14. (Syr. T. 162, 20.) I read ܩܕܡ ܡܠܟܐ.

P. 109, 17, 18. For the two proper names see Prof. Wright's Preface to the Syriac text, p. xviii. and Benfey's *Pantsch.* i. p. 308.

P. 110, 12. (Syr. T. 168, 4.) Before ܠܟܘܠܗ I insert ܩܡ.

33. For the proper name see Prof. Wright's Preface to the Syriac text, p. xviii. and *Kal. u. Dim.* p. lxxi. The Hebrew version has שנבר. This, I think, is a corruption of שירד (Sirac), and accounts for the *Sambut* of John of Capua, and the *Sambar* of the Old German translation.

P. 111, 11—15. Corresponds to Guidi's extract 41 (p. 48).

29. (Syr. T. 170, 18.) I would read ܡܠܟܝܢ?.

P. 112, 15. This illustration corresponds to Guidi's extract 42 (p. 49).

33—36. Prof. Nöldeke has pointed out that this passage rests on a misunderstanding of the phrase عداوة الجوهر, 'natural enmity' (De Sacy, p. ١١٢, l. 15), the Syriac translator having taken ܓܘܗܪ in its other sense of 'precious stones.'

P. 113, 28. (Syr. T. 174, 2.) I retain ܠܐ.

36. (Syr. T. 174, 10.) The dots represent ܡܪܝܒܐ?, which I do not understand.

39. (Syr. T. 174, 13.) I read ܩܪܬܐܘܨ.

P. 114, 12. The clause in brackets is supplied from De Sacy's text (p. ١١٣, l. 9).

P. 115, 3—13. Corresponds to Guidi's extract 43 (p. 49).

36. (Syr. T. 177, 17.) *Mahilāropya.* ܡܠܝܐ. See Prof. Wright's Preface to the text, p. xviii.

P. 117, 16. (Syr. T. 180, 1.) *Rushing.* See glossary under ܠܐ, and compare Syr. T. 188, 7 (ܡܢ ܠܒܬܪ), where I translate 'rush after.'

22, 23. The lost clause of the wolf's soliloquy corresponds to Guidi's extract 44 (p. 49), whence I supply [not].

26. (Syr. T. 180, 13.) *A vital part.* I would read ܠܐ ܡܢܗܘܢ.

38. *Began to eat some of them.* The Ar. V. in De Sacy's

edition (١١٩, lino 12), has نيه نفاك, which, of course, should be read نيه نفاك. Compare Benfey's *Pantsch.* ١١. p. 176. The Dominican fathers have corrected the mistake (Mosul edition, ٢٠٠, lino 1). For a similar but less skilful toning down of the coarseness of the original, see 38, 1, and note.

P. 118, 20. Benfey gives another illustration of this absurd idea. In a Buddhist writing a raven asks: ' Why is my voice melodious when I perch on one tree, and discordant when I perch on another?' The answer is : ' Because under the first tree there is gold ' (*Pantscha-tantra*, ١. p. 320).

P. 120, 34. (Syr. T. 185, 20.) A word seems to be missing here.

P. 121, 2—15. Corresponds to Guidi's extract 45 (pp. 49, 50).

13. (Syr. T. 186, 17.) For *enchantment* substitute 'dumbness.'

25—37. Corresponds to Guidi's extract 46 (p. 50).

P. 122, 11. (Syr. T. 188, 7.) See note on 117, 16.

16. (Syr. T. 189, 12, 13.) There seems to be some corruption or omission (or both) here.

P. 123, 17—124, 18. Supplied from De Sacy's Arabic text (p. ١٧٢, l. 6, to p. ١٧٥, l. 12). A page is missing in the MS.

P. 124, 20, 21. Read: ' And promise your soul good, though it have departed from you. So fear not &c.'

P. 126, 25, 26. (Syr. T. 193, 10—12.) I do not understand three words.

34, 35. Read: ' beloved brother, and has parted me from his sincere love, which was warmer and inflamed &c.' See Add. and Corr. 193, 20.

P. 127, 7. *Meritorious things, bad things.* Literally: ' things of the right hand, things of the left hand.' These two expressions are borrowed from the parable of the sheep and the goats (S. Matthew, xxv. 31—46).

P. 130, 20, 21. (Syr. T. 198, 16—18.) In line 18 I would omit ܚܡܨܝܢ ܚܩܛܠ ܡܐܒܕܒܐ, and read ܠܩ ܚܘܛܚ. I prefer this arrangement to that proposed in Add. and Corr.

P. 131, 20. (Syr. T. 200, 5.) I do not understand the expression ܚܡܫܘܢ ܐܟܠܐܗ ܘܠܙܝܕܝܚܐ.

26. The Ar. V. has: ' This is like a post fixed in a sunny place, for when you incline it a little, its shadow gets longer, but when you

19—2

incline it beyond a certain angle, the shadow gets shorter again.'
(De Sacy, p. ١٨٢, lin. penult.)

P. 132, 19.   Supplied from the O. Syr. (*Kal. u. Dam.* Tr. p. 62).

33.   *Fortifies.*   I would read ܠܨܡܐ ܐܘܡ̈ܝܢ (Syr. T. 202, 6).

P. 133, 14.   (Syr. T. 203, 2.)   I read ܗܕܐ̈ܝ.

P. 134, 1..   (Syr. T. 204, 5.)   See Add. and Corr.

18—21.   Supplied from the O. Syr. (*Kal. u. Dam.* Transl. 64, 9, 10).

37.   (Syr. T. 205, 14)   *Were missing* should be in *square* brackets.   I believe that a word corresponding to قَضَى (De Sacy, ١٨١, 13) has dropped out of the text.

P. 135, 4, 5.   (Syr. T. 206, 2, 3.)   I propose to read ܡܩ̈ܘܡ ܡܩܘܡܐ̈, but not confidently; and for ܡܕ ܡܠܗ to read ܡܕ ܡܚܡ.

13.   (Syr. T. 206, 10.)   I now see that the words ܐܝܠ ܘܡܠ̈ܝܐ ܠܩܛܦ have become displaced, and ought to stand earlier in the sentence.   They represent the words إِلَّا أَنْ تَرَيْنِ (De Sacy, ١٨٤, l. 2). 'But if ye please to make him king over you while ye yourselves, &c....(do so).'   See Wright's Arabic Grammar II. p. 15, rem. b.   But the Syriac translator read أَنِي instead of أَنِ.

18.   *Its springs had dried up.*   Substitute: 'the herbage in it had dried up.'   See Add. and Corr. 206, 15; and the Ar. V. (De Sacy, ١٨٤, 6).

24.   *Lake of the moon.*   See Prof. Wright's Preface to the Syriac text, p. xviii; and *Kal. u. Dam.* pp. LXIX, LXX.   It appears that the Sanscrit *Chandrasaras* (Benfey's *Pantsch.* II. p. 226) has been *translated* in all the versions except in the O. Syr. where it stands *transliterated* from the Pehlevi.   This is lucky, as it serves to prove the Pehlevi origin of that version.

26.   It is a well-known Indian idea that the lines on the moon form the likeness of a hare.

38.   *Pêrôz.*   See Prof. Wright's Preface to the Syriac text, p. xix. and specially *Kal. u. Dam.* p. LXX.   *Pêrôz* is the Persian *translation* of the original Sanscrit *Vijayadatta* (Benfey's *Pantsch.* II. p. 227), and means 'victorious, triumphant.'   The Old Spanish has *Feyrus*, which form is noticeable as tending to show that that

version is descended directly from the Arabic and not through the Hebrew, else the F would have become P.

P. 136, 6. In Guidi's manuscript M, Pērōz is afraid to go. See Guidi's extract 48 (p. 52).

P. 137, 30. See Add. and Corr. 210, 11.

P. 139, 16. (Syr. T. 212, 19.) A clause seems to be wanting in the text.

17. See Add. and Corr. 212, 20.

P. 140, 23. See Add. and Corr. 214, 18.

35. See Add. and Corr. 215, 7.

37. Read 'yet when he sees the end &c.'

P. 141, 31—33. The words in brackets are supplied from the O. Syr. (*Kal. u. Dam.* Transl. p. 67).

33. The speech of the second rogue forms Guidi's extract 47 (p. 52). It is missing in De Sacy's Arabic text.

P. 142, 15—22. Corresponds to Guidi's extract 49 (p. 53).

P. 144, 10—11. If we invert the order of the two parts of this 'saying,' the meaning comes out more clearly. Untimely effort to gain something will result in failure, and even though a man actually realise his wish, he may, by subsequent carelessness and inattention, lose what he has gained. See p. 158, 1—13.

11. For *relinquishes* substitute 'takes no care of.'

12—14. (Syr. T. 220, 18, 19.) I read

ܠܘܩܒܠ ܕܚܣܝܪܝܢ ܦܘܩ ܚܣܝܡܝܢ ܐܢܐ ܘܠܐ ܝܕܥܬ ܠܗܘܢ

I think this reading is fully borne out by the O. Syr. (*Kal. u. Dam.* Transl. p. 69).

12. For *should* substitute 'shall.'

14. For *misses* substitute 'fails to find.'

P. 145, 5. Read: 'For he who is intelligent and prudent does not &c.'

P. 146, 16—22. The passage between brackets has been supplied from the O. Syr. (*Kal. u. Dam.* Transl. p. 71). Compare De Sacy, p. ١٩٧, ll. 6—8. See Add. and Corr. 223, 23.

8—24. See Guidi's extract 50 (p. 54).

32. See Syr. T. 224, note 4.

P. 147, 16—38. Corresponds to Guidi's extract 51 (p. 54).

17, 18. For *parable* read 'word'; and for *I have told you* read 'has been spoken to you.'

P. 149, 8.   (Syr. T. 228, 9.)   For ﻭﺪ I read ﻭﺪ.

19.   Read 'Keep his daughter [at home] when &c.'   Add. and Corr. 228, 21.

P. 151, 14—16.   Corresponds to Guidi's extract 53 (p. 56).

39—152, 15.   Corresponds to Guidi's extract 54 (p. 56).

P. 152, 3—6.   (Syr. T. 233, 1—4.)   For the names ﻭﺪ and ﻭﺪ, see Prof. Wright's Preface to the Syriac text, p. xix.   On the whole passage see *Kal. u. Dam.* pp. xl, xli.

32.   (Syr. T. 234, 7.)   I do not understand ﻭﺪ.

P. 153, 7—13.   Corresponds to Guidi's extract 56 (p. 57).

P. 154, 29.   (Syr. T. 237, 12.)   Hopelessly corrupt.   The Ar. V. has : 'When fire attacks a tree, it cannot, in spite of its intensity and heat, burn more of it than stands above ground ; but water, notwithstanding its coolness and gentleness, uproots the part of it which is under the ground' (De Sacy, ٢٠٠, 6, 7).   Compare the O. Syr. (*Kal. u. Dam.* Transl. p. 76).

33—155, 3.   The first of the four things which ought not to be neglected according to the Ar. V. and O. Syr. V. is *debt*.   The mistake is accounted for in note 10 under Syr. T. p. 237.   It has thrown the preceding clause out of gear.

39—155, 2.   (Syr. T. 238, 2—4.)   I read ﻭﺪ for ﻭﺪ both in line 2 and line 4.   I would make no other changes.   ﻭﺪ need not be omitted in line 1.

P. 155, 8, 9.   An allusion to the king's horoscope.   The ' Ear ' (Virgo spicifera) and the ' Bucket ' (Aquarius) are signs of the zodiac which were in the ascendant at his birth.

P. 156, 21.   (Syr. T. 240, 17.)   I read ﻭﺪ.

39—157, 3.   Supplied from the O. Syr. (*Kal. u. Dam.* Transl. p. 78).

P. 157, 14, 15.   There seems to be a gap here in the Syriac text (p. 241, lin. ult.).

P. 158, 18.   *Pardin.*   See Prof. Wright's Preface to the Syr. T. p. xix.

P. 159, 11.   *That region.*   See Add. and Corr. 244, 22.

28.   (Syr. T. 245, 13.)   I have no doubt that ﻭﺪ is meant for a translation of ﺍﻫﻠﻪ (- his wife), just as at Syr. T. 253, 6.

If so, there is no need to supply عليها after عليهم, as is suggested in Add. and Corr. Compare note on p. 163, 8.

28—162, 16. Corresponds to Guidi's extract 57 (pp. 57—59).

P. 160, 33. Genesis ii. 24.

P. 161, 23—28. Supplied from the O. Syr. (*Kal. u. Dam.*
Transl. p. 50). The corresponding passage in our Syriac version
(246, 10—13) is hopelessly corrupt.

P. 162, 2, 3. (Syr. T. 249, 5.) The quotation as given in the
Syr. T. only extends to the word 'men.' I guess that Matt. vii. 12
was intended.

7. For my emendation (Add. and Corr. 249, 8) compare also
Syr. T. 377, 1.

29—36. Compare Guidi's extract 58 (p. 59).

38—163, 3. I think that the words in brackets are necessary to
the sense.

P. 163, 8. (Syr. T. 250, 21, 22.) No doubt قندَ صـادا ربكـ
is meant to represent أهْلي (= my wife). If so, for ربكـ we
must read أهلك. Compare note on p. 159, 28.

37. (Syr. T. 251, 24.) For صمح لك in this sense compare
Syr. T. 328, 2 and 361, 23.

P. 164, 3—16. Corresponds to Guidi's extract 59 (p. 60).

15, 16. (Syr. T. 252, 18.) I would read مكمرصينا ('we are restored') or perhaps مكمرصلك ('they are restored'). Compare Guidi.

P. 166, 23—37. Corresponds to Guidi's extract 60 (p. 61).

38. Some words spoken by the fox are seemingly omitted
here.

P. 167, 37. The insertion is conjectural.

P. 169, 14. *Jurjân.* The O. Syr. has صرجان. The Ar. V.
(خرجان) and our Syriac V. (جورجيا) merely substitute a known
for an unknown name.

P. 170, 11. See Add. and Corr. 261, 6, according to which we
should render: 'and when these had had young for five years, the
number of them would be very great.'

13, 14. For *sow my fields* read 'sow with my oxen.' Compare

De Sacy, p. ꜱɪᴠ, l. 11. ܟܝܒ may be used in either sense. A
link of the chain has dropped out, namely the acquisition of *land*.
Compare the O. Syr. (*Kal. u. Dam.* Transl. p. 54), and De Sacy (loc.
cit.).

P. 171, 7. (Syr. T. 262, 14.) I do not understand ܠܟܡ.

10. Lit. 'returned and *consoled* him &c.' But her words were
anything but consoling. Perhaps we should read ܠܗ ܐܒܝܕ ('and
chid him').

P. 172. This story appears in the Mahâbhârata, xɪɪ. (ɪɪɪ. 539)
v. 4930 ff.

11. *Banishes* should be in *square* brackets.

18. (Syr. T. 263, 15.) *Banyan tree*. On ܩܝܣܐ see Dr
Wright's Preface to the Syr. T. p. xɪx, and *Kal. u. Dam.* p. xʟ.

19. For the proper names see *Kal. u. Dam.* pp. ʟxᴠ and ʟxᴠɪ.

27. (Syr. T. 264, 3.) I would read ܚܕ ܡܢ ܬܟܕܟܘܗܝ (lit
'through one of his entrances'): or perhaps ܚܕ ܡܢ ܬܟܟܬܗ
('on some business of his').

P. 173, 23. (Syr. T. 265, 11.) I read ܐܝܕ ܡܬܟܡܝܢ ܘܡܬܟܢܫܝܢ
ܠܚܕܐ.

P. 174, 15—23. Corresponds to Guidi's extract 64 (p. 63).

21, 22. (Syr. T. 266, 24.) A clause is hopelessly corrupt.

P. 175, 1—9. Corresponds to Guidi's extract 65 (p. 64).

12—14. Supplied from *Kal. u. Dam.* Transl. p. 58, ll. 12, 13.

25. I suppose that God is meant. For ܠܗ I read ܠܗ. A
similar corruption occurs at Syr. T. 304, 23.

30. (Syr. T. 268, 20.) Six words seem to be hopelessly corrupt.

P. 176, 4. *To make an end*. Or perhaps, 'to attain to perfection.'

8. (Syr. T. 269, 16.) Professor Wright thinks that John xv. 13
was intended; but perhaps John x. 18 is more appropriate.

9—15. (Syr. T. 269, 17—21.) See Add. and Corr.

14. I doubt whether ܢܣܒ need be added.

38. Read 'cannot be expressed.' See Add. and Corr. 270, 24.

P. 177, 14—18. Corresponds to Guidi's extract 66 (p. 64).

38. There is something wrong here in the text. But see Add.
and Corr. 272, 12.

P. 178. This story appears in the Mahâbhârata xɪɪ. (ɪɪɪ. 546), v.
5133 ff.

5. For the names, see Prof. Wright's Preface to the Syr. T. p. xx. The *catra* of the Old Spanish (*Cal. é Dym.* p. 58, b) evidently reflects a form رنق (for رنق), and is one of the examples which show that this version was made directly from the Arabic. John of Capua gives *Piza*, which reflects a form פ׳יזר (for פנוה).

34. (Syr. T. 274, 2, 3.) I do not understand a clause, though the construing is easy. Perhaps ܦܘܡܐ refers to Pinzih's beak, from which both prince and bird received the fruit every day. I suspect some stupidity on the translator's part.

P. 179, 27. (Syr. T. 275, 5.) I would read ܚܠ ܚܒܠ (i.e. the punishment). Otherwise I would make no alteration.

30. Apparently a quotation. Job ix. 10, xxxvii. 5, and Rom. xi. 33, all resemble this passage.

33 and 35. The allusions are of course to Achan and Ahab.

P. 180, 33. (Syr. T. 276, 25.) The Syriac is unintelligible to me. See glossary under ܩܛܘܠܐ and ܗܪܘ. Perhaps for ܩܛܘܠܐ should be read ܩܛܘܠܐ ('carnifex,' 'lictor'), and an allusion is meant to Christian martyrdom by burning. I had thought of reading ܗܪܘܐ ܕܢܘܪܐ ܣܒܠ ܡܦܝܣ.

P. 181, 11, 12. (Syr. T. 277, 16, 17.) I would read ܐܟܙܢܐ ܕܦܝܠܐ, and render: 'And he will be like an untrained elephant, who illtreats other elephants that are trained in knowledge.'

15. (Syr. T. 277, 20.) I prefer to read ܕܥܣܩܘܬܐ and not ܕܒܝܫܬܐ, because the latter always (in this book) means 'hardship, bad times' (see Syr. T. 369, 23; 372, 11; 394, 24; 399, 2), whereas in the passage before us 'difficulty' is meant.

17. See editor's note 9 at foot of p. 277 in the Syr. T.

30. (Syr. T. 278, 18.) If ܡܪܝܪܘܬܐ (Add. and Corr.) is right, then for *virulence* substitute 'intoxicating property.'

P. 183, 33. (Syr. T. 282, 3.) I read ܠܐ without ܘ, and make no alteration in the next line. Before *he cannot* insert 'and,' and delete *and* in the next line.

P. 184, 13. A line (Syr. T. 282, 22) is unintelligible to me. But compare the O. Syr. (*Kal. u. Dam.*, Transl. p. 83, ll. 17—19).

23—25. Adopting Prof. Wright's provisional reading (Add. and

Corr. 283, 10), render 'avarice: another is lack of [greed; and the other] is perfection of conduct and holiness of life.'

20. (Syr. T. 283, 15.) For ـهـ؟ I read ـه؟؟.

P. 186. This chapter appears in the Mahâbhârata XII. (III. 509) v. 4081.

13. (Syr. T. 285, 3.) I read ـل؟؟.

P. 187, 17. Render: 'Otherwise his similitude will be that of the lion and the jackal.' See Add. and Corr. 286, 18.

22. (Syr. T. 287, 1.) Compare Syr. T. 262, 16, for the phrase حمد محلهل

P. 191, 6. (Syr. T. 293, 2.) جمرل does not seem appropriate here, for the meat was destined for the lion's eating.

8—192, 7. Compare Guidi's extracts 69 and 70 (p. 67).

15. (Syr. T. 293, 12.) There is some corruption here.

P. 192, 1. (Syr. T. 294, 11.) For *sound* substitute 'wretched.' حمدكس is inappropriate here. I would read حمدكو.

P. 193, 7—32. Supplied from the Ar. V. (De Sacy, p. رار). A leaf is wanting in the manuscript.

P. 194, 18. (Syr. T. 297, 4.) For حمدؤ, in the sense of 'disease,' see note on 35, 9. For *sebel* see Add. and Corr. 297, 4.

20. See Add. and Corr. 297, 6.

28, 29. (Syr. T. 297, 15—19.) The text presents many diffi-culties here, and is no doubt very corrupt. Add. and Corr. 297, 16, only removes one of them.

P. 196, 9. By 'the book' I presume is meant the Bible; for at p. 219, ll. 14, 15, 'the book' is appealed to as teaching that wisdom cannot be obtained except by the fear of God, apparently in allusion to Psalm cxi. 10 or Proverbs ix. 10. Throughout this book the Bible and our Lord are alluded to in covert terms. The latter is usually called 'the wise one' or 'the chief of the wise.'

18. For *slandered* substitute 'accused.'

26 foll. Compare Guidi's extract 74 (p. 70).

P. 197, 24. The words in the bracket are inserted conjecturally.

P. 198, 20. *The snare of Satan.* Compare 1 Timothy iii. 7 and 2 Timothy ii. 26.

32. *Whose god is their belly.* See Philippians iii. 19.

P. 199, 30, 31. (Syr. T. 305, 21, 22.) A clause is unintelligible.

32. (Syr. T. 305, 23.) For ܩܢܠܝܩ I would read ܩܠܩܠܩ.

34—36. Zechariah xi. 9.

39. (Syr. T. 306, 5.) For ܟܠܝܐ I read ܟܠܩܐ. Compare Syr. T. 290, 14.

P. 200, 8, 9. (Syr. T. 306, 14, 15.) The editor supposes a gap after ܝܠܩܩܪܩ, but perhaps the difficulty may be got over by omitting ܩ altogether.

P. 201, 7. The words in brackets I have added conjecturally.

14—17. The text is exceedingly corrupt here.

28. (Syr. T. 308, 18.) I am doubtful as to ܩܪܟܝܠ (θίατρον).

P. 203, 11. Read : 'By that which the king commanded concerning him.' Namely, his execution (p. 193, l. 7). The jackal means that the others will say that he bears a grudge. Compare the Old Spanish version (*Cal. ê Dym.* p. 69, b).

P. 204. This story appears in Benfey's Berlin MS. of the Panchatantra, but as a part of the First Book (our chapter of the Lion and the Ox). See Benfey's *Pantsch.* I. §§ 60—71, and II. p. 128.

10. Read: 'conferred [by them] upon.' See Add. and Corr. 312, 1, 2.

21. (Syr. T. 312, 14.) My rendering presupposes ܠܩܪܟܩ, but I suspect that a masculine noun corresponding to ܩܠܩܩ and ܩܝܠܟܝܠ (l. 13) has dropped out. See further Add. and Corr. 312, 15.

P. 205, 9—15. Supplied from De Sacy's Arabic text (۳۷۷, 1—4).

36. De Sacy's Arabic text has: 'Then the ape said to him: My dwelling is on a mountain near the town which is called Nawûdiracht (نوبردراخت). And the tiger said to him: I too dwell in a fen adjacent to this town. And the serpent said: I too dwell in the wall of this town &c.' (۳۷۷, 13—15).

P. 206, 1. *This town.* These words point to a previous omission. As the text stands, no *town* has yet been mentioned.

P. 207, 9—28. Corresponds to Guidi's extract 87 (p. 97).

P. 208. This story appears in the Berlin MS. of the Panchatantra, where, however, it forms a part of the First Book (our chapter of the Lion and the Ox), but in such a different shape that it is doubtful whether the two really have a common origin, and consequently

whether the tale as given in the Ar. V. and its offshoots is really Indian. The story is not found in the O. Syr. V. See Benfey's *Pantsch.* ı. p. 288 ; ıı. pp. 150—154.

13—16. There is some corruption in the text of this passage. De Sacy's Arabic text (ṛṿa, 6) has simply : 'Except that destiny and fate override this rule.' But the Old Spanish V. paraphrases this sentiment at considerable length (*Cal. é Dym.* p. 71, b).

31. This paragraph should be followed by a clause corresponding to one in the Ar. V. which runs thus : 'And when they got near a city called Matrûn (مطرون), they sat down in a place adjacent to it and took counsel together' (De Sacy, p. ṛṿa, l. 5). Indeed the mention of 'the city' at 209, 4, points to a previous mention of it.

P. 209, 1. For *in advance of us* read 'forward.' There is no need to read كمصرَّفْنَ (Syr. T. 318, 15).

4. *The city.* See note on 208, 31.

12. *Zûz* is equivalent to the Greek δραχμή, and the Arabic دِرهم (dirham).

23. The stars represent the following clause :

وزهدَ لِلثَّواتِى كلَ سلَاقْ.

27, 30. *Darîc* and *dînâr* are names of coins of equal value. دِينارْ, دَرِيكَ?, Gr. Δαρεικός, name of a Persian coin, perhaps derived from Pers. دارا, 'king.' *Dînâr,* of course, = Lat. *denarius.*

28. (Syr. T. 319, 16.) I read مَصروبْهَا.

P. 210, 1—8. See Add. and Corr. 320, 0.

P. 211, 20. (Syr. T. 322, 9.) I read مصْرَ رلِيسصِّر.

P. 214. This chapter (De Sacy's 15th) is undoubtedly of Buddhist origin, but seems to have fallen out of the Indian literature altogether. See Benfey's *Pantsch.* ı. p. 599.

21. Perhaps there is an omission after *gone out* ; for De Sacy's text has : 'And she went out to hunt (one day) and left them in their lair, and there passed by them &c.' (ṛṿ, 4).

23. For 'iswâr' see Glossary under سوارْ.

28. (Syr. T. 326, 13.) The name is given in the Syriac

text, but is written wrongly ܐܝܩܢ for ܐܝܟܢ. This latter is the Arabic word شعير, which again, allowing for well-known phonetic changes, is identical with the Pehlevi *shagdl* (*Kal. u. Dam.* p. LXXXIII).

P. 215, 4—6. (Syr. T. 326, 22, 23.) No doubt Nöldeke's emendation is right (see Add. and Corr.), and we should translate : ' Know that this man would not have done you this injury, had you not injured others as he has you.'

8—12. The passages quoted are Matt. vii. 2; Gal. vi. 7; Matt. xvi. 27 or Rev. xxii. 12 ; and Luke vi. 31.

38. (Syr. T. 328, 7.) *Jackal.* According to the Ar. V. a *dove*, ورشان (De Sacy, p. ٣٦٨, l. 13). I suspect that ܟܢܫܐ is a corruption of ܝܘܢܐ ('dove'), and that the following clause (ܘܡܢܩܢ ܣܥܪܐ) was added subsequently. If so, we have here a proof that not all the explanatory glosses so frequent in this book proceed from the translator.

P. 216, 12. In the Ar. V. the story concludes as follows: 'the lioness on hearing the dove say this, left off eating fruit and took to eating grass and the exercise of piety ' (عبادة, De Sacy, p. ٣٦٩, ll. 6, 7).

P. 217. Several considerations have convinced Benfey that this short chapter is not of Indian origin. The principal ones are, the mention of the eating of dates (see next note) and of the learning of Hebrew (see note on l. 25), and the fact that in Symeon Seth's Greek version the chapter is placed not only last of all but after several professedly foreign additions (Benfey's *Pantsch.* I. p. 601).

12. For *A little fruit* substitute 'a few dates.'

13. For *this fruit is* substitute ' these dates are.'

25. Instead of the next speech the Ar. V. has the following: ' Now this ascetic was talking in Hebrew. The guest admiring his language and longing to learn it, applied himself diligently to its acquisition for some time &c.' (De Sacy, p. ٢٧٠, ll. 10—12). Guidi notices no variations in his manuscripts as to the mention of Hebrew (Guidi, p. 97).

P. 218, 1—3. (Syr. T. 330, 7—10.) I prefer to read ܗܘܐ and ܗܘܝ.

P. 219. This chapter is undoubtedly of Buddhist origin. It breathes hatred against Brahmanism. It is found in the O. Syr. V., and exists also in a Tibetan version made directly from Sanscrit,

discovered by Anton Schiefner. See *Kal. u. Dam.* pp. xi, xii, and Benfey's *Pantsch.* i. pp. 585—599.

10—220, 15. Corresponds to Guidi's extract 75 (p. 72).

14, 15. Apparently a reference to Psalm cxi. 10 or Proverbs ix. 10.

P. 220, 16; 232, 27. The names of the king, his minister, and his wives assume so many different forms in the versions, that for clearness sake I exhibit them in a table. They are all discussed by Benfey in *Kal. u. Dam.* pp. l—lix, and some by Nöldeke in the *Z. D. M. G.* xxx. p. 757. Unfortunately the Sanscrit original of this chapter is lost, but Schiefner's Tibetan version usefully takes its place in connection with the names of the king and his minister. Similarly Somadeva's *Kathāsaritsāgara*, Taranga xi. helps to identify the names of the king and his wife.

Neglecting for a moment the names between square brackets, all is fairly clear. In the first column the forms reflect more or less exactly a Sanscrit name corresponding to the Tibetan *Bharata;* the second column exhibits varying forms of a name probably best represented by the Tibetan *Chaṇḍapradyota;* the third column contains forms which Benfey would identify with the *Angāravatī* of Somadeva; and the name in the fourth column is perhaps most accurately conveyed by the form ﻋﻴﺮﻣﺎﻧﺔ. Here I should remark that in the second column ﺩﺑﺸﻠﻢ؟ is no doubt identical with our old friend *Dab-shalm* (Dēvaçarman), and so is only the substitution of a known name for an unknown one. In the third column Ἡλαὸδ should be referred to a form اربك for اربل. The Tibetan names in this column and the next do not help at all or come under discussion. But the forms between brackets seem to have been *misplaced.* Thus in the first column, De Sacy's اربل is surely another variation of the favourite wife's name. In the second column De Sacy's بلار looks uncommonly like the minister's name. In the third column the forms Helbod, דרלבת, and Helebat, are pronounced by Benfey to be identical with a form like هلبة, a variant, that is, of the other wife's name; while اراخت he would refer to another variant of that other wife's name, thus, '*harqat, irqat, irakht;* though Nöldeke (loc. cit.) refers both it and ﺍﺭﻣﻲ to the Pehlevi form corresponding to *Angāravatī.* Let us, for the sake of still greater

	MINISTER	KIXA	FAVOURITE WIFE	OTHER WIFE
Tibetan	Bharata	Chandapradyota	Keçini, Çânú	Tárá
Somadeva		Chandamahácna	Augâravati	
Old Syriac	ܚܠܐ [الد] Do Sacy	ܚܠܘܦ [Do Sacy]	[ارحـت] Do Sacy and P	ܐܘܚܠܟܘܢ
Arabic	الد Guidi's M, V بلد " F	سادرم V سارم F سارات M	ارل M, V and title of F	حررناڌ Do Sacy حررناڌ F
Greek	Παλλάριος	—	Παλλά, dat. Παλλάβῃ, etc.	not named
Old Spanish	Belel (title, Heled)	Cedran, Cederano	[Helbed]	Jorfate
New Syriac	ܚܠܐ جلد	ܚܘܒܣܩ	جلد [Helbed]	ܟܠܘܚܣ
Hebrew	בלאד	אלדנש, דמנה	[הלבד]	not named
John of Capua	Beled	Sedras	[Helebat]	"

clearness, represent the king's right name by K, the minister's name by M, the favourite wife's by W, and the other wife's by w, and write out the table again, thus:

	Minister.	King.	Wife.	Other wife.
Tibetan	M	K	—	-
Somadeva		K	W	
Old Syriac	M	K	W	w
De Sacy	W	M	W?	w
Guidi's M	M	K	W	
„ V	M	K	W	
„ F	M	K	w (title W)	w
Greek	M	—	W	..
Old Spanish	M	K	w	w
New Syriac	M	—	W	w
Hebrew	M	K	w	
John of Capua	M	K	w	—

In De Sacy's text then the minister bears the favourite wife's name, while the king has the minister's name. In the Old Spanish the favourite wife's name has disappeared and been replaced in the same way, but the minister and king retain their old names. In the Hebrew version and in John of Capua the same has happened, but the other wife is called simply 'concubine.' Lastly in Guidi's MS. F the favourite wife has her right name in the title, but throughout the text is called by the other wife's name. Thus in De Sacy's edition, in the text of Guidi's F, and in the Old Spanish version, we get two variants of the other wife's name. Benfey would explain these peculiarities by supposing an Arabic copy in which the king had no name. Some copyist then gave the minister's name to the king, the favourite

wife's name to the minister. For a fuller discussion and complete references see *Kal. u. Dam.* (loc. cit.) and the *Z. D. M. G.* (loc. cit.).

P. 221, 3 ff. In the Ar. V. the Brahmans assign a reason for their ill-will towards the king, namely that he had recently slaughtered 12,000 of them (De Sacy, p. ٢٤٨, ll. 2, 3).

12. For *on* read 'in.'

13. Read: 'and then others of us wash you with water mixed with sweet basil—if you do not consent &c.'

20—28. (Syr. T. 334, 21—335, 6.) *Gûbar.* See *Kal. u. Dam.* pp. LXXXV, LXXXVI.

From this passage it appears that the *u* in the O. Syr. *Gaupar* (گَوْبَر) is owing to the fact that *au, av, au* are expressed in Pehlevï by the same sign; that no doubt Ibu al-Mokuffa' wrote not جُرْبَر but جُوبَر, which is exactly reflected in the گۆبَر of our Modern Syriac; that the G. Spanish translator had before him a form without diacritical points, as indeed is the case in Guidi's MS. F, and being uncertain how to read it, wrote down two possible forms thus: Geuir, meaning either Geuir (جُوبَر) or Geubr (جُوبَر); and that these two possibilities some copyist combined in *Geubrir*, the form found in De Gayangos' edition (*Cal. é Dym.* p. 61), except that *u* has become *n*.

Kayil. Also Klik (231, 38.) See Dr Wright's Preface, p. xxi.

Gôd. If جُوَدَل (De Sacy, p. ٢٢١, l. 5) is intended, we ought to read the word گَوَدَل (*gawdd, gawâdh*).

Qînûrôn. See Prof. Wright's Preface to the Syr. T. p. xxi.

P. 222, 26. After 'justly' continue as follows: 'because you value others as you do yourself. For though *they* perish to-day, there are many to rise up in place of them; but if &c.'

P. 223, 10. (Syr. T. 337, 15.) It is uncertain whether ܠܒܐ is fem. abs. or masc. emph. See Nöldeke's Syriac Grammar, p. 134, § 210.

29. (Syr. T. 338, 10.) I think the MS. reading ܕܠܒܝ is correct.

P. 227, 34. The words in brackets are supplied conjecturally.

37—228, 13. This passage is given at great length in Guidi's extract 76 (pp. 73, 74).

K. F.   20

P. **229**, 4—33. Benfey, in dealing with these names, did not sufficiently distinguish between the *two sets*, namely the names of the *Kings* and the names of the *Kingdoms* (*Kal. u. Dam.* pp. LXXXVII—XCII). See Prof. Wright's Introduction to the text, p. XXII.

P. **230**, 39. A reference to Psalm xl. 1.

P. **231**, 5 **232**, 25. Corresponds to Guidi's extract 78 (pp. 75, 76).

6. Read: 'and for his secretary and confidant.'

10. (Syr. T. 350, 16.) The words in brackets are inserted conjecturally. The preposition in ܟܘܠ seems to point to a clause omitted.

22. (Syr. T. 351, 3, 4.) I read ܠܘܐ without ܘ (l. 3), and retain the MS. reading ܐܠܐܩܘ (l. 4).

29—33. Compare Guidi's text (p. 75, ll. 7, 8).

P. **232**, 27. *Gilpāh.* See note on 220, 16.

P. **234**, 31. At this point, according to the Ar. V. and the O. Syr., the minister relates to the king the story of the two doves, and then that of the monkey. (Knatchbull's *Kalila and Dimna*, pp. 331 —333: De Sacy, p. ٢٠٩, 14 ٢٦٦, 4: *Kal. u. Dam.* Transl. pp. 101, 102.) De Sacy's text runs as follows:

"It is related that two doves, a male and a female, filled their nest with wheat and barley. The cock said to his mate: 'As long as we find sustenance in the fields we will leave our store untouched, so that, when winter comes and there is nothing in the fields, we may fall back on what there is in our nest, and feed on that.' This pleased the hen-bird, who answered: 'Your plan is a good one.' Now this grain was damp when they put it into their nest. And the cock-bird went away and was absent for a time. When summer came, the grain became dry and shrunk; and when the cock-bird returned, he perceived that it had diminished in size, and said to her: 'Did we not agree to abstain from eating any of it? why then did you do so!' Then she began to swear that she had not eaten any of it and to defend herself to him, but he did not believe her, and set to pecking her until she died. And when the rains came and winter set in, the grain got damp again, and the nest became as full as before. The cock-bird on perceiving this repented; and, casting himself down by the side of his mate, said: 'What

profits me the grain and the food now that thou art dead! When
I seek thee, I find thee not nor can recover thee. When I
think of thee, I know that I have wronged thee.' And he
neither ate nor drank, until he died by her side. Now a wise
man is not swift to punish and take vengeance, especially one
who fears lest he repent of his conduct, as the dove repented.

"I have heard too that a man once started up a mountain with a
vessel of lentils on his head. And he put down the vessel from off
his back to rest himself. Whereupon a monkey came down from a
tree, took a handful of the lentils, and climbed up again. But one
of the grains falling out of his hand, he came down again to look
for it; but not only did he fail to find it, but all the lentils that he
had in his hands were scattered on the ground."

P. 235, 27. Compare Matt. vii. 13.

30—34. Corresponds to Guidi's extracts 78, 79 and 80 (p. 77).

P. 236, 10—15. Corresp. to Guidi's ex. 81, 2° (pp. 79 : xLIII, 7).

16—22.   „   „   81, 3° (pp. 79 : xLIII, 14).

23—35.   „   „   81, 4° (pp. 79 : xLIII, 18).

36—237, 2.   „   „   81, 5° (pp. 80 : xLIV, 9).

P. 237, 3—14.   „   „   81, 9° (pp. 81 : xLV, 16).

15—23.   „   „   81, 7° (pp. 80 : xLV, 3).

24—31.   „   „   81, 8° (pp. 81 : xLV, 9).

25. To say should be in round brackets.

32—238, 5. Corresp. to Guidi's ex. 81, 10° (pp. 81 : xLVI, 5).

36, 37. (Syr. T. 360, 21, 22.) Substitute: 'is not deterred,
but returns to make the same replies over again;' Delete however
contemptible.

P. 238, 6—15. Corresp. to Guidi's ex. 81, 12° (pp. 82 : xLVI, 18).

10. Read: 'whether by visiting him or writing him a letter.'
See Add. and Corr. 361, 11.

16—24. Corresp. to Guidi's ex. 81, 13° (pp. 83 : xLVII, 11).

25—36.   „   „   81, 14° (pp. 83 : xLVII, 16).

29. (Syr. T. 362, 5.) Perhaps for ـحـﺒـ should be read
ﺣـﺒـﯔ. If so render: 'a man and his wife who continually seek
to be together.'

37—239, 9. Corresp. to Guidi's ex. 81, 15° (pp. 83 : xLVIII, 5).

P. 239, 10—18.   „   „   82, 31° (pp. 90 : LIV, 11).

19—25. Bears some resemblance to Guidi's extract 81. 16ᵉ (pp. 84 : XLVIII, 11).

26—240, 8. Corresponds to Guidi's extract 84. 37ᵃ (pp. 91 : LVI, 7).

29. One word puzzles me.

P. 240, 9—15. Corresponds to Guidi's extract 81. 17ᵃ (pp. 84 : XLVIII, 17).

16—23.   „   „   82. 32ᵃ (pp. 90 : LV, 1).

21. (Syr. T. 365, 1.) A word is corrupt.

29—36. Corresponds to Guidi's extract 81. 18ᵉ (pp. 84 : XLIX, 3).

37—241, 8. „   „   81. 19ᵃ (pp. 84 : XLIX, 8).

P. 241, 2. (Syr. T. 365, 19.) I think that after ܡܢܗ should he supplied some such expression as 'in her eyes.' But compare Guidi's text (ܟܪܝ ܕܡܝܢ ܕܐܠܬ ܥܠܝܟܐ ܛܒܝܠܐ ܕܐܠܡܪܝܐ) and the O. Syr. (Kal. u. Dam. Transl. p. 109) : 'eine solche, welche von edler Abstammung ist.'

8. I have inserted this clause to complete the sense, but the Syriac language having no very fine sense of syntax, I doubt whether the original text is incomplete.

9—24. Corresponds to Guidi's extract 81. 20ᵃ (pp. 85 : XLIX, 13).

25—242, 4. Corresponds to Guidi's extract 81. 22ᵃ (pp. 85 : L, 6) and 84. 40ᵃ (pp. 92 : LVII, 3).

25, 28. (Syr. T. 366, 22, 23.) For ܣܝܣܠܐ, ܩܢܣܝܣܠܐ I read ܣܝܣܠܡ and ܩܢܣܝܣܠܡ.

33. (Syr. T. 367, 2, 3.) To everybody should be in square brackets.

36. Read : 'who wheedles her son when he is an evil doer and makes excuses for him, instead of reproving him &c.' See Payne Smith's Thesaurus under ܚܢܦ, col. 1530.

P. 242, 4. (Syr. T. 367, 12.) I suspect that the text is faulty here.

5—11. Corresponds to Guidi's extract 81. 21ᵃ (pp. 85 : L, 2).

12—22.   „   „   81. 23ᵃ (pp. 86 : L, 13).

23—36.   „   „   81. 24ᵃ (pp. 86 : LI, 2).

37—243, 10. „   „   83. 33ᵃ (pp. 90 : LV, 7).

P. 243, 11—24. Resembles faintly „   83. 34ᵃ (pp. 90 : LV, 12).

25—39. Corresponds to   „   83. 35ᵃ (pp. 91 : LV, 16).

P. 244, 8. (Syr. T. 370, 11.) There is a corruption here which

baffles me. I strongly suspect that ‏ܠܩ‏ is wrong and a mere partial repetition of ‏ܠܩܠܘ‏.

10.   A line and a third is here left blank in the manuscript.

18.   Read ‘ is sorry, because when the owners...come &c.’

20—36.   Bears some resemblance to Guidi's extract 81. 26ᵉ (pp. 8ī : ᴌᴵᴵ, 3).

26.   (Syr. T. 3ī1, 7.) Perhaps we should read ‏ܡܘ ܠܘܘܠܝ ܡܠܒ‏, ‘ when he pays no attention to it.’

P. 246, 2.   For *bits* substitute ‘ buzzing.’   See Payne Smith's *Thesaurus*, col. 1132.

25.   (Syr. T. 374, 7.) If the text is correct, render ‘for you have given me Ilūr's life.’   See Payne Smith's *Thesaurus*, col. ī00. But I suspect that we ought to read ‏ܠܐܝ̈‏.

P. 248.   The superscription is misleading.   Barzōi was not an Indian, nor did he translate into Arabic.   He was a Persian physician, living in the reign of Nûshîrwân son of Kobâd son of Fīrûz, who commissioned him to obtain and translate into Pehlevî, an old language of Persia, the Sanscrit original of this book.   This he did, and the only return which he would accept for his services was that his own biography should be added to the book.   Hence this chapter.   See further my Introduction.

15.   (Syr. T. 3ī5, 21.) Read : ‘ until I acquired much knowledge of it.’   The ‘goodly harvest’ must be taken in an intellectual sense. This comes out clearly in the Old Spanish version.   ‘ Et plúgome de trabajar en saberlo, et comencé á leer sus libros fasto que los entendí ó vi las naturas de los cuerpos ó las causas de las malutías ó las maneras del su melecinamiento, et sope ende atanto que me metí á melecinar enfermos’ (*Cal. é Dym.* p. 14, b, ll. 10—14).

P. 249, 20.   (Syr. T. 377, 6.) For *mite* read ‘ scrap.’   Possibly ‏ܐܝܗ‏ may mean a small coin, but I have no authority to show that it does.

26.   A word is almost washed out at this place in the manuscript.

2ī, 28.   In each of these lines for *weeds* substitute ‘grass.’

P. 250, 14.   (Syr. T. 3ī8, 15.) *Absorbed* in.   Literally ‘choked by.’   Compare Matt. xiii. 22.

28.   (Syr. T. 3ī9, 2.) The text as it stands has : ‘No wise and rational man possesses it, or is anxious for it, &c.’

31. (Syr. T. 379, 5.) I would read ܣܝܢ̈ܣ ܘܣܢܝܣ . ܠܗܡܣ
But if the text is right, we must render : 'turn thy gaze...and live :
and pursue after the things &c.'

P. 251, 6. (Syr. T. 379, 20.) I am doubtful as to ܘܣܡܝܪ.
Should ܣܝܐܣܡ be read ?

9. (Syr. T. 380, 1.) *Go to pieces.* Better 'collapse.'

23—252, 10. Corresponds to Guidi's extract 8 (pp. 14, 15).

24. (Syr. T. 380, 16.) *Knotted bridal chambers.* A note in
Badger's *Nestorians and their Ritual* (Vol. 11. p. 271) gives an
explanation of this 'knotting.' Alluding to a certain part of their
marriage service, called the 'Setting up (lit. knotting) of the bridal
chamber,' he says: 'This latter part of the marriage service is
usually said in the evening, before the bridegroom and bride retire
to rest for the night. As it is common for families in the East to
sleep together in one room, there is generally a temporary division
raised to separate the newly married couple from the rest of the
household. This custom has doubtless given the title to the above
service.'

P. 252, 4. (Syr. T. 381, 11.) Perhaps we should read ܐ̈ܬܝܢ ܠܣ̈ܡܝܐ.
If so, render : 'How shall the physician be honoured when &c.'

8. (Syr. T. 381, 16.) The stars represent the words ܣܐܘܢ̈ܝ
ܣܝܠܘܩܐ.

25—28. (Syr. T. 382, 11—13.) The Old Spanish version makes
clear the point of this story: 'Atal como el mercador que habia
una casa llena de oro et de plata, é dijo: "Si la vendiere á peso,
alongórseme ha"; et vendióla á ojo por mal precio' (*Cal. é Dym.*
p. 15, b, ll. 4—6). So too De Sacy's Arabic text (11, 2—4). The
merchant, thinking the process of weighing too slow and wearisome,
sold at sight, guessing the value by the apparent bulk, and so lost
heavily. But how to construe the Syriac text is a puzzle to me.

33—254, 16. Corresponds to Guidi's extract 9 (pp. 15—17).

38. (Syr. T. 382, 24.) I am doubtful as to ܡܢ ܚܡܠܝܐ.

P. 253, 4. (Syr. T. 383, 3.) Perhaps we might read ܠܘ̇ ܐ̈ܡܣܐ ܠܘܘ̈ܝ ܠܢ.

33. (Syr. T. 384, 6.) I am doubtful as to ܘܐܬܟܠܐ ܐܢ̈ܝ.

36. (Syr. T. 384, 8.) I think that an adjective has dropped out
after ܠܡܐ

37—39. They say so still.

39—254, 1. Read: 'And I saw that there was a great difference of opinion among them as to the Creator and the creature.' Compare Guidi, p. 16, and the Old Spanish version (*Cal. é Dym.* p. 15). Both these versions mention another point on which there was difference of opinion, viz. the beginning and end of the world. Of such mention we have only a mangled form in our Syriac version.

P. 255, 11. *Embrace the moonbeams.* For an illustration of this remarkable proceeding see Benfey's *Pantsch.* i. p. 77.

15, 35. *Shulam.* For a guess at the meaning of this word see Guidi, p. 19, note (*a*).

P. 256, 18—257, 15. Corresponds to Guidi's extract 10, pp. 19, 20.

30, 31. (Syr. T. 388, 21, 22.) Take ܩ from l. 21 and place it before ܐܬ݀ in l. 22: compare Guidi (loc. cit.).

38. (Syr. T. 389, 4.) I read ܒܪ݁ܩ, but the corruption probably lies deeper. See Add. and Corr.

P. 257, 2. (Syr. T. 389, 7.) Read either ܠܟܘܢ ܐܬܠ or ܠܟܘܢܕ ܐܬܠ.

9, 10. (Syr. T. 389, 15.) The text seems correct, but see Add. and Corr.

12. (Syr. T. 389, 18.) I think we should read ܠܟ ܐܟܣܘܡ.

P. 258, 30—259, 19. The story is told differently in the Arabic version (De Sacy, p. ١٨, l. 7—p. ١٩, l. 3) and its other off-shoots. There it is the merchant who loses, not the workman. The latter claims his money on the ground of having done what his employer bade him do.

35; 259, 3. (Syr. T. 392, 11, 19.) *Pearls.* No doubt the Syriac translator had ܓܘܗܪ (as in De Sacy's text) or some collective singular before him, and imagined it meant a single stone.

P. 260, 32, 33. (Syr. T. 395, 19—22.) Corresponds to the second part of Guidi's extract 11 bis (p. 21). There is some bad corruption in the text. I would omit altogether from ܩܡܣܐ in line 21 to the end of the sentence.

P. 261, 3, 4. (Syr. T. 396, 8, 9.) I do not understand ܕܠܐܝ ܩܒܠ, but see Add. and Corr. In line 9 I would insert ܗܘ before ܕܠܐ.

24. (Syr. T. 397, 5.) A word has been retouched. I do not understand it.

P. 262, 2. (Syr. T. 397, 19.) I read ܣܘܪܩܠ without ܘ.

11. (Syr. T. 398, 8.) I think that for ܠ‌ܩ‌ܝ‌ܣ‌ܐ should be read some word corresponding to ܣ‌ܝ‌ܦ‌ܬ‌ܐ in the line above (ܩ‌ܠ‌ܝ‌ܣ f).

P. 263, 14—16. The translator seems to be in error here. The Old Spanish (*Cal. é Dym.* p. 18, a) has : ' Desi vive en muchas maneras de pena, asi como si ha fambre é non le dan á comer, ó si ha sed ó non le dau á beber, ó si ha dolor é non le acorren &c.' Similarly De Sacy, p. vf, l. 14.

24. (Syr. T. 400, 13.) For ܐ‌ܦ‌ܝ ܠ‌ܝ I would read ܐ‌ܩ‌ܢ‌ܝ.

P. 264, 1. (Syr. T. 401, 6.) I read ܠ‌ܩ‌ܒ‌ܝ in order to get a rendering, but the text has been so much and so badly retouched that it is impossible to conjecture with any certainty. The same remarks apply to many passages in this oldest part of the manuscript. See note 4, under Syr. T. 367.

2—265, 21. This long piece of declamation differs from the corresponding passage in the Arabic version in several points. There it is not God whose praises are declared but 'the king' (De Sacy, p. vi, l. 4), that is, no doubt, Nûshlrvân king of Persia. Next, the passage extending from 'especially in the days &c.' (264, 21) to 'dust of the earth' (l. 32) has clearly been inserted bodily by the Syriac translator. The mention of the cedars of Lebanon (265, 12) of course proceeds from the same source, as well as the final sentence (265, 18—21). Otherwise the versions substantially agree.

28. An allusion to Coloss. iii. 14. Compare also 1 Cor. xiii. and 1 Tim. i. 5.

39. I think that a participle has dropped out. But perhaps, without supposing a gap, we may translate : ' Churlishness and pride from the roofs do preach cruelty, ill-will, and love of money.'

P. 265, 27. (Syr. T. 403, 21 ; 404, 1.) I read ܣ‌ܚ‌ܡ‌ܠ‌ܝ . . . . ܡ‌ܠ‌ܝ‌ܣ‌ܐ.

P. 266, 1. The simile is borrowed from 1 Cor. xiii. 1.

28. See 263, 24.

39—267, 4. Do Sacy's text (p. vv) runs as follows : 'Then I resolved to be content to remain as I was, and to perfect my course of action as much as I was able, that perhaps in after life I might happen on a time when I should meet with a guide for my path, a power to rule my soul, and one who would order my affairs; and in this state I remained.' See De Sacy in his *Calila et Dimna*, Mémoire Historique, p. 29.

Since the above Notes were written, a review of Professor Wright's edition of the Syriac text has appeared in the *Göttingische gelehrte Anzeigen*, Nr. 17, contributed by Prof. Theodor Nöldeke of Strassburg.

He proposes several fresh textual emendations. Namely :

Syr. T. 37, 7. ܠܥܠ

„   51, 17. ܡܟܠܝ

„   178, 9. ܐܠܐ (misprint ?).

„   231, ult. ܩܘܐܠܝܪ, the right reading, is represented by ܩܘܡ ܐܡܡ, and therefore ܩܘ must disappear from the text.

Syr. T. 261, ult. ܩܠܬܗ. The plural form never occurs in old Syriac.

Syr. T. 327, 16. ܗܘܐ ܙܝܟܩܩ

„   346, 19. ܙܠ (Imperat.).

„   349, 12. After ܐܕ there is a gap, occasioned by homoeoteleuton: 'not [wisely did I act in] not &c.' De Sacy, 257, 1; Bickell, 101, 15.

Syr. T. 354, 22. ܙܬܐܪ (Peal).

„   395, 2. ܐܬܠ ܐܠܢܩ

„   398, 22. ܩܪܡܩܐ (Pass).

REFERENCE TABLE OF CORRESPONDENCES BETWEEN DE SACY'S ARABIC TEXT AND THE SYRIAC TEXT.

De S.		Syr. T.		De S.		Syr. T.	
'p. 61, l.	1 =	p. 375, l.	5	p. 93, l.	1 =	p. 27, l.	24
62,	2	377,	3	94,	1	29,	20
63,	14	378,	13	95,	1	31,	11
64,	2	382,	9	96,	1	32,	19
65,	1	385,	21	97,	1	33,	21
65,	15	387,	24	98,	1	35,	6
67,	1	390,	13	99,	1	36,	2
68,	1	392,	1	100,	1	38,	24
69,	1	392,	22	101,	1	40,	8
70,	1	394,	18	102,	1	41,	16
70,	14	395,	22	103,	1	42,	22
72,	1	399,	4	104,	1	43,	25
73,	2	400,	5	105,	1	45,	5
74,	3	401,	7	106,	1	46,	19
75,	5	403,	17	107,	2	49,	15
76,	1	404,	20	108,	1	50,	15
76,	15	406,	2	109,	1	52,	8
78,	1	3,	5	110,	1	54,	1
79,	1	4,	12	111,	1	55,	13
80,	6-⎫			112,	1	57,	18
81,	9 ⎭	missing		113,	1	58,	19
82,	1	6,	26	114,	1	60,	13
83,	1	8,	17	115,	1	61,	12
84,	1	10,	24	116,	1	62,	20
85,	1	12,	15	117,	1	63,	20
86,	1	14,	4	118,	1	66,	25
87,	1	15,	19	119,	1	68,	24
88,	1	17,	5	120,	1	69,	25
89,	1	20,	15	121,	1	71,	15
90,	1	22,	23	121,	9-⎫		
91,	1	24,	11	122,	12 ⎭	missing	
92,	1	26,	6	123,	1	72,	17

' Pp. 1-61 are not represented at all in our Syriac version. Each page of De Sacy's edition has 15 lines, and each page of the Syriac text has from 20 to 25 lines.

De S.	Syr. T.	De S.	Syr. T.
p. 124, l. 1 = p.	73, l. 18	p. 185, l. 2 = p.	206, l. 7
125, 1	74, 23	186, 1	207, 16
126, 1	76, 18	187, 1	208, 24
127, 1	78, 12	188, 1	210, 11
128, 1	80, 2	188, 15	211, 20
129, 1	86, 20	190, 1	213, 20
130, 1	87, 25	190, 8	214, 14
131, 1	89, 17	191, 11	215, 19
131, 15	90, 25	193, 1	218, 2
133, 1	92, 16	194, 1	220, 7
134, 1	94, 6	195, 1	221, 12
160, 1	166, 4	196, 1	222, 13
161, 1	167, 10	197, 1	223, 17
162, 1	168, 16	198, 1	224, 21
163, 1	170, 21	199, 1	227, 10
164, 1	172, 20	200, 1	229, 6
165, 1	174, 1	201, 1	230, 7
166, 1	175, 13	202, 1	231, 20
167, 1	177, 7	203, 1	233, 23
168, 1	178, 19	204, 1	235, 18
169, 1	179, 22	205, 1	237, 2
170, 1	181, 10	206, 1	239, 2
171, 1	183, 23	206, 15	240, 20
172, 2	182, 7	209, 1	243, 1
173, 1	187, 17	210, 1	244, 15
173, 14- } 174, 1 }	189, 4-10	211, 1	250, 20
174, 5- } 175, 12 }	missing	212, 4	251, 17
177, 1	192, 8	213, 1	253, 19
178, 3	194, 21	214, 1	255, 18
179, 1	196, 1	215, 1	257, 13
180, 1	196, 16	216, 1	259, 9
181, 1	197, 15	217, 1	260, 19
182, 1	199, 1	218, 1	261, 16
183, 1	200, 13	219, 1	262, 12
184, 1	202, 18	220, 1	262, 20
		221, 1	263, 15
		222, 1	265, 4

[1] The chapter entitled 'Dimnah's Defence' (De Sacy, pp. 135-160) is spun out to such an extent by our Syriac translator (pp. 95-160), that it is not worth while to give any correspondences.

De S.		Syr. T.		De S.		Syr. T.	
p. 223, l.	1 =	p. 267, l.	17	p. 256, l.	1 =	p. 347, L.	21
223,	15	269,	12	256,	15	349,	9
225,	1	270,	16	258,	1	353,	8
228,	1	272,	15	259,	1	354,	21
229,	1	273,	24	259,	14-)		
230,	1	276,	2	261,	4 }	missing²	
230,	15	277,	3	²263,	5	373,	4
231,	15	278,	19	263,	15	374,	1
232,	15	280,	5	265,	2	374,	14
233,	13	281,	21	266,	1	325,	9
235,	1	283,	11	267,	2	326,	4
236,	1	284,	11	268,	2	327,	6
237,	3	286,	21	269,	4	328,	16
238,	1	288,	10	270,	1	329,	1
238,	14	289,	10	271,	1	330,	10
240,	1	290,	17	272,	1	311,	16
241,	1	292,	7	273,	1	313,	9
242,	1	294,	18	274,	1	314,	8
page 243		missing		274,	15	315,	3
214,	4	298,	5	276,	1	316,	5
247,	1	331,	1	277,	1	317,	1
248,	1	334,	4	278,	1	317,	5
249,	1	334,	12	278,	14	318,	8
249,	15	336,	8	279,	15	319,	7
250,	15	338,	7	281,	1	320,	2
252,	1	340,	20	282,	1	321,	4
252,	14	342,	6	283,	1	322,	3
254,	1	344,	14	283,	13	322,	20
255,	1	346,	9	285,	1	324,	14

¹ Pp. 244–246 in De Sacy correspond to pp. 298-311 in the Syriac.
² But translated in my notes (p. 308).
³ The long conversation between the king and his minister (Syr. T. 355, 10–371, 17) is given very briefly in De Sacy's text (pp. 261-263).

REFERENCE TABLE OF CORRESPONDENCES BETWEEN GUIDI'S EXTRACTS AND THE SYRIAC TEXT.

Guidi.		Syr. T.		
¹Extract	8	= p. 380,	l. 15–p. 381,	l. 18.
„	9	382,	17– 385,	1.
„	10	388,	9– 389,	21.
„	11	394,	14–20.	
„	11 bis	395,	19–22.	
„	12	12,	20–p. 13,	4.
„	13	17,	7–12.	
„	14	18,	2–p. 20,	2.
„	15	21,	13–17.	
„	15 bis	23,	8–19.	
„	16	23,	22–p. 24,	9.
„	20²	33,	9–16.	
„	21	40,	18–p. 41,	2.
„	22	48,	2, 3.	
„	23	50,	14–16.	
„	24	65,	1–p. 66,	4.
„	25	67,	14–17.	
„	25 bis		wanting³.	
„	26		wanting.	
„	27	73,	19–p. 74,	1.
„	28	77,	2–11.	
„	29	79,	15–p. 86,	6.
„	30	80,	1–27.	
„	31	93,	14–16.	
„	32	93,	23–p. 94,	1.
„	33	92,	9–23.	
„	34	92,	25–p. 93,	1.
„	35		wanting.	
„	36	128,	12–15.	
„	37	131,	16–p. 137,	12.
„	38	141,	17– 147,	25.

¹ The first seven extracts belong to the three introductory chapters of the Ar. V. which are not represented in our Syriac translation.

² The three short extracts 17, 18, 19 are wanting in the Syriac.

³ Owing to the fact that a leaf is missing in the Syriac MS. See Syr. T. p. 72.

Guidi.		Syr. T.		
Extract	39	= p. 156,	l. 22-p. 160, l.	2.
„	40	161,	20- 163,	20.
„	41	170,	2-5.	
„	42	171,	19, 20.	
„	43	176,	4-17.	
„	44	180,	9.	
„	45	186,	5-18.	
„	46	187,	6-18.	
„	47	216,	18, 19.	
„	48		wanting.	
„	49	217,	17-p. 218,	1.
„	50	223,	15- 224,	1.
„	51	225,	8 226,	6.
„	52		wanting.	
„	53	231,	15-17.	
„	54	232,	17-p. 233,	13.
„	55		wanting.	
„	56	234,	20-23.	
„	57	245,	13-p. 249,	17.
„	58	250,	8-12.	
„	59	252,	4-18.	
„	60	256,	1-16.	
„	61 ⎫			
„	62 ⎬		wanting.	
„	63 ⎭			
„	64	266,	17-24	
„	65	267,	17-24.	
„	66	271,	12-18.	
„	67 ⎫			
„	68 ⎭		wanting.	
„	69 ⎫			
„	70 ⎭	293,	3-p. 294,	18.
„	71	296,	17- 298,	3.
„	72 ⎫			
„	73 ⎭		wanting.	
„	74		300, 20 and onwards.	
„	75	331,	10-p. 333,	2.
„	76	345,	9- 346,	2.
„	77	350,	11- 352,	18.

Guidi.		Syr. T.	
Extract	78		
"	79	= p. 357, l. 19–23.	
"	80		
Ex. 81.	1°	wanting.	
	2°	= p. 358, l. 13–18.	
	3°	358,	18–24.
	4°	358,	21–p. 359, l. 10.
	5"	359,	10–17.
	6°	wanting.	
	7°	360,	2–10.
	8°	360,	10–17.
	9"	359,	17–p. 360, 2.
	10°	360,	17– 361, 7.
	11°	wanting.	
	12°	361,	7–17.
	13°	361,	17–p. 362, 4.
	14"	362,	4–14.
	15°	362,	14–p. 363, 4.
	16°	363,	13–20.
	17°	364,	17–22.
	18°	365,	8–15.
	19°	365,	15–p. 366, 5.
	20°	366,	5–21.
	21°	367,	13–17.
	22° (40°)	366,	21–p. 367, 13.
	23°	367,	18– 368, 5.
	24°	368,	5–18.
	25°	wanting.	
	'26°	370,	24–p. 371, 17.
82.	27°		
	28°	wanting.	
	29°		
	30°		
	31°	363,	4–13.
	32°	364,	22–p. 365, 4.
83.	33°	368,	18– 369, 3.
	'34°	369,	3–15.
	35°	369,	15–p. 370, 4.

' In this case the resemblance is very faint.

320 BOOK OF KALILAH AND DIMNAH.

	GUIDI.	SYR. T.
Ex. 84.	36ᵃ	wanting.
	37ᵃ	— p. 363, l. 20–p. 364, l. 17.
	38ᵃ 39ᵃ }	wanting.
	40ᵃ (22ᵃ) = p. 366,	21–p. 367, 13.
85. 86. }		wanting.
87.		p. 316, 8–p. 317, 1.

THE END.

www.ingramcontent.com/pod-product-compliance
Lightning Source LLC
Chambersburg PA
CBHW020239110726

47898CB00004B/1326